HOLLYWOOD ANGELS

ALSO BY ALICE DUNCAN

The Mercy Allcutt Mystery Series

Lost Among the Angels

Angels Flight

Fallen Angels

Angels of Mercy

Thanksgiving Angels

Angels Adrift

Christmas Angels

Hollywood Angels

Celluloid Angels

The Daisy Gumm Majesty Mystery Series

Strong Spirits

Fine Spirits

High Spirits

Hungry Spirits

Genteel Spirits

Ancient Spirits

Spirits Revived

Dark Spirits

Spirits Onstage

Unsettled Spirits

Bruised Spirits

Spirits United

Spirits Unearthed

Shaken Spirits

Scarlet Spirits

Exercised Spirits

Wedded Spirits

Domesticated Spirits

Library Spirits

HOLLYWOOD ANGELS

A MERCY ALLCUTT MYSTERY
BOOK 8

ALICE DUNCAN

ePublishingWorks!
love what you read

Book and cover design by eBook Prep
www.ebookprep.com

October 2023
Paperback ISBN: 978-1-64457-602-1
Hardcover ISBN: 978-1-64457-656-4

ePublishing Works!
644 Shrewsbury Commons Ave
Ste 249
Shrewsbury PA 17361
United States of America

www.epublishingworks.com
Phone: 866-846-5123

ACKNOWLEDGMENTS

Thanks to Diana Jackson for the idea behind this book. Don't know what I'd do without Diana, who lives in Norwich, UK. I appreciate her input and corrections a *whole* lot.

Thanks to Margaret Cronk, too, because she read and made corrections to the book. Honestly, sometimes I don't know what I'd do without helpful people. My brain ran dry a couple of years ago, and I *need* input from other people's brains!

Thanks, too, to the real Sue Krekeler, who not only made corrections, but who let me use her name in Mercy's books.

If you enjoyed this book, please tell people and leave a review somewhere online. Thank you. Authors rely on word-of-mouth.

According to Ray Bradbury: "Writing is supposed to be difficult, a dreadful exercise, a terrible occupation."

Glad I got something right.

ONE

There's no denying I felt a little blue in the beginning of January 1927. The holidays had been swell, and everyone in Mercy's Manor—the name Lulu LaBelle had christened my very first home—had been *so* happy and cheerful.

And Ernie Templeton had kissed me. Under the mistletoe, just like men are supposed to kiss the women they care for.

What's more, I'd kissed him back.

It had been delicious.

Speaking of delicious, Mrs. Buck, my cook-housekeeper, had kept us in absolutely superb holiday meals, and the pies, cookies, candies, and cakes had been phenomenal. She promised she'd teach me to cook, too.

I also had the heartwarming knowledge that Ernie and I, working together, had done a Very Good Deed. Those caps are deserved, and I was proud of us. We'd not only saved some kidnapped girls, but we'd cleared Ernie's Chinese pal, Charley Wu, of a murder rap. I mean, how much better can life get, you know?

And then January had rolled in. Not without some difficulty, mind you. My parents, who had followed me from Boston's Beacon Hill to Los Angeles's Bunker Hill—they deplore the hallowed historical name used in so upstart a city as Los Angeles—had pestered me to go to their home for New Year's Day.

"We have a special invitation from the mayor and will be able to view the Tournament of Roses Parade from special seats. We shall attend a reception at the Valley Hunt Club after the parade," said my mother, Honoria Violet Chudleigh Allcutt. "You owe it to us to come, Mercedes Louise. Your father and I are disgusted by your recent behavior."

My disgusting recent behavior had been my refusal of their demand to spend Christmas with them. Well, that and opening my home, which I'd purchased from my sister and her motion-picture-mogul husband, to tenants, thereby creating a lovely boarding house for deserving women who had to work for their bread. My delightful home sat on Los Angeles's very own Bunker Hill, what's more.

Mother and Father had been the bane of my existence since I was born. That was all right by me, since I'd been the bane of theirs ever since I moved from Boston to Los Angeles in order to put a couple of thousand miles between us. Then they'd tried their best to thwart me in *that* endeavor by buying a winter home in Pasadena. I'd fallen in with their plans for a while, but my spine had stiffened and so had my upper lip and now, by golly, they couldn't boss me around anymore!

I hate to admit to having palpitations after I wrote that last sentence.

Still and all, I was getting much better at protecting myself from my parental bullies. It helped that I had a job I loved (my mother most certainly had palpitations when she learned I'd actually found myself a *job)*. Women in my family were merely decorative; they weren't supposed to do anything but sit in their mansions, gossip with their neighbors, criticize their servants, and sip tea. Attend the opera or an improving play from time to time.

That's not the sort of life I wanted. I wanted to be not only *with* the people, but *of* them! I wanted to contribute to the world, not suck the life from working people who hadn't been given the opportunities of wealth and position bestowed upon me from birth.

Very well, so I know most people would like to trade places with me. *I* didn't want to be a stuffy, do-nothing rich person. I wanted to be among the worker proletariat, darn it!

The Ernie of whom I spoke earlier is helping me achieve my life's goal. That's not only because we'd begun "seeing" each other away from work, either—quite often at the dinner table in my home. It's mainly because he gave me my very first job as his private secretary. He's also tall, handsome, eternally casual, with astonishingly blue eyes, and...I beg your pardon. That's not the point here. The point is that he's a private investigator, and I'm his confidential secretary. Talk about a job guaranteed to get me out of the upper echelons of Boston society and onto the mean streets of Los Angeles! I couldn't have asked for more.

But I got more anyway. I'd found friends, primary among whom was Lulu LaBelle. Lulu hails from Oklahoma, and her last name was originally Mullins, but she wanted to become a star on the silver screen, and she thought LaBelle would look better than Mullins on a theater marquee. Lulu and I were buddies. Pals. We did everything together. We even worked in the same building, although Lulu worked at the reception desk in the lobby and I worked on the third floor.

That brisk Monday morning in January, I expected a normal work day. I might have been wronger (I don't think that's a word) in my expectations, but I doubt it.

After breakfast Lulu and I, along with my other two tenants—Sue Krekeler, who worked for a dentist; and Caroline Terry, who worked at the hosiery counter at the Broadway Department Store—walked the two short blocks from my house to Angels Flight, a darling, almost vertical funicular railroad that took passengers from Olive to Hill all day, every day. There we handed the conductor of Angels Flight our respective nickels and got onto the car that would zip us from Olive Street on Bunker Hill almost straight down to Hill Street in the heart of Los Angeles. That morning we rode the rail car Sinai. The second car on Angels Flight is Olivet. They take their biblical references literally in the City of Angels, even though the citizens of Los Angeles can be far from angelic.

"I'm freezing," said Sue, hugging her coat to her chest.

"Me too," said Caroline, doing likewise.

"Me too," said Lulu. On this Monday morning Lulu wore a vivid red velvet cape, so she hugged her cape to her chest. Lulu was...colorful, I guess is the best word to describe Lulu's clothing choices.

The rest of us (Sue, Caroline, and I) wore heavy winter coats. Let me be clear that the weather in Los Angeles in January is cold, but it's nothing like Boston cold. In Boston, there would be snow and ice on the streets, piled up and getting dirty. In Los Angeles, the air nipped at our noses. If, for example, you were to, say, walk from Olive to Hill instead of availing yourself of Angels Flight, you wouldn't freeze into a block of ice. You'd walk down the hill and shiver a bit. In Boston a walk like that, if a person was clad as we were, would mean hypothermia and probable death.

Still, by that time all of us were accustomed to Los Angeles weather, and we felt cold.

When we got off the car Sinai, we walked in a clump to Fourth and Broadway, where we left Caroline to enter the Broadway Department Store. Lulu, Sue, and I then tramped to Figueroa Street. After a short walk, I turned to enter the Figueroa Building. I was surprised when Lulu didn't turn to enter with me.

"What's up, Lulu? Aren't you still working here?" I asked.

"Oh sure, but I'm going to walk on up to Sue's office and make an appointment to get my teeth cleaned." She gave me a huge smile. Her teeth looked white to me, especially as her lips were painted a vivid red. I didn't say so.

"Oh, that's a good idea," I said. "I should probably get my own teeth checked." Going to the dentist was no darned fun, but it was still important to one's overall health.

"I can make an appointment for you too, Mercy," said Sue.

After contemplating the dentist for a very few seconds I said, "That's okay. I'll make an appointment later."

"Ha," said Sue with a chuckle. She knew how most people hated going to dentists.

I grinned back at her.

"It'll only take a few minutes. I probably won't even be late," said Lulu.

"Probably not. The office isn't even open yet," said Sue. "But I can write down an appointment for you in the book."

"Thanks, Sue," said Lulu, and the two walked arm-in-arm up Figueroa. Sue's dentist had an office a mere block away from our building.

"Bye!" I called as I reached for the door handle.

The gleaming plaque proclaiming my place of work to be the Figueroa Building had been dull, smudged, and tarnished when Ernie had hired me the prior July. Today it shone like the brass it was, and the front windows sparkled in the cool sunshiny air. That's because Mr. Buck, husband of Mrs. Buck, had taken over the job of caretaker for the Figueroa Building.

The person who'd held the position before Mr. Buck was…incompetent. He was also serving a long prison sentence for murdering several women. I, with all due modesty, can claim a pivotal role in his capture. That's mainly because I'd shoved him down the building's elevator shaft. My decision to do so hadn't been mercurial or frivolous. He'd been coming after me with a big knife at the time.

However, that experience had given me a slight—truly a trivial—unwillingness to use the elevator if I were alone. If someone was with me, I'd gladly take the trip upstairs in the elevator. That morning, after leaving Lulu and Sue to make their way up the street, I climbed the staircase to the third floor where my office and Ernie were. Well, Ernie being Ernie, he probably wasn't at work yet, but he'd show up eventually.

I loved my job. I…really liked Ernie. A lot.

Sure enough, when I got to the office the door was locked. As I believe in being efficient and prepared, I already had my key ready so I opened the door. When I stepped inside the office, I let out a satisfied sigh. The place looked great and ever so much better than it had when I'd first become employed. I'd spiffed it up, put pictures on the wall and rugs on the floor, and I'd bought a cunning pagoda clock in Chinatown that sat on my desk and kept excellent time when I remembered to wind it, which I mostly did.

The only drawback to my employment was that…well, there wasn't much of it. Perhaps now the new year had begun, things would pick up. It had been mighty slow for a few weeks around the holidays, however.

As I always did on these chilly mornings, I removed my coat and hat and hung them on the coat tree beside the door. When I removed my gloves, I shoved them and my warm knitted scarf into the pockets of my coat. Then I strode to my desk to begin my day.

Before I could get there, the telephone rang. I glanced at the wall clock, which told me it was only 7:50 a.m., ten minutes ahead of my 8 o'clock start time.

That was all right. It must be a person eager to hire Ernie to solve a bewildering problem. Or a spouse who wanted him to spy on his or her other half. Unfortunately, our firm got more of the latter types of cases than the former.

But it was work, so I walked behind my desk, sat on my chair, and, before sticking my handbag into the lower right-hand drawer of my desk, I picked up the telephone's receiver.

"Mr. Templeton's office. Miss Allcutt speaking," I said in my efficient secretarial voice.

"Morning, Mercy. Are you speaking to me yet?"

Phil Bigelow was a detective with the Los Angeles Police Department and, according to Ernie, the only honest copper on the force. We'd had a bit of a conflict a little before Christmas time. The conflict had included Ernie, too.

"Of course, Detective Bigelow," I said formally. Very well, I was still mad at him for a few things he'd said and done during the Charley Wu affair. "How may I help you?"

"Cripes. You're still mad, aren't you? Ernie's forgiven me."

"Mr. Templeton has known you far longer than I have, Detective. May I take a message for Mr. Templeton?"

I heard him sigh into the receiver. "Please have him telephone me at the station."

"May I tell him what your call is about?" I asked, opening my middle drawer to grab both my secretarial pad and my message pad. I always kept sharpened pencils in a cup on my desk, and I'd already grabbed one of them.

"Yes. Please tell him he will never have to deal with Detective O'Reilly again."

I perked up slightly, although I wouldn't admit my interest to Phil Bigelow. "Oh, you mean the man who wanted to lock up Mr. Templeton for a murder he didn't commit?"

Another sigh. "Yes, Miss Allcutt. That's the one."

"I shall be happy to give him the message, Detective."

"Thanks."

"You're welcome."

I hung up the receiver without saying another word, although I felt gleeful when I wrote down the message on one of my made-for-the-purpose message pads. After placing the message on Ernie's desk, I went about my daily routine of dusting all surfaces and making sure all the clocks were wound.

Then I sat at my desk, folded my hands, placed them on my blotter, and wished Ernie would show up so I could ask him what was up with Detective O'Reilly. Ernie had worked for the Los Angeles Police Department himself for a year or two. The murder of William Desmond Taylor—unsolved to this day, five years after the fact—had finally tipped him over the edge and made him quit the force and start his own business. He'd told me more than once that the L.A.P.D. was rife with corruption.

After working with him on the Charley Wu case—in actual fact, I kind of had to drag him kicking and screaming into the case—I believed him. It was mean of me I know, but I hoped O'Reilly had been caught doing something truly dastardly. He was a loathsome man.

It was around 8:30 when I decided I might as well work on the detective novel I'd been writing. Ernie still hadn't shown up, and I was bored. I also wasn't sure what to do about the novel. I'd killed off someone, but I hadn't yet figured out why or who'd done the evil deed. Occasionally I wondered if I was cut out for writing, but only occasionally.

I had my hands on my manuscript and was about to pull it from the same bottom drawer into which I'd put my handbag when the telephone rang again. Once more I put the receiver to my ear and spoke into the mouthpiece. Before I'd even finished my usual spiel, the caller interrupted me.

"Mercy!"

"Harvey!" My brother-in-law, Harvey Nash, owned a motion-picture studio. His wife, my marvelous sister Chloe, was pregnant and about to foal. "Is Chloe all right?" He didn't sound worried, but he did sound excited.

"Yes! Chloe's fine, but we're getting ready for the baby, and I wanted to talk to you about what we'll need for the little Nashlet."

He wanted to talk to me? A single working woman? About what to do for a baby?

"Um, well, I imagine you'll need lots of diapers and so forth," I said, attempting to be helpful.

"No, no, no. I'm not talking about those kinds of things. I've already hired a nurse who will take care of the baby and Chloe. But I want to make sure our child has *everything*!"

"Um, that's nice." Befuddled about describes my condition at Harvey's call.

"Oh, I know I'm not making any sense," said Harvey, at last making some kind of sense, at least to me. "But I want to make sure our child lacks for nothing. What do babies need? And what colors should we paint the nursery?"

"Well," I said, becoming confused again. "You don't know if it's a boy or a girl yet, so you can't allow pink or blue to predominate. Is that what you mean?"

"Yes!"

He sounded so happy, I decided to allow my imagination to roam a bit. "Okay, I think soft pastel colors should be used for the nursery. Maybe a soft green or— Oh! I know! Paint nursery-book characters on the walls. You know, like from children's poems and so forth. I always loved *Johnny Crow's Garden* when I was a little girl. And *Froggy Went a-Courting* was a favorite, too."

"Um...I've never even heard of those— What did you say they are? Not fairy tales?"

"Good Lord, no! Fairy tales are horrid. The prince always gets his eyes plucked out or the mermaid dies or something. But there are some wonderful books for children with great illustrations in them."

"Really?"

"Really. Tell you what, Harvey, why don't you and Chloe come to dinner one of these nights. I'll go to the Los Angeles Public Library and check out some of my favorite children's books with pretty illustrations and show you what I mean. Wouldn't it be fun to have your child's room filled with illustrations from…oh, I don't know. Oh, wait! Yes, I do. Beatrix Potter! Oh, a Beatrix Potter room would be charming."

"Even for a boy?" Harvey sounded doubtful.

"Even for a boy. You can have Peter Rabbit hopping over a lettuce in Mr. McGregor's garden. Or Mrs. Tiggy-Winkle and Mr. Jeremy Fisher. Beatrix Potter wrote about boy and girl animals, and they're all just precious!"

"Hmm. I'll be darned. I've never even thought about having characters from children's books painted on the walls."

"Just be sure you use the correct paint," I said in warning. "Be sure whoever does the artwork isn't using paint that contains poisons."

"Paints contain *poison*?" Harvey bellowed into the phone.

"Not all of them. That's why you'll need to find an artist who knows what kinds of paints to use in a child's room."

"If there's any possibility of poisoned paint—"

"Harvey!" I interrupted him before he could carry on. "Stop it. Go to a paint store yourself and ask a proprietor what kinds of paints are suitable for a child's room." I considered my brother-in-law being chauffeured to a paint store and altered the course of my remarks. "Or I will. There's one close to the Figueroa Building here. I can pop in there during lunch or something and ask Mr. Chavez what the best paints are for a kid's room."

"You'd do that for me?"

"I'll do it for you, Chloe, and your darling baby, Harvey," I said, laughing. "But do come to dinner some night. I know we don't live close to each other any longer, but I miss Chloe so much. We used to be best friends. Well, I guess we still are, but we don't get to see each other very often since you moved to Beverly Hills."

"You're still welcome to move in with us, you know," said Harvey.

"Thank you. I appreciate the offer, and I'll always be grateful that you and Chloe allowed me to live with you when I escaped from Boston, but I love having my own home."

"I know you do. All right. I'll talk to Chloe, both about your artistic vision and about dinner, and she'll give you a call. The two of you can discuss these things."

"Sounds like you're excited about the baby," I said, happy to hear him sound so happy.

"I am. And so is Chloe, although she's always dithering about her figure."

"Having babies does affect a woman's shape. But Chloe is naturally slim, and I'm sure she'll return to her normal beautiful self not long after the baby's born."

"I don't care if she does. I've adored Chloe since the moment I first saw her," said Harvey, now sounding kind of dreamy.

"I know. And she adores you too." If we got any sappier, I might just be sick. "But I'd better get off the phone now, Harvey, because I think Ernie's finally here."

"Please give him my best," said Harvey. Both he and Chloe were fond of Ernie, who returned the compliment.

"Will do. I'm looking forward to Chloe's call and to seeing you both again soon."

"Likewise."

I hadn't lied. As I was speaking to Harvey, the outer office door opened, and Ernie Templeton himself strolled in. He looked relatively dapper, for him. By mutual consent, we didn't display any signs of our blossoming relationship in the office, which was strictly for business. Therefore I greeted him as I normally would.

"Happy Monday, Ernie."

"Happy Monday, Mercy. Did I hear you talking to Harvey? Any baby news yet?"

"Not yet. But he's dithering like a little old woman about how to decorate the baby's nursery and what colors to paint things and so forth. I thought only women went into raptures about babies."

"Depends on whether it's yours or not, I guess," said Ernie. "Phil went nuts when Rosie was born." Rosie was Phil and Pauline Bigelow's daughter.

"Sounds reasonable. There's a message on your desk that will make you happy, I think."

"We got a client?" he asked, perking right up.

"Well, no, but you'll like it anyway."

"If you say so."

"No, I mean it. Phil Bigelow called and asked you to telephone him at the station because O'Reilly has evidently been caught out in wrongdoing."

TWO

As I'd anticipated, my words produced a smile on my boss's face. What I hadn't anticipated was his saying, "You're back to calling him Phil again? I'm glad. He's an okay guy, you know."

"Phooey on him! I want to know what O'Reilly's been caught doing. So call Phil please."

"Yes, madam secretary," said Ernie. He chuckled his way into his office and gestured for me to join him. So I grabbed a secretarial pad and pencil, hopped up from my desk, and followed him. That way I could not only listen to Ernie's side of the conversation but could also take notes if note-taking seemed advisable.

As I sat in a chair facing his desk, Ernie tossed his hat on the rack beside his desk, hung up his overcoat, and revealed himself in a nice new suit! As much as I loved working for him and enjoyed his company, I must admit he often looked rather like an unmade bed. As he sat in his swivel chair, which used to have a hideous squeak until I went at it with an oilcan, he laid his copy of the *Los Angeles Times* on his desk and reached for the receiver on his telephone. Because he had a dial phone, he didn't have to go through an operator, but merely dialed Phil's number at the police station. Station Number One, if anybody cares.

"Detective Bigelow, please," Ernie said to the L.A.P.D.'s switchboard operator.

We both waited until his call was connected to Phil's office. My heart raced for a second or two for fear Phil might have bolted before Ernie called him, but it settled down when Ernie said, "Hey, Phil, Mercy said you got O'Reilly for something. Spill."

Although I listened hard and could hear Phil speaking, I couldn't make out any words from his end of the wire. I watched Ernie, though. First, he grinned. Then he lifted his eyebrows until they arched above his almost-turquoise eyes like larks ascending. Well, caterpillars, anyway. Then his mouth fell open and he said, "No shit?"

As fond as I was of my boss, I wished he'd clean up his language. But I suppose that's neither here nor there.

At last, Ernie said, "Yeah. Sure. Come on over. I'll make Mercy call you Phil, but you have to be really nice from now on and don't accuse any of her friends of doing anything bad. You know how she gets."

I think both men were laughing like hyenas when he finally hung the receiver on its hook.

"What precisely did you mean by *that*, Ernest Templeton?" I demanded. "I get like what? You were as peeved with him as I was when he wanted to send Charley Wu to the electric chair for a murder he didn't commit!"

"I know, I know. But call him Phil, okay? He slips up every now and then, but he's a lot better than most of the cops on the L.A.P.D. Trust me. I know."

"I know you know. So what's O'Reilly done?"

"He's been a bad, bad boy."

"Thanks a heap. That tells me a lot," I said sourly.

"He got caught abetting a so-called talent scout run a stable of young fillies out of a downtown office on Hill Street."

"He's illegally racing horses?" I asked, bewildered.

Ernie, curse him, was still chuckling when Detective Phil Bigelow showed up at the office.

At least I didn't have to suffer the humiliation of sitting there when Ernie told Phil about my misconception because the telephone rang again. I scooted out of Ernie's office and shut the door behind me. I heard both men hooting with laughter as I sat at my desk. Men! Insufferable creatures.

"Mr. Templeton's office. Miss Allcutt speaking."

"Mercy!"

"Chloe!" I missed my sister *so* much. "Did Harvey tell you he called? Asking me, of all people, how to decorate a nursery for a baby?"

With a laugh, Chloe said, "Yes, he told me. I love your idea about painting pictures on the baby's nursery walls, but Harvey didn't get the names properly. He said something about Froggy Crow and Jeremy Winkle. I have *no* idea what he was talking about."

"Ha! Sounds just like a man," I said, still smarting from Ernie having laughed at me. "I told him I thought it might be fun to paint pictures of characters from children's stories on the baby's walls. Or maybe there's some wallpaper that has characters from Beatrix Potter on it?" I made my sentence a question as it seemed unlikely any decorating firm would be so creative and forward-thinking.

"I doubt there's any wallpaper like that," said Chloe, confirming my suspicion. "But I love the Beatrix Potter idea. What's more, I'll bet Francis would love to paint the pictures. He's turning more to set decoration and painting than costuming lately."

Francis Easthope, a fast friend of both Chloe and Harvey, was perhaps the most handsome man alive. And that includes Ramon Navarro and John Gilbert. He might even have given Rudolph Valentino a run for his money, but poor Mr. Valentino had died in August of the prior year.

"I didn't know that about Mr. Easthope. He's so nice." And dreamy, but I didn't add that part.

"Yes, he is. I just love the idea of the Beatrix Potter characters. Mercy, you're a genius."

Tell that to Ernie, I didn't say. What I did say was, "Anyhow, did Harvey tell you I wanted to invite you two to dinner one night?"

"Yes, he did, and if I weren't as big as a house and uncomfortable all the time, I'd love to do that. At the moment, however, I'd rather we go out to somewhere we can be more private. You have those girls renting rooms and dining with you every day. I know they're all lovely and polite and everything, but I'd feel…Well, I'd feel like a hippo among gazelles. How about we take you and Ernie to the Ambassador or Musso and Frank's one of these evenings? We can get a private table and talk all we want. I won't feel out of place with only you and Ernie with Harvey and me. And maybe Francis."

"Thanks, Chloe. I understand. Well, I don't *precisely* understand, and you couldn't look like a hippo if you tried, but that would be swell. I'm sure Ernie will enjoy it, too."

"Now that he's rich, he can probably afford to take you to the Ambassador all the time."

"Ernie's not rich!" I said, surprised by Chloe's words.

"Well, maybe not rich-rich, but I'll bet he's still profiting from that job you two did in Chinatown."

I'd told Chloe all about how Ernie and I had helped Charley Wu and the kidnapped girls. "What do you know that I don't?" I asked. "If Ernie's rich because of that case, how come I'm not?"

"You're already rich," said Chloe.

"That's not the point. What do you know that I don't?" I repeated.

"Well, I honestly don't know anything for sure, but Francis and Harvey and several other people have told me that if you do a good turn for anyone in Chinatown, they'll shower you with moola for the rest of your life."

"Nobody's showered *me* with moola," I said, annoyed.

"Of course they didn't. You're a female."

"That's not fair!"

"Since when has the world been fair, Mercy? I thought that's why you moved from Boston to Los Angeles. You wanted to learn how the real world works. That's what you've told me a thousand times, anyway. That's how the real world works. Men get all the money and appreciation and acclaim. Women…don't."

"Still and all. I was the one who forced Ernie to take an interest in that case."

"I thought he and the Chinese fellow were friends. I thought their friendship was why he worked on the case."

"Well…" I'd forgotten that part. "You're right. I was the only one who believed there were people trapped in that icky old building, though. And there were, and we rescued them."

"Face it, Mercy. We're talking about men here. If those poor girls had died in that building, nobody would have cared about anything but the smell they made as their corpses rotted."

"Chloe!" I cried, horrified.

"You know I'm right."

After a several-second pause, I admitted it. "Yes. I know you're right. Will women ever claim their rightful place in this man's world?"

"I doubt it," said Chloe, not sounding as upset as I about the situation.

"Well, let me know when you want to get together. I aim to go to the library and check out some of my favorite children's stories, too. The walls don't have to belong exclusively to Beatrix Potter, after all."

"That's true. Well, pick a night that's good for you and Ernie and let me know, okay? I can't wait to see you again!"

"Likewise," I said. "I miss you so much, Chloe!" The door to Ernie's office opened, and I added, "But I guess I have to get back to work now."

"Do you have any?" she asked, having been privy to my worry about Ernie not having enough business.

"Not much," I admitted. "But I'd better go. *So* looking forward to seeing you and Harvey again!"

We hung up our receivers, and I dared face the two men walking out of Ernie's office. They both appeared pleased with themselves and the world, and they'd evidently stopped laughing about me not knowing what a stable was in terms of crime. Stupid men. Well, stupid *me*, but it wasn't my fault. I was learning.

"Thanks for coming, Phil. Your news made me really happy."

I knew Ernie told the truth because his smile was a mile wide.

"Didn't make me happy," muttered Phil. "I've known for years O'Reilly was a bad egg, but I didn't realize how rotten he was until Magruder's got raided and he got picked up with the lot of 'em."

"Hell, Phil, O'Reilly was on the take when *I* was on the force, and that was five years ago."

"I'd heard the rumors," said Phil glumly, "but we needed proof. We got it. Now O'Reilly's toast."

"Oh!" I said, butting in on the conversation. "Is he going to be electrocuted?"

I knew I'd misspoken—again—when both Phil and Ernie burst out laughing.

"You're becoming pretty bloodthirsty, Mercy," said Ernie. "Phil only meant O'Reilly's no longer welcome on the L.A.P.D., and if there's any justice in the world he'll be in for a term in the City Jail, if not the penitentiary at San Quentin."

"Oh. Very well. I'll make a mental note of that piece of slang," I said, sounding priggish to my own ears.

"You're doing swell, Mercy," said Ernie, giving me a sweet smile that made my cheeks heat up.

"Thanks, Mercy," said Phil. Quickly, I suspect to spare being told by me not to call me by my first name, he added, "Thanks, Ernie. I'm glad to get a bad copper off the force, but I wish we had more good ones to take the place of the bad ones."

"You'll have to clean house in order to do that. Starting at the top, with Davis."

"Davis isn't dirty," said Phil sounding as if he wanted to believe himself.

"Huh," said Ernie.

"Um, is Mr. Davis the police chief?" I asked.

"Yeah," said Ernie. "'Two-Gun Davis,' they call him. Wants bootleggers brought in dead, not alive."

"That sounds drastic," I said. "Not that I approve of bootleggers."

"Oh, he's drastic, all right," said Ernie. "He's hand in glove with Frank Shaw, L.A.'s charming mayor."

"Is he a crook too?" I asked, appalled. I seemed to feel appalled quite often as I learned more about my chosen home.

"As crooked as a dog's hind leg," said Ernie.

"That's a melancholy thought," I said.

"Yeah, it is," said Ernie.

"Gotta get back to the station," said Phil, putting on his hat, a nice new fedora I suspect he'd received as a Christmas present.

"Don't take any wooden nickels," Ernie told him as he walked him to the door. When he turned and walked back to his office, he said, "Was that call about a client?"

He sounded so hopeful, I hated to tell him the truth. "No. It was Chloe. She liked my idea about painting characters from children's books on the walls of the baby's nursery."

"Yeah?" Ernie's interest in the baby's nursery was faint at best.

"Yes. She wants to take you and me out with Harvey to the Ambassador or Musso and Frank's so we can be private and talk about it."

"She wants to talk to *me* about nursery walls?" Ernie stabbed his chest with his right forefinger.

"Makes as much sense as talking to me about them," I pointed out. "I don't know anything about nurseries."

"But you're a woman," said Ernie, as if being a woman automatically meant I'd want to talk about nurseries.

"Nertz, Ernie," I said, peeved. "I came to Los Angeles to learn about how the real world works, not to talk about babies. But Chloe is not only my sister, she's also my best friend, and I'm happy for her and Harvey. So I'll endure an evening chatting about nursery walls if that's what she wants me to do. I asked her to my house for dinner, but she said she'd rather go somewhere private. Said she'd feel like a hippo among my tenants."

"Chloe? Would feel like a *hippo*?" Evidently, Ernie also found the notion of Chloe looking anything other than beautiful and elegant a lengthy stretch of his imagination.

"I know, but that's what she said."

"Well, what the heck. I guess I can sacrifice an evening of my life to hearing about nursery walls," said Ernie. "Especially if Harvey's paying."

"Ernie Templeton, you're horrible!" I told him.

"Yeah. I know."

Grinning like the Cheshire Cat, he walked to his office and entered same.

"But I want to talk to you," I called, rising from my desk chair. "Chloe said something about you being rich now that you've helped someone in Chinatown. I want to hear an explanation about why she'd say something like that, Ernest Templeton."

"Oh, boy," Ernie said in a world-weary tone. "Here it comes. Women's rights. Women's money. Women's everything."

"You betcha," I said, following him into his office and closing the door after myself.

THREE

At about twelve-fifteen, Ernie and I took the elevator down to the lobby. As we entered the cage and Ernie pulled the door closed, he told me he intended to go to the Broadway to find a baby toy to give to Chloe and Harvey when we dined together. I thought that was sweet of him.

"You sure you don't want to go with me?" he asked pleadingly. Guess he wasn't accustomed to shopping for baby toys.

"Sorry, Ernie. I told Lulu I'd grab a sandwich at the diner across the street. She has something exciting to tell me, or so she said when she called me."

"Oh, yeah? What's that?"

"She wouldn't say. She just said it was wonderful, and she'd tell me about it over lunch."

"Well, good for Lulu," said Ernie.

"My sentiments exactly."

The elevator stopped at the first floor with something of a bump, and Ernie opened the cage door and took my arm to help me out. I didn't need his help, but his hand was warm on my arm and felt good there.

As a rule, when one walked into the lobby of the Figueroa Building, one would find Lulu seated at the reception desk either filing her nails or painting them. Today she'd already tucked her manicure supplies away in a drawer and was awaiting my arrival with her velvet cape already draped over her shoulders. As she sat in her stunning red cape, which I now saw she wore over a bright red-and-white polka-dotted dress with a low waist and a white fabric sash tied slightly below where her waist should have been (according to fashion designers, women were supposed to be shaped like boys and waists weren't in favor), she was chatting merrily with Mr. Buck and Junior.

As mentioned already, Mr. Buck was the building custodian. Junior was a young lad, probably twelve or thirteen, and he worked doing different chores for various offices in the building. The attorneys in the place had him running here and there most days, but every now and then Ernie or I would send him on an errand for us. For money, of course. Red-headed and freckle-faced, Junior was a jolly lad.

"Oh, Mercy! Here you are. I can hardly wait to tell you!"

"Yeah," said Junior. "Hurry up, will ya? She won't tell us until she tells you!"

"Mind your manners, Junior," said Mr. Buck, smiling at the kid.

"Yeah, yeah," said Junior.

"Okay." When she saw Ernie standing behind me, she frowned. "Did you invite Ernie to join us?"

"No," I told her. "Ernie just rode the elevator with me."

"Good," said Lulu.

"Hey!" said Ernie. "What do you have against me?"

"Nothing," said Lulu, rising and laughing. "I just want to tell Mercy first."

"Huh," said Ernie, trying to sound indignant.

"Come on, Lulu," I said, wrapping my scarf around my neck in preparation for walking outside and into the cold, cold day. For Los Angeles. In Boston, the weather might count as early spring.

"Where are you going, Ernie?" Lulu asked as he tied his own scarf around his neck and pulled on his driving gloves.

"The Broadway."

Lulu's eyes opened wide. "Whatcha gonna do there?"

I understood her surprise. Ernie wasn't known for his love of shopping.

"Gotta get a toy for Chloe and Harvey's kid."

"Aw, that's nice of you," said Lulu, picking up her handbag. She'd already slipped her gloves on. Her bottle-blond hair sported a bright red scarf she'd tied under her chin with a big bow. She looked pretty much like a Christmas present in human form.

"Yeah," said Ernie grumpily. "Mercy wouldn't go with me, so I gotta find something all by myself."

"They have a huge toy department," Lulu told him. "Get the kid one of those new teddy bears. They're real cute."

"Would a teddy bear work if the baby's a girl?" asked Ernie doubtfully.

"Sure," said Lulu. "By the time the kid's old enough to know what bears are, whether it's a girl or a boy, the bear will probably be gnawed to death by the baby teething on it."

Ew, I thought

"Ew," said Ernie.

"Yeah, you're probably right," said Lulu. "Chloe won't let her kid teethe on a stuffed toy. So get the little one a rattle or something."

"Or maybe another kind of stuffed toy," I suggested. "A stuffed horse? A horse could be for a boy or a girl, couldn't it? It wouldn't be blue or pink, anyway."

"Good idea," said Ernie. "Mr. Buck, mind helping me start the Studebaker?"

Ernie's dilapidated Studebaker was probably known all over the city of Los Angeles. I don't know what year or model it was, but it was about to fall apart completely. If the Chinese community was chipping in to give Ernie money, I hoped he'd get a new car with some of it. Heck, after our last case, I'd learned the folks in Chinatown had businesses all over their part of Los Angeles. Certainly, one member of Charley Wu's extended family owned an automobile dealership.

But Lulu was hurrying me along, so I decided to talk to Ernie about Chinese auto dealerships after lunch.

The diner across the street from the Figueroa Building was called, appropriately enough, the Figueroa Diner. Lulu and I watched for traffic and then made a mad dash across the street without getting run down. We got honked at a couple of times, but that was only normal.

Pulling open the diner's door, Lulu said, "I wish they'd put up street lights or stop signs at a few intersections in this part of town. You take your life in your hands every time you cross the stupid street."

Panting slightly as I walked into the diner, I said, "I do too. Thanks, Lulu."

"Sure." She scanned the diner.

"Want to sit at the counter?" I asked, eyeing the long counter, where several seats stood empty.

"No. I want a booth. I'm so excited! I've been wanting to tell you what happened all morning long, and I want us to be as private as possible!"

"Okay. Well, there's a booth," I said, defying a lifetime of my overbearing mother's teachings and pointing to an empty booth.

"Great." Grabbing my sleeve, Lulu tugged me toward the booth, nodding at a smiling waitress along the way.

The waitress followed us to our booth and wiped the table with her damp rag as we slithered into seats on either side. "Want a menu?" she asked us. "We have a special today. Sliced chicken sandwich with a pickle and potato chips for twenty-five cents. Get a Coke for a nickel more."

Lulu and I eyed each other across the table, then we both nodded. "Sounds good," I said. "Only I'll have hot tea, please. It's too cold for a Coke."

"Same here," said Lulu.

"Be right back," said the cheery waitress, and she bustled off to get our lunches. On a normal day, I'd have ordered a corned beef on rye, to spite my mother, but a quarter for a chicken sandwich, a pickle, and potato chips also appealed.

"So what's your big news, Lulu? I've been waiting all morning to hear!"

"Oh, Mercy, I can't hardly believe it," said Lulu, leaning across the table and keeping her voice low. "I was walking to the Figueroa Building from Sue's building when a guy in a big Chrysler pulled up next to me. He rolled down his window and asked me if I could tell him how to get to the La Brea Tar Pits."

"How to get to where?" I asked, wondering what in heck the La Brea Tar Pits were.

"The La Brea Tar Pits. You know, that big smelly, oily area where they're finding all the fossils? On Wilshire? In the middle of Hancock Park?"

"There are pits of mucky oil in the middle of Hancock Park? I thought Hancock Park was where all the rich folks live."

"It is, but the guy who originally owned it donated a bunch of the land that's full of pitch and oil and crud to the city. When scientists began finding old animal bones there, they made it a park in 1924."

"Really? And there are fossils there?" Now I was interested in the Tar Pits, if not the man who stopped to ask Lulu where they were.

"Yes. Mammoths and animals like that. But that's not the important part!" said Lulu, waving mammoths and other fossilized remains away as if they were fairy dust. "The important part is the guy sort of squinted at me and then pulled his car over to the curb and stopped."

"Good heavens! Did you run away?" I asked, shocked at such bold behavior on a Los Angeles street in the bright morning of a brisk January day.

"Are you kidding? The guy's a *talent scout*, Mercy! He said I look just like the kind of lady he's looking for. He's a scout for the advertising folks who promote the WAMPAS Baby Stars! He said he thinks I'm perfect to be a WAMPAS Baby Star!"

"Good heavens, Lulu, really?" I stared at Lulu, amazed. And faintly troubled, as I recalled former Detective O'Reilly and the so-called talent scout ruse. But I didn't want to spoil Lulu's moment by casting doubt on her dreams of stardom. "That's wonderful!"

"I know! Isn't it swell?" Lulu's smile would have brightened up the darkest day. As the lights in the diner were already on, it didn't have a chance to light up the joint in which we sat.

By the way, in case you didn't know, the WAMPAS Baby Stars were products of a promotional campaign put together by the Western Association of Motion Picture Advertisers. Hence, the name. WAMPAS: Western Association of Motion Picture Advertisers. Clara

Bow had been a baby star, as had Colleen Moore, Bessie Love, Evelyn Brent, and several other gorgeous actresses. As I peered at Lulu from across the diner's table, I decided she could, indeed, compete with such lovelies. In looks. I'd learned long ago that looks aren't necessarily what makes a star. What counts is how a person comes across on the screen. But never mind that. I was excited for Lulu and hoped the fellow who'd stopped and talked to her was a legitimate talent scout and not a rotten cad.

"What's his name? How's he going to make you a star, baby or otherwise?"

"Mr. Clint Faraday is his name. First of all, he needs to interview me. He said we can do that over lunch. He'll take me to some fancy place and see how I get along. You know, he'll check my manners and make sure I don't eat peas off my knife or anything like that."

"Good Lord, he didn't *say* that, did he?" I asked, aghast again.

"No, but I knew what he meant. If I was some silly broad from the sticks who didn't know her salad fork from her butter knife, he wants to find out about it before he put much time into me. I have you to thank for that, by the way."

"For what? For teaching you the difference between a salad fork and a butter knife?"

"No. For telling me there *were* items called butter knives and salad forks. In Oklahoma, we had spoons, forks, and knives. We used our knives for everything from cutting meat to cutting bread, and we used the same fork for everything. My mother would never let us eat peas from a knife." She giggled.

"Oh. Of course. I understand." My mother had made me learn every single name of every single piece of silver flatware she owned starting from when I was in the cradle. I'd been shocked when I'd first witnessed people plucking olives from a bowl with a plain old fork instead of the special olive tool designed for the purpose. And you couldn't use your olive fork for pickles, either. You had to use your pickle fork. I swear, the waste of time, money, and effort that went on in my mother's life was for the birds.

However, that's neither here nor there.

"Yeah. And then he'll have to get me photographed to see how I look on film."

"That makes sense," I said.

"Yeah, it does," said Lulu, looking slightly worried. "I hope I look okay in the pictures."

"I think you'll look fine," I said. Then I added something I felt was important, after having lived with my sister and her movie-producer husband for several months. "But the main thing you need to do is project your personality when you're being photographed. Some people are lovely to look at, but they're dull as dirt in the pictures."

"Yeah?"

"Yes. Believe me, I've heard all about it from Harvey and Chloe. And remember that starlet who turned out to be the murderess? The one who called herself Jacqueline Lloyd?"

"How could I ever forget her?" said Lulu.

"Well, her sister Sylvia was almost as pretty as Jacqueline was, but she didn't sparkle on the screen. So you need to project yourself. Your personality. Don't forget, because it's really important."

"How do I do that?" asked Lulu, beginning to look uneasy.

I hadn't intended to make her lose confidence, so I used a bracing tone to say, "Easy! Just look into the camera and think to yourself, 'I am Lulu LaBelle, star of the silver screen.' Don't be shy. Be *Lulu*, the Lulu Ernie and I know. The Lulu everyone in the Figueroa Building and Mercy's Manor knows! You can do it. You do it every day. Don't get shy because somebody's pointing a camera at you."

"Huh. Now I'm scared."

"Don't be scared!" I said, using an uncharacteristically wide gesture in my enthusiasm and almost knocking the tray out of our waitress's hands. Startled, I turned and said, "Oh, I'm so sorry," and leaped up to help her re-balance her tray.

"It's okay," she said, checking the items on her tray to be sure none of them had slid off.

"I didn't mean to bump you." Feeling contrite, I began helping her empty her tray.

"You don't have to do that," she said. Now *she* sounded uneasy.

This clearly wasn't my day when it came to making people feel comfy with themselves. Or me.

"Don't worry about it," Lulu told her, smiling. "Mercy's always trying to help people. She just gets carried away sometimes."

"Oh," said the waitress. "It's nice that you try to help people, but you don't need to help me. Thanks." I think her thanks were an afterthought.

"Very well," I said. "I'll sit down and be still."

"Good idea," said Lulu.

The waitress only smiled as she laid our lunches before us. "And here's your tea," she said, setting steaming mugs on the table. "I was afraid these would spill, but they didn't."

"I'm sorry," I said again. "Truly didn't mean to cause an upset."

"You didn't," said the waitress. "See? Nothing spilled even a little bit."

"Good. Thank you," I said.

She left, and I whispered across the table, "I'll leave her a big tip."

Lulu laughed and lifted the lid of half of her sandwich to peer at its innards. "Looks pretty good," she said, sounding surprised.

"Excellent." As I'd peered at Lulu's sandwich when she opened it, I didn't bother checking mine. I just lifted half of it and took a bite. "Oh, my, this is delicious!" I said. "Wonder what they put on the bread."

"Mayonnaise, probably," said Lulu. "But they seasoned the chicken with something to make it taste better than regular old chicken."

After swallowing my bite of sandwich, I said, "Mrs. Buck's chickens always taste swell."

"Well, yeah, but *she's* a cook."

"True. Anyhow, I'm glad we got the special."

"Me, too."

We both concentrated on our lunches for a few minutes, before I decided maybe it wouldn't hurt to caution Lulu about her Mr. Faraday. "You know, Lulu, Ernie had a visit from Phil Bigelow this morning."

"Yes," she said, snapping out the word. Have I mentioned Lulu didn't care for policemen in general? That's because they'd once arrested her brother, Rupert, for a murder he didn't commit.

Are you recognizing a pattern here? The L.A.P.D. arresting innocent people for crimes they didn't commit? I recognized it, and I didn't like it one little bit.

"Well, this morning, he came in to tell Ernie that one Detective O'Reilly, who's as dirty as an old sock, finally got caught doing something evil."

"Good!" said Lulu. "They should arrest about a hundred more of them and clean up the place."

"You may well be correct," I said, "But this O'Reilly character got caught abetting a so-called talent scout named Magruder, who was actually luring young women into being"—I lowered my voice, leaned farther across the table and whispered the next word—"prostitutes."

Lulu squinted at me, and her lips turned down in a frown. "So what?" she said, making the two words sound like a challenge.

"Well, nothing really. I just wanted to warn you that not everybody who claims to be a talent scout really *is* a talent scout."

"Well, Mr. Clint Faraday *is*!" said Lulu in a voice telling me I'd best not argue with her.

So I didn't. And I hoped like anything she was correct about Mr. Faraday.

FOUR

W hen we made our treacherous way across the street from the diner back to the Figueroa Building, I felt some constraint between Lulu and me. I figured it was because I might have cast some doubt on her dream. I hadn't meant to. I only wanted her to be careful.

How come when I tried to be helpful, I ended up knocking into waitresses' trays and making my friends grumpy? Darn it!

When Lulu swept behind the reception desk, more or less leaving me in her dust, I tried to rectify my error. "Listen, Lulu. I'm sure Mr. Faraday is a real talent scout. It's only because of the other guy that I was hoping you'll be cautious."

She sat, opened her desk drawer, took out her manicure supplies, and glared at me. As she put her handbag on the little shelf below the drawer, she asked, "How long have you lived in Los Angeles, Mercy Allcutt?"

"About eight months, I think," I said.

"I've been here for three years. I know a heck of a lot more about what goes on here than you do!"

"I know you do," I said. "I'm sorry, Lulu. You're right. I should just butt out. Honestly, I wish you the very best, and I hope when you're a huge star and everybody worships you, you'll remember your old pals." Was that laying it on too thick?

Apparently, it wasn't, because Lulu thawed. "Oh, Mercy, I'm sorry I was touchy. This is just so exciting for me, you know? I never thought I'd *ever* get a chance like this one."

"I know, Lulu. And I also know you'll do great. Just don't forget to project your personality when you're with Mr. Faraday, and especially if he takes any moving shots of you."

"Yeah," said Lulu, again sounding doubtful—although, thank the good Lord, not hostile. "About that. I'm not quite sure what you mean about projecting my personality."

And there, all of a sudden, I had a brilliant idea! I was pretty sure this one actually was brilliant. Sometimes you had to wait a while to figure out the overall brilliance of a thought. "I know! We can practice! At home tonight, I'll take pictures of you, and you can practice."

"Yeah? You think that might work?"

"Why wouldn't it? I mean, if you wanted to become a famous painter, you'd practice your art, wouldn't you? Why not practice projecting your personality?"

"No reason I can think of," said Lulu, back to being her good-natured self. "If I can figure out how to do it. I don't even know what my personality is."

"Well, I do! Good. I have a pocket Kodak. We can take photos with it."

"Thanks, Mercy!"

With that, I left Lulu and walked to the staircase, there being no other person around with whom to share the elevator. When I got to the office, Ernie was already back from his shopping expedition and, I assumed, lunch. I hung my hat, coat, and scarf on the rack beside the door and walked to his office.

Peeking into it, I said, "How'd the toy shopping go?"

"Pretty good." He leaned over, lifted a brown parcel, and plopped it onto his desk. "What do you think of this?" Selecting the scissors from his multi-tool pocket knife, he snipped the string. When he drew back the paper, he revealed a gigantic toy duck!

"Good heavens, Ernie, the duck will be bigger than the baby!"

Squinting first at the duck and then at me, he said, "You think it's too much? I kinda like it."

"I love it," I said, thinking any red-blooded American child of either sex would also love the enormous stuffed animal, after the child grew up enough to appreciate it. I nodded enthusiastically. "It's great! Now I should get a giant stuffed bunny to go with it."

"I could have got a stuffed rabbit," he said as if I'd criticized his purchase. "But the rabbit was pink."

"No, no. Your ducky is marvelous," I assured him. "It's precious. Chloe will love it, and so will Harvey. So do I."

"I can get one for you, too," he said.

"That's all right. I don't need a gigantic toy duck. Buttercup might get jealous."

"You're right," he said, rewrapping the huge duck in the brown paper and tying the string together again. "So what's Lulu's news?"

I sat in one of the chairs before his desk and said, "When she was walking to work from the dentist's office—"

"She went to the dentist before work?"

"No. She just walked to Sue Krekeler's dentist's office to make an appointment before walking back to the Figueroa Building."

"Oh. Good. I hate going to the dentist." I could see Ernie running his tongue over his teeth after he spoke.

"I think everybody does. Anyway, when she was walking back here, some man stopped and asked her if she knew the way to the La Brea Tar Pits."

"That's her exciting news?"

"No! Let me finish, will you?" I said, slightly irked.

Holding up his hands, Ernie said, "All right, all right. What happened when the guy stopped and asked the way to the Tar Pits?"

"Turned out he was a talent scout. He pulled over, parked his car, got out, and told Lulu he thinks she has the makings of a WAMPAS Baby Star."

When Ernie's lip curled and one of his eyebrows lifted, my heart sank a little. "I know," I said. "Especially after learning about Magruder and O'Reilly this morning, I felt a little bit like that, too."

"How does she know the guy's legitimate?" Ernie asked.

"He had a business card?" I said, making the sentence into a question.

"Hell, anybody can have business cards printed."

"I know, but I didn't want to burst her bubble. I tried to give her a little—really, a *tiny*—warning, and she got all huffy. Reminded me she's lived in Los Angeles for three years, as opposed to my eight or nine months."

"Well, Lulu's a big girl," said Ernie, evidently thrusting any qualms aside. "She can take care of herself. I'd back Lulu in a fight with a phony talent scout any day."

"You're probably right," I said, laughing.

"By the way, when we dine with Chloe and Harvey, it's possible Francis Easthope will join us," I said.

"Eh. I can stand it."

Ernie didn't care for Mr. Easthope for no good reason.

Oh, very well. Mr. Easthope was one of those men who preferred men to women. He was still a nice man and a charming companion, and he was smart and talented. So phooey on Ernie.

"Any date good for you in particular?" I asked.

"Naw. Just tell Chloe to choose one, and I can pick you up and meet the Nashes wherever they want to dine."

"Thanks, Ernie."

"Thank Chloe and Harvey. I'll just be along for the ride. I don't think I can add anything to a conversation about baby nurseries."

"I feel the same way, actually," I said.

The telephone rang, so I left Ernie's office to answer it at my desk.

The call was from a potential client! Thrilled, I wrote down the information from the speaker and made an appointment for her at nine a.m. on the next day. The case didn't sound awfully exciting, but it was a case, and Ernie's firm needed the money.

I walked into his office to find him reading the *Los Angeles Times*. He lowered it to peer at me. I waved the message at him. "New client. Tomorrow at nine a.m."

"Good. Know what it's about?"

With a sigh, I said, "Yes. Mrs. Felix Smedley, whose first name is Verna, thinks her husband has been running around on her."

"Aw cripes," said Ernie, disgusted. "I wish people would just stop getting married. Marriages never work out, and the partners end up hating each other."

"Chloe and Harvey are happy together," I said, not appreciating my boss's total condemnation of the concept of marriage.

"Yeah, well, they're the exception."

Contemplating some of the marriages I'd seen first-hand—not many—I said, "Maybe you're right. But Phil and Pauline are happy, aren't they?"

"Yeah, and so are my sister and her husband. I guess it depends on the people involved."

"I should think so." I paused for a moment. "You know, Ernie, I told Lulu that, when this talent scout of hers takes pictures of her, she needs to project her personality."

"Makes sense to me," he said, his eyes straying to the *Times* on his desk.

"So I told her we could practice this evening at home. I have a pocket Kodak, and I can take pictures of her."

"Inside? At night?" Ernie's gaze lifted from the *Times* and landed on me.

"Oh," I said, having forgotten all about the lighting situation on a January night. Indoors or outdoors, come to think of it. "Um, you don't think a bunch of lamps and so forth would provide enough light to take pictures by? By which to take pictures, I mean?"

"Your grammar's okay with me, kiddo, even when it's wrong."

I hated it when he called me *kiddo*, but I didn't take him to task because he'd put an elbow on his desk and was tapping his chin thoughtfully. If he could salvage my brilliant idea, I'd forgive him that *kiddo*.

"You know, I think there are a couple of floodlights in storage downstairs. Maybe if we can talk to Buck or Junior, they could find them for us. I can take them to your house tonight." He gave me a cheeky grin. "Especially if you invite me for dinner."

"Floodlights? What are floodlights?"

"Big bright lights. They use 'em for outdoor shots in the flickers sometimes. That lawyer who used to work down the hall used them for taking pictures of some of the Hollywood lovelies he represented."

"Ah, yes. Lulu and I were reminiscing about Jacqueline Lloyd and her sister at lunch today."

"Yeah, well I don't think he took the lights. Why don't you call Lulu and see if either Mr. Buck or Junior is hanging around the reception desk and have her ask one of them? They'll probably know about the light situation in the basement."

"Very well. Um…How do the floodlights work? I mean, do people hold them or what?"

"No. They're on stands. If the ones I'm thinking of are still there, they might require new bulbs." His brow furrowed. "Wonder what kind of bulbs they take."

"I have no idea, but perhaps Mr. Buck will know."

"Good idea. Give Lulu a ring." He picked up the *Times* and resumed reading.

So I left his office and sat at my desk, where I picked up the receiver on my 'phone and dialed 0, which would get me Lulu, who answered the few calls that came in to the reception area.

"Figueroa Building," came her voice, sounding a little tinny over the telephone wire.

"Hey, Lulu, Ernie reminded me that I can't take pictures in the dark, so he said there might be a couple of floodlights in the basement."

"Hey, Mercy! What are floodlights? And Mr. Faraday's taking me to lunch tomorrow!"

"Oh, how nice," I said, trying to sound chipper while wondering if Mr. Faraday was legitimate. "Floodlights are big, bright lights. Is either Mr. Buck or Junior around? Maybe they can go and look for us."

"I didn't even think about lighting," said Lulu. "Boy, were we dumb, huh?"

"Well…Yes. I guess so. I'm the dumb one, because I suggested taking pictures at night in the dark. But if there *aren't* any lights down in the basement, you can still practice. I'll have you pose in various postures and tell you if you're projecting your personality properly."

"I still don't know how to project my personality. I don't think I have a personality."

"*Everybody* has a personality, Lulu! It's…it's…Well, it's how you present yourself to the world. You know, if you're animated or dull and stuff like that."

"Oh, you mean like Clara Bow's a live wire?"

"Yes! Exactly. And you can tell she's a live wire from her photographs. Clara Bow never looks dull and boring."

"Ah. I get it. I think. Okay, I'll see if I can find Junior. I'll call the basement. If he's not on a run for one of the lawyers here, he's generally down there in the basement helping Mr. Buck."

"Excellent. Let me know. You don't mind if Ernie joins us, do you?"

Silence greeted my question.

"Lulu? You know Ernie. He won't be any trouble. In fact, he can help us. He knows a lot about…well, a lot of things. He's the one who suggested the floodlights."

"Oh. Well, I don't want to look stupid."

"You won't look stupid! How could you possibly look stupid?"

"I don't know, but it'll be embarrassing to pose in front of Ernie."

"Nonsense! If this works out with your Mr. Faraday, you'll be posing in front of the entire *world*!"

Silence again.

"Lulu?"

"Yeah. You're right," she said uncertainly. "I guess this will be kind of like a test, huh?"

"Exactly!"

"Okay. I'll call the basement. And I'll try not to be embarrassed if Ernie's there when I pose."

"Excellent! I told him he could come for dinner if he brought the floodlights."

"Mercy! You didn't!"

"Did too. But I guess he can come to dinner anyway, even if some-body tossed out the floodlights."

With a laugh, Lulu said, "You two are a hoot," and hung up.

We were a hoot? Ernie and me? I wasn't entirely sure what being a hoot entailed, but if it made Lulu happy, I guess it couldn't be too bad.

FIVE

M r. Buck found a floodlight in the basement. He and Ernie wrestled it into Ernie's Studebaker before Mr. Buck, who always arrived to work early, went home for the day. Because the floodlight and Mr. Buck were going to the same place, my house, Ernie drove them both there at around three-thirty that afternoon. Ernie came back to the office at approximately four.

When he walked into the outer office from the hall, I held up a message for him. "We have another potential client."

"Good! Another erring spouse?" Ernie took the message from my hand and peered at it.

"I'm afraid so, only this time it's a man wanting you to check on a perhaps-wayward wife. Did you and Mr. Buck get the floodlight into the house all right?"

After squinting at the message, Ernie glanced at me again. "Huh? Oh, yeah. We got the floodlight in the house and in a corner. You have to be careful with those things because when the bulbs get hot, they're apt to shatter easily."

"Oh. Did you plug it in and see if it worked?"

"Yes. That's why I mentioned the possibility of a shattering bulb."

"Of course."

After heaving a huge sigh, Ernie took his message and himself and walked into his own room. "I guess I'm glad people are still marrying each other. Keeps me in business."

"Kind of," I said, thinking what a sordid business a private investigator's often is. "I wish someone would hire you to find another stolen dog."

"One stolen dog per year is my quota," he called to me from his office. "You don't want that lady with the mastiffs to get one stolen, do you? Buttercup would never stand for you getting a mastiff."

"Why would I get a mastiff?" I asked indignantly.

"You got a poodle after the stolen-poodle case."

"That's because the poodle in question was so sweet. I wouldn't want either of Mrs. What's-her-name's mastiffs." In fact, the notion made me shudder.

Ernie only laughed.

In the last hour before my five o'clock quitting time, the telephone rang twice more. The first time, the calling party was Chloe, asking if Ernie and I could meet her and Harvey at the newly opened Brown Derby restaurant on Wilshire Boulevard on the upcoming Wednesday at seven-thirty p.m. I agreed after asking Ernie if he'd be free on Wednesday.

"You betcha," he said. "I haven't been to the Brown Derby."

"I haven't either, but it's cunning to look at. Just like a derby hat."

"Cunning, is it?"

"Bother you, Ernest Templeton," I told him and I returned to my desk and resumed speaking to my sister. "Fine with both Ernie and me, Chloe," I told her.

"Good. I've been wanting to try out the place, and this seems like a perfect time."

"Will Mr. Easthope be joining us?"

"Yes. Will Ernie punch him?" Chloe was making a joke, but I didn't appreciate it much.

"Of course not." My tone of voice was repressive.

"Just kidding, Mercy. Have you heard from Mother recently?"

"No, thank God. Not since the last time she demanded I go to Pasadena for the Tournament of Roses Parade. That's...Oh, my goodness, that's about two and a half weeks ago! How did I get so lucky?"

"I don't know," said Chloe, sounding glum. "But she's promised to come to our house and help with the baby when it arrives."

"How in the *world* will she help with the baby? She didn't even help with *us* when we were babies!"

"I have no idea, but I don't know how to stop her."

"Aren't they planning to return to Boston soon?" I asked, hope ringing in my voice.

"Father is. Mother said she'll join him after I'm 'well settled in' with the baby. Those were her words. 'Well settled in,' as if there was anything she would do if I wasn't. Anyhow, I'm going to have a nurse and a nanny, so Mother will just be in the way."

"She's always in the way when she's around," I said. Not particularly filial, but true.

"I know. But what can I do?"

"I just told her no when she demanded I go to Pasadena. She then proceeded to call me names, but I'm used to that."

"You always were a problem child," said Chloe, laughing.

"Not always, but I sure am now. It takes practice, though. It's not easy at first."

"You did the wise thing by not going to Pasadena for Christmas. It was pure hell."

"You knew it would be," I said, perhaps not kindly. "Now you'll have a better excuse not to do things Mother tells you to do."

"Harvey and I didn't go to Pasadena on New Year's Day, even though we'd have liked to see the parade, but I really didn't feel like sitting with Mother and Father and—"

"The mayor," I finished for her, interrupting her. Rude of me, I know.

"Yes." She heaved a huge sigh of her own. "The mayor. I have nothing against the mayor of Pasadena, but we'd barely survived Christmas at Mother and Father's place. I wasn't about to endure another spate of time with them."

"Practice saying no. Practice in front of a mirror or something."

Chloe laughed again. "Nuts," she said and hung up on me.

The second call I received between four and five p.m. that day was from another potential client! Yay for us! Maybe. I wrote the information down and frowned a bit. Then I decided to deliver it to Ernie in person.

He glanced up from the magazine he'd been perusing, lifting his left eyebrow. "Yeah?"

"You remember Mrs. Wilkes?"

"No. Who's Mrs. Wilkes?" He took the message from my hand and lifted his right eyebrow a little higher than his left.

"She's the matron of the home for the…I'm not sure what to call them, but—"

"Oh," said Ernie, interrupting me. "Yeah. The loony bin. I remember. What's the name of the guy who escaped and came here?"

"Mr. Brentwood. And it's not nice to call it a loony bin, Ernie Templeton. Those poor people can't help being…challenged, I guess."

"Crazy, is what I'd guess. Did Brentwood escape again?"

"Yes, he did, and no one can find him this time. Mrs. Wilkes is hoping you can help."

"Cripes. How should I know where that maniac goes when he escapes?"

"He's not a maniac!"

"Yes, ma'am," said Ernie in a whatever-you-say voice.

"Anyhow, she has a list of places the home has taken its guests to, and—"

Ernie interrupted again, this time with a crow of laughter. "*Guests*? They're lunatics, if they're all like that Brentwood character."

"He wasn't a lunatic," I said hotly. "He was…confused."

With a roll of his eyes, Ernie said, "He was confused, all right."

"He might have been confused," I said, still hotly, "but he was right!"

"Guess I have to concede that point," said Ernie. "So what does Mrs. Wilkes want me to do? Visit all the places they've taken the loonies and look for Mr. Brentwood?"

"I guess so. She said something about him suddenly having taken a dislike to one of the helpers there, so she doesn't want to send him after Mr. Brentwood, because if Mr. B saw the helper, he'd probably run away."

"Thought he already ran away."

"Well, yes, he did, I guess, but she wants someone with whom Mr. Brentwood feels comfortable to search for him. So that if, for instance, he should espy you at the Griffith Park Zoo or something, he wouldn't try to hide by running into the lions' dens or whatever."

"Good gawd," said Ernie.

"Well, it's money, don't forget," I said.

"Yeah. It's money. Has she given you the list yet?"

"No. She only mentioned Chinatown and the zoo. She's going to telephone tomorrow and dictate a complete list to me. She thought you might want to check out Chinatown today."

"I have plans for my evening," said Ernie.

"Yes," I said. "You do, but maybe eating and helping Lulu won't take too long."

"You know, if you take actual photographs of Lulu, you'll have to use up the whole roll of film and then take it to the camera shop or pharmacy to get the pictures developed."

My heart sank. "You're right. I hadn't even thought about that."

"But you don't really need film. This is only to help Lulu get comfortable in front of a camera, right? So if we have the floodlight, and you point your Kodak at her, it'll be almost like the same thing."

"That's a good idea," I said, happy again. "And you can tell her if she's projecting herself well. You know, we need her to look perky and not dull."

"Lulu's never dull," said Ernie.

"Not to us, she isn't, but some people look like wooden dolls on-screen. Harvey has told me he's met some gorgeous women who wanted to be actresses, but who looked like blocks of cement when filmed. Lulu has to be able to project her inner…animation, I suppose is a good way to express it."

"I imagine Harvey knows what he's talking about. It kind of makes sense."

"I think so. So we have to make sure Lulu projects her…What would you call it?"

"Beats me," said Ernie, as helpful as ever.

"Oh, you know! Her Lulu-ness! She needs to project animation."

"The film will be blurry if she's animated."

"You know what I mean!" I snapped.

"Yeah, I know," said Ernie, grinning.

"You're impossible!"

"I know. That's why you like me."

I didn't slam his door, but I managed not to laugh until I got to my desk and he couldn't hear me.

Ernie decided to leave work early and take a quick look around Chinatown in search of Mr. Brentwood before he came over to my house in the evening. Therefore, Caroline, Lulu, Sue and I had a chilly walk to Angels Flight and then on to my house. Oh, but the house smelled *so good* when we got there, though! Mr. Buck had told Mrs. Buck Ernie aimed to dine with us that night, so she'd decided to roast two chickens.

After consuming our dinners, we sat at the table, I at the head and Ernie at the foot—a portent of things to come? Oh, who knew?—looking at each other probably like overfed piglets. Then Mrs. Buck brought in dessert. Dessert! After roast chicken, mashed potatoes, green peas, a salad made with celery and carrots and I don't know what all else.

"You're too good to us, Mrs. Buck," I said, as she handed out slices of peach pie to everyone at the table.

"Nonsense. You girls need good food, and so does Mr. Ernie. Why, I'll bet your usual dinner is a cheese sandwich."

"Not always. I eat a lot of Chinese and Mexican food," said Ernie.

"Huh. Well, you're getting good, home-cooked American food in Miss Mercy's house."

I didn't tell her that I actually wouldn't mind a Chinese or Mexican meal once in a while. I could always visit Chinatown or one of the little streets that had Mexican taco and tamale stands at lunchtime with Lulu on a Saturday.

"Well, I do love eating your good cooking, Mrs. Buck," said Ernie, looking at his slice of pie as if he weren't sure it would fit.

I knew the feeling. But I didn't want to upset Mrs. Buck, so I sacrificed my waistline and ate my pie. Boy, was it good!

After dinner, Caroline and Sue went up to their rooms to do whatever they wanted to do, and Ernie and Mr. Buck set up the floodlight in the living room. Ernie made sure it was in a safe corner so nobody could knock it over by accident and shatter the bulb.

Lulu was in a dither at first. "What should I wear? Oh, Mercy, I'm so nervous! Should I change into something blue? Red?"

"It doesn't matter, Lulu. There's no film in the camera and, even if there was film in the camera, the pictures would be black and white when they were developed." I'd already explained the film-less camera situation to her.

"True, true," she said, patting her blond hair. "Does my hair need tidying?"

"You look fine, Lulu," I said. "You're perfect the way you are."

"Huh. Sez you."

I'd never seen Lulu in such a state. "Calm down, Lulu. Next thing we know, you'll be gnawing on your lip and getting lip rouge on your teeth! Take some deep, calming breaths."

"Calming breaths. Right." Lulu sat on one of the chairs in the living room and took several deep breaths.

"You two ready?" Ernie said, walking over to us from the floodlight. "We're all set for your close-up, Lulu."

"Close-up!" Lulu shrieked. "*What* close-up?"

"Calm down, Lulu," I told her, laughing. "This is just practice. You can't be this nervous when Mr. Faraday takes your pictures, or you'll never make it onto the silver screen."

"Oh," she said, exhaling a huge gust of air and seeming to deflate. "You're right. I'm being silly."

"Calm down, kiddo," said Ernie to Lulu. I was glad I wasn't the only kiddo he knew.

Or maybe I wasn't. Well, I'd think about it later.

"Why don't we have you sit in a chair first," I suggested. "Pull up that pretty blue chair, Ernie. Lulu, why don't you sit on the chair and look off into the distance pensively?"

"How do I do that?" asked Lulu.

How to explain "pensive"? "Um, sit on the chair, but with your hand to your cheek—don't cover it. Just place your fingers like this." I demonstrated by lifting my right hand and just touched my chin with my little finger, bent my next three fingers low on my cheek, and rested my thumb on my neck. "Like that."

"Oh. Okay. Is that pensive?"

"Well, no, but it'll help. While you look into the distance with your hand like that, think about something you wish you had. Or yearn to see. Something like that. That's pensive." I looked at Ernie, who sat on the sofa trying not to laugh. "Isn't it, Ernie?"

He sobered instantly. "Yes. That would be pensive, all right."

For the record, Mr. Buck was standing near the floodlight, making sure to turn it off and on when necessary.

Lulu posed. Mr. Buck turned on the floodlight. I picked up my Kodak and aimed it at Lulu.

It was Mr. Buck who interrupted us. "Wait a minute. I can get the lighting better so that the shadows are right. Miss Lulu, turn your head to the left just a little bit. There. That's perfect."

"It *is* perfect," I said, amazed. Then, because I'd sounded amazed, I tried to salvage the situation so as not to imply any insult to Mr. Buck. "Do you practice photography, Mr. Buck? You just posed Lulu perfectly."

"Take the picture, please," said Lulu. "My arm's getting tired. Do I look yearning enough?"

"Yes," said Ernie. "You're a perfect yearner."

"Yeah. I like to take pictures," said Mr. Buck. He didn't sound offended. "I like to go to Silver Lake or Elysian Park and shoot people with my own Kodak."

"Really? I'd love to see some of your photographs," I said, snapping the shot. "Okay, Lulu, now look straight at the camera and be perky. Like Clara Bow."

She did a darned good job. "Great. Now try to look sultry. Be Pola Negri next."

By golly, she did!

We used up most of an hour not taking photos of Lulu. By the end of our hour, Ernie, Mr. Buck, Mrs. Buck (who'd joined us after cleaning up after dinner), and I all decided Lulu had projected her personality perfectly.

"You did great, Lulu!" I said, delighted for her. "If you do that when Mr. Faraday takes photos of you, you're sure to be on your way."

"Mercy's right, Lulu," agreed Ernie. "You had me convinced."

"Of what?" asked Lulu, narrowing her eyes at Ernie.

"That you'll be great on the screen. You didn't once look dull or wooden or— What did you say Harvey said some actresses look like, Mercy?"

"Blocks of cement," I said. "But you know what? Maybe I should buy some film and we can take actual photographs tomorrow. It won't take much time to use a whole roll of film, and if I take the roll to the pharmacy and tell them to hurry, they might. We can have them back in a week or so."

"We can do better than that," said Ernie.

"We can?" I asked, surprised.

"Yeah. Charley Wu's got a cousin who does photography for fun and has a development set-up in his basement. He'd probably develop and print a roll of pictures in a day or so."

"Really?" said Lulu, clasping her hands to her bosom. "Oh, Ernie, that would be *keen*. Thank you!"

"Thank the guys in Chinatown. They all seem to think they owe me favors. I haven't asked for any favors yet. This will be my first."

"And you're using it on me?" Lulu said, sounding misty.

I didn't feel misty. I felt abused and mistreated. "Why won't they do any favors for *me*, darn it?"

"I expect Lily Wu and Mr. Chew's granddaughter and maybe even Charley's mother will do favors for you, Mercy. But don't forget where women fit into the pecking order in Chinatown."

"It isn't just in Chinatown," I said grumpily.

"Whoever does what, I'll be forever grateful if you can get the photos developed in a day, Ernie," said Lulu, effectively ending my most recent session of resentfulness, which was just as well. Lulu was happy, and I was happy for her.

"I'll get some film tomorrow," I promised Lulu. And we can set up again tomorrow night."

"You don't mind?" asked Lulu, looking at least as covetous as she had when I'd told her to look as if she were yearning for something.

"I don't mind. Anybody else mind?" I asked the group gathered.

"Not at all," said Mr. Buck.

"Nope," said Ernie.

"It'll be fun," said Mrs. Buck. "And I know *just* what to fix for supper tomorrow, too, Mr. Ernie."

I was her employer, but she cooked for Ernie.

You figure it out; it's beyond me.

SIX

On Tuesday morning at nine o'clock, Mrs. Smedley came to the office for her appointment. Mrs. Smedley was of medium height, was fashionably if rather loudly dressed, had dyed red hair, and apparently believed in the Lulu LaBelle school of makeup. She also wore positively *tons* of jewelry, including several bracelets and a gold watch. I think one of her bracelets held charms, because it jingled and clanked. I led her to Ernie's office, introduced them, and then returned to my desk. I didn't think the Smedley case would be any more interesting than Ernie did.

However, she left about fifteen minutes after she'd arrived, a hankie to her eyes, and Ernie at her heels. "Try not to worry, Mrs. Smedley," said Ernie kindly.

"I'll try," she said through sniffles. "But I'm so afraid Felix has begun seeing someone else."

"I'll begin working right away," Ernie promised her as he led her to the front door, which he closed behind her. Then he turned around, looked at me, and said, "Whew!"

"Not a fun client?" I asked, trying to sound sympathetic.

"No. If I were married to that woman, I'd leave the country."

"That's not very nice," I said, but I laughed.

"Well, as long as there's nothing else on the calendar, I might as well start snooping. Mrs. Smedley gave me her husband's office address and a few other places she said he's apt to frequent, whatever that means."

"If we weren't in the middle of Prohibition, it would probably mean bars and nightclubs and so forth."

"Especially so forth," said Ernie with a grin at my naïve statement. "Phooey."

But the telephone rang again, and I had to answer it because it was my job to do so. "Mr. Templeton's office. Miss Allcutt speaking."

Another client, this one a male named Lewis, who feared his wife was playing around on him. Except for a few truly fascinating cases, the job of a P.I. really was grubby. I'd never tell Ernie. Anyhow, he already knew it. Ah, well. It was still better than being an elevator operator. I made an appointment for Mr. Lewis to see Ernie that afternoon and hoped he'd be back by then.

At about ten-thirty, Mrs. Wilkes called from the home to give me a list of places her guests had been taken on day trips.

"Are you ready to write?" she asked.

"Yes, indeed," said I, the efficient secretary, who already had my pencil poised over my secretarial pad.

"Very well, here's the list." She'd barely begun before I interrupted her. I really should stop doing that.

"Oh, you went to the La Brea Tar Pits? Is there anything there to see? I mean, haven't they just begun finding things?"

"Not really. They've been excavating extensively since about 1905. Only recently has the Los Angeles Museum of History begun collecting and displaying specimens. It's a smelly, dirty, oily place, but it's interesting for our guests—and anyone else—to see how the specimens are collected and cleaned and so forth."

"Interesting. I want to visit the place myself one of these days."

"Yes," said Mrs. Wilkes, her tone telling me she wanted to get back to business. So I dutifully wrote down all the places to which her residents had been taken to visit. "I do *so* hope Mr. Templeton can find Jerome. It's not like him to stay away like this, although he does get awfully confused."

"What did the attendant do to frighten him?" I asked, thinking maybe it wasn't my business. Then again, maybe it was.

"Mr. Grafton startled him twice in one day. Jerome is terribly jumpy. Well, you probably discovered that for yourself."

"I didn't notice him being jumpy," I said. "Only confused."

With a sigh, Mrs. Wilkes said, "Yes, he's confused most of the time, but he dislikes being startled. Mr. Grafton didn't mean to frighten him, but he wasn't as careful as he should have been when approaching Jerome from behind. The poor fellow—Jerome, I mean, not Mr. Grafton—jumped a foot and screamed. That was the first time. The second time, he not only jumped and screamed, he ran for it. Unfortunately, he managed to make it to the front gate as a delivery was being made, and he got out when the gate was open. Mr. Grafton is rather elderly, and he couldn't keep up. By the time he reached the front gate and looked around, Jerome was nowhere to be seen."

"That's too bad," I said, recalling Jerome Brentwood clearly. Which is more than Jerome Brentwood was able to do, apparently. "Well, Mr. Templeton went to Chinatown yesterday. He's asked people to watch out for Mr. Brentwood. When he escaped, was he dressed as he was the day he came here?"

"In a suit and vest and carrying a cane and wearing a top hat and using a monocle? Yes. And he's still mostly bald and has a waxed mustache."

"If his mustache were black, he'd look just like Agatha Christie's Hercule Poirot," I said.

"I don't know who that is," said Mrs. Wilkes. "But he never alters his mode of dress. I just hope he's found a safe place to stay overnight. I'm terribly worried about him."

"Yes, I can imagine," I said. "Does he have any money if he needs to use a telephone or get a room for the night?"

"Yes, his family is wealthy, and he always has a wad of cash. Which is another worry. I don't want anyone to knock him over the head to get at his money either."

"No indeed," I said, thinking how helpless Mr. Jerome Brentwood would be on the mean streets of Los Angeles.

When we each hung up our receivers, I typed up a list of the various places Ernie needed to check, wishing I could go with him. I'd love to see the Griffith Park Zoo again and visit the Tar Pits. I went to Chinatown all the time with Lulu, but I'd like to visit the Los Angeles Museum of History, the Southwest Museum, and a few other places on the list.

After I'd neatly typed the list, I took it to Ernie's office. At present, as mentioned earlier, he was out hunting straying spouses (or should that be spice?) so I left the list on his desk. He was just returning to the office as I walked out of his room. He looked as if he'd been walking a lot and wanted to sit.

"I just put the list of places to which the home took its guests on your desk," I said. "And a gentleman named Lewis is coming in at four this afternoon about another case."

"Wife trouble?"

"He thinks so."

"Great. I bought you a roll of film. And Charley Wu's cousin will develop the film and have it back to us in a day."

"Thanks, Ernie!"

"Anything to help Lulu become a star," he said, laughing a little.

"I appreciate it, and I'm sure Lulu will too," I said.

"Here you go," he said, placing a brown paper parcel on my desk. "The roll of film's in there. I'll go study the list and make out a map. Searching for that guy will be a whole lot of fun." He didn't mean it. I could tell.

At four o'clock, Mr. Lewis, a timid-looking bald fellow, came in and chatted with Ernie for about fifteen or twenty minutes. He didn't appear any too happy when he left the office, but at least he wasn't crying into a hankie.

That evening, Mrs. Buck served us tamales for dinner! Along with what she claimed was Mexican rice and pinto beans. "Got the receipt for the beans and rice from a lady at the Mexican stand at the Grand Central Market," she said. "She made the tamales. They're too much trouble to make unless you have a whole family to help you make them."

"They're delicious," I told her. "Thank you"

"Glad you like them. I made a custard for dessert. The Mexican lady calls it 'flan,' but it's just a caramel custard to the rest of us."

"Oh, I love custard," said Sue.

"So do I," said Lulu, "but I'd better not eat much of it. I just read in *Photoplay* that the camera adds ten pounds to a person."

"How does it do that?" asked Caroline.

"Holy Moses," I said. "Do they mean that the camera makes everybody who poses for pictures look ten pounds heavier than they really are?"

"That's what the magazine said," Lulu told us, sounding worried.

"I've read that, too," said Ernie.

"Good Lord," I said. "Clara Bow and Anna May Wong must be as skinny as a couple of rails if they're not as big as they look on the screen. Anna May Wong looks like a toothpick. Clara Bow has some meat on her bones, but not much."

"I've got to stop eating so much," said Lulu in a fretful voice.

"No, you don't! Don't be silly. You look great just the way you are," I said, becoming a trifle concerned about Lulu's longing to be a star.

"Mercy's right," said Ernie, bless him. "Unless a director or a producer tells you to lose weight, why bother?"

"Well, but they might not choose me if I weigh too much or look fat on film."

"Eat your dinner, child," ordered Mrs. Buck, clearing a platter from the table. "I won't cook if you won't eat."

"That's a terrifying threat," I told Lulu. "Just eat a little bit of everything, and you won't get fat. You're already not fat!"

"I guess that's good advice," said Lulu. "Just eat a little bit of everything."

"Good," said Ernie. "I'll eat what you don't."

"How come men never gain weight?" asked Lulu plaintively.

"Some of them do," I said, recalling my portly father. Then I wished I hadn't. The less I thought about my parents, the better my life was.

When dinner was over, and in spite of Lulu eating a little bit of everything, she was ready for her photographic session to begin. I loaded the camera and Ernie and Mr. Buck went to the living room to make sure the floodlight still worked. It did.

I noticed Lulu fidgeting and said, "What's up, Lulu? We did this last night. You shouldn't have any nerves tonight."

"Tonight there's film in the camera," she said, still fidgeting.

"You know, Lulu LaBelle, if Mr. Faraday hauls you somewhere to have photos taken, the photographer will use film, too. You need to stop worrying. Pretend you're already rich and famous and have men falling all over themselves to wine and dine you. Well, I forgot Prohibition, but they'll all want to take you out to dinner and so forth."

"Pretend?" Lulu asked skeptically.

"Great idea," said Ernie. "Just pretend you're already a star, and act accordingly. Only don't pretend you're Mary Pickford. She's too little girly. Pretend you're Gloria Swanson. Or Theda Bara!"

"Perfect," I said, as I wound the film on the spool. "All right, Lulu Bara, pose."

"How?" she asked, sounding scared, which was most unlike Lulu.

"Just the way you did yesterday. Try putting your hand to your face like you did yesterday. Sit in the chair. There you go."

Things went smoothly from then on. Ernie and I kept encouraging Lulu to pretend she was Theda Bara, the notion of which made me want to giggle, but our advice worked. Lulu looked like a perfect vamp for some of the roll of film. Then I suggested she pretend she was Clara Bow and be bright and lively, and she did that too. I sure hoped the Faraday guy who claimed to be a talent scout was a for-real talent scout, because I thought Lulu did a great job.

When the role of film was finished, I wound it to the end and removed it from the camera, making sure not to unroll any of it and expose the film. "Ernie will take this to Chinatown tomorrow morning," I told Lulu. "And one of Charley Wu's friends—"

"Cousins," Ernie corrected me.

"How the heck many cousins does Charley Wu have?" I asked, recalling all of the Wu relations from our last case.

With a shrug, Ernie said, "Dunno. Lots, it seems."

"Very well. One of Charley Wu's cousins will develop and print the roll of film tomorrow, and we'll have it back on Wednesday. We can look at the photos before Ernie and I meet Chloe and Harvey for dinner." I'd already told my tenants and the Bucks that Ernie and I would be absent from the dinner table on the morrow.

"Oh, boy," said Lulu. "I hope they turn out okay. I guess maybe we'll be able to tell if I'm photogenic or not from that roll of film." She nodded at Ernie, who had just stuffed the film into his pocket.

"You betcha, kiddo," said Ernie. "I think you'll be great."

"I hope you're right," said Lulu, again sounding nervous.

"Cheer up!" I told her. "If you don't, pretty soon you'll be so rattled you'll bite your fingernails, and that will never do."

"Never!" cried Lulu, shocked out of her nervousness.

Ernie and I both laughed.

I walked Ernie out to his rattletrap Studebaker, and we shared a sweet kiss in the icy night air. Oh, very well, it wasn't icy, but it was darned cold. "I hope the photos turn out well," I said, shivering.

Putting his arms around me and snugging me to his warm chest, Ernie said, "We'll see tomorrow. I'm looking forward to seeing Chloe and Harvey again."

"And Mr. Francis Easthope," I said, giggling.

"Oh, yeah. Him too," said Ernie. Then he sighed and said, "But I've got to go home to my cold and lonely hovel now."

"You don't live in a hovel!" I protested.

"Maybe not, but it doesn't hold a candle to your place."

"Yes, yes," I said, irked that he'd brought up the disparity between our worldly assets again. He hadn't done so for quite a while, and I fretted sometimes that he'd allow it to come between us. "But that doesn't matter.

"If you say so," he said, not laughing. "But you'd better go inside. It's cold out here."

"Thanks, Ernie," I said, feeling a touch of despondency.

Then I told myself to snap out of it. If Ernie was so shallow a human being that he wouldn't appreciate me for who I was, regardless of my Great-Aunt Agatha's legacy, then he wasn't worth my bother.

Wish I believed my noble words.

Then I ran back to the house before I could freeze to death. Just kidding about that last part, but it was darned cold.

Buttercup met me at the door. I think she was peeved that I hadn't allowed her to go out with me to say farewell to Ernie, but she forgot her annoyance when I scooped her up and buried my frozen nose in her soft, warm fur. Lulu interrupted this fuzzy moment when she said, "Golly, Mercy, I hope those photos look all right. I'm going to be so nervous until I see them!"

With a sigh, I removed my face from Buttercup's fluffy head. Ahhh. The house was as warm as she'd been. "Really, Lulu, I wish you'd try not to be so worried. You'll either look spectacular or you won't, but I'm betting on you looking pretty darned good on film. You're lovely in person, and I can't see how you won't also be lovely on film."

"But you told me an hour or two ago—or maybe it was yester-day—that Harvey said some pretty women look like lumps of coal on film!"

"Blocks of cement, and I already know you aren't one of those."

"How?"

"Because of how much personality you displayed when I was taking the pictures! If you were going to look like a block of cement, I'd have noticed."

"You really think so?"

"I really think so."

"Well," Lulu said doubtfully, "I hope you're right."

"I'm right. And I'll prove it to you tomorrow. Providing Charley Wu's cousin comes through as promised. Just don't start biting your nails!"

"I'd *never* bite my nails!" Lulu declared, holding up her scarlet talons. "I work too hard on these babies to bite them."

"Good." I yawned. "Goodness, I'm tired. What time is it, do you know?"

"Dunno."

"Feels like bedtime. I think Buttercup and I are going upstairs to retire."

"Yeah. I think I will too," said Lulu.

"Yes. You need plenty of rest." I caught myself a split-second before I could say she needed her beauty sleep, but it didn't matter.

"Why? Do you think I look worn out? Old? I'm only twenty-three! Is that too old? Do I have any wrinkles?"

"Stop!" I commanded. "You don't look old or worn out, but if you keep fretting, you soon will."

Holding up her hands in an I-give-up gesture, Lulu said, "Right, right. You're right. I need to calm down."

"Would some warm milk help?" I hated warm milk, unless it had cocoa powder and sugar in it, but from the books I'd read it seemed something of a universal panacea.

"Ew. No, thanks. Think I'll just go read a movie magazine. That'll probably calm me down."

"Will it really? It won't make you even more nervous?"

"Naw. I've been reading them since I learned how to read. I love them."

"Good. Then I'll see you tomorrow morning, Lulu. Sleep tight."

"Yeah. Don't let the bedbugs bite," she said in return.

"I'll try my best not to," I told her, laughing and wondering what, precisely, a bedbug was. Maybe I'd look up bedbugs when I went to find children's books on the morrow. I think this meant my upper-crust Boston background was showing again.

SEVEN

Wednesday morning turned out to be every bit as chilly as Tuesday morning had been. I guess that's because the month was January. Still, I kind of resented it. I'd really enjoyed the warm weather during the summer without the hideous humidity that went with summers on the East Coast.

As ever, Mrs. Buck served us a sustaining breakfast, and then my tenants and I went back upstairs to prepare for work. As I was waiting for everyone at the front door and adjusting my cloche hat to cover my ears, I suffered an eye-popping moment when Lulu waltzed into view.

"Wow, Lulu. You're a...vision in purple today," I said, still blinking.

"Isn't this swell?" she asked, twirling in front of me.

To be specific, her dress that day was mostly bright purple fake silk with lacy cream-colored bands around the short sleeve cuffs and rounded collar. Below where her waist would have been if women were allowed to have waists, several rows of embroidered fake silk topped a shirred purple flounce. Her hat was purple, too. It went astonishingly with her bottle-blond hair.

"It's…It's amazing," I said.

"Wish I had a purple velvet cape to wear with it," she said, looking with distaste at her black woolen coat. "I want to impress Mr. Faraday when he takes me to lunch today."

"I'm sure you will," I said. Her coat was ever so much more fashionable than was my own. Hers sported a gray brushed wool collar that wrapped her neck in its warmth, and its cuffs were also brushed wool. My coat had a plain black lay-down collar and no discernable cuffs. I wore a knitted scarf with it.

"Um…Well, you look as if you're already every inch a star on the silver screen, Lulu," I said after I stopped gawping at her. If that's what she believed it took to reach stardom, I wished her luck. Once more I entertained a fleeting hope that Mr. Faraday proved to be a genuine talent scout and that perhaps he'd persuade her to tone down her wardrobe some. Today's purple sort of made me want to run away and hide.

To be absolutely frank, purple wasn't my favorite color to begin with. Lulu's purple was…well, it was *Purple*, capitalized and italicized. If I could show it to you, I would. I'm pretty sure you'd blink too.

As Lulu and I stood at the door, Sue showed up in her white uniform. She blinked at Lulu. Then Caroline arrived, demure in a black skirt and white blouse, and she also blinked at Lulu. Buttercup, who saw us off at the door as we left for work, didn't seem to care what Lulu wore. She always wanted to go with us but never sulked when I told her she couldn't. Dogs are superior to humans in so many ways.

But enough of that. We all walked to Angels Flight and then took our regular route to work. The Figueroa Building was a little chilly when we first entered it, but Mr. Buck, whom we encountered upon arriving, said it would warm up soon.

"Had to tinker with the boiler downstairs before it would start working right," he said.

"I'm sure it'll be fine in a few minutes," I said, smiling at him.

"I hope you're right and that it'll get warm soon," said Lulu, taking off her black coat and revealing her naked arms. Well, they were naked from her wrists to halfway to her neck, anyway. "It's cold for short sleeves."

Mr. Buck blinked at Lulu and said, "It'll only take a few minutes." Then he shot me a glance that told me he disapproved of Lulu's attire and took off for the stairs to the basement. The Bucks weren't precisely prudes, but they were far from flamboyant. I'd heard Mrs. Buck utter a "tsk" more than once when eyeing Lulu, although she never said a whole word.

As for me, I walked up the three flights of stairs and down the hall to the office, also hoping the building would warm up quickly. I wore a sober, long-sleeved blue suit jacket with a matching skirt over a long-sleeved white blouse. Lulu's bare arms would be goose-fleshy in a second flat, but I was relatively comfortable.

I'd read somewhere that when Mary Pickford was working for some big producer in New York State, he had her stand on cakes of ice every time he came across one to see how her being stranded on ice would look on the screen. Nertz to that. I'd rather be comfortable than a star in the flickers. I guess some people—like, for instance, Lulu—didn't mind suffering for their art.

Ernie arrived at the office shortly after I did.

"Has Lulu lost her mind?" he asked as he strode from the front door to his own office. "What's that getup she's wearing today?"

"I think she thinks stars dress like that," I said, feeling a teensy bit guarded on Lulu's behalf. "Her talent scout is taking her to lunch today, and she wanted to dress like a star."

"Good Lord," he said, as he walked into his office, threw his hat at the rack, removed his overcoat and hung it up. Then he plopped into his chair, laid the *Times* on his desk, picked up his hat—which hadn't landed on the rack properly—hung it up, and looked up at me. I'd followed him into his office.

"Don't forget we're dining with Chloe and Harvey tonight," I reminded him.

"At the Brown Derby. I won't forget. I'll pick you up at...when? Seven?"

"Seven or seven-fifteen. I don't know how long it takes to get there from my house."

"Seven-fifteen will probably do it," he said. "I took that roll of film to Charley's last night after I left your house. He said I can pick it up at noon today. Want to go to lunch in Chinatown with me?"

"Tempting offer," I said, telling the truth, "but I promised Chloe I'd look for some children's books so we can copy the illustrations. Mr. Easthope can probably figure out what characters will look good on the walls of the nursery."

"Go to the big library on Fifth and Hope that just opened last year. It's pretty impressive."

"Yes, I thought about that. Then maybe I can borrow several books instead of buying a bunch of them."

"Sounds reasonable," Ernie said in his I'm-glad-one-of-us-is-rich voice.

"Yes," I said firmly. "It's quite reasonable. Although," I added because I felt like being firm on this point, "I aim to purchase an entire set of Beatrix Potter books for the wee tot. And *Johnny Crow's Garden*, too."

"Whatever you say," said Ernie.

"Thank you."

"But why not go now?"

"Really?"

"Yes, really? What? You think I can't answer the telephone for an hour or so? Before you pirouetted into my life, I answered the telephone all the time."

"I didn't pirouette into your life," I said, slightly miffed. "I came here to secure employment."

"Yes, ma'am."

Stepping down from my high horse, I said, "And I'm really glad you hired me, because I was about to melt into a puddle on the sidewalk. I'd copied down a lot of addresses from the 'Help Wanted' section of the *Times*, and you were fourth or fifth on the list. It was hot that day. Besides, I'd rather work for you than a lawyer."

"Good Lord, did you apply for work at a lawyer's office? Ha!"

"Two of them, I think," I said, my mind wandering back to that incredibly hot July day. "But I think working for a private investigator is ever so much more exciting than working for an attorney."

"You didn't even know what a private eye was when you applied to me."

"Well, I know it, but you filled me in, and I'm a fast learner." Contemplating my parents' friends in Boston, I said, "Besides, I haven't met many lawyers, but the ones I *have* met have been toads."

Ernie got a hearty laugh out of my comment. "Okay. Well then, go to the library or a bookstore. Whatever you want to do, do it, but come back before lunchtime. Then we can both eat at Charley's place." He wrinkled his nose. "I guess I should invite Lulu, too. If Mrs. Wu sees her, she'll probably faint."

"Does Mrs. Wu faint? She looks more like she'd scold Lulu for being so…" I couldn't think of an appropriate word.

"Flashy? Obvious? Outrageous?"

"One of those words, I guess. Maybe colorful." I heaved a somewhat dispirited sigh.

"Colorful. Huh." Shaking his head, Ernie said, "Well, hell, I'll invite her anyway."

"She's dining with Mr. Faraday today. I told you that, remember?"

"Oh yeah. Well, don't invite her then. And you can go to the library this morning."

"*Thank* you, Ernie," I said, touched by his offer. "The library doesn't open until nine, so I can answer the telephone until then."

"You aim to catch a cab?"

"No. I aim to walk," I said, wondering if this was a reference to my sacks of money.

"Well, then, start now if you're going to the library."

"Good point. Thanks." I turned to go back to my desk. "Want me to shut your door?" I asked.

"What for?" he asked back.

"I don't know."

So I left the door to his office open and heard him plonk his feet on his desk and flap open the *Times*.

The telephone didn't ring as I wrapped myself in my coat and scarf and picked up my handbag and gloves. Before leaving, I went to Ernie's office to bid him a quick *adieu*. He still had his nose stuck in the *Times*.

When he heard me at his door, he lowered the newspaper and glanced up. "Leaving now?"

"Yes. It's kind of you to let me go during office hours."

"We're not precisely rolling in work here, so it's all right."

"Will you be looking for Mr. Brentwood some more today?"

"Yes. I plan to visit the Los Angeles Museum of History after we pick up Lulu's pictures from Charley."

"I'd like to see the museum," I said wistfully.

"If you didn't have to be at a job during the day, you could go with me this afternoon," said Ernie with an innocent air that didn't fit him at all.

"Thanks. I love my job."

He lifted the *Times* again. "Glad to hear it. Be back in time for lunch."

"Thank you!"

I took the stairs to the lobby and had to pass Lulu at her reception desk. She still looked goose-fleshy. In actual fact, she hadn't even got out her fingernail-grooming kit and was hugging her violently purple self and shivering.

"Still cold down here?" I asked, already having bundled up for my walk out of doors.

"Yes," she said, commencing to rub her arms. "Mr. Buck said it'll take a few more minutes. Where are you going?"

"I was going to visit a bookstore during lunch, but Ernie told me to go now and visit the new library, so I can be back in the office in time for him to take me out to lunch."

"Where you going to lunch?" asked Lulu, sounding a trifle hurt that she hadn't been invited. Then I guess she remembered her knight in shining armor was feeding her lunch today, and she brightened up again.

"Charley Wu's," I said, and grinned. "We're going to pick up the photographs that Charley's cousin developed and printed!"

Leaping a little on her chair, Lulu stopped shivering and clasped her hands to her purple bosom. "Oh, wow, *mine*? I mean photos of *me*?"

"The very ones," I told her happily.

"Oh, *thank* you, Mercy!"

"Thank Ernie. He's the one who got Charley's cousin to print the photos so quickly."

"I'll probably be too scared to look at them," Lulu said, her face scrunching into a grimace of anxiety.

"Then I'll look at them first and only show you the good ones."

"Do you think there will be bad ones?" asked Lulu, now sounding horrified.

"No! But you said you'd be too scared to look at them."

Lulu contemplated my words for a second or three, again wrapping her arms around herself in a warming self-hug. "I guess I'm still nervous, huh?"

"I guess you are. But this will be good practice. You can look at the photos, and they will give you a picture of things to come." I ran that last sentence over in my head. "Or something like that. But I'd better scoot. I have to get back by noonish."

"Thanks, Mercy," said Lulu, now sounding almost weepy.

I squinted at her. "Don't go getting emotional, Lulu LaBelle. You'll smear your makeup.

She stiffened and nodded. "Right. You're right."

"Back in a bit," I said, and I sailed out the big double glass doors of the Figueroa Building. I stopped sailing as soon as the brisk wind smacked me in the face. Then I contemplated hailing a taxi.

But no. I was a working woman, and working women—the kinds who had to rely on the money they made from their jobs—couldn't afford to take taxicabs on a regular basis. If it was this cold when I aimed to walk back to work, maybe I'd rethink the notion. After all, if I took a cab back to work, it wouldn't be one of those regular-basis things. Or would it? Crumb. I didn't know.

It was a darned good thing the library was on Fifth Street, because it wasn't all that far away from the Figueroa Building. Even then, I thought about hailing a cab every seven steps or so. But I didn't. Looking up at the beautiful building, I was glad Ernie had suggested visiting it. I know it couldn't hold a candle to the Boston Public Library or the New York Public Library, but it was an impressive place. And really, this was just a new home for the old public library that had been in existence for fifty years or more. I'd been to it before, in particular when I was studying up on various poisons, but it still impressed me.

Very well, so Los Angeles was a kid compared to Boston or New York City. This was still a lovely library, even if it did have a mile and a half's worth of cement walkways and stairs one had to maneuver in order to get to its doors. But, nobly carrying on, I walked them and opened the front door, eager to look for children's picture books.

As soon as I stepped inside the library, darned if I didn't see Mrs. Smedley. Again today she was dressed as if she were trying to mimic Lulu. This day's outfit was orange. Bright orange. It clashed terribly with her redder-than-red hair. She sat at a table near the door with a man and two other women. Their heads were tilted toward each other, and they were whispering like conspirators aiming to storm the Bastille or take over the library or something. One of the two other women was a bottle blonde and the second had black-black hair. I couldn't really see much more of any of them. I probably wouldn't have recognized Mrs. Smedley if not for her bright clothing and startling red hair.

Oh, well, I wasn't on the Smedley case. Even if I had been on it, I'd found the wrong Smedley in the library, of all odd places for an elicit assignation. Well, along with two other women.

The man glanced up and I instantly stopped staring at them and made a mental note to tell Ernie about my Smedley sighting. If Mrs. Smedley was having an affair with that man, I didn't admire her taste. He had slicked-back hair and one of those tiny mustaches that looked like a fishing worm crawling across his upper lip. I kept walking toward the counter.

Before I reached it, I stopped dead in my tracks because there, seated at a table in the main reading room several yards farther toward the books than Mrs. Smedley and company, was Mr. Jerome Brentwood, escapee from the…whatever it was. Two cases in one day. How odd. Recalling Mrs. Wilkes's mention of how he didn't appreciate being startled, I walked slowly to his table and cleared my throat.

He leaped to his feet and gasped, his monocle falling from his eye in the process. As he'd demonstrated earlier in our acquaintanceship, losing his monocle seemed a regular thing for him. He caught it deftly and screwed it back into place. He said softly—I guess he recognized libraries and soft speech went together—"It's you."

"How do you do, Mr. Brentwood? I'm Miss Allcutt. You visited my employer, Mr. Ernest Templeton, several weeks ago."

"No. Yes. Yes, I remember." He sat. "You scared me."

"I'm sorry. I didn't mean to." I put my hand on the back of a chair next to him. "May I sit here for a minute?"

"No. No. No. Yes. Sit, sit, sit. Read. I'm reading." He held up a copy of a newish edition of *The Saturday Evening Post*.

"You know, Mr. Brentwood, Mrs. Wilkes is very worried about you?"

"Mrs. Wilkes? Mrs. Wilkes? Mrs. Wilkes?"

"Yes. Do you know who she is?"

"No. Yes. Yes. She's nice. You're nice, but you scared me."

"I didn't mean to scare you. I'm glad you think I'm nice."

"Yes. Why is Mrs. Wilkes worried?"

"Because you left your home"—I almost said "the" home, but caught myself in time—"and haven't returned. Everyone there is worried about you."

"Oh. No."

"You don't want Mrs. Wilkes to be worried, do you?"

"Mrs. Wilkes? Yes. No. No. I don't want her worried."

"Would you like me to arrange for you to go back home? Then Mrs. Wilkes won't be worried anymore."

He furrowed his brow, again dislodging his monocle, which he caught and replaced. He was an ace at monocle-catching-and-replacing.

"No. I don't know. Mr. Grafton scared me. Twice."

"He's sorry he frightened you. He didn't mean to."

"No. No. Did you mean to scare me?"

"Heavens, no! I never want to scare anyone. I certainly didn't mean to frighten you, Mr. Brentwood. But I've been worried about you, too, ever since Mrs. Wilkes asked Mr. Templeton to look for you."

"Mr. Templeton. He's the private investigator."

Pleased by this display of coherence, I smiled and said, "Yes, he is. And he's worried about you too. So may I call Mrs. Wilkes and have someone from your home pick you up here at the library?"

He sat in silence, staring off into the middle distance—or maybe he was staring at one of the ornate pictures on the library walls—for what seemed like hours. It was probably not even a full minute. You know how time does that: speeds up or slows down, whichever you don't want it to do at the moment. I wanted to prod him to speak, but knew I'd only alarm him if I did.

After what seemed ten or twelve years, he said, "Yes. No. Maybe."

"I'll be happy to take you home in a taxicab, Mr. Brentwood. We can leave now if you like." And then when would I find children's books? Nertz.

"Yes. No." He glanced around and seemed a trifle startled. "It's a library?"

"Yes, this is the Los Angeles Public Library. It's a beautiful building, isn't it?"

"No. Yes. Yes. Pretty."

"Would you like me to take you home in a taxicab?"

"Don't you want books?" he asked. "In the library?"

"I came to get some books, yes, but I'll take you home first if you like."

"Go get your books. I'll wait here for you."

"Promise? You won't go anywhere else? You'll stay right here"—I tapped lightly on the table to show him where "here" was—"and not go anywhere else?"

"No. Yes. Yes, I'll wait for you. You'll take me home."

"Exactly." I thought of a more secure method of fetching books and dealing with Mr. Brentwood. "But would you like to come with me? I'm going to look at some books for children, because—" Lord. How could I explain the baby-to-be to this damaged man? I altered course a bit. "I'm going to borrow some books for a young child."

"Books? Child?"

"Yes. Would you like to come with me?"

He tilted his head one way and then the other and thought about it for another seven or eight years. At long, long last, he rose from his chair and said, "Yes."

Hallelujah!

EIGHT

Making certain Mr. Brentwood and I kept pace with each other—I sure didn't want him slipping out a door or wandering through the stacks—I navigated us to the counter at which I'd aimed myself before spotting Mrs. Smedley's posse and Mr. Brentwood. There a nice library employee pointed me to where the children's section lay, so I gently took Mr. B by the coat sleeve and guided him there.

By the way, he was as immaculately tidy today as he'd been the other time I'd seen him when he'd come to Ernie's office. I had no idea where he'd spent the night, but it had clearly been somewhere clean. A hotel, perhaps. Maybe I'd ask Mrs. Wilkes.

When we entered the children's section, I noticed a class of students who were maybe in the second or third grade sitting in a semicircle on the floor as a woman librarian read a picture book to them. Mr. Brentwood stopped in his tracks and seemed intrigued.

"Look, look, look," he said, pointing at the gathering.

"Would you like to listen to the story the lady is reading?"

"No. Yes. Yes. Yes."

Because there was a chair near the group where someone could sit and watch and listen, I walked him to it and deposited him there. His attention was so focused on the woman reading the book, he almost fell over the chair before he realized he was supposed to sit on it. Once seated, he stared and seemed to listen with all his might.

How sweet.

But I needed to find picture books for my own use—while making sure I didn't lose sight of Mr. Brentwood—so I walked to the check-out counter. There I asked yet another library helper—the people who work in libraries can't *all* be librarians, can they?—if she could direct me to the picture books. She did. Fortunately, I could keep track of Mr. Brentwood as I looked for specific books. I had planned to take my time, but I feared Mr. Brentwood would escape if I did.

Oh, but what a treasure trove I found even without dawdling. I selected several books by Beatrix Potter and even found *Johnny Crow's Garden*! I took them to the check-out desk. "May I check out all of these, or do you have a limit?"

"We allow people to check out six books at a time," said the woman behind the desk with a smile.

As an aside, I don't know why the illustrations I've seen in newspapers and magazines show librarians to be scowling, mean-faced people with fingers to their lips, shushing folks. All the librarians I've ever met have been nice people who love books and who like people who love books. School teachers, on the other hand, are a mixed lot in my experience.

"Thank you. Then I'll take all of these, please. I have a card in my bag somewhere." I'd already taken off my gloves, so I fished around in my bag until I found my little purse and removed my library card. The desk lady dutifully wrote down my card number on the number plate in each book, then stamped the return date with the date stamper clamped to the eraser end of her pencil.

"You may keep them for fourteen days," she said as she, still smiling, nudged the pile of books towards me across the desk.

"Thank you."

As I lifted my load of books, I wished I'd thought to bring a shopping basket with me. But I hadn't. Therefore, I either had to walk all the way back to the Figueroa Building with my arms full of books and Mr. Brentwood in tow or hail a cab.

I decided to hail a cab. I know, I know. But I really did *try* to live within my means. Besides, the cab was technically for the transport of Mr. Brentwood back to the home.

Speaking of which…

Fortunately, the woman reading the book just turned the last page and said, "The end," when I reached Mr. Brentwood's chair. He still stared, either at the book or the woman who'd read same. I said softly and gently, "Mr. Brentwood?"

I swear, he nearly broke his neck jerking it to peer up at me. "Me? Miss Allcutt? Mr. Templeton?"

"We're going to take a taxicab back to your home now, Mr. Brentwood, all right?"

"Home? Mrs. Wilkes. Home."

"Yes. Home. Where Mrs. Wilkes is."

"Okay." And darned if he didn't stand up and begin walking to the front door of the library. I had to scurry to keep up with him.

As we traversed the approximate mile and a half of walkway and stairs from the library to the street, I asked, "Um, Mr. Brentwood, do you know the address of your home?"

"Home? Address? Mrs. Wilkes?"

"Yes. Do you know the address of your home?"

He lowered his eyebrows. Naturally, his monocle fell and, again naturally, he caught it and screwed it back in its proper place. "Yes. No. No. I don't know."

"Oh, dear. Do you remember the name of the street it's on?" I asked, becoming a bit frustrated with this poor confused fellow.

"Street? Home? Mrs. Wilkes? No. No. No."

Great. I cudgeled my brain, trying at least to recall the street where the big white gated mansion stood.

Naturally, I couldn't. However, I spotted a row of three telephone booths at the foot of the last staircase. I could telephone Ernie and he'd know, if not the address, at least the street on which the home stood.

"Mr. Brentwood?" I said gently.

"No. Yes?"

"If you don't know the address of your home, I'll telephone Mr.

Templeton at the office, and ask him to give it to me. Is that all right with you? You don't mind waiting while I use the telephone, do you?"

"Wait? Telephone? Yes. No."

What the heck did that mean? I had no idea, so I gently clutched the cuff of Mr. Brentwood's left sleeve and guided him boothwards. "Will you please just stand still here, Mr. Brentwood? I'll use the telephone to call Mr. Templeton."

"Mr. Templeton," said Mr. Brentwood.

"Precisely," I said.

Lord. I had to set my short stack of books on the seat where a person would normally sit in order to use the telephone in the middle booth of the three. Then I had to get my purse out of my handbag again, this time foraging for a nickel. Found one. Checked to make sure Mr. Brentwood wasn't wandering. He wasn't. Good. Lifted the receiver and depressed the hook several times.

"Please insert a nickel," came the officious voice of a woman at the switchboard.

I inserted my nickel and gave the woman Ernie's office number. She put my call through. I heard the 'phone ring. And ring. And ring.

Just when I was about ready to give up and utter a blasphemous word, I heard a click and then Ernie saying, "Ernest Templeton, private investigations."

"What took you so long to answer the stupid telephone?" Very well, my frustration level was quite high just then, so I wasn't awfully polite.

"I'm fine, thank you," said Ernie sarcastically. "And you?"

Deciding not to waste any more time, I said, "I found Mr. Brentwood at the library, and I need to know the address of the home so I can get a cab and take him there."

"He was at the library?" Ernie sounded astonished.

I didn't blame him, but that wasn't the point. I'd managed to regrab the cuff of Mr. Brentwood's left coat sleeve after I set down my books and dug for my nickel, but I didn't know how long he'd stand still and remain placid. "Yes! Now what's the address?"

"Cripes, I don't know. It's on Los Angeles Street. You remember what it looks like?"

"Yes. I guess I can tell the cabbie where to stop."

"You still at the library? I'll drive down there and pick you both up."

"Won't that take too long?"

"Dunno. You see any taxicabs driving past the library?"

I looked. "No."

"Well, keep looking, and I'll drive. If you catch a cab before I get there, I'll know where you went."

"Thanks, Ernie. Mr. Brentwood takes a good deal of looking after."

"I guess so," he said and hung up.

I turned just long enough to retrieve my books before once more attaching myself to one of Mr. Brentwood's coat sleeves. I still had my handbag hanging from my wrist. While I was glad the thing had straps, I wished they were longer so I could sling it on my shoulder. Oh, well, if wishes were horses, as somebody said once. Probably Shakespeare. He said most of the things people quoted.

Still docile, Mr. Brentwood stood at the telephone booth, gazing out at Fifth Street. Traffic wasn't too bad, but there were plenty of cars zipping past. "Mr. Brentwood?" I asked carefully, moderating my tone of voice so as not to startle him.

"Miss Allcutt?"

"Yes. I'm Miss Allcutt. Mr. Templeton is going to drive to the library and pick us both up. Then we'll take you to your home."

"Mr. Templeton? Mrs. Wilkes. Mrs. Wilkes is the one."

"Yes, she is. Mr. Templeton will take us to Mrs. Wilkes."

"Ah. No. Yes. Yes. Good."

"Now as Mr. Templeton drives his automobile to the library, I'm going to keep watching for a taxicab. Do you know what a taxicab is?"

Gazing at me as if I were insane, Mr. Brentwood said, "Taxicab? Yes. No. Mr. Templeton."

"Well, if we see a taxicab before Mr. Templeton gets here, we'll take the cab and Mr. Templeton will follow us to your home to make sure you get settled safely. Is that all right with you?"

The expression on his face made me fear for his monocle for a second, but I presume he finally figured out what I meant, because he nodded. "Yes. No. Yes. Wait. Or take taxicab."

"Exactly."

"Very well."

Thank the good Lord and Mr. Buck, who always helped Ernie start his pathetic automobile by manning the crank, Ernie arrived a second or two after I saw a cab on the other side of the street. I'd just sucked in a breath in order to holler at the cabbie or race out into the traffic and hope I didn't get run over and die before I reached him, thereby giving Mr. Brentwood a perfect chance to escape again. Then everything would have been for naught, you know?

The Studebaker shuddered to a stop, and Ernie leaned over and opened the front door. "Please step in, Mr. Brentwood."

"Mr. Templeton?"

"Yes, I'm Ernie Templeton. Remember me?"

"Yes. But Miss Allcutt. Miss Allcutt should sit up front."

Eyeing Mr. Brentwood and me, Ernie said, "You can both sit up front. You get in first."

So we did. Ernie, Mr. Brentwood, and I were kind of squashed together, but at least Mr. B stayed put as Ernie drove to the home. When we reached our goal, Ernie left the car first and hurried around the wreck to open the passenger door. I stepped out, and we both grabbed a sleeve of Mr. Brentwood's coat. Still holding onto the sleeve, Ernie walked to the speaker next to the big wrought-iron gate, pressed the buzzer, lifted the receiver, and spoke to whoever answered on the other end of the wire.

Ernie explained things on our side of the locked gate.

I heard a tinny exclamation: "Mr. Brentwood? Really?"

Ernie removed the ear piece from his ear and shook his head before saying, "Yes. Mr. Brentwood. Really." He listened for a few more seconds, holding the earpiece away from his ear until he decided the person on the other end had stopped screeching. Then he again pressed it to his ear. "Yeah," he said. "We're right at the front gate." Pause. "Right." Pause. "Right." Pause. "Okay."

He hung up the earpiece and turned to Mr. B and me. "They'll be right out for you, Mr. Brentwood. It's probably better if you don't leave the premises without asking Mrs. Wilkes if it's all right first."

"Didn't ask," said Mr. Brentwood. "Scared. Man scared me."

"I understand, but…" Perceiving that to belabor the matter would be pointless, Ernie finally said, "Never mind."

"We'll wait with you, Mr. Brentwood," I told him softly. "Then you'll be home, all nice and warm. Aren't you chilly?"

"No."

All right then. "I'm glad," I said sweetly.

We didn't have to wait long. About a second and a half after Ernie decided not to explain the virtues of asking for permission, the huge door of the mansion opened, and a man hurried out to the gate.

"Mr. Brentwood!" the man exclaimed. "We're so glad you're back."

"Home," said Mr. Brentwood.

"Yes. Home," said the man. He unlocked the gigantic gate and shoved it open so the three of us could enter. I walked with Ernie, and the attendant walked with Mr. Brentwood to the big porch. I noticed a couple of people, perhaps inmates, with uniformed nurses in tow—or maybe it was the other way around—walking on the lovely manicured grounds. One nice thing about Los Angeles is that the grass pretty much stays green all year around. Huge mounds of snow don't bury it all.

Mrs. Wilkes was, if my observation means anything, thrilled beyond measure when Mr. Brentwood was returned to her. After scolding him a little bit and handing him off to an attendant who promised not to frighten him, she led Ernie and me into her office and wrote out a check to the firm for quite a large sum of money.

When another attendant led us back to the front gate and allowed us out, Ernie said, "Glad to get out of that place. Good for you for finding the guy, Mercy!" He actually gave me a hug. Right there on the street in front of witnesses!

How embarrassing. And how rewarding. However, I had to admit, "He was just sitting at a table there when I walked in. I sat beside him and talked to him a little bit. He even went to the children's room to fetch these books with me. He listened to the librarian read a story."

"Bet he enjoyed that," said Ernie, opening the passenger door for me.

"He seemed to. And I found all the books I wanted to. Mostly. I didn't want to spend too much time and lose track of the escapee."

"You know, if you *have* to live in a loony bin, that's probably the best one you could find."

"I wish you wouldn't call it a loony bin."

"Nertz."

Then I remembered the Smedley gang. "Oh, and I saw Mrs. Smedley in the library too."

"Yeah? Seems like a strange place for her to be."

"I thought so too, but she was there with outriders."

"With what?"

"Outriders. A man and two other women."

"Odd."

"I thought so, but I didn't talk to her because I spotted Mr. Brentwood."

"Doesn't matter. It's her husband we're supposed to trail."

"You're supposed to trail him. I'll stay in the office and answer the telephone."

Ernie only grinned. It was then about time for lunch, so we bypassed the Figueroa Building and went to Chinatown to have pork and noodles at Charley Wu's diner. They were delicious. They always were.

When we finally returned to the Figueroa Building, a smiling Lulu greeted us at the reception desk.

"Where did Mr. Faraday take you to lunch, Lulu?" I asked.

"To a nice little café on Temple Street," she said. "It was real nice."

"Good. Well, look what we have for you!" I handed her the parcel of photographs.

Lulu was absolutely ecstatic.

NINE

Naturally, when quitting time came and Caroline and Sue showed up at the Figueroa Building's reception desk, Lulu showed them her photographs. All three young women appeared delighted with the results of my photographic efforts. Personally, I was relieved and a bit surprised. Didn't know I was so good at taking pictures, by golly.

"Oh, Lulu, I love this one!" said Sue, holding the photo of Lulu looking chipper and perky, *a la* Clara Bow.

"This one is quite nice," said the more subdued Caroline, carefully gazing at a Theda-Bara-posed Lulu LaBelle. "I think you're better looking than Theda Bara. She always looks as if she got lost in a harem and is peeved about it."

We all laughed, and Caroline blushed. Finally, Lulu was persuaded to tuck her photographs into her handbag, and the four of us walked to Angels Flight and then on to Mercy's Manor. Buttercup met us at the door, deliriously happy as ever, and whatever Mrs. Buck was fixing for the others to eat for dinner smelled scrumptious.

At Mercy's Manor, we always dined at the unfashionable hour of six or six-thirty. My tummy was growling by the time Ernie picked me up at seven-fifteen to meet Chloe and Harvey at the Brown Derby. He

ALICE DUNCAN

looked amazingly well dressed, for him. He even wore a dinner jacket and a stiff-bosomed shirt.

As for me, I wore a black silk dress with the pearls my Great-Aunt Agatha had willed to me upon her death. Bless Great-Aunt Agatha; she'd left me not only an annuity but pearls, which were the height of fashion in 1927. With my black dinner dress, I also wore black shoes with a moderate heel and a strap, which made them quite comfortable for evening shoes.

"You look great, Ernie," I said as I greeted him at the door. "I didn't even know you had a dinner jacket."

"There are lots of things you don't know about me," he said, stepping into the black-and-white tiled entryway of Mercy's Manor. "You look pretty swell yourself."

"Thank you."

Although my black dress, small black hat, and pearls were perfect for an evening out, my black bag was larger than the one I'd usually carry on the same adventure. However, I had to take books with me that night, so I opted for a plain but nice black handbag and only stuck three of the small Beatrix Potter books in it, figuring Mr. Easthope didn't need to look at more in order to get the idea Chloe and I'd come up with, if you'll please excuse me ending that sentence with a preposition. Or even if you don't.

The English language can be *such* a problem sometimes.

At any rate, I'd brought my pretty black evening stole downstairs, and I handed it to Ernie so he could help me drape it around my shoulders. It wasn't as warm as my sturdy black woolen coat, but we *were* going out to dine with my sister and brother-in-law at the newly opened Brown Derby Restaurant, so I figured I'd just shiver in Ernie's old raggedy Studebaker until we got there.

But when he escorted me outdoors and down the porch steps to the drive, I didn't see his Studebaker anywhere. "Where's your car, Ernie? You needn't spring for a cab. We can use my car."

"Does the darkness impair your vision, Miss Allcutt?" he asked, sounding solicitous.

Very well, I knew a trap when I heard one. I pointed to the nice-looking late-model automobile parked in my drive. I'd wondered why it was there, but it had never even occurred to me that it might belong to Ernie, of all people.

"Is that lovely auto *yours*? Do you mean to tell me you actually got a new car? Oh, Ernie, it's so nice!"

"Don't get too excited. It's used. I got it from Charley Wu's cousin Fung. He has a car lot on Melrose. It's a 1924 Packard Six."

"It's beautiful!" I said. And it was. It was black, as most cars were—except mine, which was blue. I walked up and stroked its sleek fender. "When did you get it?"

"This afternoon. I went to Fung's yesterday, tried a few, and he gave me a good deal on this one. It has a self-starter, which will make Mr. Buck happy, and it's closed in and the windows work, which should make you happy." He opened the passenger's side door for me.

"Oh, it does," I said gleefully. "I'm *so* glad you got rid of that old Studebaker. I was worried for your safety every time you drove it."

"Yes, I was getting kind of scared to drive it, too. 1909 was a long time ago."

"Good heavens, was it *that* old?"

"Eighteen years isn't all that old. You're not much older than that yourself."

"I am too! I turned twenty-two in November."

"Ancient," said Ernie, shutting my door and going around the vehicle to the driver's side. When he got into the car, he said, "That poor Studebaker had been through a lot. It drove with me from Chicago, for Pete's sake."

"You drove that thing from Chicago to Los Angeles?"

"With all my goods and chattels. Which means a canvas sack and me, in my case."

"When did you get here?"

"Ten years ago. I was a copper in Chicago for a year and decided I wanted to get a job where the weather was better."

"You were a policeman in Chicago before coming to Los Angeles and joining the force?"

"Isn't that what I just said?"

"Well, yes, but I didn't know you were a policeman when you lived in Chicago. You were born there, right?"

"Right. I was mostly a kid when I lived in Chicago, but when I graduated from high school, my family didn't have money to send me to college, so I decided to join the force. Glad I left when I did. It's hell there now, with all the rum-running gangs killing each other and innocent pedestrians. Things are bad enough in Los Angeles, but there aren't as many chances of getting shot by a gangster here. You just have to watch out for two-gun Davis's uniformed gang."

"I don't like it when you sound so cynical, Ernie," I said, knowing as I did so I was displaying my naïveté yet one more time. "Although I know you've told me from the moment we met that the L.A.P.D. is corrupt. Except for Phil Bigelow. And heck, I've even seen it for myself."

"Yep," he said, maneuvering his smooth-running machine through the busy Los Angeles streets. What a change for the better from his rickety Studebaker!

"I think Lulu's right. There should be stoplights on more corners." We'd nearly been run into by someone driving a battered Ford. I think. I can't really tell one brand of car from another even in the daylight unless it has a huge name on it somewhere.

"I agree with her, too. L.A.'s catching up, though. What with all the movie money being spread around, there will be new everything cropping up pretty soon."

"You really think so?"

"I really think so. The folks with money will make it so, and the rest of us will either benefit, or L.A. will become too expensive for most of us to live in."

"That's not a comforting notion," I said. "I'm doing my part by renting out apartments in my home for women who need to work for their livings."

"Yes, you are, and I applaud you for it."

I squinted at him, but despite all the lights from various automobiles' headlamps and the streetlights erected by Los Angeles's city fathers, I couldn't see him very well. "Are you teasing me?"

"Me? Never! Would I ever do such a thing?"

"Yes," I said. "All the time."

"Well, I think you're okay, Mercy Allcutt, whatever anybody else thinks."

"All right, now I *know* you're teasing me."

"Just a little. But we're here."

We were? I glanced out the window and saw an enormous cement brown derby hat perched near the street just about a block away. The Ambassador Hotel, home of the Cocoanut Grove as well as a good restaurant of its own was directly across the street.

"I'm glad Chloe suggested this. It's a darling place. Hope the food is good."

"I've heard it is," said Ernie, squinting at the stretch of Wilshire leading up to the restaurant. "They probably have valet parking."

"What's that?"

"You hand your key to a guy in a uniform, and he parks your car in the lot. Then, when he fetches your car after dinner, you give him a tip in order to get your car back. It's extortion, but what can a fellow do? Aha, there's a spot on the street." Ernie deftly drove his lovely newish Packard Six to a parking space less than a block from the Brown Derby Restaurant. He exited the motor from his side, walked to mine, and opened the door for me.

Holding out an arm for me to grab, he said, "Please allow me to escort you, my lady."

"Thank you, kind sir," I said, hefting my somewhat heavy black bag and making sure my stole was secure around my shoulders before taking his arm and stepping onto the sidewalk. I was sure glad for concrete! I can't imagine being dressed as I was and having to walk on dirt. My heels would either sink in or I'd trip over a rock or something, and tonight I wanted to do Chloe and Harvey—and Ernie—proud. "Did you bring the stuffed ducky?"

"No. I didn't want to walk into the Brown Derby carrying a huge yellow duck."

"Don't blame you," I said, grinning at the notion and almost wishing he *had* brought the duck.

Quite a few people milled around under the awning outside the restaurant, but Ernie marched right past them and opened the front door for me. I stepped inside, and darned if it didn't look like the inside of a derby hat in there! How adorable.

I didn't have much time to gawk, however, because a hostess in a long green gown greeted us with a smile. "Reservations?" she asked in a sweet voice.

"Nash," said Ernie, offering her Harvey's last name.

The hostess gave a start of surprise. I guess we didn't look grand enough to be seen with Harvey and Chloe Nash, royalty among flicker folks. Well, phooey on her!

"Would you like to check your wrap?" she asked me after overcoming her initial reaction.

"Yes, please. It's too bulky to carry around." So I handed her my stole, she gave it to the person manning the check-in desk, he handed her a ticket, and she gave it to Ernie. Wouldn't you know it? My stole. Ernie was given the ticket with which to claim it. I tell you, it's a man's world.

Then the hostess said, "This way, please," and we walked after her as she took off through another door, out of the hat and into a softly lit restaurant. She led us to a booth in the back of the restaurant in a quiet corner. Chloe saw us first and waved. Harvey and Mr. Easthope then spotted us, too, and they both rose to greet us.

My sister is a beautiful woman. Ethereal, even in these, the latter stages of her pregnancy. She still had her gorgeous blue eyes and stunning blond hair—which, unlike Lulu, she didn't have to bleach. We hadn't seen each other for quite a while, so she shoved herself out of the booth and we hugged each other.

"It's *so* good to see you again!" she said. By golly, her eyes were shining as if there were tears in them.

"Shoot, Chloe, don't cry," I said, hugging her harder. "We talk all the time on the telephone."

"It's not the same thing," she said with a sniffle, "And oh, you just don't know how much I want to get rid of this load!" she added, patting her bulge. "I'm excited about being the kind of mother our mother wasn't, but I'll sure be glad when the kid gets here." She laughed a little and sat again, lifting a napkin to her eyes to blot the few emotional tears there.

"I'm excited for both of you," I told her. "It's great to see you, Harvey, and you, Francis. I brought some books for you to look at regarding nursery walls."

"We'll peek at those later," Harvey said with a laugh. "Good to see you again, Ernie."

"And you, too," said Ernie, shaking Harvey's hand. "Mr. East-hope," he said then without any hint of antipathy, and he held his hand out for Francis Easthope to shake, which he did.

"Good evening, both of you. It's been a long time," said Mr. East-hope, not merely one of the most handsome men on earth, but also one of the most pleasant.

"But take a seat," said Harvey. "During these benighted time, we can't have a civilized cocktail before dinner, but we can sip water and look at our menus."

We took his advice.

Recalling Lulu, I asked Harvey, "Say, Harvey, have you ever heard of a talent scout or an agent named Faraday?"

"Faraday?" He wrinkled his brow as he thought. "Faraday. No. Can't say as I have, but there are people calling themselves talent scouts and agents all over Los Angeles. I'm sure some of them are legitimate."

"Oh dear," I said, beginning to fret on Lulu's account. "I hope this fellow's legitimate, because he's got Lulu under his spell. I don't want her to be hurt if he turns out to be unsavory."

"Mercy, almost everyone in Hollywood these days is unsavory to one degree or another," said Chloe, sounding more cynical even than Ernie.

"Well, I wouldn't tar all of them with the same brush," said Mr. Easthope. "But the streets are crawling with young women who want to be stars and men who want to help them."

"Or take advantage of them," said Harvey.

"That's what I'm worried about," I said.

"Lulu's a big girl," Ernie reminded us all. "She's lived in Los Angeles a long time, and she can probably take care of herself if a guy gets out of hand."

With a laugh, Chloe said, "I'm sure you're right, Ernie. I adore

Lulu." Shaking her head, she added, "Although I don't think I'll ever accustom myself to her mode of dress."

"I won't, either," I said. "You should have seen her today." I shook my own head.

"Today's outfit was…especially eye-catching," Ernie said, grinning.

"Dear Lulu," said Chloe. "But let's look at this menu. I've heard good things from friends who have been to lunch here."

We took her advice.

"Everything looks delicious. Has anyone suggested anything especially good?" I asked my table companions.

"Not to me," said Harvey.

"Nobody's suggested anything to me either," said Chloe.

Harvey added, "The place hasn't been open very long. I think I'll take the grenadine of filet beef. Not sure what that is, but I'll try anything once."

Good heavens. That was the most expensive item on the menu, at three dollars and fifty cents, and it only came with a minute potato, whatever that was. I almost asked if it was really small or if it only got cooked for a minute but thought better of it. Not everyone appreciates my interest in our language.

"I'll take the grilled halibut," said Chloe. "I can't even bear the thought of eating a steak or anything heavy like that beef thing with the béarnaise sauce. Oh, and please order some mineral water for me, too."

"Did you notice the specials at the bottom of the menu?" asked Mr. Easthope. "I think I'll have the prime rib au Jus. And a cup of whatever their soup *du jour* is."

That one was almost three dollars, but not quite. I saw Harvey adjust his spectacles. "By George, you're right. I think I'll have that, too, only with the salad."

"I'll take the grilled halibut," I said. "And I'd also like some mineral water."

"Braised short ribs for me," said Ernie.

A waiter came by our table and asked if we were ready to order.

As we were, Harvey told the fellow who wanted what. The waiter dutifully noted everything down and went away again.

"All right, Mercy," said Chloe, "show us what you found today."

"I found Mr. Brentwood today, actually, but that's not what you want to see," I said, chuckling at my feeble wit. As we'd taken our seats at the booth I'd cleverly kept my oversized handbag in my lap, so I was able to dig into it and withdraw *The Adventures of Jemima Puddle Duck*. I opened it and passed it around the table.

Chloe was charmed. "Oh, how precious!" she said softly.

"But what if it's a boy?" demanded Harvey.

"Yeah. These look like they're all pictures for girls," agreed Ernie.

"Jeremy Fisher, whose story was written by the same author, is a boy," Francis Easthope reminded them all.

"And don't forget *Johnny Crow's Garden*," I said. "I didn't bring that one because it was bigger than the others and wouldn't fit in my handbag, but it's got great pictures of lions and hippos and giraffes and so forth."

"Who's Mr. Brentwood?" asked Chloe as if she'd only then registered my original statement.

"Just a case we were hired for," said Ernie. "He was at the library when Mercy went there to find books." He shook his head. "These illustrations still look pretty girly to me."

"Yeah," said Harvey. "Me too."

Chloe, Mr. Easthope and I exchanged a trio of glances. Then I sighed. "Men. But I think you'll all like the pictures in *Johnny Crow's Garden*, and they're suitable for a boy or a girl. Besides, maybe Francis can paint some baseball players in between the charming animals."

"That's actually a great idea, Mercy," said Harvey.

"Good Lord," said Chloe.

Ernie and I just laughed.

And dinner was delicious.

TEN

At breakfast on Thursday morning my tenants, especially Lulu, wanted to know all about the Brown Derby Restaurant.

"It's pretty inside, and the food was delectable," I said, telling the absolute truth. My halibut had been perfection itself, and so had the new potatoes and fried onions. Ernie had enjoyed his short ribs, and both Harvey and Francis Easthope had praised their prime rib. Chloe hadn't eaten all of her halibut, but she'd enjoyed the little of it she'd eaten.

"I'd love to go there one day," said Sue dreamily.

"Me, too," said Lulu. "Maybe Mr. Faraday will take me there."

"It sounds expensive," said Caroline, always the voice of economy, if not reason.

"It was," I told her.

I'd been almost afraid to look at Lulu today after yesterday's shocking purple, but she'd surprised me. Today's outfit wasn't what anyone would call subdued, but at least it wasn't bright purple. Today, she wore bright blue. Blue is a much easier color for me to tolerate than purple. I don't know why. With her bright blue low-waisted dress, she wore a couple of strands of fake pearls, and at least the dress had sleeves.

"Oh!" I cried, suddenly remembering the most interesting thing that had happened yesterday, and I'm including the discovery of Mr. Brentwood. "Ernie got a new car!"

"What?" a quartet of voices warbled in reaction. Mrs. Buck had come into the dining room from the kitchen, bearing a platter of pancakes, which made the fourth voice.

"A 1924 Packard Six. It's lovely. Black, of course, but the seats aren't ripped, the windows go up and down, and it's enclosed so you can't freeze to death when you ride in it. He got it from Wu Fung's automobile lot."

"Who's Wu Fung?" asked Sue.

"Remember Lily Wu, who worked for me around Christmastime? Well, Fung is a cousin of hers. She and Charley Wu have cousins by the dozens," I said, reminding myself of W.S. Gilbert.

"Oh, my," said Caroline. "Lily was a nice girl. I hope her cousin gave Mr. Templeton a good deal on his motor."

"Ernie said he did," I replied.

"I can't wait to see it," said Lulu. "Maybe he'll take us to lunch again today at Charley Wu's place."

"I thought you were going to lunch at the Brown Derby with Mr. Faraday," I said, nodding my thanks to Mrs. Buck as she set the platter of pancakes on the table for us to hand around. Mrs. Buck made excellent pancakes, and they went superbly with butter and maple syrup. I always had maple syrup in the pantry. I ordered it from a store in Boston, and it cost the earth but it was worth it. If you were me and had the money.

"If I'm lucky, Mr. Faraday will come by to take me to lunch," said Lulu. "I telephoned his office and told him I had those photos you took of me."

"Those pictures turned out really well," said Sue, slathering her stack of pancakes with butter, just as I'd done.

"Yes, they did," I said. "I've never taken pictures of a person before. Maybe I'll go into photography as a profession."

"I thought you were going to be a private eye," said Lulu. I noticed she'd taken only one—*one*—pancake, and she was eating it dry. No butter or syrup. I hope she'd either become a star fast or fail fast, because I hated to eat like a porker while she starved herself.

"I do aim to become good at private investigation," I said. "But photography might be a fun hobby."

We continued to chat amiably until we'd finished our breakfasts, and then we four ladies went upstairs to prepare for work. When we met at the front door, Buttercup was there to see us off, and we all— even Lulu—put on warm coats. I'd feared she might wear her red velvet cape over her blue dress, but I guess yesterday's chill indoors and out had cured her of wanting to be *that* fashionable. If her taste could be considered fashionable. But I was no fashion plate, so I probably shouldn't judge.

When I got to Ernie's office, the front door was unlocked, which was unusual. While I always arrived at the office before eight a.m., Ernie was generally less punctual. However, we did have a couple of actual cases for him to work on, so maybe that accounted for his early arrival.

"There you are," he said, turning from frowning at my desk and aiming his frown at me.

"Why are you mad at me?" Glancing at the clock on the wall, I noticed it was only five minutes until eight. "Heck, I'm early for work. Why are you here? You generally stroll in at nine or nine-thirty."

"I'm not mad at you. And you're right. I shouldn't frown at you," said Ernie, giving up the argument easily for once. "But I have a couple of spouses to spy on, so I thought I'd better get started."

"Wish you had something more interesting to do," I said with true sympathy.

"Yeah. Me too, but that's the life of a private eye for you. Anyhow, sometimes this job can get a little too exciting."

"Like when you and Charley Wu were arrested?"

"Yeah," said Ernie, shuddering. "Like that."

"Well, with any luck, somebody will 'phone with an interesting case for you."

"Right." Ernie walked to his office, and I heard him perform the morning's ritual: his hat missed the rack, as usual; he picked it up;

then he plonked his feet on his desk and shook open the day's *Los Angeles Times*.

"I thought you had work to do," I called from my desk, where I'd already retrieved my dust rag and stowed my handbag.

"It'll only take me a few minutes to look through the paper," he called back. "Today, I not only get to look out for Mr. Smedley, but Mrs. Lewis also seems to be on the prowl."

"That sounds terrible."

"Yeah, it does. Mr. Lewis probably isn't any prize, but she married him."

"Yes," I said with a sigh. "If you marry someone, you promise to be faithful. If a person isn't willing to abide by that promise, he or she shouldn't make it in the first place."

"I agree, although—this may come as a shock to your tender ears—sometimes marriages can be forced by the unexpected conse- quences of foolish dalliances."

"You don't need to be quite *that* attentive to my delicate sensibili- ties," I told him acidly. "I know girls get pregnant. I also know men sometimes marry them and sometimes run off because they don't want the responsibility. Remember poor Fritzie Mann? Nobody's ever been convicted of her murder. And have you read *An American Tragedy*, by Theodore Dreiser?"

"Yes, but I'm surprised your mother allowed you to read the news- papers or that book," said Ernie.

"Much to her dismay, Mother has seldom been able to stop me from doing much of anything at all," I spoke proudly.

"Yeah. I like that about you," said Ernie. "But let me look at the paper. The sooner I read the funny page, the sooner I can get out there on the streets."

"All right. I'll shut up now."

"Thank God."

I didn't speak again but continued my daily chores. True to his word, about fifteen minutes after I heard his feet plunk onto his desk, Ernie emerged from his office, hat on head and coat on, ready to tackle any number of straying wives and/or husbands. When I mentioned his workload to him, he said, "I'm not going to spy on anyone this morning. Need to see Fung and finalize the paperwork on the Packard."

"Oh. That's nice."

"Dunno what's nice about it." He paused in his walk to the front door when the telephone rang. I answered it and looked at Ernie. He lifted an eyebrow.

"I see," I said into the mouthpiece. "When and where did you last see Puddles?"

A grimace from Ernie nearly made me laugh, but I was a professional and didn't. "I see. And you don't believe she will come home by herself?" The woman at the end of the wire spoke some more, and I felt my own eyebrows lift. "A ransom note? Someone left you a ransom note?"

This time both of Ernie's eyebrows zoomed upwards.

"Would you like to bring it in and show it to Mr. Templeton? And what kind of dog is Puddles? A Pekingese? I see. Yes. You can come to the office at ten o'clock this morning?" I glanced at Ernie, he nodded, and I said, "That will be fine. I'll put you down for ten o'clock. You have our address?" Pause. "Excellent. We'll see you then, and I trust Mr. Templeton will be able to assist you."

The weeping woman on the other end of the wire said a muffled good-bye and hung up her receiver.

"At least it's a straying Pekingese and not a straying spouse," I told Ernie as I wrote down the woman's name and telephone number.

"A Pekingese? Aren't they those fluffy dogs with the flat faces?"

After thinking about the few Pekingese dogs I'd met in my life, I nodded. "Yes. Their faces aren't as flat as some, and they can be kind of cunning. And I think they're usually sweet dogs. Still, I wouldn't want one. I prefer Buttercup."

"At least it isn't another mastiff."

"Or an Irish wolfhound or a Russian wolfhound," I said, agreeing with my boss. A recent case had involved two mastiffs, an Irish wolfhound, and a Russian wolfhound. A Pekingese should be no trouble at all.

Ernie had no sooner left the office than the telephone rang again. That was fine. At least we were getting some jobs, which should keep the business afloat for a while, especially if the folks in Chinatown kept giving Ernie good deals on everything. Heck, for all I knew, they were showering him in money every time he walked through the place.

I didn't even get out my standard greeting before Lulu shrieked into my ear. "Mercy! Mr. Faraday is going to take me out to dinner tonight, and he wants to see the photographs you took! He said he might even introduce me to a producer friend of his."

"Tonight? I thought maybe he'd take you to lunch again first," I said, a faint niggling sensation beginning to tug at my nerves.

"What do you mean, first?"

"Well, I thought maybe he'd start by taking you to lunch a couple of times, and then maybe work up to dinner if he thinks you show promise," I said, my voice a little feeble.

"He already thinks I show promise, Mercy Allcutt!"

"Yes, yes. Of course, he does. Um, do you know where his office is?" I asked.

"Somewhere on Hill. Or maybe Broadway. I can't remember."

"Well, please give me the address before you go out tonight, all right?"

"Why? Do you still think he's a phony?"

"I don't think he's a phony," I told Lulu, who sounded as if she didn't appreciate my caution one little bit. "But I do want to be sure I know where you are, just in case."

"In case of what exactly?" Lulu demanded.

"Please don't be angry at me, Lulu. You're my best friend, and I want you to be safe. I'm sure Mr. Faraday is legitimate—"

"It doesn't sound like it to me!" she snapped.

"But it's still a good idea to tell someone where you'll be when you go out in the evening," I said in my best placating voice.

It didn't placate Lulu.

"Fine, then. I'll make sure you have the address of his office."

And Lulu hung up on me.

Oh, dear.

However, I didn't get a chance to brood about Lulu. The telephone rang about a second after I'd hung up the receiver.

"Mr. Templeton's office. Miss Allcutt speaking," I said, hoping against hope it was Lulu calling to patch things up.

No such luck.

"Oh, Miss Allcutt!" exclaimed Mrs. Wilkes, whose voice I recognized by this time. "He's escaped *again*!"

"Good heavens, how'd he get out this time?"

"I don't even know," said Mrs. Wilkes, sounding close to tears. "But he's gone again, and nobody has a clue where he might be. Will you please telephone if he shows up in your office, as he did that other time?"

"Of course, I shall," I told her, trying to convey my sympathy. For a person Ernie stigmatized as a loony, Mr. Jerome Brentwood could sure evade his keepers with finesse and alacrity.

"Thank you. You still have the list I gave you?"

"Yes, I do. It's in my file." I'd filed it as soon as I got back to the office after returning Mr. Brentwood the day before, in fact.

"Thank you. I just don't know what to do about that man."

"I'm sorry. I'm sure Mr. Templeton will be able to help find him."

"I hope so."

After a few more tense sentences on her part and a few more soothing ones on mine, we both hung up. Oh, boy. Mr. Brentwood was quite the problem fellow. When he got back to the office a little after nine, Ernie agreed with me.

And boy, was I wrong about Pekingese being sweet doggies. As soon as Mrs. Amstell walked into the outer office, the Pekingese dog with her began to snarl at me. I hadn't even moved, for pity's sake!

"Pierre, stop it," said Mrs. Amstell, who kind of looked like a Pekingese herself, with a flattish face and fluffy hair. She wore a fabulous cloche hat that had probably made Lulu drool, as it was purple. Her day dress was also purple, with black edging. "I'm sorry," she said to me.

"It's all right," I said, not daring to rise from my chair.

"Pierre knows Puddles is missing, and he knows how upset I am. He probably thinks you're to blame."

Me? Whatever would make that stupid dog think *I* was to blame for his missing friend or his owner's distress? I didn't ask. Rather, I rose slowly from my chair as Pierre's growls became sharp barks of outrage, and sidled to Ernie's office. Opening the door, I slid inside and said, "Mrs. Amstell is here. She has another Peke with her. Pierre isn't happy."

"Pierre?" Said Ernie, astounded unless I miss my guess. "Is that the werewolf howling in your room?"

Sure enough, Pierre had begun to howl.

"I'm afraid so," I told him.

"Gawd," said Ernie sounding as if he wished he were elsewhere.

"I'll let Mrs. Amstell and Pierre in. She's got him on a leash."

"She'd better have him on a leash. A short one," said Ernie, grumpy as all get-out.

I stood in the doorway to Ernie's office, took a good gander at the distraught woman and her mad dog, and decided what the heck.

"Pierre! Stop that infernal racket right now!"

Mrs. Amstell jumped about three inches off the floor. As for Pierre, he gave me one startled, scared look, let out a short scream-like yap, and flattened himself on the floor—well, as flat as he could get, given his fluff—and shut up. Golly, until that moment, I hadn't realized how forceful I could be.

"Well, really!" said Mrs. Amstell after she landed, slapped a hand to her bosom and caught her breath.

"I'm sorry, Mrs. Amstell, but we can't work with you if you allow your dog to behave in such an ill-bred manner," I told her in my Mother's best, most obnoxious, upper-crust Boston tones. "If you prefer to hire another private investigator to find your Puddles, feel free."

I saw her swallow. She glanced down at Pierre, who now whimpered. Then she tilted her head to one side and said, "No. I should like to employ Mr. Templeton. Evidently, his staff has a way with recalcitrant dogs, according to Lillian Swale."

Aha. Mrs. Lillian Swale, whose husband was a villain and whose dogs were English mastiffs, had recommended us. Good. I, as Ernie's staff, nodded regally. "Did you bring the ransom note?"

"Yes."

"Then come this way, please. And please keep Pierre on a short leash. If he should bite either Mr. Templeton or me, there *will* be legal repercussions."

"Yes," whimpered Mrs. Amstell, sounding not unlike Pierre. "I understand."

I glanced back to see Ernie grinning from ear to ear as I stepped away from his open door—toward my desk. I mean, I'm not stupid enough to think Pierre wouldn't be peeved with the person who out-howled him and attempt a quick nip. "Then come into Mr. Temple-ton's office, please," I said as I hurriedly took my seat at my desk and lifted my feet off the floor in case Pierre got any snappish ideas and managed to free himself from Mrs. Amstell's firm hold. If I had to, I could climb on my desk. That silly dog was too short to leap up and murder me.

ELEVEN

After about twenty minutes, Ernie's office door opened and Mrs. Amstell, with Pierre still held firmly on a short leash, walked out. Pierre eyed me nervously but didn't utter a whine, much less a bark.

"I'll see what I can for you, Mrs. Amstell," said Ernie, waiting to appear in his doorway until Mrs. Amstell and Pierre were almost at the front office door. "I'm glad you kept the envelope the ransom note came in. It will help me pin down the post office from which it was sent."

"Thank you, Mr. Templeton," she said in a voice clogged with unshed tears. She sure loved her dogs. "And I'm sorry about Pierre, Miss Allcutt," she said to me.

"It's all right. I'm sure both you and Pierre are upset about Puddles going missing."

"Yes, yes." She unleashed her tears (but not, thank God, Pierre) and sobbed openly.

It looked to me as if Ernie, who kept a supply of handkerchiefs in his desk for weeping clients, had already given her one, because she used it to wipe her eyes.

"Try not to worry too much," said Ernie.

"I can't *help* it!" cried Mrs. Amstell. Literally. I mean, the woman was crying.

She left and shut the door behind her. Ernie heaved a huge sigh. "Lordy, that woman is nuts."

"Maybe not," I said, although I was no fan of Mrs. Amstell. "I'd be crushed and heartbroken if anything happened to Buttercup."

"Buttercup doesn't try to bite everyone she meets or howl at the moon even on dark nights when the moon's not out."

"Heavens, do Puddles and Pierre do that?"

"Evidently." Ernie shook his head. "I'm surprised whoever took Puddles didn't get Pierre while he was at it. According to Mrs. Amstell, Pekingese are called 'lion dogs' because they look like little lions and were owned by royalty in ancient China. Lap dogs."

"Why doesn't she train her dogs?" I asked.

With a shrug, Ernie said, "Hell, how should I know?"

"What did the ransom note say?"

Reaching into his jacket pocket, Ernie pulled out the note and handed it to me. He'd put it back into its envelope, so I opened the flap and retrieved the note. It read: *If you can't keep your dogs quiet, you'll lose them both. This is a warning. Shut the other one up, and I'll give back the first one. Don't, and I'll take him, too. If I do give the dog back, shut her up too.*

I turned the note over in my hand and scanned its other side, where nothing was written. "Where's the ransom demand?"

"There isn't one," said Ernie. "I suspect this is from a neighbor who just wants to be able to sleep without hearing dogs howling all night long."

"What Mrs. Amstell needs to do is get her dogs some training. I understand there are people who will train dogs for a fee. If both of her fluffy puppies are like Pierre, they need a firm hand. Clearly, Mrs. Amstell doesn't have one."

"You sure had a firm voice," said Ernie grinning at me. "I never thought I'd feel sorry for Buttercup, but her mother is a shrew."

"Bother you, Ernie Templeton!" I snapped. "I used my horrid mother's voice on that dog, and it responded pretty much like my mother's children responded to her. According to Mrs. Majesty in

Pasadena, a person can even take their own dogs to obedience training classes."

"I think her name's Rotondo now. She and Sam got married."

"Oh, how nice," I said, feeling happy for the couple. We'd shared a harrowing experience a couple of months prior. "I didn't know you kept in touch."

"Not often, but we talk on the 'phone from time to time."

"I'm glad to hear it. I liked both of them."

"So I think I'll start in Mrs. Amstell's neighborhood. While I'm doing that, why don't you look in the telephone directory and see if there are any dog-training services advertised in the yellow pages?"

"Good idea," I said, already reaching for my right-side file drawer where I kept the Los Angeles telephone book. Now that we were getting so many more clients, I might have to find another place to store the 'phone book, by George!

The day proceeded apace. Lulu didn't telephone, so I figured she was still upset with me. A little before lunchtime, I dialed the reception desk. When Lulu answered, I said, "Hey Lulu, want to go across the street to the diner for lunch?"

After a brief hesitation, she said, "No, thanks. Mr. Faraday is taking me out for lunch again today. We're going to the Ambassador." She sounded rather snippy.

"Oh. Well then, have a good time. See you later." Probably for no reason, my feelings were bruised. I knew Lulu didn't appreciate my doubts about her precious Mr. Faraday, but still and all. She *had* told me how careful a girl had to be around people who claimed to be producers and talent scouts and so forth. The fact she was now mad at me because I cared what happened to her made me feel really crummy. Plainly, she didn't want *anyone* to cast even the faintest of doubts upon her fantasy of achieving flicker stardom. But darn it, friends looked out for each other.

Oh well. Wasn't much I could do about it. I typed the names, addresses, telephone numbers, and fees of dog trainers. The fees they charged were astronomical. Maybe they trained dogs for the movies, too, and set their prices for studio use. Shoot, I'd trained Buttercup myself, and I didn't even know what I was doing at the time. These professionals took their training duties seriously.

I'd just taken the list from my typewriter when Ernie walked into the office. "Found the kidnapper," he announced first thing.

"Already? Your sleuthing skills astound me," I said, amused. "What did the kidnapper want as ransom?"

"As I figured, he wants the Amstell dogs to shut up and be good. He works the night shift at the Pacific Electric Company, and the dogs bark all day long and howl at intervals. Also, at least one, and maybe both, of the dogs is as good as Mr. Brentwood at escaping confinement. The difference is that Mr. Brentwood doesn't chase cats or try to bite postmen and other citizens he encounters."

"Good heavens, she *really* needs to train those dogs. Or give them to someone who will train them for her. I have several names of people who do that, by the way." I waved my list at Ernie.

He walked over and sat in a chair before my desk, taking the list as he sat. "Aha. Thanks. Criminy! These people cost a fortune."

"I noticed that. Does Mrs. Amstell have a fortune?"

"One or two." He looked up from the list and grinned at me. "I think she has even more money than you."

"Lots of people do," I said grimly.

"Sorry about teasing you, Mercy. It's just so much fun. Say, why don't we go across the street for lunch? We can take Lulu if you want to."

"I'd love to," I said, feeling a little happier than I had moments earlier. "Lulu has other plans, though."

"Aha. Going to lunch with her talent scout?"

"Yes. She's also going out to dinner with him this evening."

Lifting an eyebrow, Ernie said, "Yeah? She going to show him the pictures you took?"

"Yes. And she's mad at me for asking her to give me his address before she leaves tonight."

"Sorry, Mercy. You should probably stop throwing cold water on her plans with this guy."

"I don't think asking for an address is throwing cold water on anything," I said, miffed. "I think it's only good sense."

"Yeah, I think so too, but neither of us is Lulu."

"I wonder if Rupert has met Mr. Faraday." Rupert, Lulu's brother, worked as a houseboy for Mr. Francis Easthope.

"Don't know. Didn't she just meet him a day or so ago?"

"Monday morning, to be precise," I said. "Swept her off her feet, almost literally."

Shaking his head and rising from his chair, Ernie said, "Why don't you call Mrs. Amstell? See if she can come to the office at two this afternoon. Thanks for this list." He waved it in the air as he vanished into his office.

So I called Mrs. Amstell and made an appointment for her to come to the office at two that afternoon.

Ernie and I had a nice lunch at the Figueroa Street Diner, across the street from our building. We didn't see Lulu as we walked past the reception desk on our way to lunch or when we came back. I hoped she'd be there—and be willing to speak to me—after work.

Mrs. Amstell arrived promptly at two p.m., *sans* Pierre. I ushered her into Ernie's office, where she spent approximately thirty minutes. She left, sobbing piteously, and thanking Ernie for finding dog trainers for her. Well. I sometimes get the feeling secretaries exist only to do all the things nobody else wants to do, accept blame when things go wrong and never receive any credit when credit is due.

Ernie walked the weeping woman to the door. When he turned back, he said, "I told her you found the names of the trainers. I think she's still mad at you for hollering at Pierre."

Very well, so *some* bosses will attribute credit to their secretaries when it's deserved.

"Thanks, Ernie."

When closing time arrived, Ernie came out of his office and said, "Say, do you think Lulu and those other two ladies would like a ride home in my newish car?"

"I'd love it, thanks!" I said. "I'm sure they will too. It's cold outside, and your car actually has a heater and windows that close."

"Yup. All the finest in two-year-old Packard Sixes."

So he drove Lulu, Caroline, Sue, and me home, and we all praised his Packard to the skies. I think he was pleased. I know he was pleased when I invited him to take dinner with us. Except, of course, for Lulu, who was dining elsewhere that evening. At least she'd resumed speaking to me.

About an hour after we were finished with dinner—a lovely beef stew with dumplings—at my house and Ernie had gone out to search for straying spouses and perhaps Mr. Brentwood, I went up to my suite of rooms. There I got out of my work clothes and donned my nightgown and fuzzy robe. It was kind of cold that night, so I turned the electric heater on, sat in my comfy chair, stuck my feet in their slippers on the ottoman, and picked up *Johnny Crow's Garden*. I wanted to select pictures from the book to show Ernie and Harvey that not all children's books were for girls. Huh! As if boys didn't love Beatrix Potter as much as girls did. I think. Maybe they don't.

Anyhow, I'd been sitting for maybe a half hour when a little tap came at my door. Buttercup woofed softly, and I said, "C'm in."

Lulu walked in! To say I was surprised would be an understatement. Approaching my chair, she said a little stiffly, "I came to give you Mr. Faraday's address. I'm sure there's no need for this."

"Thanks, Lulu," She handed me a thickish piece of oblong cardboard, upon which was printed in a florid font: Clint R. Faraday, Talent Scout-Agent-Producer-Director. Printed on the card, too, were Faraday's address and telephone number. I was glad to have it. "Do you know where he's taking you?"

"Yes. We're going to dine and dance at the Club Parisienne. I think it's swell."

"I hope you're right." Wrong thing to say. I could tell when Lulu stiffened further, so I hurried to add, "I'm sure it will be." But I wasn't sure of it. What's more, I didn't like it. I didn't want her to get hurt by a devious Lothario.

"After dinner and a little dancing, he wants to take another look at those photos you took to see if he thinks I'll look good on the screen." Lulu plucked at a violent red sleeve of her violent red dress with fingers the nails of which were painted a violent red matching the dress. She was truly blink-worthy that evening.

Knowing as I did so that I shouldn't, I said, "Just be careful. Remember, you're the one who told me some of these talent scouts, agents, and producers are often up to no good and try to take advantage of young women longing to be stars."

"Yes, yes, I know, but this fellow is the goods."

"I hope he is," I told her, doubt clear to hear in my voice.

"Nertz, Mercy! He's taken me out to lunch *twice*, and he's been a perfect gentleman both times. His office is in a good part of town. I've seen his office three times!"

"Good. I'm glad."

"Well, then. He's legit! He's helped lots of girls get their start."

"Oh really? Which ones?" I asked, honestly curious.

Lulu tossed her head. "I can't remember. Anyhow, he's had bad luck with them backing out at the last minute after he did all the groundwork for them, but he said he's sure I won't be like that. He's going to take more photos of me this evening and show them around as soon as he gets them developed. He *knows* some casting directors will want me!"

"But I thought you said this was a dinner date. Where is he going to take photos?"

"At his office." She pointed a red nail at the card I still held. "That's the address."

"But it's nighttime," I said, still attempting to make Lulu see reason. I'd known for months she wanted to be a big star on the silver screen, but she mostly just sat around all day fiddling with her fingernails behind the reception desk at the Figueroa Building.

"So what? That's where his camera is," said Lulu as if it made sense for her to go to his office in the dead of night. "Other talent scouts and producers are always trying to snitch the people he's promoting. He doesn't want them to get a look at me, for fear someone will steal me before he can get me established. They're all jealous of him!"

Oh, dear. This *really* didn't sound right to me.

"May I please just drive you to his location, Lulu? I'll sit in the car and wait for you. I won't get in your way, I promise."

"It's the middle of January, Mercy! You'll freeze to death if you wait in your car."

"I don't mind," I said, which was the truest test of friendship I could think of. Lulu was right. We might live in Los Angeles and not the frozen North, but the night air was darned cold.

"Nonsense. He's sending a car for me."

"It's nice he's sending a car for you," I said. "As long as he aims to bring you home early and in one piece."

"What do you mean by that, Mercy Allcutt? Do you think I'm an idiot? I've heard all the bad stories! I know what goes on. Mr. Faraday won't do anything awful to me. He just won't."

"I guess there's no use arguing with you anymore, right?"

"Right." Lulu clapped her black cloche hat with the violent red silk flowers on it on her bottle-blond hair and stuck a pretty Chinese pin with a red whatchamacallit at its end to hold the hat in place. Then she twirled in front of the Cheval glass mirror in my room, my room being the only room in Mercy's Manor to have a full-length mirror.

"Well, good luck," I said, attempting to sound cheerful.

"Thanks, Mercy. Stop worrying!"

"I'll try," I told her.

And Lulu left for her appointment with the talent scout who was going to make her a huge star in the Hollywood firmament. I wished her well.

TWELVE

It took me a long time to get to sleep that night because I kept worrying about Lulu. Buttercup finally got disgusted with my tossing and turning, leaped off my bed, and curled up on the rug beside the bed.

I don't know how long I'd been asleep when I awoke again to a sleepy "Woof" from Buttercup and a not-very-gentle shaking of my shoulder.

"M-Mercy?"

Blinking in surprise, I leaned over and pulled the chain on my bedside table's lamp. My eyes grew wide and my mouth fell open when I saw a disheveled Lulu, lipstick smeared, mascara running down her cheeks, dress torn, and the red roses on her hat dragging around her shoulders. "Lulu! You look like you've been in the Battle of the Somme! What did that beast *do* to you? What in the world *happened*!"

"I-I'll tell you. But later, okay? I h-h-had to take a t-t-taxicab home, but I don't have any m-m-*money*! Will you please lend me enough m-money for the cab fare?"

"Lulu! Of course, I'll pay your cab fare. Stay here. Don't move. I want to know what that horrible, deceitful, louse of a bounder did to

you! I'll kill him with my bare hands! I *knew* you shouldn't have gone
to see him!"

It was, probably, the stupidest and wrongest (I'm sure that's not a
word) sentence I could say to the poor girl, who knew better than I she
shouldn't have gone with Mr. Faraday that night. She collapsed onto
my bed, sobbing as if her heart and several bones were broken.
Buttercup jumped up to comfort her.

I love dogs. Well, except maybe Pierre and Puddles.

Throwing on my robe, I stuffed my feet into my slippers, grabbed
my handbag, and raced downstairs and out into the cold to pay the
cabbie. As I scrabbled in my bag for my little purse, I had the presence
of mind to ask him where he'd picked up Lulu.

"Broadway. Near Chinatown. Don't know the address. She was
running down the sidewalk and hailed me. She looked like she went a
few rounds with Jack Dempsey. She okay?"

"She will be. Was anyone with her when she hailed you?"

Shaking his head, the cabbie said, "Nope. Looked to me as if she
was running away from someone. She didn't talk when she got into
the cab. Just huddled in the backseat and cried."

"Thank you for bringing her home." Then I had another brain
wave. Recalling a Sherlock Holmes story I'd read once, I asked, "Say,
does your cab have a number or some kind of identification? And
what is your name?"

"Hey, I didn't do nothin' to her! I'm the one who brought her
home." He glanced at Mercy's Manor and sneered. "And what she
was doin' in that place if she lives here is somethin' I'll never understand. She was dressed like a—"

"Thank you!" I said, interrupting him. "Your name and cab
number, please? Just in case I need it in the future. Thank you for
bringing her home safely."

"Sid Jankowski's the name. Cab number is seventeen-fifty-two."

"Thank you very much, Mr. Jankowski. How much is the fare."

"From Broadway to here? Seventy-five cents."

I handed him a five-dollar bill and said, "Keep the change."

He took the bill and stared at it as if he'd never seen one before.
"Holy Moses, you mean it?"

"Yes. Thank you for helping my friend."

"Sure, lady. If you need me, just call the Yellow Cab number."

"Thank you again, Mr. Jankowski."

He saluted and began backing out of the drive. I didn't watch him after that, but hurried back into the house. It was *cold* out there.

When I got indoors, I stood in the entryway shivering for a bit before I went back upstairs. I almost didn't want to know what Mr. Faraday had done to send Lulu home in such distress (and in such a mess). If even the cabbie considered her attire fit for a lady of the night, perhaps Mr. Faraday had misunderstood her true nature.

But no. *He* knew she believed he was a genuine talent scout who could get her into the flickers. He hadn't misunderstood anything at all. He just hadn't realized that Lulu was a sensible girl under all her makeup and flashy clothing. I hope he didn't get to see too much of what was under her clothing. Oh, dear....

"Everything all right?" came a sleepy voice when I got to the head of the staircase. The voice was soft, but it jarred me so badly I nearly skipped a step and fell down the stairs I'd just climbed. Clinging madly to the banister, I saw Sue Krekeler, standing at her door, looking worried.

"Oh, everything's fine, Sue. Thanks for checking," I told her.

"Good. Thought I heard somebody running around and was a little worried."

"I'm sorry to have troubled you. That was me. I forgot something in the car and was afraid it would freeze if I didn't bring it inside overnight." For some reason I still don't understand, I held up my handbag, as if *it* were the item I feared would freeze if left in the automobile overnight.

"Oh. Okay. Well then, goodnight."

"Goodnight, Sue," I said, aiming for a sweet tone. Almost achieved it, by golly.

When I got to my bedroom, I took a deep breath, opened the door, and walked in. Lulu had removed herself from my bed and taken up residence on my cozy reading chair. She still held Buttercup for comfort. I didn't begrudge her the use of my dog.

Because Lulu had her knees tucked under her and the ottoman was free, I sat there in front of the chair. "What happened, Lulu?"

Sniffle. "I'm an idiot." *Sniffle.* "You were right. Faraday's a bum, and he tried—" She stopped speaking and began crying.

"I'm so sorry, Lulu."

"H-he said I dressed"—*sniffle*—"like a wh-wh-whore!"

"The cad!" Boston rearing its ugly head again. Cad? "The monster! The fiend!"

"I-I think he's *right*!" sobbed Lulu. Then she broke down again and buried her head in Buttercup's fluff. She wasn't supposed to be so fluffy. Time to get the dog to the groomer's.

"Oh, no, Lulu," I said, although I couldn't say it with conviction. "You dress in a…um…colorful manner. It's part of your personality." There. That was good.

Or not.

"Nuts on my personality! I dress like a whore, and he thought I *was* one! He tried to-toe-to—Oooooooh! I can't even *say* it!"

"Oh, Lulu! I'm so, so sorry."

She lifted her head from Buttercup's fluff and threw her arms around me. "You're my best friend, Mercy! I should have listened to you. C'n I borrow some of your dull clothes until I can find some of my own? I know I shouldn't ask because I was so mean to you, but—"

"Lulu, stop it!" I felt sorry for Lulu, but she was suffocating my dog, and my clothes *weren't* dull. Not very, anyway. They were appropriate for an office setting. "Please, Lulu. Stop. I need to know what that awful man did to you. If he hurt you in any way, maybe the police can arrest him for it."

Still sniffling, she sat back in the chair and wiped her eyes with her hands. Now her hands as well as her cheeks were streaked with mascara. Actually, so was Buttercup's back. I rose from the ottoman and hurried to my dresser, where I opened a drawer and pulled out a few hankies. I figured she'd probably need more than one. I aimed to use one on Buttercup, although if the hankie didn't work, the groomer would be able to clip off the mascara stains.

"Here. Wipe your eyes and blow your nose. Then try to be calm and tell me what happened."

"Thanks, Mercy," she said, sort of hiccupping the words. Then she took my advice and wiped her eyes and face with one of my hankies. Now it was smeared with mascara too, along with some kind of greasepaint and rouge. I hoped it would wash out. Maybe if I soaked it in water with baking soda in it…

"Do you need a glass of water, Lulu?" I asked, my voice soft and gentle. Poor Lulu.

"N-no. Thank you. He didn't really do much to me, because I fought him off," she said.

"But you did have to fight him off, right?"

"Yes, but the police wouldn't care about that."

Sagging somewhat, I said, "You're probably right."

"You know I'm right."

"Yeah. I wish we could figure out a way to punish rotten man, though. You thought he was a legitimate talent scout, and then he did *this* to you." I made a sweeping gesture meant to encompass the whole of Lulu's being.

Wrong thing to say.

"He-he said I dressed like a wh-whore! I *don't*, Mercy! I can't help it if I like bright colors!" She blinked several times, dislodging more tears, and she used a clean hankie on the new ones.

Bleach. Perhaps bleach would help.

Oh, why was I fretting about handkerchiefs? I could buy *dozens* of hankies. Friends were much harder to find, and I wanted to keep this one.

"And I didn't mean it when I said your clothes are dull," Lulu said when got her voice under control again. "It's just that you always look office-y."

"That's because I work in an office," I said, trying not to sound sarcastic.

"Yes. Yes, you're right. I've got to tone down my wardrobe in order not to look like a whore, huh?"

"You *don't* look like one of those, Lulu!" Listen to me. I couldn't even say the word "whore" out loud. "But I do think you might tone down your clothing choices some. Men are idiots. You never know when one of them will take it into his head that a woman is something she isn't because of what she's wearing."

Did that even make sense? It didn't matter.

"But please tell me what happened. Did he at least take you out to dinner before he tried to ravish you?"

"Yes, but it wasn't at the Café Parisienne," Lulu said in a sad voice. "He took me to a diner on Temple, and then we walked to his office. It's on Broadway, closer to Chinatown. It's not in the best neighborhood, to tell the truth." More sniffles. "I was so mad at you for not believing he was for real, I didn't want to tell you about where his office really was."

"I didn't mean to spoil your joy, Lulu. I was only concerned, was all."

"I know. I'm an idiot."

"You're not an idiot. Most young women in the United States want to move to Hollywood and become stars these days. They aren't all idiots, either. And Mr. Faraday gave you a really good spiel when he pulled over and stopped his car."

"Huh. I was a fool for falling for it. I know better. I've even told *you* I know better. But I didn't know better and I got suckered, too."

"But what happened when you got to his office?"

"For one thing, it was dark. We had to walk up two flights of clanky metal stairs. Then he unlocked the door to his office, which was at the head of the stairs, and turned on the light. When I walked in, he shut and locked the door."

"Oh, dear."

"Yeah. Oh dear is right. He said, 'Okay, Miss Lulu. We both know what we're here for, don't we?' Me, being dumb as a rock, said, 'Yeah. You want to look at the photos Mercy took of me.'" A few more sniffles, then, "He *laughed* at me! Said if I believed that, I was a silly fool. Then he came over and started pawing at me. Trying to get my c-clothes off me."

"Oh, no!" I was horrified. I'd already deduced this part of her story, but it still hurt to hear it. "How'd you get out? You said he locked the door."

"He left the key in the lock. When he started putting his hands all over me, I kneed him in the crotch, and he hollered and called me a b-bitch."

"And that hurt him?"

"I kneed him in the groin, Mercy!" Lulu said as if speaking to a dull child. "That's where a guy's family jewels are. Men're real protective of their balls."

"Oh," I said, feeling precisely like a dull child. "I can imagine." Ow. "Good for you!"

"He didn't think so. But he was bent over so far, clutching his groin, it gave me a chance to get to the door and unlock it. Then he hollered, started swearing like a drunk sailor, came lurching after me, and grabbed my sleeve." More tears. "Almost ripped it off."

"I'm sorry, Lulu," I said, thinking how inadequate words were sometimes.

"Then he grabbed my hat." Finally, she smiled. "And he stabbed himself with my hat pin." She plucked her wilted hat from her head and gazed gloomily at the bedraggled red roses. "I hope the hole gets infected and he dies!"

"So do I!"

"Oh, but Mercy, what will I tell everyone? I feel *so* stupid!"

"You're not stupid, Lulu. You got a little carried away when you thought Mr. Faraday was a real talent scout. You don't have to tell people anything."

"But they'll ask. You know they'll ask," said Lulu, sniffling some more.

"Yeah, they probably will," I said, patting a dampish, slightly made-up Buttercup on her back. At least Lulu hadn't damaged my dog when she grabbed me. "You can just say things didn't work out, can't you? Nobody else needs to know what that brute did to you."

"I guess so. Especially if you'll let me wear one of your long-sleeved suits or dresses or something. I'm afraid I'm going to have some bad bruises on my arms. He-he also hit me across the face. I hope to *God* I don't get a black eye!"

"The louse! What a horrible man! To hit a woman!"

"Well, it was after I kneed him in the groin. He was real mad about that."

ALICE DUNCAN

"I don't care how angry he was," I declared, firmly on Lulu's side. "He shouldn't have hit you. Let me look at your face."

She leaned toward me, and I didn't see a red mark. Then again, her face was blotchy with tears and smeared makeup, so I couldn't really tell. "I can't see anything yet," I said, tentatively, hoping a bruise wouldn't show up. "I'm so sorry, Lulu."

"Yeah. So am I." She shook her head miserably. "But most of all, I feel really stupid."

"Stop it. You might have been carried away when you thought he was a legitimate talent scout, but don't forget there are men all over the place in Los Angeles just lying in wait to take advantage of young women who want to get into the pictures."

"Yeah. I know. In fact, I'm the one who told *you* that."

"Yes, and I have a brother-in-law who's a big motion-picture executive. He's told me stories, too. Some of the stories are a lot worse than yours."

"Yeah. I guess so. Like that girl who died at Fatty Arbuckle's party. Somebody got to her. She was preggers. Probably by Faraday."

As she sat in my overstuffed chair, looking small and defeated, the spectacle of Lulu nearly made *me* cry. "But buck up. What's that they say? Time heals all wounds? It might take time, but you'll get over this."

"I wish time would wound all heels," muttered Lulu, almost making me laugh.

But this wasn't the time to laugh. "Will you be going to work in the morning?"

"Work? Wha…? What time is it?"

"I don't know. Let me have a look at my clock." I rose and went to my bedside table. The time was one-fifteen on Friday morning. "Oh, dear. It's really late. One-fifteen."

"Oh gawd," said Lulu miserably. "But I'll be cursed if I'll let that man keep me from anything, much less my job!"

"That's the spirit!" I said, glad to see some of her spunk returning. "Take a bath and go to sleep. Tomorrow you can borrow whatever you want from my closet, and over the weekend, if you really want to, we can go to that consignment shop in Chinatown. I'm sure that nice

118

lady—her name is Mary, which seems kind of odd for a Chinese woman—will have some more subdued clothes for not much money."

"Yeah. And I can take her some of my clothes. Maybe she can sell them on consignment."

"Great idea," I said, wondering who would want Lulu's flashy wardrobe. Well, who knew?

After easing Buttercup to the floor, Lulu stood, giving me an opportunity to assess her overall condition. Except for the ripped clothing and ruined hat, she didn't appear to be damaged. I suppose bruises would show up later, but we could worry about them then.

"Do you need any iodine or anything, Lulu? Any hot cocoa? Anything at all?"

"No. Just a bath. I'll check myself over for bruises. I know there will be some on my arms."

"Long sleeves will cover those," I told her bracingly.

"Thanks, Mercy. You're the best friend I've ever had."

"And you're my best friend, Lulu," I said, although Chloe was actually my best friend, but she was also my sister, so I guess I hadn't really lied. "And we'll get you all fixed up tomorrow. Nobody will ever have to know what that evil man did to you."

"Thanks, Mercy."

She came to my bedside table and gave me a hug. Then she marched, back straight, shoulders stiff, out of my suite of rooms and down the hall to her own. She had her own bathroom, so she wouldn't disturb either of the other tenants as she repaired damage to her makeup or her person.

I wished there was some way to make Mr. Clint Faraday pay for his sins, but I couldn't think of one. Darn it!

THIRTEEN

O n Friday morning, both Lulu and I were exhausted, Lulu most certainly a good deal more than I. I'm sure she was still upset by what happened to her the night before. However, you wouldn't be able to tell from her plucky spirit. She bounced down the stairs to the dining room, to all appearances the same old Lulu. She'd already put some kind of foundation makeup under her eyes to hide dark circles, but other than that, you couldn't tell she'd been through a harrowing ordeal only hours earlier. She wore one of her long-sleeved Chinese robes to breakfast.

As for me, I didn't project half as much energy and enthusiasm as Lulu. I'd checked myself out in the mirror and decided to put some powder on my cheeks before I went to work. I rubbed a little powder under my eyes, but even then my dark circles weren't as well concealed as Lulu's.

"So how did it go with your talent scout last night, Lulu?" asked an eager Sue. I'd hoped nobody would ask about her evening first off, but Lulu was prepared.

"It didn't work out," said Lulu, sounding nonchalant. "Turned out he was a phony. He didn't know *anybody* who could help me get into the pictures."

"Oh, that's too bad. He didn't…Uh…" Sue stopped speaking, clearly unable to ask a shocking question of Lulu.

"He tried," said Lulu in a clipped voice. "But I didn't let him." She heaved a huge sigh, "Darn it. I was sure he was okay, but he turned out to be a flat tire."

A flat tire? Oh! A dud. Right. "That's a shame, Lulu," I said, pretending I didn't know precisely how duddy Mr. Faraday had turned out to be. "Harvey said there are too many men like that around these days, lying to women who want to get into the pictures in order to take advantage of them. I'm glad you didn't fall for his big talk."

"No," said Lulu, not for an instant letting down her brave front. "But I'll tell you this much. I'm going to tone down my wardrobe. That man definitely got the wrong idea about me."

The conservative Caroline nodded and said, "I've thought for some time that you might want to dress more soberly." Seeing three pairs of critical gazes fixed on her, she hastened to add, "Not that you ever look bad or anything, but you do tend to wear eye-catching colors that might give certain unsavory men the wrong idea about you."

Without hesitation, Lulu said, "You're right. That's probably what caught Faraday's attention." She heaved what sounded like an honest-to-God disappointed sigh. "I do love bright colors, though."

"A little color is fine," said Caroline. "Say, a red scarf with a gray dress or something along those lines."

"Gray and I don't get along too well," said Lulu with what sounded like genuine amusement, "but if I could wear a red scarf with a gray sweater, I might survive."

Watching her closely, I didn't see a single sign that she was suffering aftereffects from her ghastly experience. Lulu was a darned good actress! By golly, maybe I'd just tell Harvey about her acting prowess. Couldn't hurt. Might help.

Conversation died as we sat at the table to eat our delicious breakfasts. This morning, Mrs. Buck served us bacon with nice omelets and half a grapefruit each. In my childhood home in Boston, our mother made us dig sour grapefruit segments out with a serrated spoon that never did the job right. Mrs. Buck had already solved the squirting problem by cutting the segments out for us but leaving them inside their skins—if that makes any sense. She'd also sugared the grapefruit halves the night before and allowed them to sweeten up in the Frigidaire before she served them. I already knew she did that because the first time I'd winced at the sight of a grapefruit half, she'd laughed and told me to try it. I had, and I'd crafted an even higher imaginary culinary pedestal upon which to place Mrs. Buck.

Caroline seemed fascinated with her grapefruit, and when Mrs. Buck came into the dining room with the coffeepot and offered refills, she asked, "How did you get these grapefruit segments so cleanly cut, Mrs. Buck?"

"Grapefruit knife," said Mrs. Buck complacently.

"I didn't know there were such things as grapefruit knives," I said, thinking it was just like my mother to make her children cut and eat sour grapefruit when there was no need to do so.

"I'll show you," said Mrs. Buck, placidly topping up Sue's cup and surveying the table and the diners' plates with a savvy eye.

"Thanks," I said. When Mrs. Buck left the room, I told everyone about the torture my mother had put Chloe and me through during our miserable childhoods.

Lulu laughed. Her laugh sounded genuine. "Poor you and Chloe!"

Sue laughed with her. Caroline stared at the three of us as if we were insane, but she was interested when Mrs. Buck came back and showed us the small, curved, serrated grapefruit knife.

"My goodness," Caroline said. "I've never seen one of those. How useful, especially here in Southern California, where one can get grapefruits almost all year long."

"Exactly," said Mrs. Buck, pleased with the success of her break-fast grapefruit.

Shortly after the grapefruit discussion, the four of us young women retreated up the stairs to get dressed for work. My rooms were the first suite at the top of the stairs, and I subtly held Lulu back from heading to her own rooms on the other side of the house. "Hey, Lulu, come in here. I want to show you a book I got for Chloe."

Sue and Caroline stopped in their tracks and turned to face us. Guess I wasn't subtle enough. I gave the two other women what was probably a sickly smile and said, "Everybody, come in. This is a really darling book."

"How nice," said Caroline a trifle stiffly.

"If you only want Lulu to see it—" Sue began, but I cut her off.

"No, no. Everybody, come in and see it. I only thought about Lulu because she was present on Monday when we were discussing painting Chloe's baby's nursery with characters from children's books."

"Oh, you mean like the Beatrix Potter books?" asked Caroline, perking up some.

"I remember those," said Sue. "They're darling."

"Yes, they are," I said. "But when I took them to show Chloe and Harvey when Ernie and I met them for dinner at the Brown Derby, both Ernie and Harvey said they looked like characters specifically for girls. I didn't bring *Johnny Crow's Garden* to show them that night, because it was bigger than the Potter books. But come on in and look at it if you want to."

Lordy, when would I ever learn to think before I speak? Never, probably. But that morning things worked out all right, because Sue, Caroline, and Lulu were all interested in *Johnny Crow*, which I'd left on the table beside my reading chair.

"But we'd best get ready for work," said Caroline after a minute or two looking at the lion in the red and yellow tie and the fox putting all the other animals in the stocks.

Lulu said, "May I look in your closet, Mercy? I want to see if I can find something subdued to wear to work today. I'm through with bright colors. At least during the week at work."

How simple had that been? No ruses required. Bless Lulu's smart heart and head.

"Sure!" I said, wishing I'd thought of so easy and uncluttered way to get her to choose a garment from my closet.

"Have fun," said Sue with a grin as she left for her room. She didn't have to worry about what to wear to work. She always wore a white nurse's uniform even though she wasn't technically a nurse, but a receptionist in a dentist's office.

Caroline always appeared well-groomed and tasteful, if not downright boring. Lulu and Chloe had both accused me of wearing boring clothes when I first arrived in Los Angeles, but I'd perked up my wardrobe some. Not to the extent Lulu had, needless to say.

"Lordy, look at my arms," said Lulu, lifting a sleeve of her Chinese robe.

"Good grief, Lulu, those bruises look painful!"

"They are, curse Mr. Clint Faraday. Do you have anything with long sleeves you can't see the bruises through?"

It took me a second to parse her sentence, but I got it fairly quickly. "Yes. Here, take a look." I opened my closet door and ushered Lulu in (it was a walk-in closet). She shuffled through my work clothes and came away with a long-sleeved white blouse and a long-sleeved black sweater with gray trim along the opening where the buttons and buttonholes were. "Is it okay if I borrow these? I'm taller than you are, and I have a black skirt I can wear these with."

"Sure. Feel free. And tomorrow we'll go to that consignment shop in Chinatown."

"You're the best friend a girl ever had, Mercy," said Lulu, sounding a little snuffly for the first time so far that day.

"You'll be fine, Lulu. The Faraday man is a monster, but you're stronger than he is, and you'll prove it. And you'll also look great in that blouse and sweater with your black skirt." I knew the black gored skirt of which she spoke because she'd worn it before.

"Thanks, Mercy."

She scooted out of my room and on to her own, leaving Buttercup and me alone. I always set out what I aimed to wear to work in the evening before I went to bed so I didn't have to fuss in the morning. That morning was no different. I went to the bathroom to brush my teeth and comb my hair and dabbed some more powder under my eyes because they were kind of puffy and discolored. Lack of sleep can do that to a person.

Caroline, Sue, Lulu, Buttercup, and I met in the tiled entryway of Mercy's Manor, prepared to walk to Angels Flight and on to our respective workplaces. However, when I opened the front door and we looked outside, darned if there wasn't a torrent of rain coming down!

"Oh, shoot," I said. "I'm glad I parked under the auto-port. I'll drive us to work."

"Boy, the rain started suddenly," said Sue. "I looked out my window right before coming downstairs and it wasn't raining then."

"Cloudburst," said Caroline philosophically.

"I didn't know we got cloudbursts in Los Angeles," I said, turning to hurry to the kitchen and utility room, outside of which the auto-port had been erected.

"Just started raining," said Mrs. Buck as I entered her realm. "I'm glad you've got a motorcar, Miss Mercy."

"So am I, Mrs. Buck! I'm going to drive us all to work."

"Good for you." She went back to washing up the breakfast dishes.

And I drove us all to work, dropping Caroline off at the Broadway Department Store and Sue at the building in which her dentist's office resided. Then I drove Lulu and me to the Figueroa Building. Because we usually took Angels Flight and walked to work, I figured I'd have a hard time finding a parking place. But darned if Mr. Buck, understanding the weather situation, hadn't cleared a space for my 1924 Moon Roadster right behind the space he always cleared for Ernie's automobile.

He even had an unfurled umbrella ready for Lulu and me when he opened our doors and escorted us to the door to the Figueroa Building.

"Thank you, Mr. Buck! You're a life-saver!" I said.

"You truly are," said Lulu, hugging her coat to her person.

"You're most welcome," said Mr. Buck, smiling at us.

After walking behind the reception desk, Lulu shucked off her black coat and hung it on the nearby rack. I saw Mr. Buck blink at her.

It was only then I noticed Lulu had removed her bright red fingernail varnish! Lulu without red talons. Flabbergastation struck me all of a heap and, without thinking (naturally), I cried, "Lulu, your nails!"

She waved her hands in the air. She had pretty hands. To my no-doubt pedestrian eyes, they looked better without having sharp red tips.

"Yeah," she said, achieving a nonchalance that would have done Ernie proud. "I decided to buff my nails instead of painting them. An article I read in *Photoplay* said nail varnish isn't good for your nails."

"I see," I said.

"You look very nice today, Miss Lulu," said Mr. Buck. He seemed pleased that Lulu had toned down her generally vibrant dress.

She did look very nice. Again in my opinion only, she looked a heck of a lot better in a nice tailored skirt and sweater than she did when she was wearing one of her staggeringly ostentatious outfits.

But I've already admitted to having pedestrian tastes.

Leaving Lulu and Mr. Buck in the lobby, I walked to the stairwell and climbed the three flights to where Ernie's office sat. I heard the telephone ringing even as I unlocked the outer office door and entered, so I raced to my desk before removing my outer garments. My gloves made handling the telephone a trifle tricky, but I managed.

"Mr. Templeton's office. Miss Allcutt speaking," I said, trying not to pant.

"Hey, Mercy," said Phil Bigelow, "is Ernie in yet?"

Looking at the clock and attempting to pull a glove off while holding the receiver under my chin, I said, "It's not even eight o'clock, Phil! Why would Ernie be in at this hour? We have several clients, so I don't know when he'll be in today. He might spend the morning looking for straying wives or husbands or both. Besides, you know he seldom comes in at eight."

Don't tell anyone, but this demonstration of Phil Bigelow's inattention to his supposed friend's habits irked me and allowed me to keep resenting him for prior misdeeds. I know, I know. Stupid. But there you go.

"Aw, crumb, I know he never comes in at eight, but I need to talk to him as soon as possible. Will you please have him telephone as soon as he gets there?"

"Of course I shall," I said, sounding snooty.

Either Phil didn't notice my tone or he didn't care, because he said, "Thanks, Mercy," and hung up on me.

Well!

I dropped the receiver on the desk, said, "Phooey!" and finished removing my gloves before hanging the silly receiver back on its hook. Because I thought I should, I wrote a note to Ernie telling him Phil urgently wanted to get in touch with him, took it to his office, and laid it on his desk before resuming hanging up my outer wear. Honestly! This was the second time in a week Phil Bigelow had called the office before our eight-o'clock starting time.

When Ernie arrived at work shortly after eight o'clock, I was still thinking black thoughts about Phil as I wound the pagoda clock on my desk. I'd already wound the one on the wall.

"Morning, Mercy," said he, sounding jaunty.

"Good morning, Ernie," I said, deciding that just because I was irked with Phil, I didn't have to take it out on Ernie. "Is it still raining out there?"

"Naw. It stopped right before I got here. What's up with Lulu this morning? Did someone in her family die? She's wearing mourning."

I whirled around. "Oh, Ernie, it was awful! That terrible man who called himself a talent scout only wanted to take advantage of her."

"So she's wearing mourning?"

"No, of course not. But she decided she should tone down her wardrobe so other men don't get the wrong idea about her."

Tilting his head and giving me a small grin, he said, "You pretty much predicted this outcome, didn't you?"

"I guess I did, but I'm sorry it happened. When Lulu came home last night, she was a mess. That horrible man ripped her dress, ruined her hat, and she had to run away from him before he could...Well, you know."

"That bad, was it?" Ernie shook his head and appeared regretful. "I'm really sorry. Poor Lulu."

"She actually borrowed some boring clothes from me this morning. Tomorrow we're going to the consignment shop in Chinatown, where she aims to buy a nun's habit if they have one."

Ernie burst out laughing and walked the rest of the way into his room, where he hung up his hat and coat.

I called after him, "Phil called. Said it was important."

"Yeah, so I see." I heard him sit in his chair, pick up the receiver, and dial Phil's number.

I went on about my business as Ernie spoke to Phil. Maybe two or three minutes later, Ernie called, "Mercy, come here for a minute." He tacked on, "Please," probably because he knew my opinion about being ordered around.

So, after picking up my secretarial pad and a couple of sharp pencils, I did. He told me to shut the door, and I did that too. Ernie looked so troubled when I sat in one of the chairs before his desk that I got worried, too. "What's the matter?"

"We've got a problem," he told me in a more serious tone than I'd never heard issue from his lips before. "Smedley's dead."

FOURTEEN

"What?" I was confused. "Mr. Smedley's one of the men you were following, wasn't he? How'd he end up dead?"

"Somebody pushed him into the street in front of a big truck. It hit him, and he died."

"Oh," I said. "Well, that solves Mrs. Smedley's problems, doesn't it? Why are you so worried?"

"Because some of those photos you took of Lulu were scattered on the floor of his office."

"*What?*" I asked, bewildered. "How'd they get there?" Then understanding struck, kind of like the big truck must have struck Mr. Smedley. "Good Lord, do you mean to tell me Mr. Faraday was actually Mr. Smedley?"

"Was Faraday the name the guy gave Lulu?" Ernie asked, still appearing dour.

"Yes. But Ernie, Lulu would no more push someone in front of a truck than *I* would, and I wouldn't! She was running away from him. Somebody else must have shoved him."

"I hope to God you're right," said Ernie. "A witness said a woman in a red dress shoved him. What was Lulu wearing last night?"

Crumb. "A red dress," I said somberly. "And a hat with red roses on it." Recalling the scene with Lulu last night—well, this morning—I said, "But Ernie, if she *did* push him, it was self-defense. You should have seen her! She was a mess!"

"Can you call Lulu and ask her to get Glynis O'Fannin to cover the telephone in the lobby for a while? I'd really like to talk to her before the police do. Phil said he'd give me forty-five minutes."

That was nice of Phil, but I didn't say so.

"Yes! Heck, I'll go down there and cover the 'phone *for* her, if I have to!"

"I need you here to take notes. See if Glennie can do it," said Ernie.

"Right."

So I raced back to my desk and called the front desk. The line was busy! Frustration gnawed at me.

Ernie must have heard my softly muttered "Damn," because he said, "What's up? Are the cops there already? I'll kill Phil—"

"No! The line's busy. I'll try again."

"Maybe I'd better just go down there and get her."

"Probably wouldn't hurt. Glynis works for Dr. Clutter, doesn't she? I can call his office and ask if Glennie can take over the front desk while you fetch Lulu."

"Good idea." Ernie didn't bother putting on his coat again before he bolted out of his office, ran through mine, and flung open the outer-office door. As I looked for Dr. Clutter's office's number in the telephone book, I heard him thumping down the hall, and I think he took the stairs.

When a woman answered Dr. Clutter's office telephone, I told her there was an emergency, and that Glynis O'Fannin was needed to work at the reception desk in the Figueroa Building's lobby.

"Oh! Oh, my. Is Lulu all right?" the woman on the other end of the wire asked, sounding alarmed, which was fine as the situation seemed plenty alarming to me.

"Yes, but we need her elsewhere for a few minutes," I said.

"Are you Miss Allcutt?"

"Yes," I said impatiently. "But we desperately need Lulu right now."

"Okay. This is Glennie. I'll go right out there," she said.

"Thank you *so* much, Glennie," I said, breathing a sigh of relief.

"You betcha. Oh!" She sounded startled. "Ernie's here. See ya!"

She hung up. So did I.

Lord, Lord, what in the world had *happened* last night? I couldn't imagine Lulu shoving anybody in front of a truck. I *could* imagine a scene in which she was running away from Mr. Faraday—Smedley. Whatever his name was. Anyhow, I could imagine him grabbing her arm on the sidewalk as she fled, Lulu struggling with him in an effort to escape and managing to push him away. He might have stumbled into a street in front of a truck. That, to my mind, would have been an accident. At least it was a clear case of self-defense. But she hadn't related such a scenario to me this morning, and I believe she would have had it occurred.

Besides, if that's what had happened, why hadn't Lulu stayed and explained herself to the cops? She was a savvy woman of the world, in a way. Surely, she wouldn't have just left Faraday/Smedley bleeding underneath a truck's wheels. If a policeman had come along, he'd have seen for himself what the ghastly man had done to Lulu, and he'd have understood instantly that Faraday/Smedley's death had been an accident and the result of Lulu trying to escape a ravening beast.

I had but a few minutes to contemplate Faraday/Smedley's death scene in my head before Lulu and Ernie rushed into the office. Lulu looked stricken. As well she should, I supposed, under the incriminating circumstances.

"Mercy! I didn't do it!"

I leaped from my chair, skirted the desk, and ran for Lulu. Throwing my arms around her, I said, "I know you didn't, Lulu! And if you did, it was self-defense."

"But I *didn't*!" she cried. "He was still bent over holding his balls when I ran down those stupid stairs and out into the street."

Vivid description. I saw Ernie wince.

"Come on, girls. Into my office. Lulu, please explain precisely what went on last night, and Mercy, you take notes."

"All right," said a terrified Lulu.

"I brung you guys some water," came the voice of Junior, hot on Ernie and Lulu's heels. "Glennie said you might need it."

"Thanks, Junior," I told the lad. I took two glasses from his hand and smiled down at him. Not too far down, as I wasn't tall and he was thirteen, but still and all. He grinned at me and remained where he was.

Then I recalled the resourceful Junior's occupation and various sources of income. Leaning down, I whispered, "I'll give you a dime later, okay?"

He saluted me smartly. "Thanks, Miss Mercy!" and he turned and left the office.

"Here, Ernie, take these, will you?" I said, holding out the two water glasses.

Seeming slightly startled at the introduction of water into this scenario, he took them and said, "Got 'em. But come in and take notes, will you?" He turned and ushered Lulu into his office a trifle less gracefully than usual, due to the impediments he carried.

"Right," I said, grabbing the same pad I'd grabbed the first time I'd entered his office. I took three pencils with me this time, just in case.

"I can't believe this," said Lulu. Except for her bottle-blond hair, she might have been any office worker in any building in any city in the United States.

"Ernie will fix it," I told her soothingly.

"We hope," said Ernie, not sounding nearly as confident as I had.

"Oh, gawd," said Lulu, beginning to leak a few tears.

Ernie had already opened his drawer, pulled out a clean hankie, and thrust it at her when I sat down, poised to take notes.

"All right. Tell me exactly what happened last night, Lulu. Don't leave anything out, even if you think it might put you in a bad light."

"Why would anything she did put her in a bad light?" I asked, indignant on Lulu's behalf.

"Just take notes, will you, Mercy?" Ernie snapped. "I know what I'm doing. More, I know how the cops think. So go on, Lulu. Spill. Everything."

So she did. Her story was pretty much the same one she'd told me last night, although she included pulling photographs out of her handbag in order to show them to Mr. Faraday. She said she did so right before he pounced on her, which was how they got scattered. Naturally, she didn't wait around to collect them when she escaped from his clutches and his office and hared down the stairs to the street.

"I'm only lucky a cab was coming along not very far away," said Lulu, her voice wobbly. "I didn't think he was going to follow me, at least not right away. I thought I'd...well, disabled him, you know?"

With a grimace, Ernie said, "Not personally, but I can imagine. So you didn't hear him run after you?"

"No. He didn't. I could swear he didn't, although I was plenty upset by then. I just ran away from him and down the street. Mercy had to pay my cab fare because I must have dropped my money when I pulled out the pictures and he grabbed me."

"Yeah?" Ernie looked at me, and I suddenly recalled last night's cabbie.

"Yes! And I have his name. It's Sid Jankowski, and he said his cab number was...Crumb. I can't remember, but I wrote it down. Just a second." I started to rise, but Ernie stopped me.

"You can do that later. Good for you for thinking to get his name and cab number, Mercy." He gave me a smile that warmed me from head to toe.

"He said if we need to get in touch with him to call the Yellow Cab Company."

"Good. That's good," said Ernie.

He grilled Lulu some more. She answered all of his questions candidly. After he'd run out of questions, he sighed and sat back in his chair. "Your story sounds clear to me. I wish you hadn't decided to dress like a nun today, though."

"Why not?" Lulu asked, as startled as I by his comment.

"Because Phil knows you and how you usually dress. Dressing soberly makes it look as if you're trying to be inconspicuous."

"But I am!" said Lulu indignantly. "I don't want any more *Mister Faradays* to get the wrong idea about me!"

"His real name was Smedley," said Ernie. "Felix Smedley. His wife came here to hire me because she thought he was running around on her."

"No," said Lulu. "Really?"

"Really."

"And he was," I said. "I'm sure you aren't the only young woman he tried to savage."

"Savage?" Ernie gave me an odd look.

So did Lulu.

"Well, you know what I mean."

"Yeah," said Ernie. "Say, Lulu, Mercy said you have bruises. You might have to show them to the police. They have matrons at most police stations these days, so you won't have to show them to a man."

As soon as Ernie mentioned she might have to show her bruises, Lulu crossed her arms over her chest and hugged her arms close to her body. "I'm not going to show any perverted copper my bruises!"

"Lulu," said Ernie patiently, "you want them to see your bruises in order to corroborate your story." He frowned. "Of course, your bruises will probably also lead them to believe you had reason to kill the guy."

"But I ran *away* from him! I *swear* he didn't follow me! I'd have heard him on those stupid metal stairs if he'd run after me. They clanked like anything." She added, "Besides, he wasn't in any condition to run once I'd kneed him."

"I expect they'll do an autopsy on his body. Not sure if they'll find anything that might help you, but his body might have bruises in…a delicate spot, which will help to prove your story." Ernie actually appeared embarrassed. I didn't know he could do that.

"This is so unfair," I said. "Who was the witness who said the pusher had on a red dress?"

"A couple of people."

"And they didn't see Lulu running down the street?"

"I guess not," said Ernie.

"That's probably because whoever pushed him did it after I got in the cab," said Lulu. "I *know* he didn't follow me. At least not right away."

"That makes sense to me," I said.

134

"It does to me too," said Ernie. "But we'll know more after Phil gets here. You should have a lawyer with you when the cops talk to you."

"Oh, gawd!" cried Lulu. "I can't afford a lawyer!"

"Don't worry about a lawyer. If you need one, I'll get you one," I told her.

"Yeah, Mercy's got the big bucks," said Ernie.

"But you've already done too much for me!" said Lulu, burying her head in Ernie's hankie. Her shoulders shook with her sobs.

"Take it easy, kid," Ernie said to Lulu. To me, he said, "Would you mind calling this guy?" He opened a desk drawer, took something out of it, then reached across the desk to hand me a business card for a Robert L. Gabriel, Esq., Attorney-at-Law. "He's a pal of mine, and he's a good defense lawyer. See if you can get him to come here this morning. If not, make an appointment." He shook his head. "I'd like him to be here when Phil questions Lulu. But if he can't come now, we can at least prevent the police from questioning her at the station until he can get there."

"They're going to take me to a police station?" asked Lulu pitifully, lifting her head from Ernie's hankie. Her poor eyes were red and swollen again, but at least she didn't have gobs of makeup smeared all over her face.

"I expect they will unless you can convince Phil you had nothing to do with Smedley's demise."

"What's a demise?" asked Lulu thickly.

"Death," I clarified for her. I'd already risen to go to my desk and call Mr. Gabriel.

"Oh, no!" wailed Lulu.

I shut the door to Ernie's office, not wanting to hear more of Lulu's woe. This was *so* unfair. As I dialed, I couldn't help feeling Lulu'd been an idiot to believe that guy. But still....

"Gabriel," came a deep voice on the other end of the wire.

"Mr. Robert Gabriel, attorney?" I asked for clarification.

"Yes," he said, sounding grumpy.

Too bad for him. "My name is Miss Mercy Allcutt, and I'm telephoning at the request of Mr. Ernest Templeton."

"Ernie! How's Ernie? Haven't seen him since before Christmas. Say, are you the Mercy he's always talking about? His secretary?"

He talked about me? How...I don't know. Nice, I guess. But now wasn't the time to bask. "Yes, I'm his secretary. Ernie has a client here who needs your services. Instantly, if possible. He asked if you could come to his office right away, and if you can't come right away, I'll be glad to make an appointment for you to see him."

"Who's the client, and what's he in for?"

"The client is a she, and the police think she killed a man last night, but she didn't. Even if she did, it would have been in self-defense," I said, still offended on Lulu's behalf.

"Murder, eh?" I heard a loud exhale. "Don't get too many of those cases. Yeah, I'm free at the moment. Ernie still in the Figueroa Building?"

"Yes. Third floor," I said. "So you'll come now?"

"Yup. It'll take me ten minutes or so to get there. I'm on Flower and Eighth."

"Oh, good. That's not far at all."

"No, but there's lots of traffic on the streets these days."

"True. Thank you for coming right away."

"Sure. What's my client's name?"

"Lulu LaBelle," I said, and then I wished I hadn't.

"You're pulling my leg, right?"

Pulling his...Oh. I got it. "No. Well, not really. Her name is Louise Mullins, but she wants to be in the flickers and thought Lulu LaBelle would look better on a theater marquee."

"Lord save me from young women who want to be stars," muttered Mr. Gabriel. "But what the hell. I'll be there as soon as I can be."

I ignored his swearing and merely said, "Thank you very much."

It only occurred to me after we both hung up that he hadn't mentioned money. Oh well. We could deal with the financial side of things after he got here and spoke to Lulu. I looked at my pagoda clock to see that fifteen minutes had passed since Lulu had come upstairs. That gave us thirty more minutes, if Phil's word was good.

After a gentle tap on Ernie's office door, I opened it and walked in.

Both Ernie and Lulu sat in their respective chairs, and neither one of them appeared the least bit happy. Lulu chewed on her lower lip, her hankie clutched in her fist, and Ernie stared out his window. At least, since he'd hired me as his secretary, he could see out of it. When I'd first been hired, the entire office was mucky. Upon my entrance, he turned to look at me with a lifted eyebrow.

"Mr. Gabriel's on his way," I told them both.

"Good." To Lulu, Ernie said, "Rob's a good lawyer, Lulu. If anybody can help you, he can."

"But I didn't *do* anything!" said Lulu.

"Yeah, I believe you. Let's hope Phil does."

"Phil." Lulu spat the word as if it contained poison.

"Yeah, I know you have a grudge against him, but he's one of the few honest coppers on the force."

"If you say so," said Lulu, sounding hopeless.

"At least you have an attorney on your side now," I said, trying to cheer her up.

"A lawyer I can't pay for," said Lulu, her lip trembling.

"Don't worry about money," I said.

"And Rob's a good guy. He won't cheat you," said Ernie.

"Wouldn't matter if he did. I couldn't pay him anyway," said a clearly miserable Lulu. "Oh, gawd, I wish I'd listened to you, Mercy!"

I wished she had, too, but I thought it wiser not to say so. Therefore, I only said, "It will be all right, Lulu. I'm sure of it."

And that was a flat-out lie. Oh, poor Lulu!

FIFTEEN

We were in luck. At least I hoped we were. Mr. Gabriel arrived no more than ten minutes after I'd telephoned him. A tall man, probably about Ernie's six feet, he had wavy brown hair, pretty brown eyes with lush lashes, and he dressed quite nicely. He didn't seem to have Ernie's devil-may-care attitude about his attire, but wore a nice suit and a fine fedora hat. He removed the hat as soon as he came into the office.

"Mr. Gabriel?" I greeted him from my desk in the outer office.

"Indeed. Miss…I'm sorry. I don't know your last name. I only know you as Mercy." Smiling, he lowered his gaze from my face to my desk, where a plaque proclaimed my name. "Miss Allcutt!" He walked over to me. I'd risen from my chair and held out a hand for him to shake.

"It's good of you to come so quickly," I said as I shook his hand.

Ernie's door opened, and Ernie stood there grinning. "Rob! Long time, no see."

Returning Ernie's smile, Mr. Gabriel took Ernie's hand and wrung it. "It *has* been a long time. Business picked up any?"

"Well, it had, but somebody knocked off a client's husband last night. I don't know who did it, although I'm sure it wasn't Lulu. But come in here and meet her." Looking at me, he said, "Mercy, will you please take notes?"

"Gladly," I told him.

Lulu had blotted her tears and stopped gnawing on her lip when Mr. Gabriel gestured for me to enter Ernie's office ahead of him. Because there were only two chairs placed before Ernie's desk, I headed to one in the corner.

Ernie said, "Miss Lulu Mullins, this is Mr. Robert Gabriel. He's a lawyer and, although it pains me to say so, he's a good one."

"How do you do, Miss Mullins?" said Mr. Gabriel, taking the hand Lulu held out for him.

"Not so good," said Lulu. She sniffled and lifted Ernie's hankie to her eyes. "Sorry."

"No need to be sorry," said Mr. Gabriel in a kind voice. "I understand you had a little trouble last night, and now the police think you're responsible for a man's death."

"But I didn't do it! He was alive when I ran from his office!"

"Calm down, Lulu," said Ernie. "Just tell Rob exactly what happened last night. He needs to know everything."

"Oh, gawd!" I'd never seen Lulu blush before, but she did then.

I felt *so* bad for her. But she pulled herself together and, gaze cast down and resting on the hands she'd placed in her lap, wringing her handkerchief, she told her story again. It didn't sound any better on the third recital, but it was consistent.

"Mercy has the name of the cabbie and his cab number," Ernie said when Lulu got to the taxicab part of her story.

Mr. Gabriel shot me a quick grin, then went back to taking his own notes. So far I'd written the story down three times. Suddenly it occurred to me that I might use it in my novel. I'd have to change the names, of course, but…

A thump came at Ernie's office door. I'd been so involved in my own thoughts—Lulu's story was old-hat by this time—I hadn't realized someone had entered the outer office.

"Ernie!" came Phil Bigelow's voice. "Is Miss LaBelle in there with you? And Mercy?"

"Yeah, they're both in here. So's Lulu's lawyer, Rob Gabriel. You might as well join us."

The door opened to reveal a grim-faced Phil Bigelow in his detective suit, big brown policeman's shoes, tatty hat, and overcoat. He glanced around Ernie's office. "There's no room," he said.

"Come in and stand," Ernie offered. "But first hang up your hat and coat out there." He pointed to my room, where the front door was. "Lulu can tell you what happened up until she ran out of that bimbo's office."

We heard grumbling as Phil went to the coat rack in the outer office and obeyed Ernie's order.

When he came back, coatless and hatless, he said, "I need to know more than that."

"I can tell you what I did," said Lulu firmly, seeming to have bucked up at the sight of a man she considered an enemy of her family, for good reason. "And it doesn't include killing anybody."

"Yeah?" said Phil in a mean voice. "So tell me."

She did. Although I had my pencil poised over my pad and listened for anything new she might say, I didn't have to put pencil to pad. Her story was her story, and it couldn't change because it was true. It seemed to me that anyone with an ounce of common sense would be able to recognize the truth when he heard it.

Phil allowed her to speak without interruption. When she got to the end of her narrative, he said, "Huh. So those photos on Smedley's floor were taken by Mercy?"

"He told me his name was Faraday," said Lulu.

"Well, it was Smedley," snarled Phil. "And Mercy took the pictures?"

"Yes," said Lulu. "She took them. Ernie was there, too."

"I was," Ernie confirmed.

"Why?" Phil turned to me.

"Why what?" I asked, not feeling inclined to help this man against whom Lulu held a legitimate grudge.

"Why'd you take pictures of Lulu? Miss Mullins, I mean?"

"Why not?" I'd been kind of peeved with Phil myself lately too, by gad. Then I reminded myself that being surly wouldn't help Lulu and might irritate Phil so much he'd arrest her out of spite.

Just as I'd opened my mouth to enlarge on my curt answer, a huge crash sounded at the outer office door. I jumped from my chair, prepared to race to see what was going on, but Phil was there first (he had an advantage, being standing at the time). A woman screamed.

"He's dead! He's *dead*!" she shrieked.

"Crumb, who's that?" asked Ernie.

"Sounds kind of like Mrs. Smedley," I said, rushing after Phil. I was mainly going by the jingles and clanks, which I assumed came from her jewelry. I couldn't tell anything by the voice, which was contorted because the woman out there was screeching like one of those banshees that inhabit various moors in the United Kingdom.

Sure enough, there was Mrs. Smedley, again garishly clad and with her jewelry clanging. Today, however, she seemed to have a grudge against her violently red hair, because she pulled at it as she hollered, "He's dead! He's dead!"

Phil caught hold of her and tried to restrain her, or at least keep her from yanking her hair out by the roots—which were dark, as opposed to the improbable red elsewhere on her head.

"Mrs. Smedley!" I bellowed, trying to cut through her noise.

"Good God." Ernie followed me, and I could hardly hear his muttered words.

"Who's that?"

I heard Lulu's question because Mrs. Smedley, deprived of her hair, had turned to pound Phil on the chest. She'd also shut up.

"Ernie, a little help here, please?" said Phil.

"Sure." Ernie approached the woman from behind and reached around her to grab her arms before she could do much damage to Phil's suit jacket. He said loudly, "Cut it out, Mrs. Smedley!"

Mrs. Smedley said, "Ooooooh!" and seemed to collapse.

Between them, Phil and Ernie held her up, Phil by the waist, Ernie by her arms.

"Bring her to the chair here," I suggested, turning one of the chairs before my desk so they could dump her in it.

They did so.

"Crumb, is she that horrible man's wife?" asked Lulu in a small voice.

"Widow now, I suppose," I told her.

"Interesting," said Mr. Gabriel, making me jump as I'd forgotten all about him.

The five of us stood gawping at the spectacle of the late Mr. Felix Smedley's widow, slumped in the chair, her arms dangling, and her legs sprawled out in front of her, her hair a wild mess—the first time I'd seen her, it had been a marcelled wonder of fake redness—and her face streaked with makeup. Except that Lulu was much prettier than Mrs. Smedley overall, she looked rather as Lulu had looked when she'd come home in the wee hours of the morning. She exuded a strong aroma of liquor as well. Yes, we were seven years into Prohibition, but even *I* knew what booze smelled like. Somehow I wasn't overwhelmingly surprised.

"I think she's zozzled," said Ernie, gazing judicially down upon the spectacle of Mrs. Smedley.

"Smells like it," agreed Phil.

"I don't blame her, if she was married to that pig," said Lulu.

"Interesting," said Mr. Gabriel again.

When Mrs. Smedley began to stir, Ernie stepped in, ready to grab her if she decided to dramatize herself some more. She pulled her legs into a more dignified position, so she was seated rather than slumped, lifted her arms, and patted her hair, which didn't do it any good. Then she put her hands in her lap, glanced up, and peered around at the five people gathered in front of her. Her expression remained blank until her gaze stumbled upon Lulu. Then she let out another screech that made the five of us step back as if our move was choreographed.

"You!" she bellowed. "*You're* the one! I *knew* Felix had a whore on the side!"

Galvanized out of her shock, Lulu said, "Don't you dare call me names!"

"Hold on!" shouted Phil. He reached out to prevent Mrs. Smedley from rising and going after Lulu, which she seemed poised to do.

"Hey, lady, calm down," said Ernie, grabbing onto one of her shoulders and struggling to keep her in the chair. Phil helped.

Recalling a couple of books I'd read in recent months, I removed myself from the group, rushed into Ernie's office, grabbed the closest water glass, took it to the outer office, and splashed its contents into Mrs. Smedley's face. Shut her right up, by Jupiter! Well, except for a gasp and a few splutters.

"Good thinking, Mercy," said Ernie, glancing up and grinning at me.

"Thanks, Mercy," said Lulu. She sounded almost awed.

"All right, now," said Phil Bigelow in his official—perhaps officious is a better word—policeman's voice. "Calm down, and tell us what the devil you're doing here, ma'am," he said to Mrs. Smedley.

The woman had taken to sobbing. I returned to Ernie's office and gave up another sacrificial handkerchief, this one to the weeping widow. She snatched it from me without even a thank-you and began mopping her face, which needed it.

"My husband is dead, and that…that…that *whore* killed him!" she sputtered.

"Stop calling me names," growled Lulu. When I glanced at her, I saw her fists clenched at her sides, and I hoped to heaven she wouldn't have an emotional breakdown of her own and begin punching Mrs. Smedley.

"Yes," I said in a tone that would have sounded good coming from my overbearing mother, "stop calling people names, and tell us why you're here and making such a dreadful scene! *Now*."

I felt rather than saw movement in the room. When I glanced around, it was to see all the standees at attention, kind of like soldiers in front of an angry general. Mrs. Smedley sat at attention too. By golly, I didn't like my mother, but she'd sure taught me how to command a room.

Mrs. Smedley's eyes were round and red as she stared at me, saying nothing.

"Well?" I demanded. "Why are you here?"

"M-my husband is dead," said the widow.

"Yes, we know. Why are you here, in Mr. Templeton's office?"

"B-because he was supposed to be following him," she said, pointing at Ernie.

"Where'd you get the booze?" asked Phil Bigelow, reverting from soldierly attention to grumpy cop mode.

"B-booze?" Mrs. Smedley lifted her chin, which still dripped, so she wiped it. "I don't know what you're talking about."

"That's beside the point," I snapped at Phil, who jerked back to attention. "Why did you come to see Mr. Templeton today, Mrs. Smedley?"

"B-because he was supposed to be following my husband," she repeated.

"I can't follow a person twenty-four hours a day, Mrs. Smedley. I told you so the first day you came here. I said I'd stake out his business for as long as I could on any given day, and keep track of his comings and goings. The two days I watched him, he didn't do anything except go to his office and stay there. He had several visitors during that time. I took as many photos as I could of the people who visited him."

"W-women?" said Mrs. Smedley in a small voice.

"For the most part," said Ernie, sounding as if he regretted having to admit it. "And don't forget that I had to stand outside in order to take the photos. If I'd gone inside the building to see which office the people went to, I wouldn't have been able to take pictures at all, so I don't know if everyone I photographed was visiting your husband."

"I knew he was ch-cheating," said Mrs. Smedley. She shot Lulu a filthy look. "And I knew he was cheating with *you*, because I saw you and him together."

"He *never* cheated on you with me!" said Lulu in a horrified voice. "Never! I wouldn't let him."

"Oooooh!" Mrs. Smedley wailed, and she buried her face in her soggy handkerchief. Well, it was Ernie's, but I don't think he wanted it back.

SIXTEEN

"You took pictures of people visiting Smedley?" asked Phil of Ernie.

"Yeah," said Ernie. "Part of the job."

"Why didn't you tell us that earlier?" Phil sounded grumpy.

"Why would I? They're part of a confidential investigation. I didn't know until this morning that someone had killed Smedley. Anyhow, the first two rolls of film are still at the pharmacy down the street being developed."

"You didn't use Charley Wu's cousin?" I asked.

"No. What was the point in that? As far as I knew, there was no particular rush on the ones I took of Smedley and the other case."

"What other case?" asked Phil.

"Another *confidential* case," I told him. "Nothing to do with Smedley."

"Right," said Ernie.

"Cripes," said Phil. "When will they be developed?"

"Don't know. I just took them in a day or so ago. I still have film in my camera, but I haven't finished the roll, so I haven't taken them in yet."

"Are there photos you took of Smedley's office on the roll?" asked Phil.

"The outside of the building. I snapped people walking up the stairs." He glanced at Lulu. "You're right about those stairs. They make a hell of a noise. Even though you were upset, you'd have been able to hear if Smedley chased you down them."

"Told you so," said Lulu with a sniff.

"Ha, that proves it," I said, not quite sure if it did or not. I mean to say, *I* knew Lulu hadn't killed Mr. Smedley, but the coppers would probably need more proof than noisy metal stairs. "I'm glad you have photographs to show us, Ernie," I said in a voice no longer my mother's.

"Did you say there were witnesses to the murder?" asked Mr. Gabriel. He had such a deep voice; it kind of surprised me whenever he spoke. He didn't look like a basso profundo, although I don't know how basso profundos (profundi?) are supposed to look. Fat and Russian pops to mind.

"Yes," said Phil.

"Who killed him?" squeaked Mrs. Smedley. "It was *her*, wasn't it?" She pointed a quivering finger at Lulu.

I noted with interest that she'd painted her long nails vivid red, leaving the tips unvarnished—which was very much the fashion. I hoped Lulu would take a lesson from this unpleasant woman and carry out her resolve to tone down her appearance.

"No, it was not me," said Lulu. She'd unclenched her fists and now stood with her hands on her hips, looking more disgusted than outraged at the widow Smedley.

"Of course, Lulu didn't kill your husband," I said, wishing I could impart a grammar lesson or two and knowing the wish to be Bostonian and unworthy. These were real people in real life, and people often used poor grammar. I decided to recall this pertinent fact when I wrote dialogue in my book.

"We don't know who killed him, Mrs. Smedley," said Ernie. "Why do you insist this lady is the killer?" He sounded honestly curious.

"Because I saw *her* pictures on the floor of his office," said Mrs. Smedley. Then she slapped a hand over her mouth.

"So you went to his office last night, did you?" said Phil, pouncing on her mistake like a cat on a mouse.

"Y-yes," said Mrs. Smedley, then sniffled and used the soggy hankie to wipe away more tears.

"And was your husband in his office when you visited him?" asked Phil.

"No! No, because she killed him!" Mrs. Smedley again pointed at Lulu, who rolled her eyes.

"Crumb, wish I'd been staking out the place last night," said Ernie. "Sounds like a real party went on in there."

"Where were you?" asked Phil. "Just out of curiosity."

"Looking to see if another client's spouse was out with a person other than the one they married," said Ernie.

"They? Don't you mean— Oh." Ernie's expression—which was quite fierce—finally made my brain click on. We were a *private* investigations office. Ernie took the "private" part of his business to heart. Therefore, so did I.

"Doesn't he mean what?" asked Phil, again pouncing. I don't dislike cats, but I wished Phil weren't so much like one at the moment.

"Nothing. He was out searching for another straying spouse," I said.

"Why weren't you watching Smedley?" asked Phil of Ernie.

"I can't watch everybody all at the same time, is why. I'd spent most of the day watching Smedley, so I scouted out another potentially straying spouse and let Smedley be for the evening." He sighed heavily. "And then there's the other guy I'm supposed to find. The one who ran away."

"Oh, yes," I said, recalling the vanishing Mr. Brentwood. "I hope you find that one soon. I worry a little."

"I know you do," said Ernie with a short grin for me.

After watching first Ernie and then me and then Ernie again, Phil asked, "Did you see anything strange when you staked out Smedley?"

"I didn't stake him out," said Ernie. "I followed him. He was a pretty boring guy. Stayed in his office most of the day. I took photos of the people walking up the stairs. You know, Phil, if he'd chased after Lulu, she'd have heard him. Trust me."

"I trust you, but I'm going to have to do my own investigation."

"Why are we all standing here in the outer office?" I asked finally. Glaring at Mrs. Smedley, I said to her, "Can you walk, or do you need someone to pick you up and carry you?"

"Wh-what? Why?" she asked.

"Because you're just sitting there, reeking of alcohol and dripping on my chair and the carpet. I'd rather you do that elsewhere. I suspect Detective Bigelow would like to question you about your husband, but he can't do it here, with the rest of us standing around and listening." Turning to Phil, I asked, "Why don't you take her to your office, Detective Bigelow? I'm sure she can answer questions just as well there as here. And, as Mr. Gabriel is representing Miss LaBelle, you can't question her without him. You also can't question both women at once. Besides," I said, thinking of something that might actually be pertinent, "Mrs. Smedley probably shouldn't be driving in her condition."

"Whattaya mean, my condition?" bellowed Mrs. Smedley, bracing her arms on the chair and looking as if she aimed to push herself out of it and lunge at me.

"Hold on. Hold on," said Ernie, pressing down on one of her shoulders so she couldn't rise. "I think that's a good idea, Phil. Why don't you take Mrs. Smedley home, so she can get cleaned up? Or to your office and show her to Two-Gun Davis. I'm sure he'd like to know about her bootlegger."

"Cripes," said Phil, scratching his head and looking as if he wished he were elsewhere. Too bad. He'd chosen his career.

"B-bootlegger? What're you talking about?" squeaked Mrs. Smedley.

"He's talking about you being drunk during Prohibition," I told her, rather brutally for me. Even my mother wouldn't speak a sentence like that one. Or she'd have substituted the word "inebriated" for the word "drunk". Not only is my mother a big bully; she's also a big prude.

"How'd you get here?" asked Ernie of Mrs. Smedley.

I noticed Mr. Gabriel tap Lulu on the shoulder and jerk his head toward Ernie's office. Lulu, understanding his meaning, nodded, and the two of them left the room, went into Ernie's office, and closed the door.

"Hey!" said Phil, taking a step after them and nearly bumping into the door.

"Let's solve this problem before you harass Miss LaBelle anymore, all right, Phil?" said Ernie.

Suddenly Junior appeared at the outer office door, which he pushed open dramatically. "Hey, Mr. Ernie, somebody ran into your new car!" He scanned the room and pointed at Mrs. Smedley. His face scrunched up and he said, "I'm pretty sure it was her what did it, only she don't look like she did when she got out of her machine. How'd she get all wet?"

"Cripes," said Ernie. "You smashed into my new car?" he growled at Mrs. Smedley.

Who instantly burst into tears yet once more.

"Aw, jeez," muttered Ernie. "Phil, can you get this Dumb Dora out of here? If she hit my car, arrest her for driving drunk. We have drunk-driving laws in L.A., don't we?"

"Since 1911, yeah," said Phil, looking with disgust at Mrs. Smedley.

"It's not my fault!" screeched Mrs. Smedley. "It's *her*"—she pointed at where Lulu had last been—"Where'd she go?"

"Never mind her," said Phil, taking one of Mrs. Smedley's arms. "Come along with me."

"Shoot," said Junior. "It ain't all that bad, but she crunched a fender."

"Great," said Ernie. "Just great."

"It's not my fault!" squeaked Mrs. Smedley again. "She killed my husband!"

"Oh, be quiet," I told her. "Nobody cares whom you think killed your horrible husband. You crashed your car into Mr. Templeton's new automobile, for pity's sake! Whilst driving under the influence of distilled spirits, which is against the law."

"Huh?" said Mrs. Smedley.

"Need any help in here?" came Mr. Buck's voice from the office door, and I turned to see him standing behind Junior. "It's getting mighty noisy."

"Yeah," said Phil. "Will you please take this woman's other arm and help me get her down to my car."

"No!" squealed Mrs. Smedley. "No nigger is going to manhandle me!"

That did it. I walked up to Mrs. Smedley, leaned over her, and said, "Shut your mouth right this second, or I'll shut it for you. Don't you *dare* call a friend of mine names!"

Even to my own ears, I sounded deadly—and I wasn't even using my mother's voice. I was fed up to the back teeth with people and their irrationalities regarding…well, everything.

"*I'll* walk with you and Detective Bigelow," I continued. "That way Mr. Buck won't have to sully his hands by touching this disgusting person."

"Cripes, Mercy," Ernie said in a low voice. "Tone it down, will you?"

"No," I said. To Mrs. Smedley, I said, "Get up. Now."

She got up, swaying. Phil took one arm and I took the other and together we walked her across the office and down the hall to the elevator. Ernie, Junior, and Mr. Buck followed us, probably to ensure Mrs. Smedley didn't attempt to escape, although I think she'd pretty much used up her store of bravado for the day. Anyhow, she was wobbling so much, I doubt she could have run if she'd tried.

When we reached the lobby and escorted Mrs. Smedley from the elevator, we noticed a whole herd of people gathered around Ernie's machine on the street. Junior had been correct. His lovely almost-new 1924 Packard-Six had a dented rear driver's side fender. What's more, Mrs. Smedley in her rage and alcoholic condition had clearly not attempted to back up or park her car, because the auto I presumed to be hers—a Chevrolet, I think—sat in the street. Its front driver's side fender still touched Ernie's Packard's back fender. She must have crashed and run. But rather than running away, she'd run to Ernie's office. Or staggered.

The woman was an idiot.

"Aw, cripes," muttered Phil. "You got the keys to your car on you, lady?" he asked Mrs. Smedley.

Junior, who had raced upstairs to deliver his news, had now raced out to Mrs. Smedley's automobile. "The keys are still plugged in," he said with glee. "Want me to move the thing?"

"Plugged in?" asked a bemused Mr. Buck.

"I think he means they're still in the ignition," muttered Ernie.

"Have you ever driven before?" I asked Junior, still holding on to Mrs. Smedley's arm.

"Naw, but how hard can it be? Everybody's drivin' these days."

"That's all right, Junior," said Ernie. "Thanks for the offer, but I think either the detective or I should move the lady's car."

"Lady?" Junior snorted. "She ain't no lady!"

Although it took her a second, Mrs. Smedley reacted to this assessment of herself. She tried to yank her arms away from Phil and me and didn't succeed. "How *dare* you!"

"Nertz on you," said the sassy Junior. "No lady drives drunk, crashes into other autos, and hollers at people. Miss Mercy now, *she's* a lady."

This, from a young fellow who'd witnessed my recent performance as a murderous changeling. I'll never understand the human race. In Junior's case, he probably thought I was a lady because I had money. He should meet my mother.

No. I take it back. Nobody I liked should be forced to meet my mother.

However, that's neither here nor there. Neither Phil nor Ernie had bothered to listen to the altercation between the lady and the lad. Phil said, "See if you can get her car started, Ernie. You can follow my machine down to the station in it. I'll stick Mrs. Smedley in the backseat."

"You'll do no such thing!" bellowed Mrs. Smedley, again trying to free herself from our grasp and again failing.

"If you don't shut up and be still I'll handcuff you," said Phil in a level voice.

"But that woman murdered my husband!" wailed Mrs. Smedley.

"And you drove drunk and hit another car," said Phil. "Let's take care of one crime at a time. The longer I have to deal with you, the longer it will be until we can figure out who killed Mr. Smedley."

"I don't quite dare let her go," I told Phil. "I'm afraid she'll either try to run off or hit me. Or maybe you. Or Junior. Or Ernie."

"I'll help," offered Mr. Buck.

"You will not," I told him firmly. "Mrs. Smedley doesn't deserve you."

A few onlookers chuckled. Phil appeared frustrated. "Aw, hell. I'll cuff her. Then she can't do anything but sit still."

"Good idea," I said.

Ernie had managed to start Mrs. Smedley's car, and he drove it to a free spot on the street and parked it. He loped up to us and said, "I'll take over for you, Mercy. Phil, you cuff her while I hold her."

"No!" bellowed Mrs. Smedley.

"Shut up," said Ernie.

By golly, she shut up. Unfortunately, it wasn't because she'd suddenly seen the light. Rather, she bumped into a stander-by and reeled away from Phil, ending up sprawled over the hood of another parked car.

"Good Lord," I said as people watched the spectacle.

"Sheesh," said Phil.

"I don't feel so good," moaned Mrs. Smedley, sounding pitiful.

"Don't you dare get sick in my car," warned Phil.

"If you gimme a quarter, I'll clean it up for you if she does," said an eager Junior.

"I won't be sick," said Mrs. Smedley, still sounding pitiful.

If she hadn't caused such a deplorable scene, I might have felt sorry for her. After all, she'd been married to a despicable man. Then again, perhaps they had deserved each other. And it might have been she who'd shoved him in front of that truck, too. She'd admitted to visiting her husband's office, after all.

This entire series of events was making my head ache. I liked it better when all we had to do was find Pekingese dogs and Mr. Brentwood.

Ah well. Such is life, I reckon.

SEVENTEEN

fter Mrs. Smedley was firmly locked in the backseat of Phil's
police car, he and Ernie held a brief discussion before they
drove to the station.

"As soon as I turn the woman over to the desk, I'll drive you back
here. I still want to talk to Miss LaBelle," said Phil.

"Right," said Ernie. "And the next time you visit, maybe you
should bring a uniform with you. I don't like it when my secretary has
to perform the duties of a copper."

Phil allowed his head to fall backward and he heaved a huge sigh.
"Yeah. You're right. I should have brought a uniform with me."

"Especially since you were going to interview a murder suspect,"
said Ernie. "After all, Lulu might have been armed and dangerous."

"Ernie!" I cried, shocked.

"Joking, Mercy," said Ernie.

"Yeah. He's only joking. I know Miss LaBelle isn't armed."

"Except with her hands," I said, grumpy at having fallen for one
of Ernie's sarcastic remarks, "with which she pushes people in front of
big trucks."

"All right, all right," said Phil, clearly frustrated. "We'll be back in a while, Mercy. Make sure Miss LaBelle and her lawyer don't go anywhere."

"Of course, Detective Bigelow," I said.

"We won't be long," said Ernie. "At least, I won't be long. If Phil gets held up at the station, I'll take a cab back."

"Very well," I said.

As I walked back into the Figueroa Building, the door of which Mr. Buck kindly held open for me, I thought about what a hideous morning it had been.

"You need me for anything, Miss Mercy?" asked Junior, suddenly appearing at my side. "Need any more water or coffee or anything?"

"No, thank you, Junior. Go on about your business. I'm sure we'll be fine now that Mrs. Smedley has been taken away."

"Sorry about Mr. Ernie's car," said Junior, sticking with me as we crossed the lobby.

"Was it Ernie's car that woman hit?" asked Glennie from the front desk. I was so unused to seeing anyone but Lulu there that I gave a slight start when I glanced at her.

"Yeah," said Junior. "But Mr. Ernie, he got it started okay. Not his car, but the lady's."

"Is Ernie's car badly dented?" Glennie wanted to know. "When I heard the crash, I rushed to the window to look, but I didn't dare go outside because I might miss a telephone call."

"That was very responsible of you, Glennie," I said, sounding kind of pompous.

Glennie grinned at me though, so I guess she didn't mind. "Well, and there were quite a few other people in the lobby, and I didn't want to leave the desk unattended, either."

"Good job," I told her, wondering who'd been cluttering up the lobby in the middle of the morning.

"Goes with the job," Glennie said dismissively. "Anyhow, that woman smelled as if she'd drunk a barrel of whiskey."

"Yeah, she was drunk as a skunk," said Junior with relish. "But Ernie's car'll be okay. He can take it to a mechanic, and it'll be easy to fix."

As I hadn't participated in the conversation between brother and sister, I continued on my way to the staircase and began climbing. When I walked into the office and on to Ernie's room, I tapped on the door.

"Lulu? Mr. Gabriel?" I said. "Is it all right for me to come in?"

"Sure," said Lulu. "Did you get rid of that woman?"

"Yes." I opened the door and entered. Mr. Gabriel sat in Ernie's chair and had a legal pad on the desk in front of him. It looked to me as if he'd written a ton of notes on it.

"Smedley was a louse," said Lulu, "but I guess his wife is one, too."

"His widow," I said. "Yes. She was…Interesting."

"That's one way to describe her," said Mr. Gabriel wryly. "She stank like a distillery. Not, of course, that I know what a distillery smells like."

"Of course not," I said.

"Mr. Gabriel doesn't think the coppers have much of a case against me, Mercy," said Lulu in a small voice.

"Well, how could they?" I asked. "You didn't do anything."

"Well, I did knee—"

"You defended yourself," broke in Mr. Gabriel, cringing. "The man tried to assault you, and you defended yourself and ran."

"Precisely," I said. "And even Ernie said you'd have been able to hear Smedley if he'd chased after you because those metal stairs are so noisy."

"Which he was in no condition to do," said Mr. Gabriel with a grimace.

Hmm. I knew the difference between the anatomy of a man and that of a woman, but I hadn't known until today that men were so protective of their dangly bits because, apparently, they were quite vulnerable to assault and hurt like the dickens when hit, kicked or, in Lulu's case, kneed. Interesting and good to know in case I ever found myself in a compromising situation from which I wished to escape.

"I see you've been taking notes," I said to Mr. Gabriel. "Would you like to compare your notes to mine? I've taken Lulu's statement about four hundred times by now."

"Oh, Mercy, I don't know what I'd have done without you," said

Lulu, suddenly breaking down, folding her arms on Ernie's desk and burying her head in them. "I was s-so stupid!"

I hurried to sit in the chair next to her and threw an arm around her shoulder. "Lulu, it's not your fault. Smedley was a beast."

"I didn't even know his real name!" sobbed Lulu.

"I know. I know." Looking up, I saw Mr. Gabriel watching us with concern. Good. He seemed to be on Lulu's side. To him, I said, "Will you please look in the drawer on your right and see if there are any handkerchiefs left?"

He did as requested, but shook his head. Oh, dear. It had already been a several-hankie day, and it wasn't even noon yet. I'd have to go to the five-and-dime and procure another dozen or so.

After a minute or two, Lulu sat up in the chair and wiped her eyes with the already-soggy handkerchief she'd been using. "I don't know what's going to happen," she said in a miserable voice, "but I don't think I want to be a star anymore. Not if girls have to meet people like Mr. Faraday or Smedley or whatever his name was. And you can't tell by looking if they're rats or not. By the time you find out, it's t-too late."

"The police really don't have any proof against you, Miss Mullins," said Mr. Gabriel in his deep voice. "It's a shame you were hoodwinked by that man, and it's too bad those photographs were scattered in his office, but there's at least one other—and I consider a better—suspect in the man's murder. His wife even admitted to visiting his office after you had left it."

"But what happened in between the time Lulu ran off and Mrs. Smedley showed up?" I asked.

"She might well have killed him," said Mr. Gabriel.

"Why'd she show up here wailing that he was dead and then accusing Lulu?" I asked.

With a shrug, Mr. Gabriel said, "She wouldn't be the first person to do something rash, instantly regret it, then try to drown her sorrows in booze and decide to blame someone else for her misdeed. She might have cooked up the notion of pinning the killing on Miss Mullins as she drank."

"How'd she know where I worked?" asked Lulu, sitting up a little straighter.

"She knew where you worked because she saw you when she came here to hire Ernie to follow her husband," I told her.

It was the right thing to say, I guess, because Lulu instantly brightened. "You're right! I forgot about that. She'd have seen me at the reception desk. I remember when she came in here on Monday."

I nodded. "Exactly."

"Good," said Mr. Gabriel. "That's good." He wrote on his pad.

Thinking about people milling about in the lobby earlier, I asked Lulu, "Um, you didn't happen to see any people on the street before you walked up to Smedley's office, did you?"

"People on the street?" asked Lulu, squinting at me.

I shook my head hard. "I don't mean on the street. I mean, did you see anyone hanging around or walking on the sidewalk near Mr. Smedley's office?"

Tilting her head to one side and then the other as she thought, Lulu shrugged and said, "I guess there were some people walking on the sidewalk. There are a couple of diners in that block and a pet store, I think." More bitterly she added, "I didn't notice if they were there when I ran away, but they sure didn't help if they *were* there."

Trying to think of a couple of follow-up questions to ask her, although I don't know why, my brain stopped functioning when a timid tap came at the outer office door. Odd. People generally just walked right in. Bemused, I rose, left Ernie's office, went to the front office door, and opened it. And there stood Mr. Brentwood, monocle in place and hat in hand.

"Mr. Brentwood!" I exclaimed.

"Yes. No. Miss Allcutt. May I come in?"

"Of course, you may," I said, gesturing for him to enter the office. "Mr. Templeton isn't here right now, but I know Mrs. Wilkes is quite worried about you. Would you like to wait here until Mr. Templeton returns?"

"Um...Yes. No. Um, I don't know."

Poor man. I had an inspiration. "Why don't you join Miss LaBelle and Mr. Gabriel and me in Mr. Templeton's office, and we'll all wait for Mr. Templeton to come back. Is that all right with you?"

"No. Yes. Yes, all right. I have a problem."

"I'm sorry. Perhaps we can help you solve it."

"Yes. No. Yes. You and Mr. Templeton. Good at solving problems."

"Indeed we are. Come with me."

So I led him, not unlike Mary's little lamb, to Ernie's office. I tapped once on the door—I'd shut it when I went to the outer office door—and let Mr. Brentwood enter the office before I did. I shut the door behind me and hoped Mr. Brentwood wouldn't bolt before Ernie got back.

As soon as Mr. Brentwood stepped into the office he stopped dead. Gesturing with his hat, he said, "He's not Mr. Templeton. I'll go now."

"No, no!" I said, grabbing his arm as he tried to turn around. "This is Mr. Gabriel. He's only sitting in Mr. Templeton's chair for a little while. Mr. Templeton will return to his office soon."

Frowning at me, Mr. Brentwood said, "No. Yes. Are you fibbing?"

"No. No, I'm not fibbing."

Mr. Gabriel rose from Ernie's chair. "She's not fibbing. I'm Mr. Robert Gabriel, and I'm an attorney."

"An attorney?" said Mr. Brentwood, squinting and dislodging his monocle, which he caught and replaced with his usual grace. "For whom?"

"For me," said Lulu. "Good day to you, Mr. Brentwood."

This time Mr. Brentwood squinted at Lulu and went through the drop-and-replace maneuver with his monocle yet again. "You belong downstairs," he said. "Somebody else is sitting in your chair. He's"— he pointed at Mr. Gabriel—"sitting in Mr. Templeton's chair." He looked at me once more. "You're not sitting anywhere. I saw you at the library."

"Yes indeed. Why don't we all just wait in Mr. Templeton's office for a minute or two until he returns." Another inspiration struck me. It would take a while to determine if these recent inspirations were brilliant or not. "Why don't *you* sit in Mr. Templeton's chair for a while, Mr. Brentwood? I'm sure Mr. Gabriel won't mind."

"Not at all," said Mr. Gabriel, scooping up his legal pad and getting to his feet. He stepped back and indicated the vacated chair. "Have a seat. You're Mr. Brentwood? Is that correct?"

"I'm so sorry," I said. "I should have introduced you. Mr. Brentwood, this is Mr. Gabriel. And you've met Miss LaBelle before, haven't you?"

"Not met," said Mr. Brentwood, for once not equivocating. "Only you were sitting downstairs. You were wearing red."

"I probably was," said Lulu, sounding unhappy with the admission.

"I like red," said Mr. Brentwood.

His words prompted the first smile I'd seen on Lulu's face since she'd come up to Ernie's office earlier that morning. "So do I," she said.

"May I sit? Yes? No?" Mr. Brentwood pointed at Ernie's chair.

"Of course, you may," said Mr. Gabriel, backing up and holding the chair for Mr. Brentwood.

After giving Mr. Gabriel a severe looking-at, Mr. Brentwood put one hand on an arm of Ernie's chair, moved over so he stood in front of it, and gently sat. Then he glanced around the office, folded his hands, placed them on Ernie's desk, tilted the chair back once, straightened it, and smiled. "I like this," he said happily.

"That's wonderful, Mr. Brentwood," I told him. "You may sit there and we'll all wait until Mr. Templeton returns to the office."

His smile fading, Mr. Brentwood said, "Then he'll sit here? Yes. No. Yes."

"Well, it is his desk," I said, smiling gently. "But I'm sure he won't mind you sitting in his chair for a while."

"Nice," said Mr. Brentwood, smiling once more. "He's nice. You're nice. I don't know if you're nice," he said to Mr. Gabriel as the lawyer moved from behind the desk and sat in the corner chair I'd sat in earlier. "You're nice," he said to Lulu.

"Thank you," Lulu and I told him. I added, "I think you're nice, too."

He beamed at me.

"Did you say you have a problem, Mr. Brentwood?" I prodded.

His smile vanished and he said, "Yes. Wait. Yes. Wait for Mr. Templeton."

"Very well. Would you like to tell us about it first?" I asked.

Giving the stink-eye to Mr. Gabriel, Mr. Brentwood said to me, "Maybe you. And her." He pointed at Lulu. "Like red better than black. Not him." His pointing finger aimed at Mr. Gabriel.

"Why don't I wait at your desk, Miss Allcutt?" said Mr. Gabriel. I was glad he didn't comment on Mr. Brentwood's clearly displayed confusion. Some folks weren't as understanding of other people's foibles as he seemed to be. "Just until Ernie—Mr. Templeton—comes back. I need to get back to my office, but I don't want to vacate the premises as long as Miss LaBelle needs me if the police come back to question her."

"Thank you. That would be nice of you," I told Mr. Gabriel.

So Mr. Gabriel went out to my desk, shutting the door to Ernie's office behind himself.

As soon as the door closed, I focused my attention upon Mr. Brentwood again. He appeared slightly troubled.

"Is something the matter, Mr. Brentwood?"

"Yes. No. The police are coming here?"

"Yes. Detective Bigelow wants to question Miss LaBelle about something that happened yesterday."

"Oh. Yes. No. I saw something yesterday."

"Did you?"

I glanced at Lulu to see if she wanted to partake in this conversation, but she looked absolutely worn to a frazzle and sat numbly in her chair, slumped over and patting her cheeks with her wet handkerchief. She might have been trying to force some color into them, but I don't know. I'd never seen her look so pale and wan. On the other hand, I'd seldom seen her without makeup, either, so maybe it was my imagination.

"Yes," said Mr. Brentwood, recalling my attention to him. Then he said, "No. Yes. Yes. Bad. It was bad."

"You saw something bad?" I asked, wondering how get any kind of coherent narrative from the fellow.

"Yes. Bad. Yes. Bad. Yes. Bad."

Well, I guess he'd seen something bad, all right. "And it disturbed you?" I figured I might as well keep talking to him until Ernie showed up. I sure didn't want him escaping again.

"Yes. Bad. Disturbed. Bad man. Night. Man fought with a lady. Not bad lady. Man bad. He hit lady. She pushed him. Truck hit him."

Egad! Had Mr. Brentwood witnessed the death of Mr. Smedley last night? How the heck could I find out? And what would happen if I did? Would anyone believe him? "Where did you see the lady push the man, Mr. Brentwood?"

He tilted his head and peered at me as if he thought I was the daft one in the room. Oh well. "On the street. Yes," he said.

"Do you know the name of the street?" I asked softly.

Lulu, I noticed, had straightened somewhat in her chair. I had a feeling neither one of us put much stock in anything Mr. Brentwood had to say, but he *had* actually witnessed a real event in Chinatown once. Mind you, what he'd seen and said then hadn't helped us solve the case, but you never knew about these things.

"Name of street?" His brow furrowed, but he lifted his hand to his monocle before it could fall again. "Name of street," he muttered. "Name of street."

"Was it on Broadway?" asked Lulu, startling Mr. Brentwood, who'd apparently expected me to speak next. He straightened in Ernie's chair and stared at Lulu as if he'd forgotten she was in the room.

"Broadway?" he said in something of a squeak. "Broadway? Yes. No. Yes. No. I don't know."

"Oh," said Lulu. She glanced at me and I gave my head a small shake, trying to convey to her that it would be better if I questioned Mr. Brentwood. I guess she caught on because she slumped back in her chair and didn't speak again.

"Is that the problem you want to discuss with Mr. Templeton, Mr. Brentwood? The woman and the man fighting and the man falling on the street?" Good grief, did that even make sense?

"Yes," said Mr. Brentwood, leading me to believe my question had at least made sense to him.

"I see. Well, Mr. Templeton should return to the office any minute now." I shook down my jacket sleeve and took a peek at my wrist-watch. Ernie had been gone for about ten minutes. I didn't know if that was time enough for him to get to the police station, deposit Mrs. Smedley and get back again.

"Yes," said Mr. Brentwood. "Wait for Mr. Templeton. He's nice. You're nice."

"Thank you," I said, "Yes. Mr. Templeton is quite nice."

"I don't know you," he said, pointing at Lulu. "But I think you're nice."

"Thank you," said Lulu in a dispirited voice.

"You're welcome," said Mr. Brentwood.

And then I didn't know what else to say.

EIGHTEEN

It seemed as if we'd been sitting in Ernie's office, none of us speaking, for several hours before we heard the outer office door open and Mr. Gabriel greet the returning Ernie. I failed to suppress my exhalation of relief. Mr. Brentwood, who'd been staring at the wall across the room from Ernie's desk, jerked in Ernie's chair.

"Mr. Templeton?" he asked, sounding scared.

"Yes, Mr. Templeton has returned," I said, speaking softly and sweetly.

Evidently, my voice wasn't sweet enough because poor Mr. Brentwood leaped to his feet and tried to hide. As he was already behind Ernie's desk, which was shoved up against a wall, he didn't have much luck, although he folded up like a concertina, drew his knees to his chest, and laid his head on his knees. His monocle, wonder of wonders, stayed in place.

"A Mr. Brentwood paid you a call," said Mr. Gabriel to Ernie. "He's sitting at your desk."

"Oh yeah? Wonder what he wants."

"Something happened to upset him."

"Ah," said Ernie. From the one word, I knew he wanted to say something more, and that if he did, it would be sarcastic. Ernie was acquainted with Mr. Brentwood, however, and didn't want to hurt his feelings, so he allowed his "Ah" to stand on its own.

That was more than Mr. Brentwood did when Ernie opened his office door. Ernie saw Lulu and me, and then he saw Mr. Brentwood, squished into the corner made by Ernie's desk and the far wall.

"Mr. Brentwood?" Ernie said in a soft voice.

"No. No. No, no, no, no," said Mr. Brentwood. Then he finally admitted it. "Yes."

"Would you like me to help you stand?" asked Ernie kindly. He removed his right glove and held the hand out to Mr. Brentwood, who stared at it as if it were a viper about to strike.

"Stand?" said Mr. Brentwood. "No. No. Yes."

"Here you go," said Ernie, benevolence fairly dripping from his voice. "Just take my hand, and I'll help you stand up. You don't look comfortable there."

"No. No. Not comfortable," said Mr. Brentwood.

Ernie stood still as Mr. Brentwood contemplated his current problem. They remained still for so long they reminded me of the tableaus we used to put on at Christmastime in my old Boston school. I got to play the Virgin Mary being annunciated once. I think the original painting was by some old Italian fellow. However, that's not the point.

The point was that finally Mr. Brentwood decided to accept Ernie's hand, and with him shoving himself and Ernie faintly tugging, Mr. Brentwood got to his feet. Instantly, he began looking around in what appeared to be panic to me.

I understood. "Here, Mr. Brentwood. Why don't you sit in this chair?" The chairs in Ernie's office weren't awfully heavy, and I managed to wrestle one of them so it sort of blocked escape from behind Ernie's desk and to the door.

"Chair?" he said. "Chair? Chair? Chair?" He gulped and finally said, "Yes." Then he sat on the chair. "Thank you."

"You're welcome," I said.

Ernie sat in his own chair. "I'm glad you're here, Mr. Brentwood. Mrs. Wilkes at your home is worried about you."

"Mrs. Wilkes," said Mr. Brentwood, fiddling with the string to his monocle. "Mrs. Wilkes. Yes. Mrs. Wilkes."

"Mr. Brentwood saw something that disturbed him last night," I told Ernie. I stood behind the chair in which Mr. Brentwood sat, hoping in that way to keep him from leaping up and attempting to run away.

"You did?" Ernie asked Mr. Brentwood pleasantly.

"Yes," said Mr. Brentwood.

Ernie, Lulu and I waited to hear more, but Mr. Brentwood remained mute. I heard Lulu heave a disconsolate sigh and decided I might have to get things moving if there were things to be moved.

"Mr. Brentwood saw a lady push a man into the street last night, Mr. Templeton," I said in a sugary voice.

"Yeah?" Ernie's sharp glance shot to me and then to Mr. Brentwood. "You saw that, did you? And it disturbed you?"

"Yes. Yes. Yes. I saw that. It disturbed me."

"I see. Well, that's too bad. Do you remember what street you were on?"

"No. No, no, no. Miss Allcutt asked me. I don't know."

"Hmmm. Well, that's interesting, Mr. Brentwood. We should probably chat about this, but I think now I should telephone Mrs. Wilkes and have someone pick you up and take you home. Is that all right with you?"

"No. No. I want to talk about the bad man. And the lady he socked. And the other lady."

"Two bad ladies?" said Ernie, clearly confused, as who wouldn't be?

"No. No. No. Bad man. Hit woman. Other woman hit him. Not bad woman. Bad man." He wrinkled his brow once more.

"He saw a bad man hit a woman," I said, hoping to prompt Mr. Brentwood into coherence. "Another woman was there, too."

"Oh?" said Ernie, sounding interested at last.

"And then," I said, looking at Mr. Brentwood in an encouraging way, "One of the ladies pushed the bad man after he hit the other lady. Isn't that correct, Mr. Brentwood?"

He nodded. Then he kept nodding until his monocle dropped from his eye, he caught it, and put it back again. The poor man. I felt sorry for him. I also wanted to shake the story out of him.

"And the man got hit by a truck?" I prodded gently. "Isn't that right?"

"Yes. Yes. Yes. Truck. Bad man. Hit woman. Another woman pushed him. He fell into the street. The truck ran over him." He screwed his face up in distaste. "It was bad. Bad. Bad. Made a big mess."

"Sounds like it," said Ernie. He gave me an incredulous look before returning his attention to Mr. Brentwood. "Do you think the woman might have pushed the man on Broadway Street, Mr. Brentwood?"

"Don't know. Street where the birds are. Pretty birds. I like birds." He produced a beatific smile.

A street with birds? Ernie and I swapped a glance. I lifted a shoulder in a shrug.

"I see. Are the pretty birds in a store?" asked Ernie.

"Pretty birds," said Mr. Brentwood. "And bunnies."

Was he recalling his visit to the library and confusing it with last night's mayhem? "Do you remember seeing birds and bunnies at the library, Mr. Brentwood?" I asked.

"Library?" He smiled some more. "I liked the lady in the library. She read a pretty book."

"Now you've done it," muttered Ernie to me. To Mr. Brentwood, he said, "Yes, the library has books with birds and bunnies. But I'll call Mrs. Wilkes now. Is that all right with you?"

Mr. Brentwood heaved a large sigh. "Mrs. Wilkes. Yes. Mrs. Wilkes. Home. Yes."

"I'll get the number for you," I told Ernie, and I flipped through one of my secretarial pads—I'd taken three, just in case—and found the number for Mrs. Wilkes and the...home for wayward innocents. Or the loony bin. Take your pick. I prefer the former.

I handed the pad to Ernie, who dialed the number. When his call was received by Mrs. Wilkes, she said she'd come to the office right away to pick up Mr. Brentwood.

"Thank you. We'll keep him safe here while we wait for you." Ernie listened to whatever Mrs. Wilkes responded to his statement and said, "Third floor. Figueroa Building. Yes. We'll keep him safe and sound."

As he hung up his receiver, the outer office door opened and I heard Phil stomp into the room. Mr. Gabriel greeted him.

"Are Ernie and the LaBelle woman in there?" we heard Phil ask Mr. Gabriel.

Standing, I said, "I'll go out there and—"

"No," said Ernie, interrupting me. He didn't mean to be rude. "I'll go out there with Lulu, and Phil can question her out there. You stay here with Mr. Brentwood. Maybe you can draw pictures in one of your notebooks." I could tell he wasn't being sarcastic or ironic.

"That's a good idea," I told him.

"Thanks," he said, sounding relieved.

So, after a tiny bit of chair reshuffling, Lulu and Ernie left his office, and Mr. Brentwood and I gazed at each other. I decided to act on Ernie's suggestion.

"Would you like to draw some of the birds you saw yesterday, Mr. Brentwood? You may use my pad and a pencil. I don't have colors, but you may draw birds if you want to."

"Birds? I like birds," said Mr. Brentwood. He took the pad and pencil I held out for him, and darned if he didn't begin sketching in my pad.

"Oh, my, you're very good at drawing, Mr. Brentwood," I said, allowing my amazement to show in my voice. Then I hoped I hadn't offended him.

"I like to draw birds," said he. "And bunnies. And other animals. I like animals."

"You're wonderful at drawing," I told him, standing so I could see better. Good Lord, the man was a by-golly artist! As I watched, he created a parrot in a palm tree.

Then he sat back and smiled at his creation. Peering up at me shyly, he said in a tentative-sounding voice, "Do you like it?"

"I love it!" I told him honestly. "I didn't know you were so good at drawing."

He heaved another sigh. "I love to draw. Want me to draw a bunny?"

"Yes, please."

For I don't know how long, we sat in Ernie's office, I watching amazed as Mr. Brentwood drew bunnies, birds, squirrels, a giraffe, an elephant and a cute little dog. I was almost disappointed when the low murmur of voices in the outer office was interrupted by the door opening and someone walking in. I figured it was the person who was going to take Mr. Brentwood back to the home.

I was correct. Shortly after the outer office door opened and a brief colloquy took place, Ernie tapped on the door. "Mrs. Wilkes is here to take Mr. Brentwood home," he said.

Frowning, Mr. Brentwood looked up from my pad. He appeared disappointed.

"Would you like to take that pad and pencil home with you, Mr. Brentwood?" I asked him sweetly. "Your drawings are absolutely beautiful."

"You think so?" he said, beaming with pride.

"I do. They're excellent. You're a talented artist."

As the door opened and Ernie peeked into his office, Mr. Brentwood carefully tore four pages, one at a time, out of my secretarial pad. He held them out to me. "Do you want them?"

"Yes!" I said. "I'd love to have them. Thank you *so* much. I'd like to see more of your artistry, Mr. Brentwood. Do you have paper and pens or paints at home?"

It was as if a storm cloud had opened up and drenched poor Mr. Brentwood in ice water. "No. I had chalk, but I was too messy."

"I'm so sorry. But I'll bet I can get some Perma Pressed Waxed Pencils for you. Would you like that? They come in different colors, and they're made of colored wax. You can draw on paper with them."

"I would like that," said Mr. Brentwood, staring at me with awe.

He wasn't the only one. When I glanced at the door, it was to see Ernie and Mrs. Wilkes also staring at me with awe. Maybe it was horror on Mrs. Wilkes's part.

"Um," she said, "Mr. Brentwood is a truly talented artist, but... Well, we found the chalks to be rather messy. Lots of dust."

"Yes," said Mr. Brentwood sadly. "Chalk makes dust."

"Perma Pressed Wax Pencils don't create dust," I said. "I'll pick some up along with some artists' pads and bring them to Mr. Brentwood, if that will be all right with you, Mrs. Wilkes."

"Perma Pressed Pencils?" she asked doubtfully.

"Yes. I promise you that, as long as Mr. Brentwood uses them on the paper on the pads, they won't make a mess." I turned to Mr. Brentwood. "Just don't draw on the walls with them. Can you be sure to use them only on paper?"

"Paper. No walls. Paper. No walls. Yes. Yes. Yes."

"Thank you very much, Miss…" Mrs. Wilkes's voice petered out.

"Allcutt. Mercy Allcutt. I'll buy some waxed pencils and artists' pads and deliver them to…your home." I still didn't know what the place was called. "And maybe an easel."

After gaping at me for a split-second, Mrs. Wilkes said, "Thank you. Would you like that, Jerome?"

Mr. Brentwood, his hands clasped to his chest and his monocle gleaming, said, "Oh, yes. Thank you. Thank you, Miss Allcutt. I'll draw birds for you. And bunnies."

"I love the birds and bunnies you drew today. Thank you for giving them to me."

"You're welcome," said Mr. Brentwood.

Mrs. Wilkes led him from the office, and he went with her as meekly as a lamb. One of which he also drew, by gad, on my secretarial pad.

When the door closed behind the two people, Ernie peered at the papers in my hand. "What're those?"

"He's an artist! A *real* artist," I said, still marveling at this discovery. "Look at these!"

He looked. So did Mr. Gabriel, Phil, and Lulu.

"Well, I'll be damned," said Phil.

"Of that, I have no doubt," I told him, still annoyed. Then something almost pertinent occurred to me.

"Could Mr. Brentwood have been visiting a pet store last night when he saw the lady push the man?" I asked the occupants of the room. "Does anyone know if there's a pet store near Mr. Smedley's office? Where it used to be, I mean. Well, I guess the office is still there, even if Smedley isn't." Before anyone could answer, I asked Ernie, "What happened to Mrs. Smedley, by the way?"

"She called her brother to bail her out."

"Ah. Did they arrest her for smashing your car whilst under the influence of intoxicating liquors?"

"They booked her, but she called her brother, and he came and bailed her out."

"Her brother, eh?" My mind, which was a slippery devil, slid back to my trip to the library. "What's her brother's name? What does he look like?"

"Raymond Oswald, and he's kind of short and skinny with brown hair and a mustache."

"One of those skinny mustaches that look like caterpillars crawling across a man's upper lip?"

Lulu said, "Ick."

After laughing, Ernie said, "Yes."

"I saw him at the library where I discovered Mr. Brentwood. He and Mrs. Smedley and a couple of other women were discussing something at a table near the front door. I didn't think much about it at the time. In fact, I fear I figured they might be romantically involved, and I thought it strange to be canoodling with a fellow right after she hired you to find out if her husband was straying."

"Canoodling?" said Ernie with a chuckle.

"You know what I mean," I said, irked.

"Yeah, I do. Apparently, the guy with the slicked-back hair and the mustache is her brother, and you said there were a couple of other women were there, so I doubt they were canoodling."

"They might have been plotting, though," I said.

"Plotting? You think she did her old man in?"

I lifted my arms in a gesture of frustration—I think the gesture is commonly known as throwing one's arms in the air, but that sounds disgusting to me. And bloody. "*I* don't know! All I know for certain is that Lulu didn't do it, and if Mr. Brentwood was there on the sidewalk at the same time the man was shoved, who knows who did it? There seem to be dozens of suspects!"

"I've only noted two so far," muttered Phil.

"Oh, bother you," I told him. Unwise and mean of me, but I was aggravated. "You have nothing on Lulu."

"We have photographs of her on the floor of the dead man's office," Phil reminded me.

"Yes, I know, and you know how they got there, too," I snapped.

"Calm down, Mercy. Phil isn't going to arrest Lulu," said Ernie.

"Oh. Good."

"Thanks, Mercy," said Lulu in a stifled voice.

"We're going to do some more investigating," said Phil.

"What a brilliant idea," I said. Quite snidely, I fear.

Ernie frowned at me and whispered, "Shut up, Mercy," so I decided to shut up.

After shooting me a nasty glare, Phil turned again to Lulu and Mr. Gabriel. "All right, Miss LaBelle, you've agreed to stay in Los Angeles, right?"

"Yes," answered Mr. Gabriel for Lulu. "She will not leave Los Angeles."

"Where would I go?" asked a plaintive Lulu.

"I don't know," said Phil. "Just don't leave Los Angeles. You live at Miss Allcutt's residence, and you work here, right? You don't normally travel anywhere else?"

"We've said Miss LaBelle will remain in Los Angeles until this matter is cleared up," said Mr. Gabriel, suddenly sounding more legal than he had to date, at least in my hearing.

"Yes, yes. I know, I know," said Phil, reminding me of Mr. Brentwood. "Just have to make sure."

"So you're sure now," said Ernie. "Go away, Phil."

"Cripes," muttered Phil, slapping his hat on his head and grabbing his overcoat from the rack beside the front door. "I'm going."

And he went. Ernie held up a hand after the door shut behind Phil, so none of us spoke until Ernie'd walked to the door, opened it, and peeked out to see that Phil had actually exited the hallway.

"Huh," Ernie said, coming in and closing the door again and locking it. "He's on the elevator."

"Good," I said.

"Now," said Ernie, "let's figure out what to do from here." He grabbed the chair where Mrs. Smedley had sat, noticed it was still wet, frowned, and carried it to the coat rack, probably so it could dry in peace. Then he snagged the chair beside my desk, turned it around, gestured for me to sit in it, and told Mr. Gabriel, "Rob, you sit between Mercy and Lulu. I'll sit at Mercy's desk. We have to talk."

So we did.

NINETEEN

"I've got to get into Smedley's office and look through his records," Ernie said as soon as we were all seated. I resented him for sitting in my chair behind my desk, but I didn't let on. He was, after all, the boss.

"The police have probably already done that," said Mr. Gabriel. "And I suspect they've barred entry to Smedley's office."

"You're giving them a lot of credit they may not have earned," said Ernie. "I was a cop once, remember? Once they think they have a good suspect, they stop looking. This time they have *two* good suspects."

"So you don't think they've checked Smedley's records?" I asked, surprised. I mean, I know the police in Los Angeles sometimes did sloppy work, but not to check Mr. Smedley's office files seemed beyond inept to me.

"Don't know, but I intend to find out." Ernie checked the clock on the wall. "It's almost noon. What say we all go out to lunch? Do you think Glennie will mind holding down the fort for you for another couple of hours, Lulu?"

"I hate to ask her," said Lulu. She still looked pretty darned ravaged.

"You need to...do something, Lulu," I said.

"What do you mean, do something?" she asked.

"If you're going to resume your place at the reception desk, you need to wash your face and dab on a little powder or something," I said, deciding discretion was uncalled-for at the moment. All three people with Lulu could see she needed help just by looking.

"Oh, my God!" she cried. "I forgot! Oh, nooooooo!" And darned if she didn't start crying again.

"Come on, Lulu," I said, rising and taking one of her arms. "Let's you and me visit the ladies' room down the hall. Ernie, open the left bottom drawer and get out my handbag, please. Lulu and I are going to need it."

He did as I asked. Mind you, I didn't keep a supply of pastes or powders in my bag, but I did have a compact and a powder puff, and they might help Lulu look less like a walking dead person than she did at the moment. "Thanks, Ernie. Come with me, Lulu."

Mopping her eyes with her soggy handkerchief—another thing I had in my bag was a clean hankie—Lulu allowed me to lead her from the office and down the hall to the ladies' room. Once there, Lulu took one look at herself in the mirror and darned near collapsed once more. I jostled her shoulder.

"Buck up," I told her sternly. "Wash your face and— Ew." I'd just noticed the towel on the rack. It was pretty darned dirty. "Well, you can use my handkerchief to dry your face. I have some powder in here. Not sure what to do about your swollen eyes, but we'll do what we can to make you presentable."

Glumly staring at her reflection in the mirror, Lulu said, "I don't think it's possible."

"Oh, sure it is!" I said in an effort to boost her spirits.

So Lulu took a good long time washing her face. Several times. Every time she splashed cold water on it and peered in the mirror, she washed it again. Poor Lulu.

A knock at the restroom door made both Lulu and me leap like a couple of startled hares. It also darned near made me utter a swear word.

"Miss Mercy? Miss Lulu."

"Junior!" I cried. "What are you doing here?"

"Mr. Ernie called the front desk, and Glennie sent some stuff up for you. It's your handbag, Miss Lulu, and Glennie sent hers, too. She said use anything you need to use of what she's got in there."

"Bless Ernie Templeton as a saint," I whispered, "and Glennie too."

I opened the door to find Junior standing with both arms held out, a handbag dangling from each wrist.

"Thanks, Junior," I said after yanking the bags from him and shutting the door in his face. If he wanted a tip for doing a good deed, he could wait for it again. If this day ever ended, I'd owe the kid a fortune.

"Bless them all," whispered Lulu, reaching for her handbag. "Will you see if Glennie has any lip rouge in her bag? I didn't even pack any this morning, but I think I need some."

"Here's another hankie," I said, holding it out for Lulu as I peered into Glennie's bag. Sure enough, she had a small pouch in her bag that, when opened, revealed a few cosmetic items. "Here's some powder and some rouge. You can use it on your cheeks and your lips," I told Lulu.

"And I have a compact that has white powder in it in here some-place," muttered Lulu, rummaging through her own bag.

"White?" I asked, surprised.

"For under my eyes. Might make them look less red. I'll put some flesh-colored powder on top of the white. I didn't bother with rouge, because I was trying to look boring today, but I might need some of Glennie's."

"Look! Glennie has one of those Maybelline cake mascara boxes," I said, plucking it out of Glennie's bag and showing it to Lulu.

"Oh, good. I don't want to look robust, but I don't much like my current dead look, either." She lifted a key from her handbag and squinted at it. "What the heck is this doing here?"

Glancing at the key in her fingers, I said, "Don't know. Is it one of yours? Maybe to a desk or something?"

"I've never seen it—" She stopped speaking suddenly and her

175

eyebrows dipped in puzzlement. Then she shrugged and shoved the key back in her bag. "Anyhow, I don't want to look dead."

"I figured you wouldn't want to look like that for the rest of the day," I said. Because Lulu didn't need anything else to think about, I didn't resume questioning her about the strange-to-her key.

Another knock at the restroom door yanked an "Eek" from Lulu and a grunt from me. "Junior?" I asked.

"Yeah," said the lad. "Glennie says she can stay at the desk for the rest of the day if you need her to. Mr. Ernie, he just sent me up here to tell you that and then he give me money to get Glennie, Mr. Buck, and me lunch from the diner across the street."

"Excellent," I said, breathing a little more easily. "Thanks, Junior." I'd taken to sitting in the one chair in the room, so I continued rooting through Glennie's handbag.

"Thank Mr. Ernie," said the impish Junior. "He's the one who arranged it all."

"We'll thank him," said Lulu.

As her voice had sounded suspiciously thick, I jerked a glance at her. I *truly* didn't want her weeping anymore today. It would take a miracle to get her looking well enough to walk out of the building without people staring at her. Fortunately, Lulu was made of stern stuff. The reason her voice had sounded odd was because she was stretching her neck to see herself more closely in the mirror and patting some white powder under her eyes.

"Golly, that white stuff really works, doesn't it?" I said, amazed.

"Yeah, it's good for if you've had a late night," she said. "Or if you've been crying all morning."

I noticed she'd begun to sound less weepy and more grumpy, and took it as a good sign. Lulu wasn't a tragedy queen as a rule. Mind you, I couldn't blame her for breaking down today, but I was glad she seemed to be regaining her gumption.

"What do you think of Mr. Gabriel?" I asked as she worked on repairing the damage to her face.

"He's swell," said Lulu, again sounding odd. That's because she had her lips pressed together as she applied powder to her face with her powder puff. She'd thought to drape the dirty towel from the rack around her shoulders so the loose powder wouldn't get on her—well, my, but who cares?—black sweater. When she stopped flapping powder at her face, she patted her cheeks with her hands to rid them of loose powder so they wouldn't appear to have been dusted with talcum.

Stepping away from the mirror, she gazed at herself with what seemed to me to be a professional's eye. "Better," she said. "Wish I had some boric acid powder so I could rinse out my eyes, but I guess they can't be helped much more."

"No, I don't have any with me, either."

"Does Glennie have a light rouge, or does she wear dark stuff?"

"There are a couple of tins in here," I said, getting them from Glennie's makeup pouch. "Oh, look here! She has some Tangee Natural. Doesn't that change color depending on your skin tone?"

"Yeah. I read about Tangee Natural in *Photoplay*. Maybe I'll try it on my lips and see what happens. I'll just dab on a little."

I handed her the small round tin. Lulu opened it, got a small amount of the product on the tip of her finger, and delicately dabbed it on her upper lip. "Better wait and see what happens," she said. "If it turns orange or something, I'll use…What's the other one she has?"

"Rose," I said, holding up that tin for her to see.

"Thanks," said Lulu, still staring at herself. After a few seconds, she said, "I think the Tangee will work." She turned to me and pooched out her lips. "What do you think? It turned kind of pink. Does that work?"

"It works better than pasty-white from crying," I told her, perhaps too candidly.

But Lulu was Lulu, and darned if she didn't chuckle. "Yeah. You're right. Okay. I'll dab just a little on my cheeks and spread it around. Wish I'd brought my Boncilla with me today."

"Golly, I don't usually carry makeup with me. Well, except for powder and a puff."

"I know," said Lulu, letting me know precisely what she thought of my makeup routine. That's because I didn't have one.

"Well, you said you wanted to look dull. I'm just trying to help."

"I know it, Mercy, and I didn't mean anything bad. I'm just used to wearing lots of makeup. Without it, I feel different. Kind of…I don't know. Exposed or something. Maybe that's a good thing."

"Can't say at this point. We just want you to be presentable. I don't know where Ernie plans to take us for lunch, but if it's anywhere other than Charley's, you probably don't want to look as though you've been sobbing for hours."

After heaving a huge sigh, Lulu said, "You're right. Okay. I think I've done all I can do for my cheeks and lips. Let me have the mascara now, please."

So I took the Tangee tin from her and handed her the cardboard Maybelline box. Then I watched as she withdrew the tiny brush, ran some water on it, and dipped it into the black cake. She brushed the resultant pasty liquid on her upper eyelashes. She allowed the cake to dry for a few seconds and peered at herself some more.

"There," she said at last. "I'm only going to do the upper lashes. If I do the lower ones, too, it'd be too trashy."

"Trashy?" I asked, astonished. Lulu generally wore mascara on both her upper and lower lashes along with blue or green cream shadow, or sometimes a combination of both, on her eyelids. "You never look trashy."

And I'd just fibbed to my dear friend. Darn.

"Yes, I do. You don't have to be polite with me, Mercy. I know I've been sashaying around and all but screaming, 'Look at me!' for a couple of years now. And somebody looked, and see where it got me. Arrested for murder."

"You haven't been arrested," I said, nobly leaving off the "yet" dangling on the tip of my tongue. "And if Ernie and I have anything to do with it, you never will be."

"Thanks, Mercy. I owe you and Ernie a lot. And Mr. Gabriel. I'll owe him a lot more if he can get me off this murder charge."

"You didn't do it," I told her. "Ernie and I will make sure Mr. Gabriel can prove it."

"You think Ernie will let you help him?"

"He'd better," I said. I said it firmly, too, what's more, because I aimed to snoop whether Ernie wanted me to or not.

Lulu gave her face another good looking-over before turning and squaring her shoulders as she flipped the dirty towel from them and hung it back on the rack. "There. Do I look presentable?"

I got up from my chair, having packed everything away in Glennie's handbag. Giving Lulu a close once-over, I said, "Turn around." She turned around. She hadn't got any powder on the back of my black sweater. "You look good," I said at last. "And I'm not even stretching the point very far, either."

"Gawd, I love you Mercy!" Lulu cried, flinging her arms around me.

After giving each other a big hug, we prepared to go out and face the public.

When we got back to Ernie's office and walked in, Ernie and Mr. Gabriel stopped chatting and looked critically at Lulu and me. I'm sure I looked pretty much as I always did. It was Lulu everyone was concerned about.

I don't know how long Lulu and I stood there being stared at, but it was fully long enough for me to feel like a mannequin at a fashion show. "Well?" I demanded at last. "Can Lulu be seen in public?"

"Yeah," said Ernie. "I'm surprised." He sounded it, which might or might not have been flattering. It was up to Lulu to decide that one.

"You look very good," said Mr. Gabriel in a more reserved tone.

"Considering what I looked like before?" asked Lulu.

"Well, yes," said Mr. Gabriel.

"You looked like hell before you and Mercy took off for the ladies' room," said Ernie. "I'm impressed."

"Thanks, Ernie," said Lulu crisply. "And thanks for thinking to get Junior to fetch Glennie's and my handbags."

"Figured you'd probably need whatever women carry around in them," said Ernie, standing from where he'd been lounging on my desk chair. "You girls ready? Rob and I think Chinatown's our best bet. Nobody cares what white women look like there."

"Gee, thanks, Ernie," barked Lulu. "I thought you said I looked okay."

"You do. But I didn't know you would until you walked in here."

"True," said Lulu. "Charley's?"

"I was thinking Hop Luey's," said Ernie. "It's darker in there, and we can sit in a corner and talk. I want to figure out how to get a look at Smedley's records."

"Why don't you drive to his office, climb the stairs, and see if you can open the door to his office?" I said, being a smart aleck.

Tilting his head to one side, Ernie stared at me for fully long enough for me to feel like an idiot. Then he said, "I'll be damned, Mercy. That's a really good idea."

It was? Well, how about that.

TWENTY

T he four of us took the elevator down to the lobby, and Lulu handed Glynis her handbag.

"Thanks so much, Glennie. I don't know what I'd have done without your Tangee. Do I look like death warmed up, or am I okay to walk outside in the daylight?"

"You look better than I expected," said Glennie candidly. "Junior said you'd been bawling your eyes out."

Ernie and Mr. Gabriel laughed. I said, "Your little brother is an impertinent boy, isn't he?"

"Don't know what that means, but he's sassy as heck."

"He's also useful," said Ernie. "Don't forget that part."

"Yes, he is," I admitted. "He's quite useful."

"He's getting my lunch now," Glennie added. "Thanks, Ernie. Appreciate it a lot." Glancing again at Lulu, she said, "Try not to worry, Lulu. Nobody with a brain in his head would think you killed anybody!"

"I hope you're right, Glennie. I didn't do it, you know."

"I know it," said Glennie, sounding adamant.

"We can take my machine," said Ernie. "Thanks to Mrs. Smedley, it's got a smashed rear fender, but it still runs."

"Or we can take mine," said Mr. Gabriel, pointing to a nice-looking, highly polished blue sedan parked close to Ernie's. "We can all fit in it."

Squinting at the automobile, Ernie said, "You lawyers make too much money."

"Maybe just a little more than private eyes," said Mr. Gabriel, laughing. "Got this baby about three months ago. She's a Flint E-55. And I take good care of her."

"Her?" I said, thinking the pronoun an odd one for an automobile.

"Susie," said Mr. Gabriel. "Named her after my Aunt Susie. Great gal, my Aunt Susie." He walked up and opened the passenger side doors, gesturing for Lulu to take the front seat. "Miss Allcutt, you and Ernie can sit in the back if you don't mind. It's supposed to seat five passengers comfortably, but I mainly only have to drive clients around in it, and that's usually one at a time."

"Huh," said Ernie, holding the back door open for me. I got in, and he shut the door and walked around the car to get into it so I didn't have to scoot myself over to the driver's side of the backseat. "Nice car," he told Mr. Gabriel. The backseat was plenty big enough to hold another passenger. Under other circumstances, I might have been disappointed Ernie and I weren't sitting closer to each other, but not that day. That day my attention was devoted to Lulu.

"Thanks," said Mr. Gabriel, who had seated himself behind the wheel. "I like it. When did you get rid of your old Studebaker? I thought you'd never get rid of that death trap."

"Don't say mean things about my car, Rob," said Ernie in a funning voice. "I loved my old wreck." More somberly, he said, "I bought it the day before yesterday. And today, that idiot woman bashed its fender."

"Sorry, Ern," said Mr. Gabriel. He'd pressed the starter and was craning his neck out the driver's window in order to find a space in the traffic flow into which he could insert his car so he could get us to Chinatown.

Once the Flint was in the street among all the other autos, it didn't take long to get to Chinatown. Mr. Gabriel drove to Hill Street and parked on the other side of the street from where Charley Wu's noodle shop was located. The men—I hesitate to call both of them gentlemen, although I figured Mr. Gabriel was one—opened the doors for Lulu and me, and we all walked through the plaza to Hop Luey's. It was in the shape of a Pagoda, and when you entered, light ceased. Well, not entirely. But the interior was dim. A waiter recognized Ernie and said, "Mr. Templeton! Good to see you here again."

"Thanks, Henry. There will be four of us for lunch today. In a dark corner if you have one."

"Sure we do," said Henry with a grin.

Whoever Henry was, he led us up the mutedly lit staircase to the restaurant's main dining room. The dining room was pretty full, but Henry led Ernie to a booth in a by-golly dark corner. Lulu and Mr. Gabriel sat on the bench—I think those seats are called banquettes—and Ernie held a chair for me and sat in the other one so we faced the other couple.

"Would you like to start with tea?" asked Henry politely as he handed menus to us.

"Yes. Thanks, Henry," said Ernie, smiling at the lad.

As Henry drifted off to get tea I leaned toward Ernie and whispered, "Who's Henry?"

With a shrug, Ernie said, "He's one of the five million people I talked to in Chinatown when we were trying to figure out who killed the bozo the police arrested Charley Wu for killing."

"Aha. Probably a cousin of Charley and Lily Wu," I said.

"Probably," said Ernie with a chuckle.

It did seem the Wus—and the Fongs—had tons of relatives living in and around Chinatown in Los Angeles. They'd all been extremely helpful to Ernie—not so much to me—in solving Charley's case. They still lauded Ernie—not so much me—for having cleared Charley's good name, too.

Because I knew women weren't valued at their true worth no matter *what* culture they were born into, I tried not to take it personally, but I did anyway. Heck, I made a bet with myself as we sat there that Ernie wouldn't even have to pay for this lunch for four.

Besides, it had been my perseverance—Ernie called it bull-headedness—that had actually led to the case's solution and the clearing of Charley's good name. The world is an unfair place, but I think we've covered the topic before.

By the time Henry came back with our tea, we'd decided what we'd like to have for lunch. Henry took our orders, removed the menus, and glided off, allowing us to whisper to each other.

"Very well," said Ernie, getting us started, "so we know what happened to you last night, Lulu. What we don't know is what precisely happened after you fled from Smedley's office. Do you recall seeing anyone on the sidewalk when you ran away?"

"Well, yes," said Lulu. "There were people walking on the street. It was dark by then, but the street lights were on and there were still a few shops and businesses open. Not everybody keeps the same hours around here these days. Back in Enid"—Lulu originally hailed from Enid, Oklahoma—"they roll up the streets at seven p.m."

"Yeah," said Ernie. "Los Angeles is getting bigger and busier all the time. But you didn't notice, say, that strange man with the monocle who claims he saw a woman shove a guy in front of a truck?"

"Mr. Brentwood?" said Lulu. After taking a second to think, she shook her head sadly. "No. I didn't look at anybody in particular. I just ran. And I *know* Mr. Faraday—I mean Mr. Smedley—didn't follow me down those metal stairs. They're noisy. I'd have heard, even with traffic noises."

"I agree with you about the stairs," said Ernie. Turning to me, he asked, "Where do you want to get Mr. Brentwood's art supplies?"

"Um...I don't know. I think you can probably get pads of paper and colored wax pencils at variety stores. Heck, there's a Woolworth's right there on Broadway. I think they sell stuff like that."

"Good. We can go there after lunch, and I won't have to make up an excuse for being on Broadway if Phil finds out we were near Smedley's office."

"Why would you need an excuse?" I asked, getting all hot and bothered until I realized Ernie was trying to rile me. As usual. "Never mind."

"Darn it, Mercy, you're getting to know me too well," said Ernie. "You don't take my bait at all anymore."

"Phooey. Anyhow, I don't know if Woolworth's is near Smedley's office. What's the address, Lulu? I can't remember."

"The office is on North Broadway. I think Woolworth's is on South Broadway."

"Doesn't matter," said Ernie. "Same general neighborhood."

"Give or take seven or eight blocks," said Mr. Gabriel, laughing.

"What're a few blocks among friends?" said Ernie.

Henry came back pushing a metal trolley upon which sat plates mounded with food. He placed them all on the turntable in the center of the table, handed out plates, chopsticks, and flatware to each of us, and asked if we'd like anything else.

"Don't think so. Thanks, Henry," said Ernie, giving the boy a big smile.

"Not a problem, Mr. Templeton," said Henry, smiling up a storm. Everybody adored Ernie. It was a gift, I guess. Heck, even *I*…Never mind.

"So you know a lot of folks in this district, Ernie?" asked Mr. Gabriel as he scooped noodles onto Lulu's plate and placed it back in front of her. "I'll let you get whatever else you want," he told her. Huh. I should hope so.

I'm sorry. Mr. Gabriel seemed to be an extremely nice man, and just because he didn't think Lulu could serve herself was no reason for me to become irked with him.

"You want me to help you get your food, Mercy?" asked Ernie, sounding innocent.

"No, thank you. I'm fully able to fill my own plate," I said with something of a snap to my voice.

Mr. Gabriel held up both hands in an "I surrender" gesture. "I'm sorry. Didn't mean to be officious."

"These two are modern women, Rob. You can probably get away with opening doors for them, but don't do any more than that. They'll scratch your eyes out."

"I won't either," said Lulu in a small voice. "Thank you, Mr. Gabriel. I couldn't reach those noodles."

"The table turns," said Ernie dryly, demonstrating.

"I don't care," said Lulu. "I think it's nice of Mr. Gabriel to help me. I haven't had a lot of luck with men lately."

And nobody said another word for several minutes as we slowly spun the table and each took tidbits from it. I absolutely love Chinese spareribs and fried shrimp, so I took three of each. I know, what a pig, huh? But there was enough food on that turntable to feed an army or three. I'm almost positive the Hop Luey's folks gave us more than we ordered, thanks to Ernie.

The food was, as ever, delicious. I noticed Lulu seemed to have little appetite, although she pretended.

"It'll be okay, Lulu," I said when we'd been chewing and swallowing for several minutes. "We'll find the truth."

"I sure hope so," she said, sounding kind of dismal.

"They don't have much of a case against you," said Mr. Gabriel.

"True," said Ernie. "Try not to worry. You and I both know the cops don't look farther than the most obvious suspect, but it seems to me that there's at least one other obvious suspect, and that's the fellow's missus. And if he tried his charms on other innocent women, there may be seven or eight more."

"I wonder what she and her brother and those other women were doing at the library that day," I mused after having demolished my second sparerib.

"Don't know," said Ernie.

"They might have been plotting," I said. "If I hadn't noticed Mr. Brentwood sitting there, maybe I could have snooped on the Smedley gang."

"Gang?" Ernie turned to give me an open-eyed astonished look I didn't believe for a second.

"You know what I mean. Yes, she came to you because she said she thought her husband was running around on her—and she was right—but why was she plotting with her brother and those other women the next day?"

"How do you know they were plotting anything?" asked Lulu.

"Well," I admitted, "I don't, but she didn't look like the library type to me, and that guy she was sitting with, who I guess is her brother, didn't either. Nor did the other two women. They probably met there because nobody would ever suspect them of being there. If you know what I mean."

"I know what you mean, but I can't think of a reason for them to be plotting. If they were plotting to do away with Smedley, they did a lousy job of it. Right there on Broadway? That's a little public, don't you think?"

"Darn you, Ernie," I said, not entirely feigning annoyance. "You're always poking holes in my theories."

"Am not."

"Are too. How long did I have to prod you before you went to that horrid building in Chinatown with me?"

"All right, all right. You got me there."

"Mercy was right about that one, Ernie, and you know it."

"Yeah. I know it. Let's finish and go to Woolworth's. I want to go to Smedley's office after that and see if we can get in."

"It's probably locked," I said. "And do you really think the police won't have confiscated his files?"

"Don't know. That's why I want to look. I do know they can be mighty sloppy when they think they have a suspect. Or even if they don't. I quit the force after the Taylor fiasco."

"That's so unfair," I grumbled. "Why, I'll bet anything Lulu isn't the only girl that horrible man tried to bamboozle."

"Bamboozle. Yeah, that's what he did," said Lulu, sounding sad again.

"Oh, Lulu. Try to cheer up. Ernie and Mr. Gabriel will get you off. And I'll help."

"For some reason," said Lulu, "I trust you more than I do the fellows. You never give up."

"Hey!" said Ernie, truly offended. "I won't give up either."

"Sorry, Ernie," said Lulu. "But Mercy has had to push you a whole lot sometimes in order for you to work on cases."

"Hey!" said Ernie again. "I have to earn a living here. I work for people who pay me. I have to pay Mercy, and then she goes haring off on her own all the time."

"I do not," I said. "It's not my fault you let me go to the library and I saw both Mrs. Smedley and Mr. Brentwood there."

"Yeah, yeah," said Ernie. "I guess so."

Shaking his head, Mr. Gabriel chuckled and said, "You two make a good team."

It was really dark in our corner, but when I took a peek at Ernie, I could have sworn he blushed. I didn't even know he could.

I said, "Thank you," formally, and continued dining.

As I figured would happen, when Ernie asked for the bill, Henry said the meal had been taken care of, and asked if he'd like them to save the leftovers for him to pick up later.

"Thanks, Henry. And please thank Mr. Hop. I won't need the leftovers, so please give them to some deserving orphans or something."

"Thank you," said Henry with a slight bow.

So we left Hop Luey's on a mission. First to the Woolworth's on South Broadway and then to Mr. Smedley's office on North Broadway. I found precisely what I needed at the art-supply section in Woolworth's. I discovered more than mere Perma Pressed wax pencils, but also discovered that a company called Munsell sold a product called Crayolas that came in a box with lots of different colors of wax sticks. So I bought two of the largest Crayola boxes for Mr. Brentwood along with three artists' pads, which contained large white pages.

"That should make him happy," said Ernie.

"I hope they do," I said, meaning it sincerely. As I'd shopped for the odd Mr. Brentwood, it occurred to me that he might be able to draw faces as well as birds and bunnies. I didn't tell Ernie, Lulu, or Mr. Gabriel my thoughts on the matter.

Then Mr. Gabriel drove us up to North Broadway, and he found a parking space directly in front of the building housing the late Mr. Smedley's office. That metal staircase even *looked* noisy.

TWENTY-ONE

W e exited Mr. Gabriel's Flint motorcar and stood in a clump on the sidewalk, all of us looking around in an attempt to find stray coppers.

"I don't see a police presence," said Ernie.

"They're never around when you need them," I said.

Ernie laughed. Nobody else did. Then I spotted the pet store two doors north of the metal staircase. I even pointed at it, taking one more opportunity to disobey the teachings of my childhood. "Hey, look! I'll bet that's where Mr. Brentwood was when he witnessed Mr. Smedley and whoever it was who pushed him into the street." Leaving the clump, I trotted to the store and said triumphantly, "See? Birds and bunnies!"

Sure enough, through the big glass window, we saw cages holding pretty birds and a cage with three cute little white rabbits in it. Next to it was another cage with a whole lot of white mice. They were playing on little circus wheels and runways and looked absolutely adorable. Fancy that. Mice. Looking adorable. If Mrs. Buck ever found one of those in our house, she'd probably whack it with a broom or call in Buttercup, who could savage a mouse in a minute flat. I found that out by accident one day when I took her to Echo Park.

"Huh," said Ernie. "I'll be. He really *was* here, I guess."

"Well, I wasn't," said Lulu bitterly. "I was long gone by the time Smedley got killed. I ran so fast I didn't even notice the pet store."

"Do you have any idea which businesses were open when you ran past them?" I asked her, wondering why Mr. Brentwood might have been lingering on a street looking at a closed pet store.

"Don't have a single clue," said Lulu. "There were street lights on, and some businesses had lights on inside. I guess they might have been open. Or they keep the lights on to discourage crooks."

"That might be the reason he was here," I said. "If there were lights in the pet-shop window. How do the poor animals sleep at night?"

"They've got boxes to go into," said Ernie, pointing in his turn. He didn't have my mother to disobey, so either he was disobeying his own mother, or his mother hadn't been as strict as mine.

"Ah, yes. I see them."

"Well," said Mr. Gabriel. "I suppose we should go upstairs and see if we can gain entry to Mr. Smedley's office. That's why we're here, after all."

"True," said Ernie. "Come along, Mercy. Enough bunny-watching for you today."

"Yes, I know we're here to find Mr. Smedley's client records if we can. If they can be called clients," I said, a trifle irked with my employer. I didn't think it was a waste of time to discover the reason Mr. Brentwood might have been on this street and in a position to witness the murder. Accident. Whatever it had been.

"I don't want to go up there again," said Lulu glumly. "But I guess we have to."

So we walked up the metal staircase, making a good deal of noise without even trying. "You know," I said as we reached the top, "if we can get a coherent account of what happened last night from Mr. Brentwood, we can probably clear Lulu with no trouble at all."

"What do you mean, 'no trouble?'" asked Lulu. "I haven't heard that guy make sense during any of the times I've seen him."

"Well, I kind of have," I said in a not-awfully-confident voice. But really, if one took one's time, one could coax some kind of sense from the poor man.

"Let's hope we can find an easier way," said Mr. Gabriel.

"Amen," said Ernie.

He led the way down the hall until we got to an office with the painted legend *CLINT FARADAY, Talent Scout, Agent*, on the smoked glass window. Ernie tried the doorknob. It didn't turn.

"Locked," he said. "Let me see if any of these keys work." And darned if he didn't fish in his jacket pocket and come away with a ring full of keys, all different. "These come in handy from time to time."

"I hope one of them works," said Lulu.

"Me too," I said. Then I turned to her. She appeared wan and exhausted, although she still looked much better than she had before we visited the ladies' room in the Figueroa Building. "Say, Lulu, that key you found. It couldn't be to the cad's office, could it?"

"What? No! I turned the key and left it in the lock when I ran out," she said. "I don't know where the key in my bag came from or what door it's for."

Ernie and Mr. Gabriel, both of whose attention had fixed on the door, turned to stare at Lulu.

"What?" said Lulu, sounding scared.

"You found a key in your bag?" asked Ernie.

"Well, yeah. When Mercy and I visited the ladies' room to fix my face." She hugged her handbag to her chest.

"Interesting," said Mr. Gabriel, giving Lulu a slanty-eyed look.

"Yeah, very interesting," agreed Ernie.

I didn't like the expression on either man's face, and I wish I'd kept my big mouth shut. "I'm sorry, Lulu. Shouldn't have mentioned the stupid key."

"Me, too," said Lulu. "But it's not the key to that horrible man's office! It can't be! *That* key was in the lock when I ran away from him!" She lifted her handbag away from her chest and said, "Look for yourself! Try the stupid thing! I don't know where it came from or what it's to, but it *sure* isn't the key to that man's office!" She kind of shoved her bag toward Ernie.

"Why don't you get it for me?" said Ernie.

"Fine. I'll get it," said Lulu. She opened her handbag, dug in it, and produced the same key she'd found when we were in the ladies' room. "Here." She thrust the key at Ernie.

He said, "Thanks," stuck the key in the lock, turned it, and the door opened.

"But…But that's impossible!" said Lulu, sounding as if she might start crying again.

"You're absolutely certain you didn't take the key with you when you left Smedley's office?" asked Mr. Gabriel, tilting his head and narrowing his eyes as he gazed at Lulu.

"Yes," she said in a choked whisper. "I didn't *leave* his office, I *escaped* from it. I don't know how that key got in my handbag."

I put a hand on one of her shoulders. "Don't fuss about it now," I told Mr. Gabriel, my expression as fierce as I could make it. "Something weird is going on. Lulu did precisely what she said she did last night. We'll figure out about the key later. Now let's look inside the bum's office."

"Good idea," said Ernie, who didn't seem as flustered about the key as Mr. Gabriel, Lulu and I were. Good old Ernie. He didn't let himself get bothered until he knew for certain there was good reason to be. He walked into the office and stood still, hands on hips, gazing around. "The cops haven't bothered searching this place yet," he said in a flat voice.

"How can you tell?" I asked.

"Because none of the cabinet drawers are hanging open. The police aren't tidy when they search."

"Oh," I said.

"But they'll probably be here soon, so let's start looking." He strode to a tall file wooden cabinet and tried to open the top drawer. "Damn." He yanked on it harder, but evidently, it was locked.

"I'll look in his desk drawer. That's where I keep cabinet keys," I said, and scurried to the desk where I opened the top drawer. Sure enough there, in a little glass holder, lay a bunch of little storage-drawer keys. I just picked up the glass holder, carried it to Ernie, and handed him the top key.

"Nope," he said after he tried it. I took the key from him and handed him another. "Somebody try this key in another drawer," I told Lulu and Mr. Gabriel. I held out the key Ernie had just tried to use.

After a significant period of hesitation, Mr. Gabriel took the key. Perhaps because I glared at him. "We probably shouldn't be here and doing this," he said a trifle lamely. Not to mention far too late.

"Too bad," I said. "We're here now, and we need to see if Smedley had photographs of other women. If he treated them all as badly as he treated Lulu, any one of them might have done him in. And then there's his wife and her brother."

"You still think the siblings conspired to kill him?" asked Ernie, grinning as he tried the key I'd just handed him. "Why?"

"I don't know, but they might have had a reason," I said, annoyed that he found my theory so amusing.

Lulu had roused from her misery to take the first key from Mr. Gabriel, and she was trying it in keyholes in other file cabinet drawers.

As for Mr. Gabriel, he just stood there, looking uncomfortable. Clearly, he'd never been detecting with Ernie Templeton before.

"Got this one open," said Lulu from across the room. "Golly, look here. There are names written on a lot of folders in here. They don't look like they're in any particular order."

"They aren't stored alphabetically?" I asked handing Ernie the glass key box and going over to where Lulu knelt in front of a wooden storage cabinet with three drawers. "Oh, I see what you mean." A bunch of folders were stacked on top of each other with names written on the tops of the folders.

"Want to look through them?" asked Lulu, handing me a stack of folders.

"Might as well." I opened the top one and shut it again instantly. "Good Lord, the man was a perfect *fiend*!"

"Huh?" said Ernie, turning from his storage cabinet, the upper drawer of which he'd finally managed to unlock.

I slapped my hand on top of the folder I'd just opened and closed. "I think he was every bit as bad as Lulu believed him to be. If the photograph in this folder is anything by which to judge, there are probably a hundred young women in Los Angeles—not to mention their parents—who wanted the man dead."

"Golly," said Lulu, "do you think he was maybe blackmailing some of those poor girls? They probably didn't have any money."

"I'm sure he made them pay one way or another," I said, my tone grim.

"What are you two talking about?" said Ernie, walking over to Lulu and me. I didn't want him to see what I'd just seen, but I knew he needed to if we wanted to find out who'd actually done in Mr. Smedley.

"Here," I said, more or less shoving my stack of file folders at him. As luck—bad luck in this case—would have it, he fumbled the stack, and the files fell to the floor, spilling papers and photographs everywhere.

Only most of these photographs weren't of young women in pretty frocks attempting to look like Clara Bow or Pola Negri. Most of the young women in these photos were stark naked. I hate to admit to my state of shock, but it was severe.

"Holy Moses," muttered Ernie, staring at the display on the floor.

"Pick them up!" cried Lulu, who stood there, her hands pressed to her cheeks, in no position to do any picking up of her own.

Therefore, as Mr. Gabriel strode over to see what we were all distressed about, I got onto my knees and began grabbing photos and documents as fast as I could.

"Hold on, Mercy," said Ernie, sounding not at all titillated but extremely Ernie-like. "Don't shuffle them all together. Try to separate them, so we'll know which documentation goes with which photo. I'd like to interview some of these poor girls if we can find them. And if they'll talk to me."

"Maybe they'd talk to Lulu and me. They might be ashamed to talk to a man."

"They'll probably be ashamed to talk to anybody," said a quavery-voiced Lulu. "I know I am, and I kept my clothes on."

"The man was a disgusting skunk," I said, attempting to follow Ernie's instructions. I *really* wanted to get those poor naked girls covered up, but I knew he was correct that it would be wise to figure out who was whom and if they still lived in Los Angeles and could be found and interviewed about Mr. Smedley.

"Good God," muttered Mr. Gabriel, standing and staring down as Ernie and I attempted to arrange pictures and papers in some kind of order in the various folders.

"I don't think God has anything to do with this mess," I growled.

"I'll help," said Lulu, finally snapping out of her mesmeric state, getting down on her hands and knees and shoving papers into folders, too.

"I'll look in these other drawers," said Mr. Gabriel. Guess he'd finally decided to do something worthwhile for a change.

I'm sorry. The poor man was as surprised and horrified as the rest of us, and I didn't mean to snarl about him, but I didn't appreciate the way he'd questioned Lulu about the key either.

"Good Lord, there are more folders over here," he said.

"Just grab them and let's take as many as we can find," said Ernie. "The cops might finally decide to investigate the case, and I'd rather be gone if they show up today."

"You don't think we should take these to the police?" asked Mr. Gabriel, sounding worried.

"Not until I get as much information as I can from them," said Ernie, working quickly. "You see any canvas sacks or empty cardboard boxes or anything like that around here?" he asked me.

"I'll look. It'll be difficult to carry all these folders as they are," I said, wishing I'd bought a couple of net shopping bags when I was at Woolworth's.

But what the heck. I rushed around the office, pulling open unlocked drawers and opening cabinets, and I actually did find a couple of string bags in a closet. I hauled them out, looked inside them, saw items of clothing, decided they might be important, but could be more easily carried in Lulu's and my arms than could paper folders. Therefore, I dumped the clothing on the floor, not entirely surprised to see women's undergarments in the pile.

"You can use these," I said, dropping the string bags at Ernie's feet. "Lulu, why don't you and I get these clothes organized so we can carry them to the automobile."

"For pity's sake! Look at all those frilly underthings!" cried Lulu. "I expect they're trophies. Oh, what a *fool* I was!"

"Don't worry about that now. Just get this stuff picked up," I told her. "Do you have those folders ready to go, Ernie?"

"Almost. Let me check a couple of these other drawers. They aren't—damn. This one's locked. But this one isn't," he said, reaching for the bottom of the three drawers in the cabinet. "Shoot, it's full of folders, too. Rob, help me scoop these out and stuff them in the sacks Mercy found."

"I don't think this is a good idea, Ernie," said Mr. Gabriel. "I'm sure this is against the law."

"Yeah, yeah, I know," said Ernie. "The cops in this city break the law more than most of L.A.'s real crooks do."

"But—"

"Dammit, if you don't want to help, at least go out and start the car!" snapped Ernie. "We've got to get this stuff out of here. Then we can take it back to…Aw, crumb, I don't know where to take it."

"Take it all to my house," I suggested. "We can go through it there. In my office or in a spare room or something."

"Good idea, Mercy," said Lulu, picking up a huge pile of folded clothing and stuffing it under her arm. "I can hold another bundle under my other arm if you'll get it for me," she said to me.

So I did. I got a pile for me to carry as well. Then, with Mr. Gabriel muttering tut-tutting sounds, we scrammed out of Mr. Smedley's office. Both Ernie and Mr. Gabriel, for all his tuts, carried files in those sacks. Ernie set his string bag on the floor long enough for him to relock the door. Then we scuttled down the hallway and took those noisy metal steps to the sidewalk on Broadway. Fortunately, we didn't have far to go to get to Mr. Gabriel's auto.

Mr. Gabriel opened the passenger doors, and Lulu and I got in. I set my own pile of ladies' clothes on the seat beside me. Ernie dumped his string bag on my lap and went to the back door on the driver's side.

Mr. Gabriel, shaking his head as if he knew he were doing something wrong, nevertheless started his car and pulled it out into traffic, which had lessened after the luncheon crowds had gone back to work or home or wherever they went.

"Where to?" he asked as he tootled the Flint up Broadway.

"Hang a left at the next street, then take another left on Hill." He gave Mr. Gabriel the number of my house and then said, "Go there."

"Why?" asked Mr. Gabriel.

"That's Mercy's place. It's where we're headed. We'll dump this stuff there, lock it up and then go back to the Figueroa Building. God alone knows what Phil's doing. He might be camped out in my office."

"Oh, my Lord, I don't want to see him again!" cried Lulu.

"Don't worry. The next time you talk to the coppers, Rob will be with you," said Ernie.

Giving Mr. Gabriel a beseeching look from the front seat, Lulu said, "I don't know if he believes me any longer."

She sounded so pathetic I darned near cried for her.

"Doesn't matter," said Ernie. "He's a defense lawyer."

I thought that was kind of a depressing statement, although I didn't say so.

TWENTY-TWO

We did precisely as Ernie had suggested and emptied our evidence—I presumed it was evidence—at my house. We placed it in my downstairs office in no particular order.

"Can you come over tonight, Ernie?" I asked. "You can look for Mrs. Lewis tomorrow. We need to get this stuff sorted out and see if we can make contact with any of these poor girls Mr. Smedley duped."

"Yeah," said Ernie. "Rob, you want to go through this mess, too, or are you too prissy to do any detecting of your own?"

"I'm not prissy!" Mr. Gabriel snapped. "I'm an attorney, I have other cases, and I'm not supposed to break the law."

"Nobody's supposed to break the law," said Ernie. "But I'll bet anything this Smedley character ruined more girls than Fatty Arbuckle. I'm glad he's dead, but I don't want Lulu to fry for killing him. If we need to find another lawyer—"

"No!" said Mr. Gabriel. "I'm sure you're right, and I believe in Miss LaBelle's innocence. I just question your methods." He finished his last sentence on a lame note.

"Thank you both," said Lulu in a tiny voice. "Thank you, all three of you."

"We'll get you out of this mess, Lulu," I said bracingly. "You just wait and see."

"Guess I'll have to," she said, still sounding forlorn.

"All right," said Ernie after he'd set both string bags full of paperwork on my desk and Lulu and I had deposited our armloads of clothing on the various chairs. "Lock this room, okay, Mercy?"

"I always lock this door," I said. "Not that I don't trust people, but…Well…"

"You don't trust people." Ernie grinned at me.

"I guess. It just seems prudent." I turned to Mr. Gabriel. "So you'll not be coming back today, right? You prefer to be left out of the search and read a report or something after we get it all organized?"

His cheeks puffed out as he blew air through his lips. "You've put me in kind of a quandary," he said. "I will do my very best for Miss LaBelle, but I don't want to twist the law any more than I already have. I can get disbarred for doing this sort of thing."

"Okay. You come back to the Figueroa Building with us," said Ernie. "Don't worry about the evidence. Mercy and I are a good team when it comes to compiling evidence. Then your conscience will be clear." He didn't sound sarcastic, and I was impressed.

On the other hand, Mr. Gabriel evidently had a legitimate concern. It hadn't occurred to me that he might be disbarred for going through Mr. Smedley's office. But if Ernie, Lulu, and I did it, he'd still use the results but his conscience would be clear?

Very well, so I didn't understand anything, but I wasn't sorry Mr. Gabriel wouldn't be joining us that evening.

"Ready?" asked Mr. Gabriel, who stood next to the door of my home office, watching us worker bees.

"Yeah, I think so. Mercy?" Ernie cocked an eyebrow at me.

"I think so," I said. "Lulu?" I cocked an eyebrow at Lulu.

"As ready as I'll ever be," said Lulu, who stared at the rug on the floor and didn't even blink.

"All right. I'll go tell Mrs. Buck to expect Ernie for dinner and join you at the front door," I said. And I did.

"I already prepared enough for Mr. Ernie, Miss Mercy," said Mrs.

Buck with a big grin. "I figured he'd be comin' here for supper tonight."

"You're a jewel, Mrs. Buck."

She only laughed, and I rushed to the front door.

So Mr. Gabriel, after telling me I had a lovely home, which I already knew, drove us back to the Figueroa Building. Ernie's poor Packard looked forlorn parked at the curb with a smashed fender. "Sorry about your car, Ernie," I said, reaching across the backseat of Mr. Gabriel's Flint to give his arm a brief squeeze.

"It'll be all right," he said. "Another one of Charley's cousins has a service station where they do body work."

"The Wus work in mysterious ways their wonders to perform," I muttered.

"They do indeed," said Ernie.

Mr. Gabriel double-parked in front of the Figueroa Building, which I thought was breaking a law, but I didn't ask. Double parking seemed at least rude to me. Perhaps dangerous, because people would have to swerve to avoid a car stopped in the street.

Nevertheless, we walked into the lobby to find Glennie, Junior, and Mr. Buck chatting amiably. Other than the three of them, the lobby was empty. When I looked at the clock on the wall, I saw it was about two-thirty, which surprised me. I thought we'd been gone a lot longer.

"Want your job back, Lulu?" asked a grinning Glennie.

"Yeah. Don't know how long I'll be able to keep it," Lulu told her.

"Buck up, kiddo," said Ernie. "Mercy and I will find the real culprit, and Rob will go with you if the police want to question you further."

"Really?" Lulu glanced from Glennie to Mr. Gabriel, who nodded briskly.

"I am your attorney. If the police want to question you, don't say a word until I'm there with you."

"Thanks," said an unhappy Lulu. She and Glennie traded places, and Glennie went back to her own job in the doctor's office as Lulu sat at the reception desk.

"You have my card," Mr. Gabriel said to Lulu. "Call me if you need me, and I'll be in touch."

"You're leaving now?" she asked him.

"I have an office of my own I have to keep operating," he said. "I'm sorry. But I'll be available any time you need me."

"Thanks," said Lulu as if she didn't mean it.

Mr. Gabriel left the building and Ernie and I took the elevator up to the third floor.

When the elevator cage bumped to a stop, I was almost sorry we hadn't chucked going back to the office and remained at my house when we both saw an extremely annoyed Phil Bigelow pacing in front of Ernie's office. He charged at us as soon as he spotted us.

"Where the devil have you been?" he more or less yelled.

"We went to lunch," said Ernie after we'd walked to the office, he'd unlocked the outer office door and ushered me in first and then indicated that Phil should enter. "You want to talk some more? You'll have to wait for Lulu's attorney if you want to question her again."

"I *do* want to question Miss LaBelle some more," grumbled Phil. "But I guess it can wait until tomorrow."

"Good idea," said Ernie. "She's exhausted. She had a terrible experience last night, and this morning you came here and accused her of a murder she didn't commit."

I scuttled behind my desk, threw my coat over the chair next to the desk and put my handbag in the bottom right drawer. Then I sat on my chair, folded my hands on the desk, and attempted to appear official and efficient as I listened to the two men snarl and snap. They reminded me of dogs circling each other, and I wasn't sure if they were going to go for each other's throats or wag their tails. If you know what I mean.

"Gawd," said Phil, sounding as frustrated as I've ever heard anyone sound. "Is she downstairs at the reception desk?"

"Yes, but her attorney isn't. He went back to his office. Did Mrs. Smedley get sprung by her brother?"

"Yeah. He picked her up. Do you want to file charges against her for driving drunk and hitting your car?"

"Sure. She broke the law. We can't have that, can we? Besides, maybe I can get her to pay for repairs to my car. I'd also pick her over Lulu as a murderer any day of the week."

"Cripes," said Phil. "All right. I'll send in a uniform to take your statement."

"That's the berries, Phil," said Ernie with exquisite sarcasm. "Don't talk to Lulu on your way out of the building. She doesn't have her attorney present."

"Cripes," said Phil again. Then he whirled around and stamped out of the office.

"I think he's mad at me," said Ernie.

"You think so? He seemed quite serene to me," I said.

Ernie carefully pushed my coat aside and plopped himself in the chair beside my desk. "You want to go back to your place? It's going to take some time to go through all those photos and papers, and we'd better do it today. I have a sick feeling that Phil's going to take Lulu in tomorrow unless we can give him a viable alternative."

"You really think so?"

"I do. Unfortunately, she's a logical candidate. And how the hell did that key get into her bag?"

"I don't know. Was Mrs. Smedley as…incapacitated as she seemed to be?"

"Incapacitated?" Ernie repeated. "Mercy, you slay me! She was drunk!"

"Well, I know, but that sounds so…unladylike."

Ernie lowered his head and shook it from side to side. "I swear…"

But he didn't. He stopped speaking entirely, so I said, "I mean, if she was not quite as inebriated as she seemed to be, she might have bumped into the reception desk and dropped the key into Lulu's bag or something. Or maybe her brother was downstairs, and during the hubbub she created *he* put the key in her bag."

Ernie didn't speak for a moment or two as he—I presume—contemplated my suggestions. Then he said, "Does Lulu lock up her handbag, or does she just stick it on the floor or in a drawer or something?"

"I think she puts it on a shelf under the drawer. I think she always puts her manicure stuff in the drawer. I'm pretty sure she doesn't lock it unless she has to leave the desk unattended."

"She wasn't painting her nails today," Ernie reminded me.

"True." Lulu had worn my dull black-and-gray sweater and had left her fingernails naked.

"Well," said Ernie after a substantial pause during which I thought about all sorts of things and I have no idea what Ernie was thinking, "can we go to your house and begin digging through that pile of junk?"

"I drove my car to work today because of the rain," I told him. "I'd hate to leave Lulu and the others stranded."

"The sun came out hours ago, Mercy. Don't you usually take Angels Flight? Why can't they take Angels Flight? I'm sorry Lulu can't come with us, but I guess that can't be helped."

"I wish Glennie could work at the reception desk for the rest of the day," I said. "Poor Lulu is not only suspected of murder, but she didn't get more than three hours of sleep last night."

"Wait here," Ernie said, getting to his feet once more. "I'm going to have a chat with Dr. Clutter. Maybe he'll let Glennie take over for Lulu for the rest of the day."

"Good idea. I..." Would Ernie jump down my throat if I made the offer I was considering? Oh, to heck with him. "I'll be glad to pay Dr. Clutter for Glennie's day if he balks at paying her for doing somebody else's job."

"Don't worry about it," said Ernie, not getting mad at me. I was glad, although I wasn't accustomed to his nonchalance when it came to me offering to pay for things. On the other hand, since we'd cleared Charley Wu of murder charges, he'd been showered with monetary gifts from his friends in the Chinese community.

"Then Glennie can tell Sue and Caroline they'll have to take Angels Flight home," I said. "Tell Glennie to do that, okay?"

"Yes, ma'am," said Ernie, saluting.

Well, really!

On the other hand, probably Glennie would have told Sue and Caroline they'd have to take Angels Flight in order to go home even if Ernie didn't tell her to do so. It's a ghastly notion, but perhaps I occasionally act like my detestable mother, who doesn't believe anyone can do anything unless directed by her. Oh, dear. Well, I could work on my many flaws later. I probably wasn't as worn down by last night and today as was Lulu, but I felt sort of like a rug that had been hung on the clothesline and battered with a big stick.

How the *heck* did Mr. Smedley's office key get into Lulu's handbag?

Who'd shoved the evil man in front of a truck?

Were Mrs. Smedley and her brother and those other women in a conspiracy? To do what precisely? Murder her husband? Wouldn't divorce be less...I don't know. Illegal? I mean, divorce was an unpleasant thing, but it wasn't as bad as murder if you wanted to get rid of an unsavory spouse.

Hmm. If Mrs. Smedley and her brother were involved, the motive probably had something to do with money.

But how?

Darned if I knew.

I folded my arms on my desk and rested my head on them. Thinking was starting to hurt.

By golly, I dozed off! I know I did because when Ernie opened the office door, I nearly fell out of my chair. Fortunately for me, my chair had arms and kept me from hitting the floor.

"Wake up, sleepy head," said an unnecessarily cheerful Ernie. "Lulu's coming home with us. Want to take her in your car?"

Blinking furiously and deciding it wouldn't be kind of me to yell at Ernie for startling me, I said, "Sure. Want to stop by Charley's cousin's body shop and leave your car? You can come to my place with Lulu and me in the Roadster." My lovely blue Moon Roadster had been given to me by my sister Chloe and her husband after Harvey bought Chloe a Rolls-Royce Silver Ghost (complete with chauffeur) several months back.

"Good idea," said Ernie. "Lulu's getting her stuff together downstairs."

"Do you have the address of the service station?"

"Yes, Mercy. I know where it is."

Was I acting like my mother again? Hideous thought! I decided I wouldn't speak again until I absolutely had to. Maybe Mother's blather was coming out of my mouth because of my weary state. Therefore, I got up, put on my coat and hat, retrieved my handbag, and walked out from behind my desk. Ernie was still dressed for the out-of-doors, so I took the arm he held out for me, and together we walked out of the office. Ernie locked the door behind us, and we toddled down the hall and took the elevator to the lobby.

Lulu was already in her hat and coat, and Glennie sat behind the reception desk when we got to the ground floor.

As we walked to the reception desk, Ernie said, "Hey, Lulu, where do you stash your handbag during the day?"

"My bag?" said Lulu. "Right here on this shelf." She pointed to a shelf under the desk.

There was also a drawer, but it was a small one, so I understood why Lulu kept her handbag on the shelf: it wouldn't fit in the drawer. So it might be considered sort of out in the open, except that the reception desk was shaped like the letter L, only with both sides the same length. There must be a better way to describe it. It sat more or less in the middle of the lobby, only it was a two-sided triangle? No, that's not right either. But you can probably picture it in your mind.

"Ah, I see," said Ernie. He turned to Glennie. "When the woman who smashed my fender came in here, were there other people in the lobby?"

"Huh?" said Glennie, evidently caught off-guard by Ernie's question. "Oh, sure. Lots of people were in here, either heading to or leaving offices or coming in or going out of the building. It's pretty busy in the morning."

"You didn't notice anybody go behind the desk, did you?" asked Ernie.

After hesitating for a couple of seconds, Glennie said, "No," uncertainly. "But that woman had just created a scene, so people were going every which way, and I ran to the window to see what had happened outside. Somebody might have walked behind the desk. I don't know."

"Thanks, Glennie," said Ernie. To Lulu and me, he said, "Let's go, ladies. We're going to take both cars, Lulu. I'm going to drop mine off at Wu Han's service station and then ride with you and Mercy to her place."

"Okay," said a subdued Lulu.

ALICE DUNCAN

Honestly, by then, she looked as if she'd not quite risen from the dead, poor thing. She was pale and tired-looking and clearly low in spirits. I felt *so* awful for her.

Because I couldn't seem to help myself, I said to Glennie, "Will you tell Sue and Caroline they'll have to take Angels Flight because Lulu and I had to go home early?"

"Sure," said Glennie. "Ernie already told me to do that."

"I should have known," I muttered.

"Yes," said Ernie. "You should have."

"Thanks, Glennie," I said. Then I renewed my vow not to speak unless I absolutely *had* to for the rest of the stupid day.

TWENTY-THREE

On the corner of Seventh and Grand, Wu Han's Service Station and Body Shop announced itself in both English and Chinese, and it was a busy place. However, as soon as Ernie drove his Packard to the office, a Chinese man hurried out to serve him. Nobody seemed to notice my little blue Moon Roadster right behind Ernie's Packard. I was used to it.

In almost no time at all, Ernie walked back to Lulu and me. "Want me to drive you or do you want to drive me? Hank said he'll have the Packard's fender all fixed by tomorrow at noonish."

"Hank?" I asked, surprised out of my vow of silence almost before I'd made it.

"Wu Han," said Ernie. "He said to call him Hank, so I do."

"Makes sense," I said, again speaking when I didn't have to. Just can't shut me up sometimes. "And he'll have your car ready so soon?"

"Special service." Ernie glanced at the innards of my car, and I knew precisely what he was thinking.

Therefore, I opened my door, got out, and again broke my vow of silence. "You drive. I can fit in the backseat better than you can."

"Thanks, Mercy. Appreciate it," said Ernie.

Lulu remained silent and gloomy, as was only her due.

It didn't take long to drive to my home on Bunker Hill. Ernie parked beside the front porch, and we all piled out. Although the rain had stopped hours earlier, it was still darned nippy, so we hurried to the front door, and I shoved it open. Buttercup, whom we'd unconscionably neglected when we'd brought home the things from Smedley's office an hour or so earlier, received her full share of pats and greetings this time.

She appreciated them all.

"I'm going upstairs to get into something more comfortable," said Lulu. She patted Buttercup first, though, so I guess she wasn't totally down in the dumps.

"If you need to take a nap, Lulu, go ahead. You didn't get any sleep last night, and today has been hideous for you," I told her, again entirely forgetting to be silent.

"I can't let you guys do everything for me. I at least have to help," she said.

"Applesauce," said Ernie. "You look like hell, Lulu. Lie down for fifteen minutes, and if you can catch forty winks, more power to you. We're just going to be putting photos with corresponding information. I hope we can, anyway. Then I'll get in touch with some of the poor girls and see what they have to say about that so-called talent scout."

"Thanks, Ernie," said Lulu with the merest hint of indignation. "So glad to know I look like hell."

"You deserve it, kiddo," said Ernie, grinning at her.

She didn't grin back. "I'll be back in a few minutes."

I'd already taken off my hat and hung my coat on the rack beside the door.

Ernie did likewise with his outer garments, and together we watched a defeated Lulu walk beneath the archway leading to the living room. From there she'd take the stairs up a floor and go to her suite of rooms.

"We have to help her, Ernie. I know she didn't kill Smedley."

"You don't have to convince me," he said. "Let's start organizing."

So we went to my office, I unlocked the door, and we entered. I decided the printed information and the photographs were more important than the items of clothing, so I piled all the ladies' underthings in a corner, retrieved a secretarial pad and pencil from my top desk drawer, and Ernie and I each picked a folder out of a string bag.

"Ah," said Ernie. "This one is more or less together. Guess it's not one of the ones that spilled." He laid a photograph of a fully clothed (thank God) young woman on the desk and laid a filled-out form beside it. He squinted at the form, then glanced at me. "You taking notes?"

"Happy to," I said not entirely truthfully.

"Good. So take down this information. Miss Sylvia Brown. Address is 341 West College, #24. No telephone number listed."

"That's near Chinatown, isn't it?" I asked as I wrote.

"Yeah. Not a great neighborhood, but lots of boarding houses and so forth."

"Kind of like those behind the Figueroa Building?" Lulu and I had visited a couple of those boarding houses once. It wasn't any fun, and that's only partly because we suspected—and were eventually proved correct—that a murderer lived in one of them.

"About like those, yeah. All these young kids coming to Los Angeles to become stars have to live somewhere." Ernie sounded almost as defeated as Lulu had.

I understood. Virtually every waitress, elevator operator, or receptionist you encountered in Los Angeles in those days was an actress waiting to be discovered. Kind of like Lulu.

Fortunately, Ernie had begun his search with a sack full of folders that hadn't had their contents scattered on the floor of Mr. Smedley's office. So we'd already compiled a list of seven women's names and addresses by the time a timid tap came at my office door.

"C'm in," I said, looking up and seeing Lulu, still appearing listless and miserable, standing in the doorway. She'd put on an old house-dress I'd never seen her wear before. Guess she didn't want to wear one of her bright Chinese silk robes.

"I'm here to help however I can," she said, sounding as melancholy as she looked.

"Sure," said Ernie. "I'm working on this sack. It's pretty well organized, so I suspect that one"—he pointed to the other string bag on the chair next to him—"might need closer observation in order to get pictures, names, and addresses put together properly."

"That's okay. I'll look through it." Glancing at me, she said, "You taking notes?"

"Yes," I said. "I don't know what to do about the clothes. They're in a pile in the corner." I chin-pointed to the heap of clothing. "Not sure if we'll learn anything from them."

"Probably won't," muttered Lulu. "They'll just prove there are women stupider than me in Los Angeles."

"You're not stupid, Lulu," said Ernie, sounding matter-of-fact. "And you're sure not the first person to fall for a lousy man's line."

"Exactly," I said. And, believe it or not, I said no more. Lulu didn't need words; she needed help to get out of the mess she was in, and compiling the information we had into a usable format would do that better than a million words. I took my pencil and pad to the corner where the women's clothing was and began a desultory examination of the various items, stopping my work to take notes when someone spoke.

Silence, broken by the shuffling of papers and Ernie's occasional recital of a woman's name and address, prevailed for quite a while.

Suddenly Lulu said, "Oh, my gawd, these pictures are just…just… Oh, my gawd, that man was *evil*! Look at this! This kid can't be more than thirteen or fourteen!" She waved a photograph of a young girl who, as Lulu had said, plainly wasn't out of her teens, stark naked and staring slyly at the space in front of her. "Look at the child! She's trying to be seductive, and she probably doesn't even know what the word *means*!"

"Hey, Lulu, it'll be all right. With any luck at all, most of these young women are back home with their families," said Ernie.

Bowing her head and leaking tears, Lulu whimpered, "I hope so. How could I have been so *dumb*?"

"Stop it, Lulu," I said from my corner chair. I didn't say it in a mean voice, but right now we didn't need Lulu moping over her un-lost virtue. "You're a lot smarter and luckier than the girls who took their clothes off for that villain."

"I'm probably a whole lot older than most of them, too," said

Lulu, bucking up slightly.

"So be glad he didn't find you when you were straight off the bus," said Ernie. "And if you can connect a girl with her information, tell Mercy. She's writing lists of names and addresses. Wish we had more telephone numbers."

"Well, you can go out tomorrow and knock on doors," I told him. "Mr. Lewis can wait for news about his wife for a few days. And that idiot Pekingese woman is all taken care of, right?"

"If she called those numbers you gave her, she will be. If she didn't, her dogs are probably living in El Monte by now. The man I talked to about Puddles and Pierre didn't have anything against the dogs themselves; he just wanted them confined and shut up. He as much as told me he had a brother in El Monte who'd be happy to take a couple of purebred Pekes off his hands."

"Good heavens. Purloined pooches. Well, if his brother in El Monte will train them, more power to him. And the dogs, too," I said.

"My sentiments exactly," he said, picking up another folder. "Shoot, this one's from England." Ernie shook his head. "Los Angeles has a lot to answer for. Anyway, the name is Millicent Entwhistle." He gave me her address which was, naturally, in Los Angeles.

"I wonder if she came all the way from England to L.A. in order to get into the pictures," I mumbled.

"Probably," said Ernie.

"It's not Los Angeles itself," said Lulu, rummaging through her sack. "It's the flickers. They've turned everyone's heads."

"I guess my brother-in-law is part of that," I said, feeling bad for Harvey, an exceptionally nice man who didn't take advantage of others.

I hoped.

Crumb. I didn't even know. I decided not to think about it, but continued writing names and addresses as they were read out to me and peering at underthings. "There are initials written in India ink on these frillies," I said. "Maybe we can connect them with the women in the folders."

"Cripes, the man was a toad," said Ernie.

"Toads are good for eating bad bugs," I told Ernie. "I don't think

211

Mr. Smedley was good for anything."

"You're right about that," said Lulu.

By the time Mrs. Buck knocked at the office door and told Lulu, Ernie and me it was time for dinner, we'd compiled a list of thirty female persons who had, we believed, been exploited by Mr. Felix Smedley.

When the three of us exited my office, I locked the door again. Although I trusted everyone who lived in my home, I didn't want to inflict those photos—and all those female undergarments—on any of them.

"Sure smells good out here," said Ernie, rubbing his hands together as we walked toward the dining room.

"Mrs. Buck's meals are always good," said Lulu.

"Indeed they are. We're lucky to have Mr. and Mrs. Buck working for us."

"Us?" said Lulu.

"Us," I repeated firmly. "We all benefit from their good work."

"There you are!" said Sue, glancing up from her place at the table. "When Caroline and I got home, Mrs. Buck said you were working in your office and couldn't be disturbed."

"Not that we'd have disturbed you," said Caroline.

"I know you wouldn't have," I told them both with a big, fake smile. "But we're trying to figure out another one of Ernie's cases. Lulu knew one of the parties involved, and we were going through some paperwork."

"Oh, my," said Sue eagerly. "What kind of case is it?"

Stumped, I said, "Uh..."

Ernie said, "Believe it or not, a woman hired me to find a lost dog." He laughed.

"And you need Mercy and Lulu to help you?" said Caroline. She sounded skeptical, blast her.

"Sure do. Lulu knows a fellow who trains animals for the flickers. He thinks he might know something about this particular dog, so we were calling people. Mercy took notes."

"My goodness," said Sue. "You get some interesting cases, don't you?"

"Not very often," said Ernie with perfect truth.

"This one is interesting," I said, embellishing. "So's the man who keeps disappearing from the home in which he's supposed to live. I guess it's a place where concerned relatives send family members who aren't quite able to care for themselves. Today I discovered the fellow is not merely a magician at disappearing from places, but he's also a splendid artist."

"Really?" said Sue. "What's he in for?" She frowned for a second. "That sounds like he's a criminal. I mean, why can't he take care of himself?"

"I have no idea if there's a word for his condition, but he can't express himself very well verbally." And I had another one of my perhaps-brilliant ideas. "But he sure can draw. He gave me some of the pictures he drew while we waited in the office for someone to come pick him up."

"Interesting," said Caroline. "I've heard that sometimes when a person isn't good at one thing, he or she will develop another skill to compensate for the one lost. I'm thinking mostly of people who are deaf, but I guess the same principle applies."

"I hope it does," I said before thinking. Happens a lot with me.

"Why do you hope that?" queried Caroline.

"I was…just thinking about having him draw a portrait of Buttercup for me," I said improvising madly. "He's extremely talented, and his drawings are amazing."

"I'd like to see them," said Sue.

By then we were all in the dining room. Because I'm a considerate hostess, I guided Ernie to the head of the table where I usually sat. I sat at the foot. My tenants sat in their regular places. I noticed that Lulu, although she wasn't chatty, didn't look nearly as hopeless and miserable as she had before we dove into those Smedley records. I had a feeling, later proved correct, that she was now more eager to help some of the other women he'd trifled with than feeling obtuse about having almost been one of them.

Mrs. Buck's pork chops, mashed potatoes, green beans, cornbread and apple pie with ice cream diverted everyone from Ernie's lost dog and my artistic odd duck.

TWENTY-FOUR

B ecause Ernie's newish Packard was in the auto-repair shop and he couldn't drive himself home, he slept in a spare bedroom in my house that night. My big house had enough rooms to house six or seven Ernies—except that there was only one of him. And he was mine. Maybe. I mean, we hadn't officially announced anything, but we seemed to be a couple.

Anyway, as he didn't bring a change of clothing with him, after he bathed—I know he bathed, because he smelled like the sandalwood-scented soap I bought in Chinatown—he dressed in yesterday's shirt, suit, and trousers. He didn't bother with his tie, at least not yet. At any rate, he didn't appear wrinkled when he loped down the stairs, but he sure smelled good.

"Good morning, all," he said cheerfully to those of us who had managed to get out of bed and dress.

It was Saturday and sometimes Sue slept late on Saturday mornings. Caroline, who was prim and proper and didn't believe in coddling herself, never slept late. I was surprised to find Lulu walking down the hall to the staircase when I left my bedroom. She still appeared tired but she wasn't a total wreck of herself, as she'd been the day prior, and she even gave me a big smile when we met outside my door.

Anyway, we walked downstairs together, and we were sitting on the sofa in the living room playing with Buttercup when Ernie joined us. Caroline sat in an armchair, reading a book.

Mrs. Buck always fixed breakfast for us on Saturdays, although we were on our own for the rest of the day. At about seven-thirty, she walked into the living room to tell us we could dine if we felt like it. We did.

So did Sue, who ran downstairs in her robe and slippers, then screeched to a stop when she saw Ernie.

"Oh!" she cried, slapping a hand to her cheek, which had turned pink with embarrassment. So had the other one. "I forgot you'd be here this morning."

"Don't mind me," said Ernie with a relaxed smile. "I promise I won't look."

We all laughed when she realized she was so bundled up there was nothing to see if he *did* look. "Thank you," she said and continued to the dining room. There Mrs. Buck served us ham and eggs and biscuits, along with a little bowl each of mixed fruits, mostly pieces of orange and grapefruit. It was all delicious, as ever.

"Do you want me to drive you to Hank Wu's station to pick up your automobile?" I asked Ernie at one point.

"Sure, but I'd like to go over some of those names first."

I wasn't sure what he meant by "go over" some of the names, so I just said, "Fine with me."

"I'll go with you, if you don't mind," said Lulu.

"That's right," I said, thanking my lucky stars I'd remembered what our agenda had been before we discovered somebody'd killed Mr. Smedley. "We still need to go to Chinatown and visit the consignment shop."

"What are you looking for?" asked Sue, slathering raspberry jam on a buttered biscuit. Mrs. Buck made the *best* jams and jellies.

"Dull clothes," I said. "Lulu wants to tone down her wardrobe."

"Not entirely," said Lulu with a wee bit of animation. "I mean, I'll still wear colorful scarves and so forth, but I'm through with trying to look like a Christmas ornament. According to an article I read in *Motion Picture Story Magazine*, the 'new' look is tailored and not...too bright."

I think the word she wanted was "flamboyant," but I didn't say so.

"I think that's a good idea," said Caroline. "Sometimes, although you always look nice, I think you maybe went a little overboard on the...um..."

"Spit it out, Caroline. I dressed like a...circus performer."

I'm pretty sure that wasn't the first descriptive noun that popped into her mind, but Caroline would likely have fainted if she'd said it out loud.

"I love your clothes," said Sue. "I have to wear white uniforms. Talk about boring."

"You're all lovely ladies," said Mrs. Buck, carrying the coffeepot into the dining room in search of empty cups. "And I'm glad you're going to tone it down, Miss Lulu. You're so pretty; you don't need all those flashy colors to look good."

"Really?" said Lulu, surprised. "You think so?"

"I know it, child," said Mrs. Buck firmly.

"Exactly," said Ernie.

Evidently, his word settled the matter, because no more was said about Lulu's wardrobe. I swear, women can suggest things from now until the cows come home—not that I know anything about cows—but once a man says the same thing, the conversation is over.

Anyhow, breakfast was great and, except for Ernie, who went outside to get my copy of the *Los Angeles Times* (I had it delivered every day), we all went upstairs to brush our teeth and change clothes. Well, except for Mrs. Buck, who went to the kitchen to wash up. Then I guess she'd do whatever she'd planned to do on this Saturday.

We joined Ernie downstairs around nine a.m. When he saw Lulu and me descend the staircase, he rose and walked over to us. Speaking softly, he said, "My car won't be ready until around noon, so let's see if we can find any of those poor women Smedley duped, if they still live at the addresses on the forms."

"Sounds like a good plan to me," I said.

"You guys are so nice to me," said Lulu.

Her voice sounded odd, so I told her perhaps too snappishly, "Don't you start crying again, Lulu LaBelle. You have a murder rap to beat, and we need you to be in tip-top shape."

"Mercy!" said Ernie, laughing. "Give the girl a break."

"No," said Lulu. "Mercy's right."

Right or wrong, I unlocked my office door and fetched my list of names along with my secretarial pad and a few pencils in case I had to take notes. While I was there, I also retrieved the sack of art supplies I'd purchased on Friday. "We'll have to stop by the home when we're in the area so I can give these things to Mr. Brentwood," I reminded Lulu and Ernie.

"One of these addresses is on Los Angeles Street," said Ernie. "We can go to the loony bin after we check that one out."

"I wish you wouldn't call it that," I grumbled.

"The home for itinerant eccentrics? That any better?" asked Ernie.

"A little," I told him. Lulu giggled, which was a step in the right direction.

"There's still a whole lot of paperwork in here," I said as we exited my office. "We should probably finish going through it. There might be more papers of interest."

"More poor girls who got tricked, you mean?" said Lulu.

"Probably, but maybe there's other stuff in there." An idea occurred to me. Happens a lot. "I mean, maybe Mr. Smedley had a huge life-insurance policy that would pay off when he died. That would give his missus a swell motive for doing him in. She wouldn't get much if she divorced him. Probably."

"There's a thought," said Ernie, making me feel validated, if that makes any sense.

"Huh. Never thought about stuff like insurance policies," said Lulu. "I figured somebody killed him because of his nasty dealings with young women."

"That might be true, too," said Ernie, who seemed to be validating everyone that morning.

We managed to get out of the house without anyone except Buttercup noticing, and I promised I'd take her for a walk later. I'm not sure she believed me.

We didn't have a whole lot of luck at first. Miss Sylvia Brown no longer lived at the boarding house on College Street. The rather formidable landlady who answered our knock claimed she didn't know where she went after she left her place.

"She wanted to be a *star*, don't you know," she said in a waspish tone. "They all do. Got herself involved with a man who claimed to be a talent scout, and I don't know what happened after that. She just up and left one day. Crying. I think the man did something to her."

"And you have no idea where she went when she left your boarding house?" Ernie asked.

I stood silent, pencil poised over my pad.

The landlady, Mrs. Groggins, shook her head. "No. She didn't leave a forwarding address." With a shrug, she said, "Never got mail anyway. A letter or two from someplace called Fresno. Think it's in California. Guess that's where she was from. If she had any brains, that's where she went when she left."

"And you can't think of any names of people she was close to when she lived here?"

Mrs. Groggins shook her head. "Kept herself to herself except when she went out with her *talent scout* fellow."

"Do you remember his name?" asked Lulu. Because she stood behind me and had been silent so far, she startled me but I tried not to show it.

"Lordy, that was almost a year ago," said Mrs. Groggins. "Can't remember. Farris? Fleming? I think it started with an F, anyway."

"Faraday?" asked Ernie.

After tilting her head to one side and then the other, I presume to jostle her brain into action, Mrs. Groggins said, "Might be. Sounds kind of familiar. But I can't say for sure. There are almost as many *talent scouts*"—she put a world of hateful meaning in the two words—"as there are innocent young gals wanting to be stars in Los Angeles these days."

"Yes," said Ernie. "There are. Well, thanks, Mrs. Groggins."

"You're welcome. Hope you find Sylvia and she's come to no harm. She was a nice girl."

So we went to the second address on our list—Ernie and Lulu, who knew more about L.A. than I did, had sorted out the addresses more or less geographically—and had no luck with the next name. Again, there was no forwarding address.

Same thing happened with the third name.

"This might be a waste of time," said Lulu as we walked back to the Roadster.

"And it might not be," said Ernie. "The private investigation business is often full of boring work, dead ends, and tramping around. Hard on the feet."

"It can also be rewarding, don't forget," I said, trying to pep up Lulu.

"You're right," said Lulu. "I'm sorry. You're doing this for me, after all."

"And for the sake of justice," I said

After several seconds of silence—well, except for street noises—the three of us burst out laughing.

We had better luck with the fourth name. A girl named Florence Mandrake still lived in a crummy boarding house on Temple Street. When we rang the doorbell, she actually answered it. She didn't look as if she were feeling well.

"Miss Mandrake?" Ernie said in a friendly voice.

"What do you want?" she said, making the words sound like a challenge.

"We'd like to speak to you for a minute or two if we may," he said, still friendly.

"About what?"

"Mr. Clint Faraday."

She tried to slam the door in our faces, but Ernie prevented her from doing so by sticking his foot in the door and pushing it. I'm glad he pushed it, too, or the little minx might have broken his foot. She was a small woman, but she seemed strong.

"I don't want to talk to you!" Miss Mandrake said in a furious whisper. "I don't know who that person is!"

Lulu stepped up to the door. She had to peer over Ernie's shoulder, as the door was only open a crack. "Listen, Miss Mandrake, he fooled me too. He was a miserable louse, and his name wasn't even Faraday. It was Smedley, and somebody murdered him the night before last. We're trying to find as many people as we can who had anything to do with him, and we know you did, because we found paperwork in his office."

"I don't want to talk to you," Miss Mandrake repeated in a voice that had begun to quiver.

"Please," said Lulu. "We need to gather as much information as we can about the guy, or *I'll* be charged with his murder. And I didn't do it!"

"You didn't?" asked Miss Mandrake, not as emotionally as before.

"No, I didn't. But he was a horrible person and, even though I honestly don't care who killed him because I'm glad he's dead, I don't want them to pin it on *me!*"

"Well," said Miss Mandrake, "I didn't kill him either."

"I'm sure you didn't, but we're gathering as much information as we can about the man and his practices," said Ernie. "We don't think you had anything to do with his murder, but we would like to talk to you about your dealings with him. Please. It won't take long, and the only people who will ever know about this conversation are the three of us and you. Unless, of course, your information leads us to the real killer."

Ernie's foot remained in the door, but Miss Mandrake was no longer trying to close it. After a couple of seconds, she stepped back. Ernie nobly suppressed his sigh of relief, but his face lost its pained expression.

"All right," said Miss Mandrake. "Come in. I still don't want to talk to you. But if you"—she nodded at Lulu—"were suckered by that man, too, I'll give you a few minutes."

"Thank you," said Lulu.

Miss Mandrake led us to what looked to me like a communal gathering place for tenants of the house. It seemed to serve the same function as the living room in my house, but it was nowhere near as cozy, comfortable, or inviting. The walls were a dirty white, the furniture sagged, and merely looking at it made me sad.

"Very well," said Miss Mandrake when we were seated, she on a sofa and the rest of us on chairs. "What do you want to know?"

Ernie started. "Lulu, why don't you tell Miss Mandrake your story? You might have had similar experiences, or perhaps Miss Mandrake was introduced to other men or women who might have a connection with the man and his racket."

"Racket," muttered Miss Mandrake. "Good word."

So Lulu told her story. As she spoke, Miss Mandrake nodded almost constantly. When Lulu reported running away from Smedley's office, Miss Mandrake looked miserable.

"Wish I'd done that," she said somberly. "But I didn't have wits enough. I still honestly thought he cared about me and wanted the best for me. He said he loved me."

"Good Lord, really?" said Lulu, amazed. "He said I looked like a whore!"

"I guess he didn't string you along for as long a time as he did me. He didn't try anything with me until he'd been…I don't know what you call it. Courting, is what they called it in my grandma's day. I honestly thought he was courting me. He paid me compliments, told me I was beautiful, took me out to eat, and said he knew he could make me a star."

"That's what he said to me, too," said Lulu unhappily. "But I think he thought I was a fallen woman when he met me. Guess he figured he didn't have to spend as much time and money on me as he did on you."

"He lied to both of us," said Miss Mandrake, also unhappily. "I didn't figure it out until he'd…Well, never mind." She sniffled a couple of times before bursting into tears. "I-I-I'm only lucky I didn't get pregnant!"

Lulu scooted from her chair, joined Miss Mandrake on the sofa, and put her arms around her. "Golly, kid, I'm so sorry!"

"M-me, too," whimpered Miss Mandrake.

"Are you still trying to find an agent or something?" I asked. "I mean, do you still want to get into the pictures?"

"No. I don't want anything to do with the flickers. All the people are horrible, and girls have to do awful things in order to get anywhere."

"I've heard that before," I said. Now *I* was unhappy. "But my brother-in-law isn't a bad man, and he owns Nash Studios."

"I've heard about him," said Miss Mandrake, alarming me. "But he's all right, according to the gossips. It's the people who pretend to be agents and talent scouts who are the bums."

Whew! My alarm bells quit clanging.

"Can you think of anyone else who could help us find out who might have hated Mr. Faraday enough to kill him?" asked Ernie, getting us back to the point.

"Me, for one," said Miss Mandrake. "But I'm not brave enough to do anything like that."

"It's a good thing you aren't," said Lulu. "That oaf wasn't worth going to prison for."

"True," said Miss Mandrake. "I knew one other girl who fell for his tall tales, but she moved back to Idaho. She hasn't lived in L.A. for six months or more."

"May we please have her name?" said Ernie gently. "Just so we can check her off the list we've been making. He fooled a lot of women."

"That's for sure," said Lulu.

Miss Mandrake gave us the name of a female whose file we hadn't found yet. I wrote it down, just so we could check to see if we had her folder in my office. If she was really in Idaho, however, she was out of the murder scenario.

We drove to a few other addresses to no avail, and finally, Ernie said, "I'm going to pick up my car. I'm tired of this. It's not getting us anywhere. But let's go to that Los Angeles Street address, and then we can take the art supplies to the loony bin."

"All right by me," I said. "I want to go through the rest of those folders. All we've found so far is photographs and women's names and addresses. I want to look in the folders not containing photos. Maybe we'll find what other dirty tricks Mr. Smedley was up to."

"Not sure it'll do any good," said Ernie. "The man's dead."

"I *know* he's dead, but maybe he's been blackmailing some of the women he seduced. Or maybe he's got seven other names he's used in seven other states or something."

"Hmm," said Ernie. "You have a point. Too bad we didn't collect all the folders in his office while we were there," said Ernie.

"We could go back and see if we can get into the office again," I said.

"I never want to see that place again," said Lulu.

"I don't think we ought to press our luck," said Ernie.

"You two are no fun," I said, only half-joking.

TWENTY-FIVE

We decided to have lunch before picking up Ernie's Packard and, since we were nearby, we chose Charley Wu's Noodle Shop in which to dine. The food was, as always, delicious.

As we plied our chopsticks, we chatted.

Lulu, who had seemed to be flagging as the morning progressed, finally said, "I know you want to get those pencils to the crazy fellow, but would you mind taking me home first? I'm about to fall over from exhaustion. I really need a nap."

"Of course!" I told her. While she no longer looked half-dead as she had on Friday, she still appeared worn to a nub.

"Okay by me," said Ernie. "We can drop you at home, take Mr. Monocle his art supplies, and then pick up my car."

"Brentwood, Ernie. His name is Brentwood, and I want to spend some time with him," I told them both, then turned to Ernie. "So if you don't want to stay there with me, we'd better pick up your car first."

"Why do you want to spend time with him?" asked Lulu. "He's kind of loopy."

"I don't think he's precisely loopy," I said, having pondered Mr. Brentwood and his peculiarities a lot in the past day or two. "I think he has trouble expressing himself in words. Maybe he has some kind of mental disorder, but he's not crazy. He's also a spectacular artist. I want to see if he can draw people as well as he can animals. If he can, maybe he can recall the faces of the people he saw on the sidewalk when Mr. Smedley was shoved. We can also show him some of those photographs to see if he recognizes any of the women in them. If he does, maybe he can duplicate them on paper."

Neither of my counter-mates spoke for enough seconds for me to wonder why they hadn't. I finally lifted my head from my noodle bowl to find them both staring at me.

"What?" I said. "What's wrong with asking him for help?"

Ernie heaved a huge sigh. "Not a thing," he said.

"Crumb," muttered Lulu. "Wish we'd done that first. Take my photo with you, too, okay? I know he didn't see me there when the truck hit Smedley, because I *wasn't* there."

"Oh, you mean you think it's a good idea?" I asked, feeling brighter than I probably was.

"I wish you'd had it sooner, actually," said Ernie. "Would have saved the soles of our shoes and a lot of gas."

"Oh." Now I felt guilty. "Well, I did think of it earlier, but I wasn't sure if it was a good idea or not."

"It's a great idea," said Ernie.

Feeling better about the day, I said, "I'm glad you think so. We can pick up more photos while we're at my house."

"Make sure you write names on the backs of them," said Lulu. "If he recognizes somebody, you want to know who it is."

"Right," I said.

"Will do," agreed Ernie.

So we did. After Charley Wu hadn't taken money from any of us when we finished eating our delicious pork and noodles—not sure about Ernie, but I was starting to feel guilty about not paying for meals—we drove Lulu home. Everyone else was gone. Except, of course, for Buttercup, who naturally assumed I was there to take her for a walk.

"Oh, Buttercup, I'm so sorry!" I told her after I unlocked my office, feeling dreadfully guilty. Kneeling down to speak lovingly to her, I went on, "I'll have to take you for a walk later, though. Is that all right with you?"

"Mercy," said Lulu, heading for the stairs. She was really dragging by then. "You make me laugh."

"Well, but I promised her," I said in my own defense.

"Cripes, Mercy, Buttercup is a nice dog, but she's a dog, not a baby," said Ernie, chuckling at me.

"She's my baby," I said, picking up my lovely apricot-colored poodle and giving her a hug, which she evidently didn't appreciate a whole lot as she squirmed madly. "And she needs a good clipping." My brain stopped functioning for a second and then swerved onto a whole 'nother road. "Say, I wonder if that pet store near Mr. Smedley's office has a pet-grooming service."

With a shrug, Ernie said, "Dunno. We can find out after we talk to Mr. What's his name—"

"Brentwood," I said with some exasperation.

"Yeah, Mr. Brentwood. Then we can pick up my car."

"I thought you said it would be ready by now," I said, carefully putting Buttercup on the pretty Oriental rug in my office. She didn't seem to be unduly upset by my not offering to take her for a walk instantly. "Don't you want to get it now?"

"That's what Hank told me. Maybe we'd better pick up the Packard first, and then drive back to Los Angeles Street and Mr. Brentwood."

"If you want to. Or you can telephone Mr. Wu and say you won't be able to pick up your automobile until later in the day."

"He probably doesn't care," said Ernie.

"But it would be the polite thing to do," I reminded him. "Especially since everyone in Chinatown seems to be feeding you for free these days."

"Yeah, you're right," said Ernie.

So, while I searched for photographs of fully clothed women—I didn't want to shock Mr. Brentwood—Ernie telephoned Wu Han's Service Station and Body Shop and told whoever answered the call that he'd be in late to pick up his Packard. He spoke a bit of Cantonese to whoever was on the other end of the wire.

"How much Cantonese do you know?" I asked when he'd hung up the receiver.

"About as much Spanish as I know."

"And how much is that?"

"Not much," he said. "Need any help?"

"Why don't you go through that one last stack? The one on the chair over there." I indicated the chair and stack of papers I meant. "I've just about finished here. I've written the names of the girls on the backs of their photos. Smedley sure went through a lot of women. I'm glad he's dead."

"Yeah. I'm sure a lot of people are," said Ernie, shuffling through the papers in the stack I'd mentioned. "Hey, look at this," he said, lifting a paper from the pile.

"What is it?"

"It's a marriage certificate, uniting Mr. Felix Smedley in holy matrimony with Miss Harriet Bowlus."

"Is Mrs. Smedley's first name Harriet?"

"Don't remember," said Ernie. "But here's another one."

"Another one what?" I asked, confused.

"Another marriage certificate. This one unites Mr. Felix Smedley with Miss Mary Williams."

"What?" I put down the stack of photos I'd been compiling and walked to the chair where Ernie stood plucking papers.

"And this unites Mr. Felix Smedley with Miss Verna Wilson."

"That's her name," I said.

"Whose name?" asked Ernie.

"Mrs. Smedley's."

"Which Mrs. Smedley? Evidently, there are several of them."

"Our Mrs. Smedley. The one who hired you to find out if her husband was running around on her."

"Looks like he was running around on more than just one wife. Unless there are some divorce papers in here somewhere."

He handed me the three marriage certificates. I read the first one. "He and Harriet were married in Chicago," I said. "He and Mary were married in Nevada. He and Verna were wed here in Los Angeles."

"Here's another one," said Ernie, his voice holding a quality of astonishment I had never heard before. "Good Lord, the man married someone named Virginia Harkrider in New York City."

"He's a...what would you call him?"

"A son of a bitch," said Ernie.

"Aside from that. I mean, he's more than a bigamist. He's a quadrupist. Or another word along those lines."

"I don't think there's a word for it," said Ernie.

"I think you're right." I took the other marriage certificate from Ernie. "Are there any more of these in there? Or any other legal documents? Maybe he got divorced from three of these women, and he's not a quadrupist after all."

"I don't see any other legal stuff in here. Oh. Except for this." He shook out a thick wad of papers he'd withdrawn from a large brown envelope. "It's an insurance policy."

"Ha! Maybe that's why his latest missus killed him!" I said.

"It's on her, not him," said Ernie.

"I beg your pardon?"

"It's an insurance policy he took out on her. Verna, I mean. Cripes, I wonder where the rest of his wives are now?"

"What do you...? Oh, my Lord, do you think he killed them all for the insurance money?"

"I have absolutely no idea," said Ernie. "Crumb. How the devil can we find out?"

"Um...I don't know." I stood in my office with four marriage certificates in my hands, pondering how one man could get four different women to marry him. And how he could get so many young women, like Lulu, to believe he was a legitimate talent scout. After several fuddled moments, I asked, "How old does it say Mr. Smedley is? Was?"

"Well, it says here on this insurance form that he was born on August 4, 1881."

"So that would make him..." I tried to do the math in my head, but my brain was swirling with marriage certificates.

"Forty-five," said Ernie.

"Gee, he was pretty old to be seducing young women like Lulu, wasn't he?" I said.

"Cripes, Mercy, forty-five isn't all that old. Lots of men look good at forty-five. Lots of women do, too."

"Really? I don't know how old my father is, but he sure doesn't look good to me."

With a laugh, Ernie said, "I'm glad of that. But if you want to get those art supplies to Mr. Brentwood, we should probably do that pretty soon. Have you been through all the photographs?"

"Yes, and I've found several women's photos whom I can identify, so I wrote their names on the backs."

"Good. Take the pictures you've identified, and let's go. We can look through more of this paperwork later."

"Very well," I said. "This case is getting more complicated by the second, Ernie. I don't like it."

"I don't either," he said.

So, after bidding Buttercup another farewell and feeling guilty some more, we went out to the Roadster, Ernie got behind the wheel, and we took off back to Los Angeles Street and Mr. Brentwood's home. Honestly, I don't know how the fellow managed to escape it so often. It looked positively impenetrable from the outside. After we went through the necessary rigmarole, a fellow in a uniform came out and unlocked the gate for us.

As the three of us walked to the huge white building, the uniformed fellow said, "I hear you're bringing some supplies to our resident artist. That's very nice of you."

"I was surprised by how well Mr. Brentwood can draw," I said. "Do you know if he can draw portraits?"

"Have no idea. He likes drawing rabbits and birds and other animals. That time he got out and went to the library, we finally figured out he went there to look at books with animal pictures in them."

"Really? I can get him some books with pictures of animals in them," I said, thinking a trip to the bookstore would probably be advisable, not merely to get children's books for my soon-to-be-born niece or nephew, but for Mr. Brentwood as well.

"He's already got a lot of them," said the man. "He just wanted to see some he hadn't looked at yet, I guess."

"Interesting," said Ernie.

"He's an interesting guy," said the other man. I never did learn his name.

When we entered the place, we visited Mrs. Wilkes in her office first. She was pleased to see us and was overjoyed that I'd kept my promise to Mr. Brentwood.

"You're all he's been able to talk about since he came home yesterday," she said. "He's so excited to see the colored wax pencils you mentioned."

"I got two boxes of them for him, in case he runs out. And I bought four big artists' pads."

"You're extremely kind, Miss Allcutt."

"Nonsense," I said, embarrassed. "I like Mr. Bentwood, and I feel bad for him because he has such a difficult time making himself understood."

With a sigh, Mrs. Wilkes said, "Yes, he does. I wouldn't say he's in any way insane, but there's probably a condition from which he suffers that doctors haven't identified yet. I know there are others like him, because I've seen two other cases. In those cases, though, the sufferers weren't as well able to function in other areas of life as is Mr. Brentwood."

"Interesting," I said. "I don't think Mr. Brentwood is crazy, either. He just can't quite make his brain form proper explanations. Or something like that."

With a chuckle, Mrs. Wilkes said, "Something like that indeed." She rose from her desk and said, "Why don't you come with me? I believe Mr. Brentwood is in the garden. He likes to sit out there even when the weather is chilly, as it is today."

So Ernie and I went with her. She led us down the hallway from her office. I noticed there were pretty pictures on the walls. A few nurse-type people were wheeling infirm tenants of the home here and there. About halfway down the hall—halfway to a door in another wall, I probably should say—she turned right and led us to a pretty area that might have been termed a lobby or an atrium. From there, two glass doors led to a huge garden area.

"He likes to sit in the winter garden at this time of year."

"Do you have gardeners who take care of the grounds?" I asked.

"Believe it or not, while we do have gardeners, many of our guests like to help care for the garden. Mr. Brentwood isn't a gardener, but he loves to sit outside and look at the flowers."

"Are there flowers blooming this time of year?" asked Ernie, who sounded surprised.

"Yes," said Mrs. Wilkes. She went on to explain, "Nasturtiums, snapdragons, pansies, and calendula often bloom in our mild winters. And stock, which smells heavenly. Mr. Brentwood is particularly fond of stock."

"I had no idea," said Ernie.

"I didn't either," I said. I knew Mr. and Mrs. Buck tended a vegetable garden and that Mr. Buck was proud of the rose bed he'd just created. I'd never heard of a bare-root rosebush until he asked if I'd like a rose garden in the backyard. Naturally, I'd said yes. He'd cleared an area for a rose bed and planted several rosebushes in it, but so far nothing had bloomed.

Sure enough, as soon as Mrs. Wilkes led us outside and into a patio area, we saw Mr. Brentwood sitting on a bench several yards away. He had what looked like a plaid blanket wrapped around his shoulders and his attention was fixed on a pretty garden full of plants flowering like mad. In the middle of January, for Pete's sake! Crumb. Where I came from, there was still snow on the ground and nothing grew except children, and then only if they were lucky.

"Golly," said Ernie, using the mildest term in his vocabulary, "that's a pretty garden. There's still ten feet of snow in Chicago, where I'm from."

"Ten feet?" I said, shocked.

"Exaggeration, Mercy," he said in a pitying voice.

"Oh. Well, good. I'm sure there's still snow on the ground in Boston, too, but we rarely get ten feet of it."

"I'm from the San Diego area," said Mrs. Wilkes. "If I want to see snow—and I don't—I have to drive up into the mountains."

Because we all knew how Mr. Brentwood hated to be startled, we walked a long way around the blooming winter garden so that we could approach him from the front and not the back. His gaze was fixed with fascination on the various flowering plants, but he saw us eventually, smiled, and rose to his feet.

"Mrs. Wilkes. Miss Allcutt. Mr. Templeton," he said, getting all of us in.

"How do you do, Mr. Brentwood? I've brought you some colored wax pencils and some paper for you to draw on."

"Oh. Oh, oh, *thank* you, Miss Allcutt. You're nice. Mrs. Wilkes is nice. Mr. Templeton is nice. That other lady is nice. I like her better in red."

Another endorsement of Lulu, who was *not* a murderess.

"I think you're nice, too, Mr. Brentwood," I told him. "Would you like to take these colored pencils and the paper indoors so you can begin to use them? It's a little breezy out here." Not to mention cold.

"Yes. No. Yes. Yes. Yes. Thank you."

So we all walked together back inside the home, and Mr. Brentwood led us to his apartment, where he had a snug sitting room with a couple of doors leading to, I presumed, a bathroom and a bedroom. This place really was a first-class establishment. If I ever had to be confined to a loony bin, I hoped it would be like this one.

"Where would you like to look at these?" I asked him when we walked into his sitting room.

"Desk. Table. Desk. Table."

"Here," I said, taking the matter into my own hands. "Why don't I set them down on this nice desk here?" And I did. The desk sat against a wall, and it had an electric lamp on it with a lovely shade. It might even have been made by Mr. Tiffany. I'd seen his work back east before.

"Yes. Yes. Thank you. Miss Allcutt. Thank you. Miss Allcutt."

"You're welcome, Mr. Brentwood."

I pulled a pad from my bag and laid it on the desk. Then I put a box of wax pencils on the desk next to the pad. Mr. Brentwood pulled out the desk chair, sat in it, and instantly opened the box of Crayolas. He stared into the box for about infinity and a half, but he eventually took the wax pencils out of the box, one at a time, and set them on the desk with their points facing the wall right above the blank white paper on the pad.

"Do you like them?" I asked tentatively, as silence seemed to stretch out forever.

"Like? Like? Like?" he said. "Yes. Yes. Love them."

Whew!

TWENTY-SIX

After the guard unlocked the main gate of the home for us so we could return to my Roadster and pick up Ernie's Packard, a disgruntled Ernie griped, "Well, hell, that didn't accomplish anything."

"It did too," I told him, although I have to admit to being a trifle disappointed myself.

"Yeah? What did it accomplish?"

"It made Mr. Brentwood happy. And he gave me some beautiful pictures to show Chloe."

"That sure was my goal," grumbled Ernie.

"But all isn't yet lost," I said as I struggled in my mind to climb over a boulder of disappointment and reach for something helpful.

"No? Seems like it to me. I don't think your Mr. Brentwood is going to be able to help us, Mercy. You did something really nice for the poor guy, but I think about all you're going to get for it is a feeling of virtue and some pretty pictures."

"Applesauce. He thinks of us as friends now. And we can compile more photos and take them back tomorrow to see if he can remember any faces."

"We also have to go through the rest of the pile of documents," said Ernie. "So far we've found records of a whole lot of women he fooled, but I think it's the marriage certificates and the insurance documents that are going to help us most of all."

"You may well be right." Another thought struck me, kind of like a blow to the side of my head with a baseball bat. "You know whom we should talk to?"

"No," said Ernie sarcastically. "Whom should we talk to?"

"It's actually to whom we should talk, but never mind that. We ought to talk to Mrs. Smedley. The latest one. Verna, your client."

"The one who smashed my fender?"

"Precisely. If she learned about any of her late husband's other wives and knows *we* know about them and the insurance policy, maybe she'll cooperate with us."

"Seems to me she's the most likely killer," said Ernie as we reached the Roadster and he held the passenger door open for me to climb in.

I waited until he got to the driver's side and entered the machine before saying, "According to Mr. Brentwood, there were two women on the sidewalk and a bad man. The bad man hit one of the women and got pushed into the street for his efforts. Maybe neither of the women he saw during the altercation was guilty of murder, but it was just a big, fat accident."

"How the devil can we prove any of that?"

"There's no need to sound so vexed, Ernie Templeton. After we pick up your Packard, come back to my house. We need to go through the rest of those papers."

"You're right," said Ernie unenthusiastically. "Sounds like a fun afternoon."

"It'll probably take all evening," I pointed out. "And I don't know what to do with the pile of clothing."

"Throw it out would be my suggestion."

"Fiddlesticks. We have to figure this whole thing out before the L.A.P.D. decides the case is too complicated for them to deal with and arrests Lulu for murder."

"Rob doesn't think they have enough evidence against Lulu." After a second Ernie added, "Although there's that key to Smedley's door she found in her handbag."

"Indeed. The key someone planted there."

We'd arrived at Wu Han's service station and Ernie pulled up to the office. After he shut off the Roadster's engine, he turned to me. "You don't think there's any chance at all that Lulu really *did* shove the guy in front of that truck, do you?"

"What?" I stared at him. "No! She didn't! Ernie, when she came home two nights—well, mornings—ago, she was terrified. That man had tried to...ravage her! She ran away from him, precisely as she said she had. I don't know what happened after that, but it didn't involve Lulu!"

"All right, all right. I believe you. And Lulu." He shook his head and shoved his door open.

I exited the car too and walked to the driver's side. "I wish I could have taken a picture of Lulu that night," I told Ernie. "You'd have believed her too."

"I do believe her. And you," he said as he walked to the office door. A Chinese man saw him and opened the door to greet him. Then both men walked to Ernie's Packard.

Golly, they'd not only taken the crunch out of the fender, but they'd smoothed it out and painted it, too. You'd never know the car had been hit. If I ever needed to get a car fixed, I knew where I'd take it. However, unlike Ernie, who was holding his wallet and arguing with the Chinese man who was shaking his head adamantly and waving his hands, palms down in front of him, I would have to pay for them to fix it. Shrugging in defeat, Ernie finally shoved his wallet back into his trouser pocket and got into his automobile.

When he'd driven over to my Roadster and rolled down his window, he said, "Let's go to your place."

"All right by me," I said.

So we both drove to my place. By then the afternoon was well advanced, and Lulu had awakened from her nap. She and Buttercup greeted us at the door.

"Feel any better?" I asked as I knelt to pet Buttercup.

"I'm not as exhausted as I was, but I'm every bit as worried as I was," she said, sounding it.

She stepped back so Ernie and I could enter.

"We're going to go through the rest of the paperwork we took from Mr. Smedley's office," I told her as I hung up my coat and put my hat on the shelf. "So far it looks as if he's been married four times, and we didn't find any divorce paperwork."

"We have to inspect everything we took from Smedley's office," said Ernie. "The guy was a piece of work, but we still don't know who shoved him in front of that truck."

"It wasn't me."

"We know that, Lulu," I said. Then I looked down at my adorable, fluffy dog. "Before we start shuffling through that junk in my office again, does anybody want to go for a walk with Buttercup and me? I need to clear my head."

"Of what?" asked Ernie. He would.

"Of clutter and evil people. I'm sick of thinking about Mr. Smedley and his cruelty to women. There must be a way to figure out who did what to whom. So far we've found four marriage certificates and an insurance policy *he* took out on *her*. There's something wrong about this whole thing."

"No. Really?" said Ernie, being sarcastic again.

I didn't appreciate his sarcasm one little bit. "Yes. Really," I snapped.

"Wait a minute," said Lulu, sounding confused, which made sense. "Four marriage certificates, no divorce records, and an insurance policy on her? His *wife*? His *now* wife?"

"Yes."

"Golly," Lulu whispered. "You're right. Something's really screwy."

"Aw, cripes," said Ernie. "All right. Let's all bundle up and take Buttercup for a walk. Maybe one of us will think of a brilliant solution to this problem as we walk. In the freezing weather."

"It's not freezing," I said, grabbing for my coat again. "Lulu, get a coat or something. Ernie, stay here."

"Yes, ma'am," said Ernie, saluting me. I didn't appreciate that, either, darn it.

"Nertz to you, Mr. Templeton," I said.

Lulu actually giggled a bit before she took off for the stairs in order to fetch her coat and hat. Buttercup and I walked through the house to the utility porch where her leash and collar hung. Buttercup was ecstatic, which made me happier than I'd been for days. It's amazing what dogs can do for a person's mood.

Buttercup, Lulu, Ernie, and I all gathered in the tiled entryway of my home shortly thereafter, and we went for a walk. Buttercup was absolutely thrilled to be taking a walk through our nice neighborhood with three of her favorite people. She watered plants here and there, barked at a cat, wagged her stubby tail at a couple of other dogs and their humans, and just had a great old time.

After we'd been walking for quite a while without talking, Ernie began to speak in a musing sort of voice. "You know, Mercy, you might have had a good idea when you suggested talking to Mrs. Smedley."

"You want to talk to *her*?" said Lulu, shocked.

"It occurred to me, yes. But we need to finish going through the mess in my office first. If she found out about her husband's other wives and that insurance policy, she might have…I don't know."

"She might have killed him?" said Lulu.

"Well, maybe. But maybe she just confronted him and things got out of hand. According to Mr. Brentwood, there were two women involved in the incident that ended with Smedley being run over by a truck—and a good thing, if you ask me. Maybe one of his other wives hunted him down."

"And she and the latest Mrs. Smedley did him in?" asked Ernie.

"Maybe. Maybe not," I said. "The whole Smedley death scenario is crazy. I wish Mr. Brentwood had been able to help us today."

"He wasn't?" Lulu sounded disappointed.

"He was so excited about his new Crayolas and paper, we couldn't get through to him about the Smedley-truck incident," I told her.

"He was so busy drawing animals, he didn't draw any people," Ernie told her.

"Can he draw people?" said Lulu.

Shaking my head and beginning to feel vexed once more, I said, "I don't know. He's a wonderful artist. If he can draw animals, maybe he can draw people. Not sure how good his memory is, either, although he was disturbed enough by the scene on that sidewalk that he sought out Ernie's office. I mean, he remembered where it was and what Ernie did for a living."

"That's one way to put it," said Ernie.

"He did!" I insisted. "You weren't there when he came in yesterday. Before you got there, he told us he'd seen something that had upset him, and then he described a fight on a sidewalk featuring a bad man and two women, and then he said the man got pushed into the street and got hit by a big truck. Then he said there was a big mess in the street."

"Yeah. I remember him saying something like that," said Ernie.

"It's kind of difficult to keep up with his train of thought, but he has one and it works. It just veers off track sometimes."

"A whole lot of the time," said Ernie.

"Yeah," said Lulu. "I don't think the coppers would take his word for anything."

"No," I said, "They probably wouldn't. But perhaps we can find someone who can verify what he saw. That's why I was contemplating talking to Mrs. Smedley."

"Huh," said Lulu. "Well, if we all work on it, we can probably finish going through everything we took from his office tonight."

"Boy, I'm really looking forward to doing that," I said, lying through my teeth.

"Got anything at your house to eat for supper?" asked Ernie, the practical.

"Um…I don't know. Mrs. Buck generally has bread available. Not sure what else is in the Frigidaire."

"You and your tenants are on your own for dinners on Saturday? How do you survive?"

"Generally by making a cheese sandwich," said Lulu. "Or a chicken or ham sandwich. Soup. Whatever's left over from whatever Mrs. Buck cooked last."

"Precisely," I said. "Mrs. Buck always has food available for us to eat. Nothing fancy, but that's okay."

"Yeah. It works out fine," agreed Lulu.

"Do your other tenants dine with you on Saturdays?" Ernie asked.

"Sometimes," I said. "Not always. They know the house rules, and they can both cut bread." They could cut bread a whole lot better than I could, in truth, but I didn't tell Ernie that.

"Yeah. We get along just fine," said Lulu. "At the boardinghouse I lived in before Mercy, the landlady gave us meals for breakfast and dinner every day, but they were lousy. Mrs. Buck's a good cook. She's a heck of a lot better than any of the other cooks I've met in my life in L.A."

"I know she is," said Ernie. "I'm not disparaging anyone, just wondering what we can eat for supper."

"Are you hungry?" I asked him. Seemed to me as though we'd just had lunch, although I guess it was later than that.

"Naw. Just asked. If there's nothing much to eat at your place, I can go to Philippe's and pick up sandwiches."

"Oh, I like their sandwiches," said Lulu.

"Me too," I agreed. "So dinner's taken care of. Any other questions, Mr. Templeton?"

"No, but I like to make sure about these important things."

"Right," I said. "Let's go home. I think Buttercup has had a long-enough walk, and I want to finish sorting through Mr. Smedley's papers. If we find anything interesting, how the heck are you going to tell Phil? You can't admit we stole stuff from Smedley's office, can you?"

"No. I've been wondering the same thing."

"Great," said Lulu. "If we find a written confession, does that mean the police can't use it?"

"Why would we find a written confession?" asked Ernie.

"*I* don't know," Lulu snapped. "But if we find all the evidence in the world that I didn't kill him, what good will it do me if we can't tell the police about it?"

"We'll probably just learn more about what a stinker Mr. Smedley was," I said. "We can figure out strategies after we get the goods on him."

"Right," said Ernie.

"If you say so," said Lulu, sounding unhappy.

I didn't blame her. She was suspected of having committed a

heinous crime. Well, it would have been heinous if Mr. Smedley hadn't been heinous all by himself. Whoever killed him did the world a favor.

Golly, that doesn't sound very nice, does it?

Well, never mind. We turned around and went back home. Buttercup seemed satisfied that I'd finally kept my promise to her.

TWENTY-SEVEN

When we got home again, Sue and Caroline were there too. Buttercup bounded to the living room to say hi to them as Lulu, Ernie, and I hung our coats on the rack and put our hats on the shelf in the entryway.

"Where'd you guys go?" asked Sue, who leaned over a hat box she'd set on a table in the living room and seemed to be showing Caroline its contents.

"Just took Buttercup for a walk," I said. "Did you get a new hat?"

"Yes!" said Sue happily. "Look. I went to that hat shop on Broadway. Near the Woolworth's there."

Ernie, Lulu, and I exchanged various glances. Evidently, the entire population of Los Angeles had been on one part or another of Broadway in the last few days.

"It's really pretty. And it will go with that nice blue suit you bought when you visited your parents at Christmas," said Caroline.

"Let's see," said Lulu, whose attention was easily captured by fashions.

Ernie and I strolled over to the hat box after Lulu. Sue lifted the hat out of the box. It was quite pretty: a beige cloche with a small brim, a beige band, and a blue flower. Dressier than one would wear to work, but perfect for visiting her parents, who lived in Riverside and whom she didn't see very often. Caroline, on the other hand, visited her parents every weekend. They only lived a short trolley ride away, in Alhambra. She went to church with them every Sunday too.

"Very nice," I said. "And it looks as if you can change the flower on it, depending on what color you're wearing."

"Exactly," said Sue, satisfied with her purchase. "I even went to Woolworth's and got a couple more flowers. The way it is now, I can wear it with my blue suit. I also got a white flower and a yellow one." She shot a glance at Lulu. "I didn't get a red one because I don't wear red very often."

"I won't either anymore," said Lulu firmly. "That's nice, Sue. Good for you. Mind if I ask how much it cost?"

"Not at all! It cost a dollar and a half."

"That's not bad," said Lulu. She turned to me. "We didn't make it to the consignment shop today, so we'll have to go on Monday, I guess. Mind if I borrow clothes from you again in the meantime?"

"Feel free," I told her.

"Thanks, Mercy."

"You're more than welcome."

"Well, this is nice," said Ernie, bored. "But how about we do some work, you two?"

"Right," I said. "Let's get to it. What time is it, anyway?"

Ernie shook his jacket sleeve down to look at his wristwatch. "Five-thirty."

"That late? I guess we've done a lot today, haven't we?" I unlocked my office door.

"Yeah," said Ernie. "We did a lot, but I'm not sure how much we accomplished."

"We seem to accomplish more going through Mr. Smedley's junk than walking around visiting people," I said. And we'd spent so *very* much time driving and walking and knocking on doors, too. "Oh well. Let's hope we discover more information now."

"I'm not sure I want to know," said Lulu. Then she said, "What am I saying? Yes, I do! I want to find out what that creature did and who he did it to. There must be women all over L.A. who wanted him dead. Heck, all over the U.S. of A."

"I think you're right," I said, refraining from correcting her grammar. I did a whole lot of refraining sometimes.

"Yeah," said Ernie with a discouraged sigh as he gazed at my still-messy office.

"It's not quite as daunting a task as it seemed yesterday," I said, sounding more hopeful than confident.

"If you say so," said Ernie. "Why don't I finish going through that pile where I discovered the wedding certificates and insurance papers?"

"Good idea." I glanced at the heap of women's things in the far corner of my office. "Lulu, maybe we should go through that clothing and decide if anything's of use to your case. If an item is relevant, we can log it in on my pad and keep it in a separate pile. If it isn't, we can give it to a charity somewhere."

"There are lots of them in Los Angeles," said Lulu. "The Salvation Army is always asking for donations."

"Good. They help people, too, so that's a great idea."

Sitting in my desk chair, Ernie pulled a stack of folders and papers in front of him and began picking them up and looking at each one.

"There's something on this one," said Lulu, picking up a pair of ladies' drawers. "Oh, ew, I think it's blood."

I squinted at the stain. "I think you're right."

"This probably means he raped a poor girl and kept the evidence," said Lulu. "I'm so glad I got away from him!"

"Me too," I told her. After considering the frilly, stained drawers for a moment, I said, "Let's log that one in. I don't suppose there's any way of knowing to whom they belonged."

"How are you going to log it in?" asked Lulu.

It was a sensible question, and one I'd thought of myself. "I'll just write a brief description and...crumb. I don't know how many we'll be logging in. I suppose we should number them. Maybe with sewing pins and little pieces of paper? Um, I don't have any sewing pins."

"I do, and that's a good idea," said Lulu.

So she exited the office, went upstairs, and came down with several papers with sewing pins stuck in them.

"Thanks, Lulu. I should probably get some of those for when I need to mend things, huh?"

"You haven't had to mend anything since you moved to L.A.?" asked Lulu, sounding surprised.

"I hate to admit it, but Mrs. Buck always mends things for me."

"Moneybags," said Ernie from behind his pile of papers.

"Idler," I retorted. Then I relented. "Okay, you're not an idler, but you're perennially casual."

"A sin, for sure," said Ernie.

Lulu and I went back to sorting and logging various pieces of ladies' underthings. It took a long time, and we didn't find much of interest. We did come to the conclusion that Mr. Smedley was a deplorable human being who treated women like dirt, but we already knew that.

"Oh, look here," said Ernie after several silent minutes.

"What?" asked Lulu.

I'd been busy shoving underwear into an old canvas sack I'd found folded and tucked away in the utility room. I'd find some charity to which I could donate them. I glanced up from my task to see Ernie holding a brown notebook. He had a strange expression on his face. "What's that?" I asked.

"Evidently, Smedley kept records of his conquests. Listen to this: *Verna's becoming a real pest. Got an insurance policy on her. Maybe she can fall out a window or something. Got a live wire on the hook this time. Won't have to spend a lot on her. Calls herself—*" He stopped suddenly.

When he didn't resume, I thought I knew why. I only wished he hadn't started reading aloud.

Lulu caught on, too. "She calls herself Lulu LaBelle? Is that what the stinker wrote?"

"I'm sorry, Lulu. I hadn't read the whole thing before I began reading it to you two."

"It's all right," said Lulu. "I know what a fool I was. At least now I know I'm not the only one."

"Do you really think he was contemplating throwing his wife out a window?" I asked, although I don't know why I was surprised. The man was a cad, a louse, and a cockroach. Nothing he did or planned to do should shock me.

"Don't know. But I also found one more marriage certificate."

"Good Lord," I muttered, "So that makes him a quintomist?"

"Is that word?" asked Lulu.

"Is now," said Ernie.

"Do you know if the police ever bothered to search his office?" I asked.

"Don't know," said Ernie. "But maybe Rob does. Okay if I use your telephone, Mercy?"

"Of course it is."

So Ernie telephoned his friend Robert Gabriel, the lawyer. From the side of the conversation Lulu and I could hear, it sounded as if Mr. Gabriel had actually been doing research into Lulu's case, which made me feel a little less annoyed with him.

Finally, Ernie said, "All right. Thanks, Rob." He hung up the receiver and looked at Lulu and me. "Nope. They haven't bothered."

"Why the heck haven't they?" I asked Ernie.

"They think they already have a couple of good suspects in Lulu and Mrs. Smedley. After you get all that stuff logged and bagged and I finish going through this mess, I think we're going to take it all back to Smedley's office. Rob is going to put pressure on Phil to get a warrant to search the office. Rob will be sure he's there when they go through the place so they don't accidentally lose anything important."

"What about all the records we've got?" I asked, not particularly wanting my efforts to go to waste.

"Don't worry. Rob will make good use of them."

"He will?" said Lulu, frowning. "How?"

"He'll pretend they're his after he goes through Smedley's office with the coppers. Everything you wrote down, he can use in Lulu's defense case."

"This is so stupidly complicated," I said, grumpy. "If Phil and his gang had done their job in the first place, we wouldn't have had to steal this junk."

"True, but at least we know the cops didn't find it first and now have it hidden under desks, stuffed into cardboard boxes that will never be opened again because they don't want to complicate their lives with more suspects. We now *know* what Smedley was up to."

"I already told you what he was up to," said Lulu.

"You're just lucky you managed to get away from him," said Ernie. "He clearly wasn't nearly as benevolent as your experience would have people believe."

"*Benevolent!*" I screeched on Lulu's behalf.

Holding up a hand, Ernie said, "Irony is wasted on you, Mercy."

I said, "Oh."

Along about seven that evening, Lulu and I finally finished going through the pile of women's clothing. Most of what we'd found and logged were benign, but a few of the things had what seemed to be bloodstains on them. So those we pinned tags on and kept. Ernie would have to ask Mr. Gabriel what he wanted to do with them. Ernie had read through two of Smedley's diaries. He didn't read us further passages from them, and I was glad of it.

"Ick," I said after I stuffed the last frilly brassiere into the canvas sack, "I'm glad the man's dead. He was a louse." I kind of wished I didn't know there were people like Mr. Smedley in the world.

Then I took myself to task. One of the major reasons I'd left my ivory tower in Boston and moved to Los Angeles was to learn about the real world and write about the mean streets. Still and all, I wished the streets weren't quite *so* mean.

"Yeah, he was," said Ernie. "How about we go to Philippe's? I'm hungry. Or would you rather I go out and bring sandwiches back here?"

After exchanging a couple of looks, Lulu and I both said, "Let's go out."

So we did. Even at past seven o'clock on a cold winter evening— cold by Los Angeles's standards—Philippe's was a busy place.

We each got a French dip sandwich, which is a sandwich you dip into a cup of stuff that looks like meat juice. Ernie got an order of potato salad and three forks, so we each ate some of that, too. It was delicious.

After we ate and went back to my place, Ernie telephoned Mr.

Gabriel again and told him what our search had produced. I heard an exclamation on the other end of the wire, but I couldn't make out any words.

"So," said Ernie after Mr. Gabriel had quit exclaiming. "We aim to put all this stuff back in Smedley's office, and *you* make sure Phil gets a search warrant. You go with him. Hell, I'll go with him, too. I don't want any of Phil's incompetent uniforms to miss anything."

I didn't hear anything but rumbles coming from Mr. Gabriel's end of the wire, but evidently whatever he said got Ernie's approval. "Will do. Want to go with me tomorrow to put the stuff back, or do you want Mercy, Lulu, and me to do it tonight? We have full records of everything. I'll fill you in tomorrow."

Rumble, rumble.

"We'll use the key from Lulu's handbag," said Ernie, grinning at Lulu, who stuck her tongue out at him. After a comment from Mr. Gabriel, Ernie said, "We don't know. Lulu sure as hell doesn't know. It's possible Mrs. Smedley put on a big show for us yesterday and she's the one who planted the key. Or maybe it was her brother."

Rumble, rumble.

"Yeah," said Ernie, grinning. "You too. See you tomorrow." He hung up the receiver and sighed heavily. Turning to Lulu and me, he said, "Okay. Rob and I will return all this junk tomorrow."

"Are you going to put it back in the drawers?" I wanted to know. "That might be difficult."

"No. Why bother? The police haven't considered the place worth searching so far. For all they'll know, Smedley left it the way they'll find it."

"But you'll try to be kind of neat?" I said in a small voice.

"We won't just dump it on the floor," Ernie promised. "That might look a little suspicious, even to L.A. coppers."

"Good," I said.

"After Rob and I go to Smedley's office—I think we should go early in the morning—and return this paperwork, do you want to go with me to Mrs. Smedley's place? I actually have a reason other than her husband's death to talk to her, you know."

"You do?" said Lulu.

"She's his client," I said. "Oh, well done, Ernie! And tomorrow's Sunday, so she'll probably be at home. She doesn't strike me as a fervent church-goer."

"Unlike you and Lulu," said Ernie.

"We went to church together for a while," I said. As I'd been forced to attend church every Sunday of my life when I was growing up, I still felt a trifle guilty for not attending church services in Los Angeles. Not guilty enough to try to find a church I wanted to attend, but still....

"I think we should tell her something akin to the truth," said Ernie. "We know he was at least a bigamist, so there are more women than merely Lulu and she who hated him."

"Oh, that should make her feel swell," said Lulu.

"Don't you start feeling sorry for that woman," I told her. "She's probably the one who planted the key in your handbag, and I want to know why. If she did it, of course."

"Of course," said Ernie.

He was laughing at me again. "Oh, bother you."

"Help me take this rubbish out to my car, will you? Just stuff it in the front seat. No. Better stuff it in the back, because when I pick Rob up, he'll probably want to sit up front."

"Will do," said Lulu.

"What about the ladies' things?" I asked.

"Dump them in there, too. I want the police and Rob to know Smedley took trophies of his victories over gullible women."

"What a dirty skunk he was," I said, growling slightly.

"I don't think skunks are all that dirty," said Lulu. "They sure stink, though. And Smedley stank too."

"Amen," I said, which didn't make me feel less guilty about not attending church.

TWENTY-EIGHT

Lulu and I were yawning over coffee and toast when Buttercup raced to the front door and barked ecstatically. We looked at each other.

"Ernie?" said Lulu, checking the clock on the kitchen wall, which said it was seven-thirty a.m.

"Don't know. It's early."

"Yeah, it is."

I shoved myself away from the table. "Well, I'd better go let him in if it is Ernie."

"I suppose so," said Lulu, sounding halfhearted about it.

Buttercup hadn't fibbed. It was Ernie. And Rob. Gadzooks! And here Lulu and I were still in our bathrobes and slippers. Oh well, they deserved it because they were so early.

"H'lo," I said to the two men. I stepped back. "Come on in. There's coffee."

"And a bright and perky hostess to serve it," said Ernie, taking in my bathrobe-clad, messy-haired self.

"Yes," I said. "And there's another perky hostess in the kitchen with the coffee. Unless you want to wait until we get dressed and made up and—"

"No," said Ernie. "We'll have coffee now, thanks. Got any toast?"

"Yes," I said. "Mrs. Buck always makes sure we have bread on weekends."

"Excellent woman, Mrs. Buck," said Ernie.

"Good morning, Miss Allcutt," said Mr. Gabriel.

"Is it?" I asked. Impolite of me, but who cares?

"Actually, it is," said Ernie, answering for Mr. Gabriel as both men hung their coats on the rack and flipped their hats onto the shelf. "We got all that junk stashed in Smedley's office around six o'clock this morning."

"Then we had breakfast at the Pantry," said Mr. Gabriel.

"Oh. I'm glad you returned Smedley's records. Why do you want toast if you already had breakfast?"

"Rob wasn't supposed to tell you that part," said Ernie as we walked to the kitchen. "I wanted you to feel sorry for us."

"Why would anybody feel sorry for you?" asked Lulu, looking up from the kitchen table, where she'd been studying a cup of coffee. "You've been taking care of yourself for donkeys' years. Besides, you're men. Men get all the breaks."

"Hey," said Ernie. "I'm a poor lonely bachelor. And so is Rob."

"Uh," said Lulu, who wasn't quite awake yet. Well, neither was I.

"Have a seat," I said, waving my arm to indicate the empty chairs around the kitchen table.

Both men sat.

"Want coffee?" I asked them.

"Yes, please," said Mr. Gabriel.

"Who made it?" said Ernie.

"I did," snarled Lulu.

Ernie laughed. It figured.

So I poured both men cups of coffee and took them to the table. The milk and sugar were already there.

"Where are your other ladies?" asked Ernie. "You the only two here this morning?"

"Caroline always goes to Alhambra to visit her parents on Saturday evening and comes back Sunday. Sue's upstairs getting ready to go to that Presbyterian church on Hill."

"So you're the only two sinners in the place, eh?" said Ernie after stirring some sugar and milk into his coffee cup.

"Yeah," said Lulu. "Wanna make something of it?"

"You're in a snarly mood today, aren't you?" said Ernie, lifting his cup.

"Yes, I am," said Lulu. "You would be too if the coppers were trying to pin a murder rap on you."

Swallowing coffee and tilting his head slightly, Ernie said, "You're right. They did, and I was. Peeved was what I was."

"I'm more than peeved," said Lulu. "I'm mad as hell."

"Makes sense to me," said Mr. Gabriel.

"Me too," I said.

Lulu and I finished our toast and coffee, and then we went upstairs to change into daywear. We met Sue in the upper hallway. She was all dressed for church and greeted us cheerfully.

"Any time you want to go to church with me, feel free," she said. "I don't know what churches you went to before you moved here, but the Presbyterian church down the street is full of really nice people."

"Episcopalian," I said.

"Baptist," said Lulu.

"Oh. Well, I'm sure there are both of those kinds of churches close by."

"I'm sure there are," I said. "Haven't looked yet. I might do that."

"I'd be happy to have you come to church with me if you want to," said Sue again.

"Thanks," I told her. "The only reason I wouldn't go to a Presbyterian church is because they forgive people their debts, and I grew up forgiving trespasses."

"Huh?" said Lulu.

Sue laughed. "Oh, well. Whatever you want to do is all right with me."

"Have a lovely time," I told her as Lulu and I went our separate ways to our rooms.

It didn't take me long to get into my skirt, blouse, and sweater. Nothing fancy. I met Lulu in the hall as I exited my door. She, too, was clad simply in a skirt, blouse, and sweater. She wore a black cloche hat and shoes and carried a black handbag. As my skirt and sweater were sort of a cinnamon brown and my blouse cream-colored, I wore brown accessories. Neither one of us had used more than powder on our faces.

"I'm not used to seeing you clad so soberly," I told Lulu.

"I'm not used to being clad so soberly," She said. "What was that you told Sue about debts? I don't get it."

"Oh. It was a joke. In the Lord's Prayer, the Presbyterians say, 'Forgive us our debts as we forgive our debtors.' The Episcopalians say, 'Forgive us our trespasses as we forgive those who trespass against us.' Just a different interpretation, I guess.

"Oh. Yeah, the Baptists say 'trespasses,' too."

I shrugged. "I don't understand anything. Maybe different translators used different words. The Bible's more than two thousand years old, after all."

"Yeah. I'm only twenty-three, and I feel at least two thousand."

"I'm sorry, Lulu. We'll get this all straightened out."

When we returned to the kitchen, because that's where the two men had remained, darned if Ernie hadn't washed our cups and plates! Such consideration on his part surprised me. "Thanks, Ernie. You didn't have to do that."

"Only fair," he said. "Besides, Lulu's in such a rotten mood I was afraid she'd hit me if I didn't."

"I might hit you anyway," growled Lulu.

When I turned to smile at her, I saw her face had begun to pucker up, as if she were about to cry. I hurried to her and gave her a hug. "Try not to worry, Lulu. We'll get you out of this mess."

"I h-hope so," she said, sniffling a bit. She dug a hankie out of her handbag and dabbed at the corners of her eyes. Then she sucked in a deep breath and squared her shoulders. "Okay, so what are we going to do now?"

"We're going to visit Mrs. Smedley's house," said Ernie. "I went to the pharmacy last night—they stay open late on Saturdays—and picked up the photos I took outside of Smedley's office."

"Oh, and did you find anything interesting?" I asked. "I want to see them before we go out. Is that all right with you?"

"Yup," said Ernie, pulling an envelope from his inside jacket pocket and pulling out a chair for Lulu and one for me. "Figured we should look at them, just in case we find anything interesting."

So Lulu and I sat and so did Mr. Gabriel and Ernie. Ernie took the photos out of the envelope one at a time and handed them around. Most of them showed women climbing those noisy metal stairs. Some of them showed the same women climbing down again.

"Oh, look!" I said at one point, about three photos in. "Isn't that Mrs. Smedley's brother?"

"Looks like him to me," said Ernie.

I passed the photo along to Lulu, who said, "Huh."

"Look! This is one of the women I saw with Mrs. Smedley and her brother at the library! She's going up to Mr. Smedley's office in this picture, isn't she?"

"Let me see that," said Lulu, leaning in to see the photo I held.

"She was," said Ernie.

"Well, that's interesting," I said, relinquishing the photo to Lulu. "Wonder why she and Mrs. Smedley and her brother were plotting together in the library."

"You don't know what they were doing in the library," Ernie reminded me.

"Spoilsport," I said. "I wonder if Mr. Brentwood would recognize any of these women as being on the street when Smedley hit the truck."

"I think the truck hit Smedley," said Ernie.

"Oh, who cares, as long as he's dead," said Lulu, which pretty well summed up the situation.

"Maybe we can stop by and see Mr. Brentwood before we visit Mrs. Smedley," said Mr. Gabriel.

"That would be nice," said Ernie, "but I want to visit Mrs. Smedley's place before she wakes up and goes anywhere. We can see Mr. Brentwood later."

"Very well," I said, dissatisfied, but realizing Ernie was correct. If we wanted to see Mrs. Smedley and catch her off-guard, it was best to get to her place early.

I knelt to say goodbye to my poor dog. "You take care of the house while we're gone, sweetheart," I told her. She wagged at me, even though I knew she didn't approve of all these comings and goings. Actually, she approved of the comings. She loved company. But she didn't like it when we all went away again. Poor Buttercup.

"Want to take her to Echo Park later? She'd probably like that," said Ernie.

"That would be lovely. Thanks, Ernie," I said.

"Lucky Buttercup," said Lulu sounding mournful.

"If you want to, we can go to Echo Park, too," suggested Mr. Gabriel.

Lulu gave a tiny start of surprise and whipped her head around and up to stare at Mr. Gabriel. "You want to talk about the case?" she asked.

"Well, we could do that. But we could also just take a couple of hours to enjoy the day."

When Ernie opened the door, the day intruded rather abruptly.

"Shoot! Let's none of us go to Echo Park," I said. "That wind is sharp."

"Might calm down later," said Ernie. "It's early, after all."

"I guess," I muttered as I pulled my coat collar up to keep my neck warm.

"We'll take my machine," said Mr. Gabriel, heading to his Flint motorcar. "Ernie and I drove past the Smedley house before we came to your place, Miss Allcutt, because we wanted to make sure where it was."

"Makes sense," I said.

"There were three or four cars parked in the drive and in front of the house," said Ernie. "Wonder if the owners of the cars are inside with Mrs. Smedley."

"Guess we'll find out," I said. "Where does she live? I can't remember from her interview with you."

"Glendale Boulevard in the Silver Lake neighborhood. Kind of a nice place, really."

"Hmm. Wonder if Smedley made lots of money," I muttered. "Probably via blackmailing the poor young women he ruined."

"Huh," said Lulu.

"Don't know," said Ernie. "Maybe Mrs. Smedley can tell us."

Ernie was correct in that the house in which Mrs. Smedley lived was nice. The whole area was pretty, kind of hilly with streets lined with pleasant houses and shrubbery. The lake itself started out as a reservoir, or so Ernie had told me. Gradually people began building homes there. By this time, 1927, some of the homes were truly grand.

The Smedley residence wasn't one of the grand ones, but it was pleasing enough. A smallish stucco number with a nice porch and several bushes lining the walk to the front door. And yes, three automobiles sat in the driveway leading to a garage in the back, and another car sat at the curb. At this hour on a Sunday morning— approximately 8:15—people had begun to stir, judging by the smoke coming from various neighborhood chimneys, but folks weren't streaming to their cars in order to catch early services at any churches nearby. That's only an assumption on my part, of course. I didn't knock on doors and ask.

However, after we exited Mr. Gabriel's Flint motorcar, the four of us walked up to the Smedley front door and rang the doorbell. Twice. After several minutes during which nothing happened, Ernie rang the doorbell again. He also pounded on the door.

Finally, the door opened a crack and a bleary-eyed, tousle-haired woman I'd never seen before stuck her face in the space made by same. "What? Who are you? What do you want?"

"We want to see Mrs. Felix Smedley," said Ernie. "Ernest Templeton here."

"Well, you're seeing her," said the woman. "What do you want with me?"

I felt my eyes open wide. Oh, my Lord, was this one of the Mrs. Smedleys whose marriage certificates Ernie had found?

"Any more Mrs. Smedleys in there?" asked Ernie. "One of them hired me."

"What?"

"What's going on, Mary?" asked a familiar voice from behind the woman at the door.

"Mrs. Verna Smedley?" Ernie said, raising his voice. "Ernie Templeton here. We need to talk."

"Oh, damn!" said the Verna voice.

"What's happening?" another woman's voice chimed in.

"Cripes. Better step back, Mary," said Verna. "I guess we'll have to let him in."

"And don't forget the rest of us," said Lulu in a voice like flint. "We need to talk, too."

"Dammit, what're *you* doing here?" asked Verna. She took the door from Mary and, I think, tried to slam it, but Ernie's flat palm on the outside of the door stopped her.

"It's over, Mrs. Verna Smedley and the rest of the Mrs. Smedleys, if they're in there. And your brother, too," said Ernie. "Now move aside."

"You got no right—"

"You hired me," said Ernie. "Under false pretenses, if I'm not mistaken. That gives me every right, especially since I understand there are many more Mrs. Felix Smedleys running around loose. I want to know why and what's going on, and why you tried to pin your husband's death on Miss LaBelle. We know you were there on Broadway when your husband was pushed. We have a witness who saw you there."

"Aw, cripes," said our Mrs. Smedley, sounding pitiful. "But he was going to kill me!"

"Let's all go inside and talk about it, all right?" said Ernie in a reasonable voice. "My secretary, Miss Allcutt, will take notes for us."

"Gawd. Very well. Come in." Clad in a robe and slippers, and with her red hair in a scarf, she looked…worn out, is the best way I can think of to describe her overall demeanor. I got the feeling these past few days had been almost as hard on her as they'd been on Lulu.

When it was my turn to walk into the house, I stopped short, nearly causing Mr. Gabriel to bump into me. Four women, all wearing robes and slippers and looking as if they'd just awakened, stared at us. I recognized two of them as having been with Mrs. Smedley at the library. And there, by golly, was Mrs. Smedley's brother.

Well, well, well. What did this mean?

Beat the heck out of me.

TWENTY-NINE

"You might as well sit down if you can find a seat," said our Mrs. Smedley, waving vaguely at the living room furniture. A sofa and three chairs were placed tastefully in the room, and I noticed a dining room with a table and chairs off the living room, so I doubted we'd have trouble finding places to sit.

"Thank you," said Mr. Gabriel. "Mr. Templeton and I will fetch a couple of chairs from the dining room, so we'll all be able to sit and chat."

"Yeah, yeah," said Mrs. Verna. "Do what you have to do."

"Thank you," said Ernie. "What we want to do is get to the bottom of your late husband's death. There seem to be several Mrs. Smedleys in the United States. Are these other ladies some of them? And I see Mr. Oswald is staying with you, is that right?"

"Yeah," said Mrs. Verna. "But nobody here killed the bastard."

"Was he a bastard?" said Ernie sounding interested and innocent. I knew the innocence to be faked. Not sure about the interest part.

"You know what I mean," said Mrs. Verna. "Yeah, these ladies and I were all fools enough to marry Felix Smedley."

"May I have your names, please?" asked Ernie politely.

"Yeah." Mrs. Verna turned to the other three women, all of

whom sat on the sofa. Verna had yet to take a seat. "Tell the guy your names, gals. We got nothing to worry about."

"I'm not so sure about that," said the black-black-haired lady. "But I guess there's no getting away from it now. I'm Virginia. Maiden name Harkrider. Married Felix in New York City seven years ago. He ran out on me a couple of months later."

"And I," said the woman who'd opened the door and whom I'd never seen before, "am Mary. Married Felix in Nevada three years back. He ran out on me about a month after we were married."

"Harriet here," said the bottle-blonde whom I'd seen with Mrs. Verna at the library. "Felix and I married in Chicago. After he took all my money, he ran out on me about a month after we got hitched."

"Oh, yeah," said Mary. "I forgot that part. He took all my money too. Then he scrammed out as fast as he could go."

"Same here," said the woman named Virginia. "Took me for all I had."

"Thank you, ladies," said Ernie. "You have all that, Mercy?" He glanced at me, as I'd been furiously taking down names and places on my secretarial pad.

"Yes," I said. "Mrs. Verna Smedley, did you marry Mr. Felix Smedley here in Los Angeles?"

"Yeah," she said.

"I found one more marriage certificate," said Ernie. "For a woman named—"

"Olive," said Verna, interrupting. "Yeah. We know about her. She's dead. He wised up after marrying Virginia, Harriet, and Mary. He took out an insurance policy on Olive. Then she mysteriously fell out of a window in San Francisco."

"Good heavens," muttered Lulu.

"Heaven's got nothing to do with that devil," said Mrs. Verna. "And when I went through his office, I saw he'd taken out a policy on me. If somebody hadn't killed him, he'd probably have thrown me out of a window, too."

"Excuse me, ladies and Ernie," said Rob Gabriel, sounding official. "We've seen the paperwork about which you're speaking. It's quite damning of Mr. Smedley being the worst sort of human being, but I doubt we can prove he committed murder."

"Only because he died before he could do me in or we could find witnesses in San Francisco," said Verna.

"That's probably the truth," I said. "Golly, I'm so sorry, ladies."

"Yeah, same here," said Lulu. "I thought he was a legitimate talent scout, so he suckered me too. But that doesn't give you the right to accuse me of killing him." She frowned at Mrs. Verna.

"Yes, you're right. But when we found those photos of you on the floor of his office when we went there to confront him, I got mad."

"Was he in his office when you got there?" asked Ernie.

"No. Virginia, Harriet, Mary and me went there. We were going to call the cops on him, because he was a...Whattaya call them? Bigamist? He was a bigamist and then some."

"Yes, so we discovered," said Ernie drily.

"So he wasn't in his office when you got there, but Miss LaBelle's photos still lay on the floor. Is that correct?" asked Mr. Gabriel, sounding official.

"Yeah. Then we heard a bunch of screaming and horns blowing on the street, so we ran down and saw Felix dead in the street in a puddle of blood, and a blonde running away." She turned to Lulu. "Honest to God, honey, I thought she was you."

"Well, she wasn't," said a disgruntled Lulu.

"All right. Let me get this straight. Verna, you're the one who hired me. Did you honestly want me to find out if your husband was running around on you, or was that some kind of ploy? If it was a ploy, what did you hope to achieve?"

"It wasn't a ploy, whatever that is," declared Verna. "I already knew he was a bigamist because I wrote to these ladies." She waved a hand to include the three women on the sofa. "What I wanted to know was if he was trying to get somebody else to marry him. I found the insurance policy he had on me."

"When?" asked Ernie. "When did you find that?"

"I stopped trusting him about three months ago," said Verna in a disgusted-sounding voice. "So I'd visit his office when he wasn't there and go through his files."

"You had keys to all the cabinets and his desk?"

After hesitating slightly, Mrs. Verna said, "Not…exactly. My brother is useful for getting into locked places."

"And I'm not a thief," declared Mr. Oswald. "I'm a legitimate locksmith. So I made keys for all the doors and cabinets in Felix's office after Verna told me she suspected him of running around on her and maybe even plotting to kill her in order to get the insurance money on the policy he took out on her. After she showed me those other marriage certificates, we both knew he was a rat, so I helped her."

"Very well," said Ernie. "Thank you. What you did is probably illegal, but I'm not about to turn you in."

"Thanks," said Mr. Oswald, who didn't sound particularly grateful.

"So," Ernie continued. "I managed to get the photographs I took of people walking up those metal stairs to your husband's office developed. Well, all your husbands, I guess. Will you look at these and see if you recognize anyone as the blonde you saw after Mr. Smedley was killed?"

"Yeah," said Mrs. Verna. "Let's look at 'em at the dining room table. You can spread 'em out there."

"Sounds all right to me," said Ernie. "Please bear in mind that there's another witness, so don't finger someone just to make your lives easier. You've all got a lot of explaining to do to the cops."

"Crumb. That louse wasn't worth it," muttered one of the Mrs. Smedleys. I didn't see which one.

"No, he wasn't," said Mrs. Verna. "But if one of these pictures shows the woman who shoved him, it might help us."

"If anybody *did* shove him," said another Mrs. Smedley. "Maybe he bumped into somebody and stumbled into the street."

"Maybe," said Ernie. "But please look at the photos. Scrutinize them carefully. My secretary will take notes. If you see anyone who looks familiar, or if you see a photograph of someone you know, give Miss Allcutt the photo."

"Right," said Mrs. Verna.

Various murmurs of assent came from the other Mrs. Smedleys, and I heard a low-pitched mutter from Mr. Oswald. They trundled into the dining room, along with Mr. Oswald. Ernie, Lulu, Mr. Gabriel, and I followed them. Mr. Gabriel stood at the door to the living room, I guess to make sure no one made a bolt for the door, although they all seemed relatively docile now that their secret had been discovered and *they'd* been discovered clustered together in one house.

The women and Mr. Oswald took up places on the far side of the dining room table, which was an oblong wooden affair that had a nice shine to it. Cherry wood? Mahogany? I didn't know one wood from another, but it was a nice table. A figurine of a black cat sat in the middle of the table on a white doily. I glanced around the room and realized that what little I could see of the house was quite well-decorated.

"This is a nice place, Mrs. Smedley," I said, forgetting for a moment there was more than one Mrs. Smedley in the room.

"Thanks," said Mrs. Verna. "Virginia, Harriet, and Mary used to have nice places too, until Felix got his mitts on them."

"Really? Interesting," I said.

"Very interesting," said Ernie. "But we can talk about that later. Right now I want all of you to look at these pictures. Miss Allcutt, please take notes."

That was Ernie's polite way of telling me to shut up, so I did.

He withdrew three envelopes from his coat pocket, opened one of them, and laid a total of twelve photos in a pile on the table.

Mrs. Verna, standing at the living room end of the table, began the process by picking up one photo, squinting at it, and handing it to the next Mrs. Smedley. The line ended with Mr. Oswald, and he too peered closely at each picture. After Mrs. Verna picked up the third photo and peered at it, she said, "I've seen this one. Can't remember where. Check it out, gals. You too, Ray. Have you seen her anywhere?"

The photo made its way from hand to hand down the line, ending up with Mr. Oswald. One of the Mrs. Smedleys said, "I've seen her too. In fact, isn't she the one who was at Musso and Frank's with Felix a couple of weeks ago?"

"Might be," said Mrs. Verna. "Oh, and look here. I've seen this one, too."

"Let me have the first one," said Ernie. "Lulu, would you mind being the fetcher and get all the pictures of women they recognize? I want to keep them separate."

"Sure," said Lulu, walking to Mr. Oswald and taking the first photo, which she carried to Ernie, who handed it to me. Then she went back to Mr. Oswald.

"Mercy, will you please make some marks on these as the Mrs. Smedleys recognize their photos? On the backs of them or something?"

"Sure," I said, and did as requested.

By the time the ladies and Mr. Oswald had finished looking at all the pictures from the three envelopes, they'd identified five individuals—four of them female—as people they'd seen before.

Naturally, as I took them to mark, I also peered at them. They all looked like eager young girls. Mr. Felix Smedley had been a scoundrel.

"All right," said Ernie when the viewing was complete. "Let's go back into the living room and get comfortable. I want to get stories from each of you regarding how you got involved with Felix Smedley, how he fooled you, and what happened. And how did you all find each other?"

"Told you," said Mrs. Verna. "After I went through Felix's papers and found all those marriage certificates, I wrote to all of his wives. They were all happy to help me bring Felix down."

"But you didn't intend to kill him?" asked Mr. Gabriel, being lawyerly again.

"No!" said one of the other Mrs. Smedleys. "I wanted to, but that would only get us into trouble. I wanted to get dirt on him so the cops would arrest him. He swindled all of us, except Verna. She was smart enough to catch on to his dirty little game before he could take everything from her." This Mrs. Smedley—I think it was Virginia—sniffled dolefully. "He played the rest of us for pure suckers."

"And I'm sure he murdered Olive," said Mrs. Verna. "Then, when I found the policy he'd taken out on me, I figured he was going to do the same to me. The filthy pig."

"It seems to me that you were doing some good investigating on your own," said Ernie. "Why'd you hire me?"

"We figured the police would pay more attention to a licensed private eye than they would to a bunch of women who'd been tricked by a rat. You know how much attention coppers pay to women," said Mrs. Verna. "None, is how much."

"That's the truth," said Lulu.

"Yes, it is," I agreed.

"You really think so?" asked Ernie, as if he actually meant his question.

All five of us females in the room stared at him. After a couple of seconds, I said, "You recall how much attention the police paid to Calvin Buck and Charley Wu?"

"Yeah," said Ernie, catching on.

"That's about how much attention the police pay to women who have problems."

"That's right," said Mrs. Verna. "They won't even believe a girl if she said a man assaulted her! The dumb coppers will blame it on *her*! I know it for a fact, because something like that happened to a friend of mine."

"It's the truth," confirmed Mr. Gabriel. Good for him.

"There you go, Mr. Templeton," I said with satisfaction marred by the grim truth. "The only people the police will pay attention to or believe are white men." I glanced at Mr. Oswald. "Is that why you're here? To help the ladies get some kind of justice?"

"Sort of," said Mr. Oswald. "Verna and I have always been close to each other. She more or less reared me when our folks died. So I wanted to help her, especially when she told me what kind of man she'd married."

"Is that why you were in the library?" I asked.

"The library?" exclaimed Mrs. Verna. "You saw us at the library?"

"Yes. I'd gone there to look for some books and wondered why you were all gathered at a table there. But then I got distracted." My explanation petered out at the end because I didn't want to bring Mr. Brentwood into the conversation.

"Yeah, we were there discussing what to do," said Mrs. Verna. She fixed her gaze upon Ernie. "So, since I hired you, what do you expect us to do now? None of us killed Felix, and neither did your friend over there"—she gestured at Lulu—"so what now?"

Ernie explained about Mr. Gabriel's planned visit to Phil's office on the morrow, and about how he aimed to go with the police when they searched Smedley's office.

"After we leave here," he continued, "we're going to visit the witness to your…Oh, hell, I don't know what to call him. The witness to Mr. Felix Smedley's death. I want to see if he can recognize any of the people in these photographs."

"If that blonde killed him, she deserves a medal, not a prison sentence," said Mrs. Verna.

A chorus of "Amens" followed her statement.

"The police probably won't see it that way," said Ernie. "But I'll see what I can do in order to solve the matter without anyone else getting hurt by…Felix."

"Stupid name, isn't it?" asked a Mrs. Smedley. Again, I'm not sure which one.

"Not a favorite of mine," said Ernie.

"Nor mine," I agreed.

"I hate it," said Lulu. "He told me his name was Clint Faraday when he said he was going to make me a WAMPAS Baby Star."

"Used that line on you, did he?" asked Mrs. Verna. "He was a horrible man, and I'm sorry. I'm sorry I fingered you, too. I didn't know you were all right."

"Are you sorry for crunching my fender?" asked Ernie.

By golly, Mrs. Verna's face turned red! She seemed so hardened an individual I didn't know she had a blush in her.

"I'm sorry about that. It was a stupid thing to do: play drunk and hit your car. I guess we thought we'd get the coppers' attention, and they'd look into Felix's life. To hell with his death."

"Police work doesn't operate like that as a rule," said Ernie drily.

"Yeah, I found that out," said Mrs. Verna. "But I'll pay for the damages to your car."

"Don't worry about it. A friend fixed it for me."

"And he didn't charge you anything?"

"Not a cent," said Ernie.

"Well, take this anyway. For your trouble," said Mrs. Verna, reaching in her handbag and pulling out a wad of bills.

"Wish I had friends like that," muttered Mr. Oswald.

Another chorus of agreement went up in the room. We left shortly thereafter and decided to pay Mr. Brentwood a visit.

THIRTY

"I don't want to visit that loony fellow," said Lulu to Ernie. "Would you mind if I went home, and you and Mercy visit him?"

"All right by me," said Ernie.

"Likewise," I told her.

"Why don't I drop Miss Allcutt and Ernie at his place?" said Mr. Gabriel. "They can fetch his automobile. Now that it's warmed up so much, perhaps we can take a stroll in the park, Miss LaBelle?"

"Oh," said Lulu, flustered. "Oh. Um…Sure, that'd be nice."

"Excellent." Mr. Gabriel sounded satisfied. He added in a more lawyerly voice, "We can discuss your case in the park."

"Sure. Thanks," said Lulu.

I'd have tipped Lulu a wink, except she seemed a bit confused already. She'd been through a whole lot in a very few days, and I didn't want her to think I was playing matchmaker or, worse, busybody.

So Mr. Gabriel drove to Ernie's apartment on Yale Street, almost right smack in Chinatown, and drove off with Lulu to Echo Park. Unless he decided to take her to another park.

"Ready for a visit to the loony bin?" asked Ernie as he opened the passenger-side door for me.

"Don't call it that. Mr. Brentwood isn't a lunatic. He's got…something else wrong with him."

"Right." Ernie shut my door and walked to the driver's side of his nice almost-new Packard. As he got in, he said, "I have the photos, including the ones you marked as having been recognized by the Mrs. Smedleys. And you've got your notebook and pencils, so I guess we're ready."

"I hope Mr. Brentwood recognizes one of the photographs as that of at least one of the women he saw on the street arguing with Mr. Smedley. Even if he can't say for sure which one pushed him."

"If he was pushed. I'm beginning to think his death might have been caused by accident and that, if it was an accident, he was probably to blame for it. Didn't your pal Mr. Monocle say he hit one of the women?"

"Mr. Brentwood," I snapped, although I'm pretty sure Ernie only called him by the wrong name to tease me. "And I think you may be right. And if he hit one of the women and she shoved him, he deserved it, so it's still not her fault."

"According to you."

"According to me."

Mr. Brentwood was overjoyed to greet Ernie and me. By then it was almost eleven a.m., and I was feeling a little tired and grumpy, but Mr. Brentwood's good mood made me happy. He was truly a pleasant, nice person, if perhaps a trifle confused. Very well, a good deal confused. But he wasn't stupid.

He wanted us to go to his room, and Mrs. Wilkes came with us.

"Miss Allcutt, Miss Allcutt, Miss Allcutt," he said as we walked.

"Yes?"

"Miss Allcutt, Miss Allcutt, Miss Allcutt," he repeated.

I didn't speak again, figuring he'd eventually make his way to his point, if he had one, without my help.

"Miss Allcutt."

We got to the door of his apartment, and he opened the door and rushed inside, straight to his desk. There he swept up a piece of paper from one of the pads I'd given him, carried it to me, and handed it over with a bow. "For you."

"Thank you!"

Ernie, Mrs. Wilkes, and I stared at the paper, upon which Mr. Brentwood had created an absolutely amazing scene that might have come straight out of a spectacular springtime flower garden. Not only were there roses and irises, freesias and snapdragons, but dahlias, delphiniums, and carnations abounded. Mr. Brentwood's garden had hydrangeas and gardenias around the edges. Playing among the abundant floral growth, bunnies hopped—without nibbling any of the plants, a display of respect most gardeners would envy—birds flew, and bees dipped their toes in the pollen. A happy toad peeked out from behind a decorative rock formation, and a couple of sheep frolicked in a pasture in the background.

"This is…" I couldn't for the life of me think of an appropriate word. Then suddenly several tumbled out of my mouth. "This is gorgeous, it's beautiful! It's amazing. You're the best artist I've ever known. In person, I mean. Mr. Brentwood, you have a perfectly astounding talent!"

"It's for you," said Mr. Brentwood, pleased.

An idea occurred to me, but I didn't blurt it out (for once). Turning it into a *brilliant* idea would require some deep thought and planning and might ultimately be impossible, although I hoped not.

"May I keep it?" I asked.

"It's for you," Mr. Brentwood repeated.

"Thank you! I'm going to have it framed, and I'll hang it in my home. This is just beautiful, Mr. Brentwood."

After we'd finished oohing and aahing over Mr. Brentwood's many art projects—the man was a genius when it came to his art—we finally settled down and Ernie took out the envelopes containing photographs. Because I seemed to be Mr. Brentwood's special friend at the moment, I explained to him what we required of him. Hoped from him would be a better way of expressing it, I guess.

But by golly, the man came through for us! He picked out four photographs, two of one blonde and two of one brunette.

"These," he said positively.

"These are the women you saw with the bad man? On the sidewalk?"

"Yes, yes, yes. He hit this one." He pointed at the blonde. "This one," he said, pointing to the brunette, "hit him back. Then he fell in the street in front of a truck." He wrinkled his nose. "Lots of blood. It was ugly. I left."

"And the two women left as well?"

He shook his head. "No. Yes. No. Yes. I don't know."

"So you left and didn't see if the women also left?" asked Ernie, although I don't know why. I thought Mr. Brentwood had been as clear as he ever was.

"Yes. Yes. Yes."

"Thank you," said Ernie.

"Do you think you can draw pictures of other people who were on the street that night?" I asked for the heck of it.

"Yes. Yes. Yes." Abruptly, Mr. Brentwood rose from the chair he'd been sitting on and returned to his desk where he sat in the chair. Then he pulled the chain on his desk lamp, spread a clean paper in front of him on the desk, selected a black Crayola, and began to draw.

Ernie, Mrs. Wilkes, and I exchanged a trio of glances. I was *so* glad I'd offered to allow Mr. Brentwood to draw pictures when we were waiting in Ernie's office last Friday!

It didn't take Mr. Brentwood more than five or ten minutes to complete whatever he was drawing. Then he carried it over and handed it to me with another bow.

Darned if he hadn't created a Los Angeles street scene at night! And I recognized the blonde, the brunette, and the man I presumed to be Mr. Smedley. Other people looked as if they were walking past the scene, some staring, some trying not to stare. It was an astonishing picture. To me anyway. Maybe other people have artistic skills I lack, and such renderings might be old hat to them, but to say I was impressed would be a serious understatement.

"Thank you, Mr. Brentwood," I breathed. "Thank you so much."

"This is what you saw on the street the night the man got hit by the truck?" Ernie asked, I suppose to be sure.

"Yes. Yes. Yes. Bad man. Hit woman. She wore red, but I drew her in black." His brow wrinkled, and he dropped, caught, and replaced his monocle. "Do you want me to draw her in red?"

"No, thank you. This is fine. Thank you very much, Mr. Brentwood."

Hallelujah! Ernie finally remembered the poor man's name!

We left shortly thereafter, after thanking Mr. Brentwood about three hundred more times. I promised to bring him more artistic pads and keep him supplied with Crayolas, and he seemed happy. So did Mrs. Wilkes.

"Will that help you, do you think?" she asked as she escorted us to the door. "I doubt Mr. Brentwood would be able to handle a court-room situation, but if you can use the drawing and his identification of those women to assist in your investigation…Well, I hope it helps."

"Thank you," said Ernie. "I think this will actually be quite useful."

I carried my drawing carefully so as not to wrinkle it and said, "I think so, too. And I'm going to take this masterpiece to a framer as soon as I possibly can."

"He truly is an exceptionally talented fellow," said Mrs. Wilkes. "His…disability doesn't seem to affect his artistic gift, does it?"

"Not at all," said Ernie.

"He's brilliant," I said.

Ernie slanted me a skeptical look, but I meant what I'd said.

When we got into his Packard, he said, "I suppose you want to take that home before we go to the park, right?"

"Of course I do!" I exclaimed. "Anyhow, we need to fetch Butter-cup. You promised her you'd take her to the park."

"Did I?" said Ernie. He shrugged. "I guess I did. Anyhow, I'm hungry. Want to get something to eat before we go to your place?"

I stared at my gorgeous picture and contemplated options. Hunger pangs gnawed at my innards, too, but I didn't want to take a chance on ripping, wrinkling, or otherwise damaging Mr. Brentwood's artwork.

Ernie, recognizing my hesitation for what it was, said, "Let's take your picture home, pick up Buttercup, and get some sandwiches at a deli or somewhere and take 'em to the park with us."

"Wonderful idea!"

"Should we take lunch to Rob and Lulu?"

After thinking about his question for a second or three, I said, "No. I don't even know for sure what park they're going to. And if they're hungry, too, I'm sure Rob will feed Lulu."

"He seems to have taken a shine to her," observed Ernie.

"He'd better be a nice man," I said, growling a little. "Lulu's been through enough lately. She doesn't need another cad to torment her."

"Hey, Rob's not a cad," said Ernie.

"Sez you," I muttered.

"He's not," said Ernie.

I said, "Huh."

When we got to my place, I handed Ernie the key to my abode and the one to my office and carried Mr. Brentwood's picture so I wouldn't wrinkle it while trying to unlock the front door. Naturally, Buttercup met us at the door, but Ernie quickly scooped her up and began petting her before she could put her little puppy paws on my picture. Not that she regularly jumped on people, because she was a well-trained poodle, but I appreciated Ernie's thoughtfulness.

Fortunately for all three of us, Ernie was able to do two things at once. He didn't drop Buttercup as he unlocked my office door and opened it. "Buttercup, you're such a good girl," I cooed at her as she rested in Ernie's arms, straining slightly to get to me.

"Hey, what about me?" asked Ernie in a fake-offended voice.

"You're a good boy, Ernie."

"Thanks." He laughed.

As soon as I laid my picture on my desk, after moving various items out of the way, Ernie set Buttercup on the floor. She ran to greet me and, after I stuck the telephone on one edge of my picture and my ink stand on another so it wouldn't accidentally get blown off my desk and onto the floor, I bent to give her the greeting she deserved.

"Do you want to go to the park with Uncle Ernie and me, Buttercup?" I asked her in a silly high-pitched voice.

"Uncle Ernie?" said Ernie incredulously.

"You don't want to be uncle to this adorable pooch?"

After thinking about the matter for a second or two, Ernie shrugged and said, "Better than being uncle to a few human kids I know, I suppose."

"I knew you wouldn't mind! Let's go to the utility porch and get her leash, and take her to the park. I'm glad the day's warmed up some."

"I'm glad it's warmed up a lot," Ernie said.

So we fetched Buttercup's collar and leash. She was ecstatic, especially when she realized we weren't merely going to take a walk around the neighborhood, but were going somewhere in an automobile! Because the day had turned into a warm one, I allowed her to sit on my lap and stick her pretty little nose out the window as Ernie drove us to Echo Park.

As luck would have it, we passed a little sandwich shop on the way to our destination. Traffic was relatively light that late Sunday morning—probably because most of the good citizens of Los Angeles were still in church and the not-so-good ones were still abed—so Ernie found a parking place at the curb right in front of the shop.

"What do you want?" he asked me before he left the car.

"Whatever looks good to you," I told him.

"I like lots of different kinds of food," he warned me.

"Surprise me. If I don't like it, I'll just starve."

I saw his mouth quirk as he left the machine and hoped I wasn't in for too much of a surprise.

But Ernie was a good food-picker. He returned to the Packard about five minutes after he'd left and set a paper sack on the floor of the backseat.

"What did you get?" I asked. Then I sniffed. "It smells good, whatever it is."

"It's a surprise," he told me. "But the café owner gave me some clean rags to use as napkins."

"Messy then?" I asked.

"You'll see."

And I did. Ernie carried the paper sack and I held Buttercup's lead as we walked from his Packard into the grassy park. Fortunately, the people who ran the park had placed picnic tables and benches here and there, so we found one near the lake, and Ernie set the paper sack on it. Buttercup was busy sniffing here and there, and when she spotted a little boy and a man I took to be his father attempting to launch a toy sailboat along the shore of the lake, she tugged on her leash and looked back at me eagerly.

"How about you set out lunch, and I'll let Buttercup meet that kid and his dad and his boat?"

"Okay, but don't be long. Lunch might get cold."

"It's warm now?" I asked, intrigued. Gee, the place where he'd picked up lunch didn't look as if it might sell Mexican food, which is about the only food I could think of that might be warm—I'm thinking about tamales here, which you could purchase from street vendors from time to time.

"Yes, it is, so don't dawdle," said Ernie. He was grinning, so I guess he wasn't too worried about Buttercup and me wasting time.

Buttercup and I meandered over to the kid who, I learned, was named Allan. Allan and his father, Mr. Jensen, were indeed attempting to launch a toy sailboat. They'd just got it underway when Buttercup and I joined them. Allan was absolutely thrilled that his boat seemed to be sailing quite well.

"Don't let her go too far out, Allan," warned his father. "We want to be able to bring her in again."

"I won't," promised Allan.

"That's a lovely boat," I said to the two males, both of whom turned and smiled. When Allan saw Buttercup, his smile turned into a beam of delight.

"Thank you," said Allan's father. "My son and I built it." As Allan and Buttercup made friends, Mr. Jensen whispered to me, "I was afraid it might sink, but it seems to be doing pretty well."

"It's a lovely boat on a lovely day," I said.

That's actually when we introduced ourselves.

Anyway, Buttercup and I didn't stay long watching the Jensens' boat sail serenely on Echo Park Lake. After a very few minutes, we walked back to the picnic table where, sure enough, Ernie had set out waxed-paper-wrapped sandwiches, little bags of potato chips, and two Coca-Colas for his and my enjoyment.

He was absolutely correct in that the sandwich was warm. What's more, it was delicious!

"I've never had anything like this before, Ernie," I said after taking my first messy bite.

"We're just lucky we chanced upon that sandwich shop. The owner is a Jewish fellow named Baumgarten, and he hails from New York City. He has a pal named Kulakhofsky who runs a delicatessen there, and he created this sandwich for some actress or other several years back. According to Baumgarten, he's about the only person in Los Angeles who makes Reubens. That's what he calls the sandwich, because Mr. Kulakhofsky's first name is Reuben."

"It's delicious! I never had anything like this when I went to New York City." As I chewed, I thought how silly my statement had been. After I swallowed, I said, "Of course, my mother wouldn't allow me to set foot in a Jewish delicatessen."

"What a surprise," said an unsurprised Ernie. "I've never had one either, if that makes you feel any better."

"I don't think anything can make me feel better than this sandwich."

In case you wondered, the sandwich was made with ham, turkey, cheese (I think it was Swiss cheese), some kind of salad dressing, and sauerkraut. All of that stuff was piled between two slices of rye bread and then toasted on a griddle. I knew that last part because Ernie told me about the griddle. I don't think I'd ever had such a delicious sandwich in my life, and that includes the corned beef sandwiches I'd been devouring, much to my mother's displeasure, since I'd moved to L.A.

Buttercup, who had been taught not to outright beg at the table, did look upon Ernie and me with soulful eyes as we dined. So I threw her a piece of turkey and a potato chip. I'm sure Ernie slipped her a couple of goodies too.

We didn't stay at Echo Park very long. After we ate, we took Buttercup for a walk around the lake. I waved at the Jensen males, pointed out their sailboat to Ernie, who approved with a smile and a nod, and then we decided to go back to my house.

"I'm too full to walk anymore," Ernie announced. "Besides, I don't see Rob and Lulu anywhere, so maybe Rob's taken her home. I hope they're both there because I want to find out how he plans to tackle the search warrant and the police department tomorrow."

"Good idea," I said. I didn't mention that I, too, was stuffed to the gills and walking wasn't much fun at the moment.

THIRTY-ONE

L uck was with us, and so were Mr. Gabriel and Lulu when we got
 back to Mercy's Manor. Sue and Caroline had also returned
home by then too, but Ernie and I were more interested in Rob and
Lulu. Therefore, after we'd greeted the two church-goers, Ernie, Mr.
Gabriel, Lulu and I retired to my office, where things were much
tidier than they'd been the day before, although I still felt a frisson of
evil when I entered. Perhaps it was my imagination, but I don't think
so. The office had been tainted with the paraphernalia of Mr. Felix
Smedley, and his essence still lingered.

Rubbing my hands over my arms, I said, "I still feel lingering
tendrils of Mr. Smedley's evil in here."

Lulu said, "Huh?"

Mr. Gabriel said, "Beg pardon?"

Ernie said, "Somebody go get one of those shaman-fellows from
India to purify Mercy's office, will you?"

I frowned at him and got a big grin in return.

Very well, so it had been my imagination. I took my rightful place
in the chair at my desk, made sure nothing had happened to Mr.
Brentwood's spectacular artwork, and said, "What are you going to do
tomorrow? Mr. Gabriel, you plan to visit the police first thing, right?"

"Yes, and I wish you'd call me Rob," he said.

After a brief hesitation, I said, "Thank you. And please call me Mercy."

"Good God, cut out the formalities all around, okay?" said Ernie. He turned to Rob. "You're going to Phil's office and will get a warrant executed right away?"

"I even have the judge lined up and talked to him already. Judge Havers. Good man, all things considered. Anyhow, he said he'll sign a warrant as soon as it hits his office."

"Don't know him," said Ernie. "But I don't hang out in court-rooms if I can avoid them."

"He's one of the better judges in L.A.," said Rob.

"While you do that, what do you want us to do?" Ernie asked.

"Gather all the evidence you have—and by evidence, I mean all the notes Mercy's taken and so forth—and be prepared."

Lulu chimed in, "Rob suggested we call all the Mrs. Smedleys and Mr. Oswald together and be prepared to storm Detective Bigelow's office as soon as the warrant is served and ex...executed?" She glanced at Rob, perhaps to be sure she'd used the correct word. He nodded and smiled, and Lulu relaxed.

"Interesting notion," said Ernie. "Wonder if they'll go for it."

"They seemed amenable to clearing their names and pinning all possible dirt on Smedley when we talked to them this morning," said Rob. "Lulu and I even stopped by their house after we left the park today, and they said they'd be available at ten o'clock Monday morn-ing, but they'll wait if it takes longer than that."

"Oh, hell, we can all go the station at ten and wait for you and Phil and his tame coppers to get back if it comes to that," said Ernie.

"Even Lulu and me?" I asked. "I mean, we're supposed to go to work."

"Believe me, this will be work," said Ernie. "In fact, corralling all those women and keeping them in line will be more work than usual."

"But Lulu has to be at the reception desk."

"Aw, hell, I'm sure Glennie won't mind serving for another day at the desk," Ernie said.

"Maybe not, but what if Dr. Clutter is getting tired of Glennie being away from his office? Is there anyone else who can handle the phone there?" I glanced at Lulu, who shrugged.

"For all anybody knows, the police will *make* me go to their offices tomorrow," she said in a woeful voice.

Why was she sounding woeful?

"Why do you sound so sad, Lulu?" I asked, figuring why shouldn't I?

"Because I feel sad," she said.

I turned to glare at Rob. "Did you and Lulu get some lunch while you were out and about today? What park did you go to?"

"Elysian Park," said Rob. "And I didn't even think about food. We discussed her case."

"You're an idiot, Rob," Ernie told him.

"There was nowhere to sit anyway," said Lulu. "We just walked for a couple of miles."

"Rob Gabriel, you're more than an idiot," said Ernie. "You're an insufferable cad. Why the hell didn't you and Lulu get something to eat? *You* had a nice breakfast this morning. Poor Lulu had toast and coffee."

"Oh, no!" cried Lulu. "It's all right. I should have said something. Probably." She sounded embarrassed.

"Nertz," I said. "Let's raid the kitchen."

"To hell with the kitchen," said Ernie. "Let's go to Chinatown. Mercy and I actually *ate* lunch, so we'll just watch the two of you dine."

"But—" said Lulu.

"No buts," said Ernie, interrupting. "Rob has treated you shamefully. I didn't believe Mercy when she said you were a no-good so-and-so, Rob, but I guess she was right."

"I did not!" I cried. "I mean, I was kind of hoping he wasn't a rat, but I never said so."

"Good Lord!" said Rob, sounding and looking mortified, ashamed, aghast, and a whole bunch of other awful things. He swirled on his chair and gawped at Lulu. "I'm *so* sorry, Lulu! If I'd—"

"If you had the brains God gave a gnat," said Ernie, interrupting, "you'd have made sure your client had something for lunch and somewhere to sit and eat it." He looked at me. "Isn't that right, Mercy?"

"Yes, that's right," I said fiercely.

"Mercy!" said Lulu, horrified. "Honestly, it's all right!"

"No, it isn't. You've been through too much already lately, without your own attorney trying to starve you to death."

"Now wait a minute—"

"To hell with that," said Ernie, who seemed determined to interrupt Rob every time he tried to say anything at all. "Lulu and Mercy, get your wraps. Rob, get your hat and coat. You're taking us all out to dinner in Chinatown."

"I am?" Rob said, standing up and evidently ready to take direction from Ernie.

"Yes, you are," said Ernie. "Come along, Lulu. Mercy and I care about what happens to you, even if your attorney doesn't."

"Hey!" said Rob.

"Nertz," I told him. "Come on, Lulu, get your coat and hat on."

So she did. And the rest of us got our own coats and hats on. Then we bade Sue, Caroline, and Buttercup *adios* (as we live in Los Angeles), and went to Chinatown. Because we all seemed to be following Ernie's directives that evening, we went to a restaurant I'd never been to before. The name of the place was written in Chinese characters, so I don't know what it was called, but it was a nice place. The atmosphere was dim, and the decorations were pretty, and the Chinese waiter led us to a table in a corner, as if Ernie had planned it that way. Maybe he had. By this time, his ways had become kind of mysterious to me. He was being quite forceful. Generally, he was relaxed and casual.

Honestly, I think he was play-acting for Rob and Lulu. Whatever he was doing, we finally got Lulu some food. And Rob paid for it. Ernie and I each had hot tea and a couple of almond cookies because we were still full from those exceptionally delicious Reuben sandwiches.

When Rob and Ernie ultimately deposited Lulu and me home and left, we chatted briefly with Caroline and Sue and then went upstairs to bed. Buttercup joined me.

"I'm so tired, I think I'm going to collapse before I get to my bedroom," muttered Lulu as we got to the top of the staircase.

"I'm sure you are," I said, oozing sympathy. "I can't believe Rob didn't get you something for lunch." While I aimed to give him the benefit of the doubt because Ernie vouched for him, I wasn't ready to like or approve of him yet.

"Not his fault," said Lulu in a weak voice. "I should have said something."

"Nonsense. He's being paid to help you, and he should help you."

Lulu heaved one of the bigger sighs I'd heard in my life. "I'm not the one paying him, and I don't feel right whining about feeling hungry when everyone's being so nice to me."

"Stop that right this minute, Lulu LaBelle," I told her sharply. "It doesn't matter who's paying him. He's being paid to take care of you, and he should take care of you."

"Well, he is helping with the case."

"And if you drop dead from starvation before the case is over? What about then?"

"I'm not going to starve, Mercy!" said Lulu. "Give the guy a break, will you? He's being nice to me. We had a good time at Elysian Park, and he told me exactly how he's going to handle the police and Mrs. Smedley. All of the Mrs. Smedleys, I mean, tomorrow."

"Huh. Well, all right. But speak up for yourself if you need something, okay? There's no need to suffer any more than the police are making you suffer."

"Thanks, Mercy."

I saw tears standing in her eyes. "Oh, Lulu! Don't cry!"

"I won't. I'm just so glad you're my friend. And Ernie's my friend, and that you and Ernie got together, and…I don't know. Just everything. If I'd listened to you in the first place, I wouldn't be in this mess."

"Old news, Lulu. Don't worry about it. You have lots of friends, and we're all on your side. So get some sleep and…Oh, crumb, do you need something boring to wear to work tomorrow?"

She shook her head. "I think I can manage. Thanks, Mercy. I appreciate you so much."

"Fiddlesticks. Go to bed. Do you need Buttercup?" I hated to ask, because if Lulu needed the comfort of Buttercup that would mean I wouldn't have it for myself. If that makes sense.

"Don't be silly. Buttercup belongs with you."

Thank God for that!

THIRTY-TWO

Monday morning dawned, as Monday mornings almost always do, too early for me. However, as I'd chosen to move to Los Angeles and become one of the worker proletariat, I didn't even gripe to Buttercup when my alarm clock went off. I just got out of bed.

Buttercup, who could sleep all day if she wanted to, was bouncing like a wind-up toy, and I realized I'd neglected to take her outside before we went to bed. Whoops. Buttercup was a wonderful dog and beautifully trained, but even the best of us have physical needs.

"I'm sorry, Buttercup," I told her as I shrugged into my robe and shoved my feet into my slippers. Then we both hurried out of my room, down the stairs, and raced through the house—giving Mrs. Buck a wave as we tore through the kitchen—to the back door which I opened for my dog. She raced out of there as if she were being pursued by demons.

"You're sure in a hurry this morning, Miss Mercy," said a puzzled Mrs. Buck.

"I forgot to take Buttercup outside to piddle before we went to bed last night," I told her. "Poor dog had to hold it in all night."

"She's a good dog," muttered Mrs. Buck as she went back to whatever she'd been doing before Buttercup and I flew past her.

It was darned cold outside, but I figured my dog deserved my company as she snuffled around the yard, watering plants here and there and depositing some manure near the plot of land Mr. Buck had been grooming to become the rose garden. Like the mostly dutiful dog owner I was, I retrieved an old newspaper from the utility porch and tidied up after my pooch. Mr. Buck had been hired to do repairs, etc., in my home—and plant roses if he wanted to—but I figured he didn't need to clear the yard of dog poop, too.

Although Buttercup deserved a good romp that morning, I finally got tired of shivering outside and called her in again. She came, good doggie that she was, and didn't even look at me reproachfully.

"You're such a good girl," I told her.

She told me she knew it, and we both went back upstairs, where I bathed and prepared myself for work. As I looked in the mirror and adjusted my scarf, I decided Buttercup wasn't the only household member who could use a haircut. My bob needed to be trimmed. Fortunately, I could merely hie myself to the nearby barbershop in order to take care of my own hair. I'd have to make an appointment with a groomer for Buttercup.

Buttercup gave a sharp yip when someone knocked at my door. I jumped a little myself. "Come in!" I called, turning to sit on my bed and pull on my stockings.

"C'n I borrow another sweater or a blouse or something?" asked Lulu, walking into my room. "I thought I was all set, but today I realized the sweater I thought would go with my skirt won't."

"Sure," I told her, waving at my closet. "I think there's a gray cardigan and pullover set in there that would go with your skirt. You're talking about your black skirt, right?"

With a sigh, Lulu said, "Yeah. I really have to go to that consignment shop in Chinatown and get some boring clothes."

"I know. We can do that..." My words trickled off as I realized I had no idea what the day would hold for either of us. "Well, we can do that sometime."

"Yeah," said Lulu. She picked my gray sweater set from the shelf upon which they lay and shook them out. "This should do. Thanks, Mercy."

"You know, you can wear a pretty scarf with that so you won't be totally dull and boring."

"I dunno. I don't feel very cheery at the moment. I think I'll stick to gray and black."

"All right. I hope the Smedley mess will be cleared up today."

"I only hope the Mrs. Smedleys meant it when they said they'd go to the police station."

"I do too," I said. "I've got all my notes tucked into a portfolio in my office. Don't let me forget to fetch it before we go to work."

"Don't worry, I won't," said Lulu listlessly.

"It'll be all right, Lulu," I said, looking up from my bed where I was attaching a black stocking to a garter clip.

"I hope so," she said, and turned and slumped out of my room.

I shook my head in sympathy as I grabbed the second stocking and carefully pulled it on. As I was heading to work, I wasn't wearing sheer rayon or silk stockings, but practical lisle hosiery for my practical working life. Lulu might consider me dull, but at least no horrid man had pretended he wanted to make me a WAMPAS Baby Star and then tried to ravish me.

Heck, no man had ever tried to ravish me. Why did that make me feel a little down in the dumps?

Oh, pay no attention to me.

"Let's get our breakfast, Buttercup," I said brightly to my darling poodle as I rose, slipped on my practical black shoes, and headed for my bedroom door.

Mrs. Buck served us ham and scrambled eggs that morning, along with sliced oranges and some of her delicious biscuits. As she was a mistress of the art of jams and jellies, she also provided us with a variety of each. That morning, I slathered my biscuit with butter and peach jam. I thought about having another one and slathering it with apple butter, but restrained myself. After yesterday's Reuben sandwich and almond cookies, I figured I should refrain from stuffing myself for at least a couple of days.

Sue and Caroline were both chipper that Monday morning and oohed and aahed over Mrs. Buck's breakfast, as was only Mrs. Buck's due.

Lulu, I noticed, stared at her biscuit, scrambled eggs, and ham for a moment, then split her biscuit, cut a piece of ham, slapped it on the biscuit, and made a sandwich out of it.

"Want some mustard for that, Miss Lulu?" asked Mrs. Buck as she came in the dining room to refill coffee cups.

"No, thanks. I'll just eat it like this. Thank you, though," said Lulu. She sounded as if she were trying not to come across as dismal but didn't quite make it.

"If you're sure," said Mrs. Buck doubtfully.

Lulu sucked in a lungful of air, and for a second I feared she might just shriek at my housekeeper, but instead, she let out three-quarters of her lungful and said merely, "I'm sure. Thank you."

Oh, dear. I truly hoped today would signal the end to Lulu's troubles. And that the Mrs. Smedleys and Mr. Oswald would do as they'd promised. And that Mr. Gabriel—I beg your pardon; Rob—would already be haunting Phil Bigelow's office. Or maybe Judge What'shis-name's office. Havers. I think that was it.

"It's cold today, ladies," I said to my tenants as we finished our breakfasts. "I'm going to drive us to work, if that's all right with you."

"Sounds perfect," said Sue.

"Thanks," said Caroline.

"Sure. Thanks, Mercy," said Lulu, giving me a significant glance. I wasn't quite sure what it signified, but I had my suspicions.

So we all trooped back upstairs to brush our teeth and do whatever else needed doing before gathering in the tiled entryway to go outside and head to work. Buttercup kindly saw us to the door.

Then I nearly suffered a spasm when I opened same to discover Ernie and Rob standing there, Ernie with his finger pointed at the doorbell.

"*Eeek!*" somebody—I think it was Caroline—cried.

"What are you doing here?" I asked. Impolite I know, but crumb.

"And a bright and cheery good morning to you too, Miss Allcutt. Ladies," said Ernie, grinning at all of us. "We just thought we'd pick you up and take you to work."

Pressing a hand to my thundering heart—I could scarcely feel it through my thick woolen coat—I said, "Thank you, although I wish you'd warned us you'd be picking us up. You almost gave me an apoplectic fit."

"Me too," said Caroline, giving credence to my theory that she'd been the eeker.

"I told you we should have called," said Rob at Ernie's back.

"Aw, nuts. Give 'em a surprise to start their day," said Ernie. "Wake 'em up. Get the old ticker started."

"You woke us up, all right," I said, not gratefully. "My own personal ticker nearly stopped."

"Sorry," said Ernie. "Rob's right. I should have called. But I figured we might have to drive places today, so we brought both machines."

"It's all right," said Lulu. She *did* sound grateful. "Thanks. I appreciate it."

"Sure. Fine with me," said Sue, always game.

"Thank you," said a subdued Caroline.

"Mr. Buck's got two places saved for you in front of the building," called Mrs. Buck from the living room.

Buttercup only wagged.

Sue, Caroline, and I rode with Ernie. Lulu rode with Rob. That was as it should be, as he was her attorney and could fill her in on what was going to transpire that morning.

Following the familiar routine, Ernie dropped Caroline off near the Broadway at Fourth and Broadway, drove Sue to her dentist's office on Figueroa Street, then backtracked to the Figueroa Building where, sure enough, Mr. Buck had saved two parking places for Ernie and Rob. Rob had already parked his Flint in one space, and Ernie maneuvered his Packard into the space right behind the Flint.

Mr. Buck opened the door for me, so I didn't have to wait for Ernie to do so. Not that I would have, being perfectly capable of opening car doors on my own, but still, it was a nice gesture on Mr. Buck's part.

"You've got people waiting for you inside," he said to Ernie, Lulu, Rob, and me as we gathered on the sidewalk.

"Oh, no, please don't tell me it's the coppers," moaned Lulu.

"No. No police. Bunch of ladies and a gentleman were waiting outside the building when I came up from the basement to unlock the front door." Mr. Buck had many duties in the Figueroa Building, several of which he performed before the place opened to most of its tenants a little before eight o'clock.

Sure enough, when we entered the building, four Mrs. Smedleys and Mr. Oswald stood in front of the reception desk, all dressed and ready for a trip to the police department. I presumed that's why they were there, in any case.

"I thought you were going to have the police execute a search warrant first thing," said Mrs. Verna as soon as she saw Rob.

"I am," he said.

"Then why are you here?" she demanded.

"I'm going to the police station right now," said Rob, turning around and heading back to his automobile. Lucky duck. We had to stay here and deal with the multitude of Smedleys.

"Um, I'm not sure why you came here so early," said Ernie. "But you might as well come upstairs to my office." Turning to Lulu, he said, "Why don't you call Glennie? See if she can cover the reception desk for you."

"Okay," said Lulu. She eyed the group of Mrs. Smedleys. "Which one of you planted the key in my handbag?"

"Crumb," said Mrs. Verna with a sigh. "I did it. I'm sorry."

"Yeah," said Lulu, "so am I. Why'd you do it?"

"So they'd finger you instead of me for that rat's death, of course."

At least the woman was honest.

"Well, take it back, okay? I don't want it." Lulu, who'd dug the key from her handbag, thrust it at Mrs. Verna, who took it.

"Sure. Sorry if it caused you any trouble. Honest to God, we didn't know what to do. I thought for sure the cops would pin the murder on me."

"So you decided to frame me instead," said Lulu, justifiably crabby. "I understand, and thanks heaps."

"All right!" said Ernie loudly to get everyone's attention. "Let's all go upstairs. Except for you, Lulu. But if Phil or any other member of the L.A.P.D. shows up and tries to cart you off, don't go. And call me. Rob's probably already at the station."

"Okay," said Lulu, forsaking crabbiness for loneliness.

"I'll just stay here with you for a while, Miss Lulu," said the kind-hearted Mr. Buck. "I won't let any coppers take you away."

"Thanks, Mr. Buck." Lulu sounded a tiny bit less forlorn.

"It'll be all right, Lulu," I told her. Then I spoke to the mob. "You take the Smedleys and Mr. Oswald in the elevator, Ernie. All right? I'll take the stairs. Hope you don't get stuck."

"Whattaya mean, stuck?" asked Mr. Oswald.

"I don't know if the elevator has ever had to carry so many people at once before," I told him.

"I'll take the stairs with you," said Ernie. "You folks can handle elevators, right?"

"Well, all right," said one of the Mrs. Smedleys. "Verna, do you know what office we're going to?"

"Third floor," said Ernie. "Mercy and I will probably get there before you and unlock the door to my office."

Muttering amongst the Smedleys broke out, but Ernie grabbed my hand and headed to the stairwell. I heard Mr. Buck assuring the assemblage he'd show them the intricacies of the elevator. There weren't many of them. Intricacies, I mean. There seemed entirely too many Smedleys in the building.

Ernie and I got to the third floor before the elevator did, and we hurried to the office. Ernie unlocked the door. The stupid telephone was already ringing, so I ran to my desk before removing my outer garments. I had to pull off my gloves in order to answer the phone. "Mr. Templeton's office—"

A bellow on the other end of the wire interrupted me. Instantly, I saw red.

"Don't you swear at me, Phil Bigelow! Why are you calling the office before eight o'clock, when we open? Have you no respect for—"

Another bellow from Phil infuriated me. I was about to slam the receiver into the cradle, but Ernie snatched it from my hand so I couldn't, curse it.

"Why are you swearing at my secretary, Phil?" he said. "And why the devil are you calling this early?"

The door to the office opened, and the Smedley ladies and Mr. Oswald entered, all chattering.

"Be quiet, please. Mr. Templeton's on the telephone," I snapped at them, which was unfair. It wasn't their fault Phil Bigelow was a pig. But my snap shut them up, so it worked out all right.

"Yeah?" Ernie said into the receiver. A wicked grin curled his lips. "Is that so? Well, well, well, how about that?"

I heard angry grumbling on Phil's end of the wire, but I couldn't make out the words. I turned to walk to the coat tree and hang up my hat and coat, but Ernie held out a hand to stop me.

"Well, how about that?" said Ernie.

More grumbling.

"We'll be there in a few minutes," said Ernie and hung up the receiver. Then he turned to face the Smedley gang. "Keep your coats on, ladies and gent. We're going to the police station. Unexpected events have transpired."

"What the hell does that mean?" snarled a Mrs. Smedley.

"Follow Miss Allcutt, Miss LaBelle, and me to the police station, and you'll find out," said Ernie, being mysterious.

After looking at each other for a second or three, the Smedley contingent gaped at Ernie.

"That your Packard out front?" Mr. Oswald asked.

"Ask Mrs. Verna Smedley," said Ernie bitingly. "She crushed its fender a few days ago."

"Cripes," said Mrs. Verna. "I'm sorry."

"Yeah, well, follow us to the police station."

"What's going on?" asked another Mrs. Smedley.

"You'll find out," said Ernie.

So we all left the office, and the Smedley clan walked to the elevator. As Ernie paused to lock the door, I whispered to Ernie, "You'd better tell *me* what's going on, or I'll never speak to you again, Ernie Templeton."

"Promise?" he asked sweetly.

So I hit him with my portfolio. Childish I know, but darn it, Lulu's very *freedom* was at stake.

Ernie said, "Ow."

But once he, Lulu, and I got into the Packard—Glennie's doctor agreed to let her woman the reception desk again—and we made sure the Smedleys and Mr. Oswald were following us, he told Lulu and me what was up as he drove us to the police station.

THIRTY-THREE

By golly, Ernie, Lulu, and I weren't the only ones who'd been greeted by unexpected visitors before office hours. When we entered the station on First Street, Phil, Rob Gabriel, and three uniforms were gathered in the lobby, along with two sobbing young women: one blonde, the other brunette.

"Those are the girls who were fighting with Mr. Smedley!" I cried, bringing all conversation to a sudden halt. Whoops. I hadn't meant to blurt that out.

Phil wheeled around and glared at me. "What do *you* know about it?" He saw the Smedley gang and added, "Who're they?"

In a sweeping gesture, Ernie said, "Detective Phil Bigelow, please allow me to introduce you to Mrs. Smedley, Mrs. Smedley, Mrs. Smedley, Mrs. Smedley, and Mr. Oswald."

Phil opened his mouth, probably to yell some more, but his mouth just kind of hung open as he took in Ernie's words. After snapping it shut and squinting at the crowd, his shoulders slumped and he said, "Cripes. Will one of you please tell me what's going on here? And how did you know about these two ladies?" He aimed the last question at me.

"Is there anywhere we can all fit?" I asked, not eager to help Phil out of his predicament.

"Yeah. Got a conference room around here, Phil?" asked Ernie. "This might take a while."

After heaving a huge sigh, Phil said, "Yeah. Conference room one is empty."

"What about the search warrant?" asked Rob gruffly. "It's been signed by Judge Havers, and I want it executed this minute."

"Hold on a bit, Rob," said Ernie. "We might not need it."

"Eh?" said Rob, clearly confused, which made sense to me.

"Follow me," said Phil. "Bloom and Richards, keep track of all these people and get them to conference room one."

"Yes, sir," said one of the uniforms.

The four Mrs. Smedleys, Mr. Oswald, Lulu, Ernie, the two weeping maidens, and three uniformed coppers—including Bloom and Richards, I guess—followed Phil down a dingy hallway to a room. He shoved the door open and stood aside. A long, scratched table sat in the middle of the room surrounded by a bunch of rickety chairs. Evidently, the L.A.P.D. didn't spend a lot of money on its conference rooms.

Everyone entered the room. I waited to see where Phil and Ernie would sit because I wanted to be near Ernie. The uniforms stood with their backs to the various walls, I expect so they'd be prepared to pounce on anyone who got out of hand.

Ernie seated Lulu beside Phil. She didn't want to be there, but he made her do it anyway. Then he took the seat next to her and patted the one next to him for me. So I sat there and placed my portfolio on the table in front of me. Rob seated the blonde and the brunette on the other side of Phil, and he sat next to them. I thought he should have sat with Lulu, but nobody asked me.

Apart from shuffling and scuffing and the noise of people clearing their throats, etc., silence more or less prevailed for several seconds. Then Phil began things.

When we finally all left the police station a little after noon and got back to the Figueroa Building, Ernie prevailed upon Junior to get sandwiches from the diner across the street. The story related in that crowded conference room comported precisely with Mr. Brentwood's tale about what he'd witnessed the night of Mr. Smedley's death, which had been an accident, pure and simple. Although I doubt either "pure" or "simple" could be used about any other aspect of Mr. Smedley's duplicitous, devious, and downright devilish life.

Not sure about Ernie, Lulu, and Rob, but I felt limp as a rag as we waited in the outer office—my room, in other words—for our lunches to arrive. I sat at my desk, Lulu and Rob sat in chairs set before my desk, and Ernie draped himself over the chair next to my desk as we waited.

"I feel as though I've just slogged five miles through a swamp," I muttered at one point. "And I'm not even the one who was accused of murder."

"I am, and I feel like I've slogged ten miles through the same swamp," said Lulu. She looked it, too, poor thing. My gray sweater set didn't suit her fair skin and bottle-blond hair and, as she hadn't worn any makeup except for a bit of face powder to cover aging bruises, her bare face appeared washed out. In fact, if you'd tied a black scarf over her hair, she really would have looked like a nun.

"At least Phil apologized," I said.

"Huh," she said.

And that was it as far as conversation went until Junior bounced in with our lunches packed away in paper sacks. Ernie, who had already given him enough money for our lunches and one for himself, tipped him lavishly, and he was a happy boy when he left the office. He whistled all the way down the hallway.

We all perked up slightly when we moved ourselves into Ernie's office and gathered around his desk. After Ernie had handed out sandwiches and Coca-Colas to each of us, Lulu was the first to break the silence.

"So nobody murdered the louse after all," she said in a wondering tone of voice as she unwrapped her chicken sandwich.

"Those poor girls must have been terrified," I said, doing the same with my own sandwich. "They were pretty brave to turn themselves into the police this morning."

"They were scared to death someone would rat them out, I expect," said Ernie. "That drawing Mr. Monocle made of them was amazing. You could recognize them perfectly."

"His name is Brentwood," I snarled.

"Yeah, I know," said Ernie, grinning at me as he unwrapped his own sandwich.

"I didn't know the fellow was such a good artist," said Lulu. Then she closed her eyes, shook her head, and said, "I can't believe it's all over."

"Yup," said Rob. "Thanks to those girls, that drawing, and all the Mrs. Smedleys."

"I still think it stinks that Mrs. Smedley tried to pin it on me," said Lulu.

"Your feelings are justified," I told her. "And she smashed Ernie's fender, too."

"She paid for it, though," said Ernie after taking a sip of his cola.

"Which is more than you did," I said.

He snickered.

"But it's not really funny," I went on. "Those poor girls were hoodwinked just as you were, Lulu. They only went to see Mr. Smedley that night in order to demand he return their photos. It was pure bad luck they met him on the street after he recovered enough to run after you."

I saw Ernie and Rob grimace in sympathetic pain. Nuts to that. Mr. Smedley deserved Lulu's knee to his groin.

"And Mr. Brentwood drew the scene perfectly, too," I went on. "The two girls said so. He might not be able to express himself very well in words, but he sure got the point across in his drawing."

"I'll give him that," said Ernie. "He might be nuts, but he's an excellent observer and artist."

"He's not nuts," I growled.

"You're right," Ernie conceded.

"True," said Rob.

"And thank God for it," said Lulu.

We all agreed.

After we'd finished our sandwiches, Rob left to go to his office, Lulu left to go down to her assigned spot at the reception desk, and Ernie and I sat and stared at each other for a few minutes. I gathered the empty waxed paper, crumpled it up and stuffed it into the paper sack, and handed it to Ernie. He obligingly crammed it into his waste-paper basket.

"So," I said after a few moments of silence. "What now?"

With a shrug, Ernie said, "Guess I'd better go back to snooping on Mrs. Allen."

"Any news from Puddles and Pierre?" I asked.

"Nope. I guess Mrs. Amstell had a servant take them to a dog trainer."

"She couldn't train them herself?"

Ernie gave me a pitying look. "Did Mrs. Amstell look like the type of woman who does things when she can have servants do them for her?"

"No," I admitted. "I still want to get the drawing Mr. Brentwood gave me framed. Maybe I can do that at lunch tomorrow or something."

"Sounds good to me," said Ernie, lifting his arms and stretching them over his head. "Crumb, I've been sitting too much. That conference room and all those pitiful women about did me in."

"They were kind of pitiful, weren't they? All taken in by a miserable lout of a man."

"Yeah. I'm glad girls aren't forced to remain in their houses unless chaperoned these days, but somebody ought to give the Bright Young Things lessons on how to avoid monsters like that Smedley goat."

An idea I'd had the prior day—or maybe it was on Saturday—crept into my head again and I rose from my chair. "Do you mind if I call Chloe?"

"Why should I mind if you call your sister?" asked Ernie as if he was surprised I'd even asked the question.

"I don't know. I just wondered, was all."

"Go ahead. Say hi to Chloe for me."

"I shall. Thanks, Ernie."

"Not a problem, Mercy," he said grinning at me. "Okay, I'm going to go on a Mrs. Allen hunt. Hold down the fort."

"Will do."

———

It took a little persuading on my part, but eventually, Chloe came around to my way of thinking. Then, of course, I had to clear the matter with Mrs. Wilkes and try to explain it to Mr. Brentwood, which took more time than Chloe or Mrs. Wilkes combined.

In the end, however, the little Nash baby—boy or girl—was going to come into the world and live in the most gorgeous nursery I've ever seen in my life. With Mr. Francis Easthope and me supervising him (more or less), Mr. Brentwood created an absolute wonderland of trees, flowers, bees, bears, bunnies, and other creatures.

Chloe and Harvey were thrilled with the result. So was Mr. Brentwood. So was Mrs. Wilkes. So were Mr. Easthope, Ernie, and I.

So that makes at least one of my ideas that turned out to be positively brilliant!

Oh, and Lulu and I visited the consignment shop in Chinatown on Tuesday after Lulu's day of redemption, if it can be called that. Anyhow, Lulu came back to Mercy's Manor with quite a nice wardrobe of office wear that didn't scream at the onlooker.

Another one of my ideas that turned out to be pretty good too, by Jupiter!

CELLULOID ANGELS

MERCY ALLCUTT MYSTERY, BOOK 9

It wasn't until Wednesday of that week that things became sticky again. Only this time the things weren't at the Nash residence, but rather on Harvey's set for the production of *Helen of Troy*.

Chloe and I had taken the baby outside to sit in the fragile sun on the Nashes' magnificent patio. The baby was still technically nameless, although Heather Rose, Helen Grace, and Melanie Eve were top contenders so far. I preferred Heather Rose, but she wasn't my kid.

"If you name her Helen, everyone will think it's because of Harvey's movie," I pointed out.

"That's true," said Chloe, who was regaining her strength such as it was and who couldn't seem to stop staring at the baby's various body parts.

I had to admit they were wee and cute. I loved it when I held my hand to her and she grabbed one of my fingers. It wasn't as much fun when she drew the finger to her puckered mouth and started sucking on same. Baby spit wasn't my favorite thing in the world, although Chloe didn't seem to mind. Heck, the kid even burped up on her shoulder from time to time, and she only laughed. I could only stare as such behavior seemed so unlike my glamorous, delicate, ethereal sister. Speaking of which…

"What about Esther?" I asked. "Esther is a pretty name."

"It's not bad," said Chloe. "Esther Rose." She tilted her head, her blond hair gleaming in the sunlight and making me sigh.

"Ma'am?" Molly's voice came from the back door.

Chloe and I turned to look at the maid.

"What's up, Molly?" asked Chloe.

"It's Mr. Harvey, Mrs. Nash. He said he needs to speak with Miss Mercy."

After sharing a startled glance with Chloe, I rose from my chair and headed for the door. "Wonder what he wants with me?" I muttered as I walked.

"He's been having trouble on that wretched set," said Chloe. "Maybe he wants you to investigate."

I laughed.

Silly me.

"Mercy," said Harvey Nash, producer, director and owner of the Nash Studios, as soon as I'd greeted him on the telephone, "can you call Ernie and ask him to get out here? A door came unhinged today and nearly killed Francis Easthope. I think there's actual sabotage going on here on the set."

"Good heavens! Is Mr. Easthope all right?" Mr. Francis Easthope was a costumer and a set designer and probably the most handsome man in California.

"He's all right, but it was a close call. But these so-called accidents are happening all the time. There's something going on, and it's not natural. I've never had this kind of trouble on a set before. I only hire the best of the best, and they know their jobs and what they're doing. I can't imagine who would want to sabotage my studio, but I fear it's happening."

"I'm so sorry, Harvey."

It was true that he'd been coming home every day with tales of trouble on the set. Scaffolding fell; a wall collapsed, nearly beaning two grips; a few tacks had "accidentally" been left on John Gilbert's chair; Miss Anita Page's Helen-of-Troy wig had magically caught fire and might have seriously injured the actress had she not been quick enough to avert disaster by flipping it into a prop fountain. It certainly did sound as if these happenings weren't merely random.

"I'm sorry too, and I want to get to the bottom of it. So I'm hoping Ernie can come out here for a week or two and maybe you and he can pretend to be extras and snoop around. Bring that Lulu person who wants to be a star with you. The more people we have working on the problem, the sooner we can solve it. I hope. I have to admit I'm worried, Mercy, and I don't want to worry. I want to leave everything to Sidney and be home with Chloe and the baby."

Sidney Lafayette was Harvey's second in command, and an able producer and director in his own right. But I understood Harvey's reluctance to turn a troubled production over to him while everything seemed to be at sixes and sevens.

"I'll be happy to call him, Harvey. And Lulu too. She'd love it!"

"Well, she might not love it so much after she lives it for a while. Most of the studios don't treat their actors as well as we do, you know."

"I know, Harvey. That's why everyone wants to work for you."

"Yeah, I know," he said sourly. "I paid a fortune to get John Gilbert and Anita Page from MGM to work for me, but I'll be ruined if they both get killed on the bloody damned set."

As Harvey seldom swore, I knew he was truly desperate. "I'll telephone Ernie right now," I told him.

"Thanks, Mercy. Call me as soon as you can. I'm going to shut down production for the day. Every day we waste is money down the drain."

"Right." Everything revolved around money, and not just in Hollywood. It was a fact of life.

So I put a call through from Beverly Hills to the Figueroa Building in downtown Los Angeles.

"Templeton," Ernie snarled into the receiver on the second ring.

"Golly Ernie, you sound grumpy," I said.

"When are you coming the hell back here?" He barked. "You were supposed to stay until your mother left. Well, she left and you're still there."

"It's only been three or four days, Ernie," I said. "Anyhow, I'm calling because Harvey needs you. He wants to hire you. And maybe even Lulu and me."

"What? What the devil are you talking about? Soft soap won't work with me, Mercy Allcutt. You're my secretary, and I need you here, not there."

"It's not soft soap. All sorts of accidents are happening on the set of *Helen of Troy*, and Harvey honestly believes someone is deliberately sabotaging the production. He asked me to telephone you and maybe even Lulu too. He wants all of us to pretend to be cast members and snoop. John Gilbert nearly sat on a seat full of tacks and Anita Page's wig caught fire. If someone is interrupting the production on purpose, they're being vicious about it. Poor Francis Easthope nearly had a door fall on him today."

"Good God. Are you serious?"

"Yes, I'm serious! For crumb's sake, Ernest Templeton, do you think I'd kid about something like *this*? If anything truly catastrophic happens to that production, Harvey's studio might be ruined!"

"Shoot."

"So far, no shooting," I said, trying to be funny and not succeeding.

Available in Paperback and eBook from Your Favorite Bookstore or Online Retailer

ABOUT THE AUTHOR

Award-winning author Alice Duncan lives with a herd of wild dachshunds (enriched from time to time with fosterees from New Mexico Dachshund Rescue) in Roswell, New Mexico. She's not a UFO enthusiast; she's in Roswell because her mother's family settled there fifty years before the aliens crashed (and living in Roswell, NM, is cheaper than living in Pasadena, CA, unfortunately). Alice would love to hear from you at alice@aliceduncan.net

www.aliceduncan.net

www.ingramcontent.com/pod-product-compliance
Lightning Source LLC
Chambersburg PA
CBHW021955010726
47494CB00003B/739